THOMAS R. McDONOUGH is Coordinator of the Search for Extraterrestrial Intelligence Program (SETI) at The Planetary Society. He has worked in NASA's Jet Propulsion Laboratory and has served as science adviser to writers Frederik Pohl, Parke Godwin, and the team of Larry Niven and Steven Barnes. He belongs to numerous professional organizations and was awarded a Special Citation by NASA for his work on the Pioneer spacecraft flyby of Saturn.

Dr. McDonough is the author of two nonfiction books, *The Search for Extraterrestrial Intelligence: Listening for Life in the Cosmos* and *Space: The Next Twenty-five Years*. His short works have appeared in *Analog* and other magazines. THE ARCHITECTS OF HYPERSPACE is his first novel.

Worlds of Science Fiction from Avon Books

Avon Books are available at special quantity discounts for bulk purchases for sales promotions, premiums, fund raising or educational use. Special books, or book excerpts, can also be created to fit specific needs.

For details write or telephone the office of the Director of Special Markets, Avon Books, Dept. FP, 105 Madison Avenue, New York, New York 10016, 212-481-5653.

THE ARCHITECTS OF HYPERSPACE

THOMAS R. McDONOUGH

AVON
PUBLISHERS OF BARD, CAMELOT, DISCUS AND FLARE BOOKS

AVON BOOKS
A division of
The Hearst Corporation
105 Madison Avenue
New York, New York 10016

Copyright © 1987 by Thomas R. McDonough
Front cover illustration by Ron Walotsky
Published by arrangement with the author
Library of Congress Catalog Card Number: 87-91602
ISBN: 0-380-75144-5

First Avon Printing: December 1987

To the memory of my father,
Lt. Col. Redmond A. McDonough,
and to my mother,
Sophie T. McDonough,
for providing my life-support system
on a primitive planet far from
the Galactic Center

PROLOGUE

In the year A.D. 2087, explorer Alexandros Zepos was dying on an alien, artificial world unlike any before seen by humans.

"For you, my little Ariadne," he whispered in Greek as he programmed a viewcrystal. He worked slowly, painfully, awkwardly, one-handed. Only bloody bandages showed where his left arm had been. Doped with painkiller, the silver-haired man desperately connected wires to an alien video transmitter, his eyes aching from ultraviolet burns.

Angrily, he fought the fog threatening to cloud his mind forever. Why had those creatures built this bizarre world, roaring around a neutron star a thousand times a second? Where had they vanished to? Now he would never know, and the pain of having come so close to solving the mystery was worse than the agony of impending death. If only this accursed world hadn't killed his entire crew!

The transparent wall revealed a vast panorama in which unfamiliar stars drew colored streaks in a faintly pink alien sky. The very fabric of space and time was warped by the Herculean pull of neutron-star gravity. Only the unknown powers of alien technology kept Alexandros from being squeezed into molecular cream by the star's tidal force. The transparent floor showed the forbidding surface of the star just meters away, filling the room with flashes from lightning powerful enough to vaporize a planet. Each burst roared with unearthly thunder as its plasma hit the station.

His vision blurred. He spoke briefly into the viewcrystal recorder, then switched it off.

"Twenty light-years to Earth," he whispered as he connected the recorder to the transmitter. "Twenty years from now, Ariadne, you may get my message, when I'm a corpse, with a neutron star for a tombstone.

"What will you look like then? Will you remember me? I'd give anything to know . . ."

He hit the transmission key. The viewcrystal began to broadcast endlessly at the faint circle in the sky where spun a tiny star called the sun and a small planet called Earth.

"Ariadne!" he whispered.

CHAPTER 1

Twenty years later and many light-years away, the battered old two-man starship *Shillelagh* entered the atmosphere of planet VII of the star Luyten 789-6. The *Shillelagh* was piloted by Sean O'Shaughnessy and Pelham "Plum" Chalmondeley III, who were visiting for the second time a frigid, alien world where only a dozen humans had ever walked.

They landed by the shore of a lake of lox—liquid oxygen—and emerged from their battered starship in cryosuits that protected them from the star's cosmic rays and from temperatures that made the coldest winter night of Antarctica seem tropical. On his shoulders, Plum carried a quantarifle and Sean a cryogun of his own design. Each bore a roidknife—the sign of the experienced asteroid miner—sheathed on his thigh.

They were greeted by the sight of giant three-eyed reptilian cryocrocks swimming lazily offshore while a flock of frisbeebirds whirled noisily overhead. Little three-footed fluffniks, like hairy orange tennis balls, lapped at the liquid oxygen with their duck bills, making little *org-org-org* sounds.

Sean knelt and studied the many tracks in the green crystalline sand. The fluffniks scurried out of the way. Plum lay down on his back, joyfully giving his rotund body a rest from the two-gee gravity. The extra weight was made tolerable by anti-gee pills that temporarily strengthened muscles at the expense of slowed bodily processes and strains that would be felt for days after the drug wore off.

Sean pointed at several huge three-clawed prints and spoke on his suitradio: "Cryocat." He studied the stride and size of the paw prints. "Young one, maybe half a year from full grown."

They were searching for *felis abboudi,* a great six-legged catlike creature as large and vicious as a tiger, with three corrugated heat-sensing ridges growing from its back like stubby wings. Popularly called cryocats, they were prized on Earth, but were known to the public only by the single example captured by an exobiological expedition five years previously. Private owner-ship of extraterrestrial life-forms being prohibited on Earth, there was a thriving underground market for such beasts.

Sean and Plum were two smugglers who catered to that market.

Sean looked back along the track, then pointed into the frigid jungle. "She came along that path and stopped to drink. Then she went off along the shore. There aren't many fluffnik prints on top of the tracks, so they're fresh."

"Then shall we pop off after her?" said Plum.

"That's what we came shopping for," agreed Sean, setting forth with a great stride across the green sand. The Irishman seemed to make no note of the added gravity, but Plum had to drag himself up with the help of his quantarifle.

They were on the edge of a frozen jungle of multicolored crystalline plant life, dusted with snow and inhabited by vicious, hungry animals. The men's heavy backpacks contained lox for breathing and powerful heaters to protect them from the cold that threatened to seep through the bulky insulation. The heaters were all that separated them from a quick death as human Popsicles. Unknown to the men, two kilometers behind them, two blue catlike eyes in a massive red head observed them, tracking the trackers. It was a massive, full-grown cryocat, a beast weighing close to a ton in the terrible gravity. A third eye in the back of its head stared behind it. To the large infrared-sensitive eyes, the cryosuit heat-leakage made the astronauts stand out in the ulrafrigid landscape, like bonfires at twilight. The cat's two forward eyes squinted at the brilliance; its great jaws yawned, revealing two sharklike rows of teeth. It stretched gracefully and padded for-ward, its six legs rhythmically moving in a complicated cadence.

"Nice thing about this planet," said Sean, waving toward the lox lake. "We may freeze to death, but at least we can get our beer decently chilled."

"Small comfort," said Plum, "especially since I do not be-lieve in spoiling good beer by excessive refrigeration." His well-educated British tongue hinted at a bemused tolerance of Sean's eccentricities.

Sean shook his head uncomprehendingly. "I'll never under-stand your fondness for beer warm enough to wash a man's hands with." He spoke in the mild brogue of his hometown of Galway, Ireland.

They followed the animal path along the shore, past violet crystal vegetation. A scarlet auroral curtain shimmered in the sky, like a blanket of the gods waving in a cosmic breeze. Crystals crunched under their feet; something brown and slimy slithered away into a pile of white crystals. Waves of pale blue lox lapped softly at the shore, their gentle sounds picked up by the suit microphones.

"It was very kind of her to leave us such a nice trail."

"Sean, my friend, I know you're quite the whiz at this game, but how can you possibly know this cryocat is a she?"

"Instinct, me boy, from years of experience on a multitude of worlds."

"In other words, a wild guess."

"You could put it in that way, if you were determined to be unflattering."

They trudged on along the shore, taking care not to step into the lox, which might overtax their suit heaters and freeze them solid.

"Bloody awful planet, if you ask me," said Plum. "Fit only for ice cubes and penguins." Unaware of his faint resemblance to the latter, he stoically marched after Sean, taking smaller strides, falling ever farther behind. A blue wave rippled through the aurora overhead.

The star's dim light made the glacial planet seem even colder. Subarctic though the planet was, it teemed with life, unique virus-based life-forms that had first evolved when the planet was warmer—though still fiercely cold by Earthly standards. As its star cooled to the point where oxygen liquefied, the life had adapted to ever colder temperatures, growing steadily more complex until it positively flourished, turning the world into an icy jungle.

The original virus had a threefold symmetry in its quasicrystalline structure, giving rise to similar symmetries in many of its descendants. In the high gravity, three-legged and six-legged creatures had the advantage of the extreme mechanical stability of the tripod to protect them from dangerous falls.

The distance between Sean and Plum slowly grew until the latter could barely see his companion. "I say," said Plum, puffing, "couldn't you slow down just a tad?" He began to sweat, as the unaccustomed exertion overloaded the old suit's life-support systems.

Sean paused, glanced back and said, "Isn't it just like an Englishman to let an Irishman set the pace and then complain about it? I'm anxious to find us that cat. She could get away from us if we're the smallest bit late. Twenty thousand roidbucks—that'll pay for a lot of sore muscles." He plunged on.

A cryocrock roared from the lake, his groans traveling half a kilometer with ease. Plum shivered at the sound.

The shore was the terminus of numerous trails, trails of animals that thrived under conditions that would quick-freeze any Earthly creature; animals superbly insulated by layers of silicone fat. Here, ice-eater viruses had evolved long ago, using the energy of the star's intense cosmic radiation. The viruses broke down several types of ices, building hydrogen compounds and releasing oxygen vapor, which condensed into lox. Animals drank lox instead of breathing air and oxidized the hydrogen into water, later excreted as crystals, then eaten by the viruses. The reaction heat kept their bodies well above the average equatorial daytime temperature of $-190°$ Celsius.

Sean stopped suddenly. "Whoa!" he whispered. "Something big, on the other side of that pink crystalbush." The bush tinkled as the crystals rattled and hundreds of multicolored frostflies buzzed around it. Sean unslung his cryogun and slowly approached the bush. Plum trudged on, still far behind.

A live animal was worth far more than a dead one, so capturing one without killing it was the purpose of their eleven–light-year journey. Sean carried the expensive custom-made cryogun he had designed expressly for this world. The meter-long gun would paralyze local animals by shooting hypersonic helium atoms. The atoms penetrated skin harmlessly, but filled the silicone fat with helium, increasing the heat conductivity so much that the animal would cool down and go into hibernation. At least, that's how it worked in theory. They had yet to try it in the field.

Plum's powerful quantarifle was meant to kill anything Sean's gun could not stop. Roidknives were their ultimate backup weapons. Similar in appearance to Bowie knives, the long blades were actually two parallel knives, angstroms apart. The handle's power supply generated a high voltage across the blades, and the field-ion effect tore atoms out of any material it came into contact with, ejecting them out the end of the handle and performing a mass-spectroscopic analysis in the bargain. With its ceramic coating to keep it from short-circuiting, it could cut through a nickel-iron asteroid like a laser through salami.

As Sean came within a meter of the pink crystalbush, a creature stepped out and stared him in the face. Its head was massive, with three soft, huge blue eyes mounted equilaterally around its head, poised above a stout, green, cowlike body with six legs. It took one look at Sean, moaned, and ran clumsily in the opposite direction.

Sean laughed. "A cryocow!"

"Maybe we should bag the blighter and go home. Any creature from here is worth a pretty penny back home."

"I didn't come eleven light-years to bag a cryocow," said Sean. "We'd be the laughingstock of the roidbelt."

"I say, this really is rather more than I bargained for." He tried to brush away a droplet of sweat from his forehead. "I was looking forward to a pleasant sojourn in an exotic vacationland, a bit of hunting, and then a spot of tea. I'd very much like that cuppa right now."

Sean pointed to the star overhead. "But look at that sun."

Plum stared at the small reddish star. "What about it?"

"Nearly overhead. You Englishmen are *supposed* to be out in the noonday sun."

"Yes, along with you mad dogs."

Sean chuckled.

"I rather doubt," said Plum, "that the principle applies to extraterrestrial planets."

The cryocat was now a kilometer behind them and closing.

A wind started to blow, tugging at their cryosuits and howling in their exterior microphones. Crystalbushes tinkled like wind chimes. Sean stared at the red clouds on the horizon. "Looks like a hailstorm coming."

Plum shivered. "Wouldn't want to get caught in one of those."

"No sir, thank you kindly. Hailstones the size of your fist, falling like cannonballs on this high-gee planet. Knew a man who got his skull cracked by one." He mimicked his companion's accent: "No place for two *civilized* gentlemen like us."

Sean stopped at the edge of the green beach, twenty meters ahead of Plum. "I see something," he whispered over the radio, afraid the sound might carry through the faceplate.

"What, pray tell?"

"There's some motion in a blue crystalplant about five meters ahead. Move slowly." Sean unslung the cryogun and crouched.

Plum slowed his already languid pace, using his quantarifle as a walking stick.

The blue crystals stirred; several broke off and fell to the ground. A large red catlike head was visible, its three eyes glowing blue. "Cryocat!" whispered Sean. "Young one, all right." He aimed the cryogun at the creature, centering her head in the cross hairs of the gun's microscreen. "Move out a little more, me darlin'," he murmured.

The cat stepped back behind the bush.

"Jesus, Mary, and all the saints!" exclaimed Sean.

Plum slowly crept up toward Sean, keeping to the left to avoid shooting his friend if he had to fire. "Patience, old chum," he said.

Sean crept forward.

The cat suddenly stuck her head back out and looked inquisitively in their direction, then slowly nodded in a circular motion to cool the cauliflowerlike infrared sensory organ in the center of her forehead, overloaded by Sean's heat. Hesitantly, she stepped out, revealing a red, muscular body the size of a small tiger, six thick legs, and three stubby corrugated "wings" with serrated edges. In this gravity, she weighed close to half a ton.

Sean aimed for her midsection and squeezed the trigger. Helium atoms shot out invisibly, silently, penetrating the thick hide. The cat snarled, leapt—and landed on him, knocking him down. She roared angrily and bit at his hot cryosuit.

Plum jerked his quantarifle up and aimed it at the animal, shouting, "Scan!" The quantarifle radio picked up his command and its central processor radioed back, "Scanning." The two-centimeter disk at the end of the rifle sprayed the landscape with infrared. An array of trillions of microscopic lasers pumped infrared photons, automatically adjusting their phases to scan the scene and amplify the reflected photons.

Plum couldn't find a clear target as the two wrestled in his screen. Every time the cat's dark image eclipsed Sean's bright one, he hesitated for fear of shooting his friend. Even a minor wound in this supercold world could be fatal.

The cat and the Irishman struggled fiercely, rolling over and over. The cat tried to bite through his suit, at first recoiling at the hot touch, then toying with Sean as if he were a finger-lickin' good drumstick hot out of the microwave. Sean's muscles strained as he grabbed the cat's ears, twisting it away each time it tried to bite his neck.

Plum's tiny quantarifle screen showed a false-color holographic image of the scene. By far the brightest image was the red picture of Sean, his metallic suit-lining strongly reflecting infrared. The cryocat glowed blue on the screen, merging with Sean's struggling image. Plum held the gunstock in his left hand and twisted the joystick trigger with his right, trying to keep the cursor over the cat's blue image. Once he squeezed the joystick, the power to the microlasers would increase a thousandfold, their phases would lock and all beams would converge wherever the cursor pointed, vaporizing a deep hole into the target. But the blue and red blobs changed places too rapidly for a safe shot.

The cat tried to bite through the metal collar at Sean's throat, while man punched beast in the underbelly. She roared horrendously, puffs of fog shooting out of her throat like dragon's breath. Plum aimed the cursor at her head, at the center of an infrared haze.

Suddenly the cat let go and rolled over on her side, on top of Sean's legs. Her snarls softened as she fell asleep.

"I say," said Plum, "that's quite a right hook you have."

"I wish I could take the credit," said Sean, pulling his legs out with difficulty. "It's the helium at work." He flexed his legs and grimaced with pain, but was relieved to find no signs of broken bones. Plum helped him up, brushing green crystals off his suit. Sean puffed hard, catching his breath. "She's hibernating now. Took a little longer than I calculated, that's all. And she is a she, as you can see."

"How long will it last?"

"Maybe half an hour, maybe an hour. Too many variables. I'll leave you here with the cryogun while I go get the ship. Just shoot her again if she wakes up." He handed the gun to Plum.

"I'm glad she's only a young one. It would have been rather unpleasant for you if she'd been fully grown."

"It wasn't a picnic as it was."

"I wish we could hunt directly from the ship. It would be far more civilized to float above the bushes and shoot from the comforts of home."

"That wouldn't be very sporting, and the ship's engine noise would scare all the game away."

"Alas, that's—"

A tremendous blow threw the men to the sand, weapons flying. The creature that had been trailing them had jumped: a huge, fully grown cryocat. This was Mother, and she was not pleased with the treatment of her kitten.

Her claws slipped on their suits. She rolled over and crouched in front of the two battered men. While Plum lay stunned on his back, Sean staggered to his feet.

The cat roared deafeningly and slammed Sean with a massive paw, like a cat playing with a mouse. He staggered. She arched her back and ran the serrated edge of a wing across his chest. Sean fell into the lake, his suit ripped.

He lay there a moment, half submerged in the lox, and an alarm went off. "*Heat leak!*" shouted the suit's alarm voice.

"Air leak! Heat overload!" The messages repeated until he groggily hit the mute key.

Lox boiled all around him where it came into contact with the relatively warm suit. He stood up with enormous difficulty, every bone hurting in the heavy gravity, and felt a great chill in his chest.

Looking down, Sean saw insulation powder pouring from the gash. Only the thin innermost metal layer was unbreached. He pushed the edges together, but whenever he breathed, a cloud of fog emerged as trapped air escaped, condensing in the frigid atmosphere. "Holy Mary, mother of God!" he exclaimed. His feet were starting to freeze as the boiling lox carried away more heat than his suit could provide.

"God damn!" shouted the Englishman over the radio.

Sean glanced at Plum, who was struggling to stand up. The giant cat knocked the Englishman down on his belly and tried to bite off his helmet.

Sean looked around for their weapons, but could not see them in the lox steam. He stepped onto the dry land and unsheathed his roidknife.

The cat, unsuccessful at eating Plum's helmet, turned her attention to his backpack and poked at it with a paw. She tore open a line and a pale blue fluid gushed out: the liquid oxygen of his air supply.

Sean held the roidknife overhand, holding the gash closed with his other hand, and staggered up behind the cat. He squeezed the handle and stabbed her in the abdomen. The blade hardly made a dent in the rocklike silicate threads of her skin.

"Christ almighty!" he shouted and stared at the roidknife. The indicator light was dead. "Frozen!" He threw it down. The knife relied on the field-ion effect and was all but worthless with the high-voltage supply in the handle dead from the cold.

The cat snarled, turned, and slammed him onto his back.

The animal put her two huge front paws on his chest and began to tear away at the gash. The weight, the cold, and the pain were unbearable. Sean screamed, then forced himself to think through the pain. Plum shouted, "Air!" and struggled to close the lox valve.

The cat paused and stared at Sean, two of her blue eyes just centimeters away. Her breath formed snow puffs, vaporizing when they hit his suit. She pawed at the insulation again. Powder flew out and the gash grew bigger. Fascinated, she pawed the gash again and again, deepening it and chilling Sean more each time. Once she ripped through the inner lining, he would be dead.

"Need oh-two!" shouted Plum.

Sean slugged the cat in the belly with no effect, then had an inspiration.

As she pounded him with jackhammer blows, he took a deep breath and unlocked his faceplate. As it swung open, the supercold atmosphere hit his face like a meteor shower. The moisture and carbon dioxide in his suit air froze into snow; oxygen became fog.

The cat looked at him quizzically. She was so close, he could see every crack in her red, diamondlike teeth, though ice glazed his eyes painfully and his vision blurred.

He blew into her face like a storm god.

His breath shot out in a cloud of snow and fog. To another human, his exhalation would have been frigid, but cold as it was, it was incomparably hotter than anything the cat had ever experienced—like a blowtorch in her face.

She screamed and jumped away, blinded.

Sean slammed the faceplate back on. The alarm was screaming its warnings again.

The cat ran around in circles, then splashed into the lake, swishing her face in the cold liquid and swimming away fitfully.

Sean collapsed onto his back and Plum staggered over.

"Help!" whispered Plum, falling to his knees. "Reserve. Air. Going!" He pointed at the torn lox line.

On his knees, Sean reattached Plum's lox line, sealing it with cryotape. The gauge on the lox cylinder was in the red. "No lox in your tank!" he whispered through frozen lips.

"Bloody hell!" exclaimed the Englishman, falling on his face as the air ran out and his mind became foggy.

Sean thought quickly and struggled to his feet. "Come here!" He dragged Plum over to the edge of the lake and yanked the lox cylinder off. Unscrewing the lid, he dipped the cylinder in the lake. The lox boiled furiously. He held it under until it was half-full and his fingers began to freeze.

He reattached the cylinder to Plum's backpack and hit the converter key. The pump started the lox on its way to the heat exchanger, where the liquid was heated to body temperature for breathing.

After two endless minutes, Plum stirred and smiled weakly. "Good show," he muttered.

Sean collapsed on the ground, his torso numb from cold. "I could do with some repairs myself," he said with difficulty.

Plum struggled to his feet and examined Sean's suit. He grimaced when he saw the huge gash, got out the repair kit from Sean's backpack, and poured insulation powder into the hole. Then he stretched cryotape over the gash, sealing it. Sean stared at him, too weak to move.

"I shall get the ship," said Plum. He glanced at the sky, which had become an angry red. "It does appear that hailstorm is coming."

Plum picked up Sean's fallen roidknife. Patting him on the shoulder, Plum added, "I might have known an Irishman would have breath that could stun a tiger."

"I'll drink to that," Sean said feebly.

CHAPTER 2

A few days later, while Sean and Plum traveled on their return trip toward the solar system, two scuba divers were swimming over an ancient Phoenician shipwreck in the Mediterranean Sea.

"We've only just excavated to the hull at this point," said Ariadne Zepos, her breath hissing with soothing regularity over the communicator. "We're following the ultrasonic scan." The divers spoke in Italian, though either would have been comfortable conversing in English, French, Latin, or Greek. "We have to be extremely careful, of course, or the wood will crumble." The woman was the beautiful young hydroarchaeologist known to some of her colleagues as the Greek Goddess, whose office was in the Italian undersea city of Delphinus, near Sicily.

"This not being my specialty," said Stefan Draganescu, "I leave the details to you. I am more at home in an office, but I am grateful for the opportunity to visit my grantees out in the field." Stefan was the Deputy Minister of World Culture, a handsome, mature Romanian.

"I'm so glad you came," said Ariadne, looking lovingly at the ancient wood.

"So am I," said Stefan, looking with similar intensity at Ariadne.

In their flippered envirosuits, they were warmed and air-conditioned like spacemen. Low-power laser beams crisscrossed the site, forming a giant reference grid. Several green-encrusted ribs of the vessel lay exposed like a skeleton, mingled with ballast stones. Three small fish swam among the ribs, mimicking the scuba divers; and the suits' hydrophones picked up the squeaks of two amorous dolphins.

"Sometimes," said Ariadne, "it is difficult for us out here in the field, not knowing whether the ministry appreciates what we're doing, or whether you're going to shut off our funds and sink the project like this ship."

"I know how hard it is to be unappreciated." He nodded

against the languid resistance of the cool water. "Sometimes I think the minister thinks I'm just another clerk. But one day, they'll need a new Minister of Culture, and there'll be just one obvious choice." He tapped his chest.

Ariadne grasped a barnacle-encrusted oarlock, while the gentle current slowly swept her flippered feet over her head. "Just think—more than two thousand years ago, men were sweating on this trireme, breaking their backs over the oars. Perhaps one of them was your ancestor."

Stefan smiled and said, "Perhaps he was on his way to attack one of your ancestors." He awkwardly grabbed a ballast stone to anchor himself.

Ariadne smiled and Stefan added, "I hope we shall have a friendlier relationship. *Much* friendlier." There was a gleam in his eye.

"So do I," said the woman—but without the gleam.

Her speaker began to beep. She touched her wrist-panel and shut it off. "I have an urgent message. We'd better get back. The last time this happened, there was a sunken tourist submarine. I helped rescue them." She released the oarlock and swam effortlessly toward the submersible. Stefan followed slowly.

They jetted to Delphinus, that collection of underwater cottages, offices, hotels, aquaculture farms, and casinos sprawling across the bottom of the Mediterranean, interconnected by glasstex tunnels made of a transparent silicate strong enough to maintain one atmosphere of air pressure against a water pressure as much as three times that. At an average depth of fifteen meters, the complex grew out of the seafloor like an artificial coral reef. Enough greenish sunlight penetrated the depths so the aquanauts could see the spheres and domes of the nearer buildings, but so vast was the city that even in the clear waters only a small part could be viewed from one point. At the limit of vision, where water absorbed the delicate light, the city seemed a futuristic castle, its outlines soft and misty in the distance.

They docked the little submersible by Ariadne's office, a little hemispherical bubble on top of a short cylinder, much like an astronomical observatory. Mowed kelp surrounded the office, and schools of tiny fish were darting among the blades. A glasstex tunnel ran to the oceanography complex forty meters away, a giant Tinkertoy of spheres interconnected by similar tunnels.

They passed quickly through the airlock and removed their helmets, remaining dressed in dripping envirosuits. A humid, salty tang penetrated the city's air. Ariadne sat down at the console, facing the open sea.

The entire hemisphere of the office was transparent glasstex, giving an uninterrupted view of the sea in all directions. To Stefan, watching the fish swim mere centimeters in front of his nose, there was an uneasy sense of claustrophobia, as if the ocean were about to crush him. But to Ariadne, the feeling of being a part of the sea, of almost breathing the very water that flowed by, was exhilarating.

In front of her console, she glanced affectionately at her garden of living sponges just outside the dome. She shook out her long, brunet hair as she hit the keyboard. Small, colorful fish darted in and out between the sponges like butterflies among flowers. Stefan carefully combed his black hair and pointed beard in the window's reflection.

Ariadne listened to the English message on the viziphone: "Call Lunar Farside Operator. You have an interstellar message. Dial white-gray-purple, black-red-green."

"What is this, some kind of joke?" she said.

"You get interstellar phone calls?" said Stefan. "I didn't think it was possible."

"Of course not. I don't even know anyone off Earth, much less from another star. Except for one family friend I haven't heard from in years. But I might as well see what this nonsense is all about." She dialed the color code and an operator came on the screen after a momentary delay.

"Lunar Farside, Operator Red," said the man in English.

"I'm Ariadne Zepos," she replied in Greek-flavored English, "and I had a message saying you had an interstellar call for me." When no reply came at first, she tapped her fingers with irritation, forgetting that it took three seconds to get to the moon and back.

The operator replied, "Glad to get you at last."

"Is this some kind of prank?"

"This is the first time I've ever heard of an interstellar call," said the operator. "It's new to me too. After all, radio communication is limited to the speed of light. No, this is not a prank. And please pause at the end of each question, due to the three-second delay."

"I'm not used to talking to the moon."

"This is the situation. One of our antennas on lunar farside monitors for interplanetary distress signals. We got an alarm when it picked up a signal today. At first, we thought it was a ship on the asteroid run, but when we cleaned up the signal—it was very noisy—we found it had been transmitted from some interstellar location twenty years ago!"

Ariadne looked at Stefan uncomprehendingly. "So why did you call *me?*"

"Because he specifically asked for you. His name is Alexandros Zepos."

She turned pale. *"Patera mou!"*

"What the hell is going on?" asked Stefan, touching her shoulder.

"Daddy!" Her knuckles were white as she gripped the keyboard. "He disappeared when I was a little girl. Went on an interstellar expedition. Never returned. Mommy said he died."

Stefan embraced her and stroked her hair.

"Let me hear the message!" she shouted at the viziphone, her face bent just centimeters from the screen.

The operator said, "This call will cost 340 geodollars, including special processing. Do you accept the charge?"

"Of course!"

"I recommend you record this."

Ariadne stabbed the record switch.

After a moment, the image of a man's head and shoulders filled the screen. The picture was blurred and streaked with electronic snow, but the pale, handsome features of a middle-aged man with silver hair and a noble, aquiline nose stood out, his dark eyes piercing the screen. He winced with pain. One shoulder was covered with blood. Thunder roared and the background flared erratically.

"It really is Daddy!" exclaimed Ariadne, turning even paler. Her eyes fastened hypnotically on the screen.

The image spoke in English: "I am Alexandros Zepos of Athens, Greece, Planet Earth. By the time you get this, I will be dead. Just find my wife, Katerina, and my daughter, Ariadne, and give them this message. When last I saw them, they were living in Zaragoza, Spain, but if they are no longer there, try Athens or Piraeus, Greece."

He shifted from English to Greek and spoke slowly, painfully. "Dearest Ariadne and Katerina, I wish that I could be with you now. We never got all the way to Beta Hydri. We found an anomaly in hyperspace and stopped to investigate. It turned out to be this diabolical world. All of the crew have died. I am alone now, and I too will join them soon.

"Katerina my darling, I want you to know that from the moment I fell in love with you, I have never betrayed you, even though I was gone most of the time, and even though we argued ceaselessly. You called me cold and distant, and you never understood why I could never be happy at home. You could not accept the fierce drive I have to explore, to see what has never been seen, even if it kills me—as it is doing now. But I will love you as long as my spirit remains. Nevertheless, you must find another man, for your own sake and for our daughter."

He shook his head wearily. "It is strange to think that you will receive this message twenty years, five months, and three days from now. Probably you have remarried and my daughter has forgotten me, though it was but seven weeks ago that I saw you both." A vast sadness was written on his noble face.

The face softened. "And to my sweet little Ariadne, I want you to know that I loved you more than you could ever dream. But I could never be the father you needed, so I hope your mother found a better man. I treasure each memory of your words and your smiles and your splashing in the ocean like a little dolphin. I left you not long after your sixth birthday, and my biggest regret is that I can never be there again to comfort you when those beautiful blue eyes fill with tears.

"Take comfort in the thought that the men and women of this expedition died while seeking knowledge—and a better reason to die has not yet been found. But humanity is not ready for what we found. If any came here again, they too would probably be killed, and if any survived, I'm sure someone would use the knowledge to kill and enslave their fellow beings. I do not want anyone following in our steps. I found the answer to that question you always asked me, Ariadne, but it killed seven good men and women, and I do not want it to kill anyone else.

"So take care of each other, Katerina and Ariadne, and think of me when you see the stars at night." The screen went blank.

Ariadne began to cry. Stefan held her close.

The operator returned to the screen and said, "I couldn't locate Katerina Zepos."

Between sobs, Ariadne said, "My mother remarried. Changed her name."

"You'll give her the message?"

She nodded and cried some more.

Stefan shut off the viziphone and said, "What was that question you always asked your father?"

She shook her head and sobbed in his arms.

"What question," murmured Stefan, his mind whirring like a computer, "could a six-year-old girl ask that could kill seven people twenty light-years away?"

CHAPTER 3

"Prepare for four-space," said Sean O'Shaughnessy as he pulled the *Shillelagh* out of hyperspace.

"Ah, practically home," said Plum as they passed Pluto. He switched on the Kawasaki engine for sublight travel.

Sean's face was uglier than Pluto's now, black and blue where the regenerating tissue could be seen under yellow frostbite cream. Plum painfully moved to a hammock, his bruised round body rejoicing in the lower gravity.

They decelerated at one gee through the solar system for two days, aiming for the asteroid Vesta, one of the main cities of the Asteroid Federation. After they passed Saturn's orbit, they swallowed gee pills, put on geesuits and reluctantly switched to high-gee deceleration. After many hours of painful gee forces, they could see the features of Vesta in the viewscreen.

Sean smiled through cracked lips at the old, familiar rock, remembering his days as an asteroid miner. The Main Bubble over the major buildings of the colony was clearly visible, covering almost a tenth of the surface of the five-hundred-kilometer-diameter spinning stone. He delicately put the battered old vessel in orbit around Vesta, a tricky procedure thanks to the weak gravitational field and the clutter of tourist, freighter, and mining vessels orbiting there.

Plum powered down the Kawasaki engine and called a roidtaxi while Sean unstowed a large metal crate. Two meters on a side, it contained their prize, the hibernating young cryocat, along with a cryonic life-support system for her. Sean changed into overalls and Plum into his favorite black suit with a maroon and black rep tie.

The taxi took them and their crate down to the Main Bubble of Vesta, an industrial airlock. Had they been in Earth orbit, they would have had to go through Customs, but in the asteroids no one cared who came and went or what they brought with them.

Inside the huge transparent geodesic bubble was a spectacular view of the black, starry sky and the cool, distant sun. They took the "ski lift," never meant for skiers but erected by the Downtown Vesta Merchants' Association to speed potential customers from the airlocks to the heart of the city. The two spacemen grabbed adjacent slings, holding the crate between them, duffel bags tied on top, and let the ski lift take them away. On Earth, the crate would have weighed more than two hundred kilos, but here in Vesta's one-fortieth–gee gravity it weighed just five.

The lift whisked them toward the civic center, their feet almost touching the ground, past pedestrians kangarooing five meters into the air. They rushed by dozens of the flimsy, garishly colored, twenty-story plastic buildings that give asteroid architecture its distinctive quality, sprouting up among the endless tall trees and bushes like gaudy cubist flowers.

They zoomed through the seedy section known as Barftown, where smugglers, criminals, government agents from Earth and other unsavory types hung out. Only the more successful of these could afford downtown bubble rents. The least successful of all hung out in the mine shafts that make a map of Vesta look like Swiss cheese.

In the heart of Barftown, Sean and Plum dropped off the ski lift in front of a violet fifteen-story building and listened to the synthetic voice of the directory: "Schwartz, Adolf. Hydroponic repair. If your veggies could speak, they'd shout 'Schwartzie!' Eighth floor, gray . . . Tokyo Sam. Restaurant. Martian-style teriyaki just like Mom used to make. Second floor, red . . . Tournier and Willoughby—"

"That's it," said Sean.

"Import/Export. You want it, we'll get it. Earth smuggling a specialty. Twelfth floor, brown-red . . ."

Sean grabbed the metal crate with one hand and started climbing the handholds on the outside of the building. In the asteroids, only luxury buildings have elevators. Plum followed behind, pushing the crate up while the directory continued: "Upham, Mwamunga, and Feldman. Arbitrators. Practiced on two planets and three moons. Seventh floor, purple . . ."

They reached the brown-red mark of the twelfth floor and climbed into the corridor. Each door continually muttered its occupant's name. Sean set the metal crate down in front of the one saying, "Tournier and Willoughby," and pushed on the doorplate. A live voice but no picture emerged. "Whaddaya want?"

"Willoughby, this is O'Shaughnessy and Chalmondeley. We've got your cargo, but it won't fit in the door."

"Use the cargo door outside," said a voice from within.

They took the crate outside, dangling it from the twelfth floor, and a large section of the wall slid open. Sean shoved the crate inside and followed with Plum.

The office was a large room filled with crates of all shapes and sizes. On one crate sat Willoughby, a fat bald man with a droopy mustache. Tournier, a thin, tall man with eyes as droopy as his partner's mustache, stood in a corner, leaning on another crate.

"Let's see it," said Willoughby, noting silently the wretched appearance of the Irishman's face.

Sean pushed a button on the side of the crate. The side turned transparent and revealed the red, muscular young cryocat motionless in a pile of green crystals. Only the fog rising from the cat's mouth showed it was still alive.

Willoughby kicked the crate around and watched as the cat slowly bounced inside like a rubber toy, still hibernating. "Nice," he said.

Tournier nodded. "Have any trouble?"

"A little," said Sean.

Plum chuckled. "We very nearly got killed," he said in his finest Oxbridge tone. "The little rascal's mother did not want her to go to Earth. Can't say I blame her."

Willoughby grunted.

Sean said, "There's about a month's life support in the crate, plus instructions on how to bring her to and keep her alive. You'll get her to Earth by then, won't you?"

"Sure, it's all set." Willoughby smiled. "The terry who's buying him can't wait to get his cold cat."

"Who is he?"

"He's a big 'crat in the Ministry of Agriculture with a private chalet and enough power to keep the C-cops away."

Sean nodded. "That'll be twenty thousand roidbucks."

"I'm afraid there's been a slight change in the terms," said Willoughby.

Sean stiffened. "How slight?"

"It seems this terry has financial problems. He didn't get the big bribe he was planning on to pay for this. He can't pay the whole amount. I'm afraid I can only afford to pay you ten thousand."

"Ten thousand!" exclaimed Sean. "That'll barely pay for the repairs to my ship!"

"A spot of rough weather," said Plum. "High-gee hailstorm, you know."

"Them's the breaks," said Willoughby, shrugging.

"The hell it is!" said Sean. "I know you, Willoughby. You wouldn't have arranged this deal unless you had at least half the money in your nosecone. And I know I could get at least a hundred K for this on Earth. In hard roidbucks, too, not flabby geobucks."

"So why don't you?"

"Because I don't have the contacts there, and you know it!"

Willoughby's right hand touched the back of his neck.

Sean whipped out a quantagun and aimed it at him. "Put your thievin' hands on your ample belly!" he snarled. The bald man did so and Sean reached behind him and pulled out a microgun from its neckholster. He threw it behind a crate.

Tournier reached inside his jacket and suddenly became aware of the quantagun Plum had aimed at him. "I shouldn't do that if I were you," said Plum. "Really, I shouldn't."

"Tune into me, Willoughby," said Sean, "you taxin', Earth-eatin' pile o' moon dust! You're going to pay me twenty K or I'm taking the cryocat and leaving!"

"And what," asked Willoughby, "would a roider like you do with a cryocat? Teach him to sniff out diamond roids?"

"I know a few Earthrunners besides you, and I can get twenty K for a cryocat easy." Sean started to lift the crate with his free hand.

"Oh, all right," said Willoughby. "Such a fuss. I'll trim my margin and cut my losses, though Einstein knows, I barely make enough in this business to survive."

"My genes mutate for you," said Sean.

Willoughby turned businesslike. "My bank is the First Interplanetary of Deimos," he said. "They have a branch here."

"Good. Mine is the Bank of Ceres."

Willoughby spoke into the viziphone and a clerk appeared on screen, saying, "First Interplanetary Bank and Trust of Deimos, Vesta business office."

"I want to transfer twenty K from my account to a customer's account with the Bank of Ceres."

"May I have your ID, please?"

Willoughby pulled out his bankcard and stuck it into the viziphone slot.

"Account is in good standing. Voice confirm, please."

"Jeremiah Mortimer Willoughby."

"Mortimer, is it?" said Sean. Willoughby ignored him.

"Voice confirmed," said the clerk. "Customer's account?"
Sean stuck his bankcard into the slot.

"Voice confirm, please."

"Sean Seamus O'Shaughnessy."

"Mr. O'Shaughnessy, today the nearest branch of the Bank of
Ceres is nine light-minutes away. It will take eighteen minutes to
make the transfer and confirm."

"Roger," said Sean.

Twenty thousand roidbucks flew on photon wings from one
asteroid to another. This capped yet another successful business
transaction beyond the bounds of Earth's laws, rules, regulations,
requirements, taxes, and bribes.

CHAPTER 4

While on Vesta Sean and Plum celebrated their success with numerous libations, on Earth Ariadne was having an intense discussion with Stefan in her underwater office.

Ariadne wore the close-fitting one-piece silver suit favored by underwater workers. It covered her from ankles to neck, but its lines made loving detours, hinting at the athletic build beneath. Stefan had on an expensive pale blue four-piece Italian suit appropriate to one who spent his days swimming through red tape. A tuna-harvester submarine swam by outside, the hum of its powerful engines vibrating the walls.

"Did you call your mother?" said Stefan.

"Yes. I played the whole recording over the viziphone. She was shattered." Ariadne winced with the memory. "Their marriage had been on the rocks." Dim recollections of her parents' verbal fights floated through her mind, arguments that had terrorized the six-year-old Ariadne. "But for two years she waited for Daddy's expedition to return. They were only supposed to be away for six months. Everyone said they must have died."

"Why were they going to Beta Hydri?"

"No one had ever visited the system before. No one's been there since. But Daddy's message said they never got there."

"What exactly was your father's background?"

"He was an exobiologist. He'd been on many interstellar expeditions to new worlds, cataloguing life forms and capturing some of them for Earth's zoos. This was his first trip as expedition leader."

"Did you ask her about that question you had always asked your father?"

"Yes, but she couldn't recall anything special. Just the usual children's questions: Why is the sky blue? What's it like on a starship? Where did I come from?"

Stefan pondered. "None of those seems to be anything that could kill a whole starship crew."

23

"Of course not."

"I could not sleep last night," said Stefan. "I lay in my bed thinking of your father's message. Somewhere in space, he made a great discovery, and if we could retrace his steps, we might uncover something that would make the world sit up and take notice of the Ministry of Culture and its noble but unappreciated workers."

"We could also get thoroughly killed."

"With twenty years more knowledge and equipment than your father had, we might have a chance at greatness, and survive to enjoy it."

"This is all academic. There's no way we could hope to find Daddy's discovery. He didn't tell us where to look. We don't even know what to look for. It could be anywhere between here and Beta Hydri. Thousands of cubic light-years."

"That is true. But last night, I had an idea. Why not go see a mnemologist?"

"A mnemo? I can't stand those brainoids. All they do is attract immature people who want to live in the past."

"Certainly, but they can let you relive your memories of the time your father left. There may be a clue there."

She thought about what it would be like to have her brain stimulated, evoking long-dormant memories of sights and sounds.

"It would be a chance to see your father once again, Ariadne."

"I'll do it!"

"I knew you would. I've contacted an Italian mnemologist right here in Delphinus. I've made an appointment for eleven o'clock."

She cocked her head and looked at Stefan in a new light. "You certainly plan ahead, don't you?"

Smiling his smoothest smile, he said, "For you, I plan nothing but happiness." He touched her shoulder sensuously.

Ariadne shifted uncomfortably.

At eleven o'clock, they were in the office of Giorgio Bisaglia, licensed professional mnemologist, conversing in Italian. He was a short, wiry man with intense black eyes. A faintly unpleasant medicinal smell tinged the air.

Giorgio gave a drink to Ariadne, then seated her in a reclining chair, while Stefan watched from a stool. "Now, I'm going to put the helmet on you, and I don't want you to be afraid." He placed the heavy white helmet on her head, draping its fiber and power cables over her shoulder.

"Me, afraid of a helmet?" said Ariadne. "I've been wearing diving helmets since before I could walk!"

"Perhaps—but so many people who come to me have misconceptions about mnemology. They think we stick needles in your brain."

"You don't? I'm glad to hear that."

"No, that liquid you are drinking has certain chemicals that are now traveling to your brain. We stimulate them selectively through magnetic resonance."

"Ah," she said, "that makes sense. We also use that technique in archaeology—to analyze material composition and to date artifacts."

Stefan spoke. "Can you trigger a memory precisely by date? We want October 4, 2087, the day her father left."

"No," said Giorgio, "it is not that easy. Each brain is different, and each is enormously complex. Each one is wired differently by nature and by the experiences during the growth phase. We must start by triggering selected, labeled nuclei and see where they are in the brain, and you must report to me what memories you experience. Gradually, we make a map of your mind and can tune in more accurately to particular events and dates."

He rolled a terminal screen over next to her and touched the keyboard. It lit up, displaying:

```
HELMET OK
OSCILLATOR STABLE
PROGRAM INITIALIZED
READY
DATE OF BIRTH?
```

"First, Ariadne, I need your birth date."

"September 16, 2081."

He entered the date into the computer.

"You're using a silent terminal, aren't you?" said Ariadne, unable to see the screen.

"Yes. It's distracting to the subject to hear the computer speaking."

She nodded with difficulty under the heavy helmet.

They continued with questions about handedness, gender, and her medical, psychological, and genetic history. Then the screen requested:

MEMORY TARGET PARAMETERS?

He typed in

    4 *OCT* 87.

"All set?"

"Yes."

"Now I am going to cover your eyes with a mask, to block out visual noise." He rolled down the clinging, flexible faceplate of her helmet, covering her eyes with blackness.

"First memory." He pushed a key. Coordinates flashed on his screen. The helmet generated an intense, slowly rotating magnetic field, subtly aligning the atoms of her brain. A radio signal swept rapidly through a large range of frequencies, some of which were absorbed by different atoms, giving signatures of the brain's many molecules, a technique known since the twentieth century. The isotopically encoded organic chemicals in her drink found their way to different segments of her mind, adding their resonances to the natural atoms, helping to map the unique geography of her brain, a technique developed in the twenty-first century.

Then the computer compared the resonance maps with thousands of previous patients and estimated the probable location of memories from the age of six. It oriented the magnetic and radio fields and turned on a complex set of simultaneous radio frequencies matching the selected molecular resonance-absorptions. The responding groups of atoms vibrated vigorously in a microscopic region within Ariadne's head, triggering the electrochemical reactions of memory.

For a moment, her mind was a jumble of random thoughts and memories. Then, suddenly, she was outside of a Greek house, in a wooden chair, eating some sticky, freshly baked *karithopita*. It smelled wonderful, and tasted even better. Olive trees swayed in the breeze. A teenage boy was plucking a bouzouki, rather poorly—trying to impress her. A goat walked by in the street, braying. Ariadne licked honey from her fingers—

—and she returned to the present. Her mouth dropped open. "I had no idea it would be so real!"

"What did you see?" said Giorgio.

She described the vision. "That was when my mother and I visited Kíthira."

"How old were you?"

"Let me see, I was twelve—no, thirteen then."

"What time of year was it? The more precise you can be, the better."

"It was early summer. That's the best I can do."

"Good." He entered the data.

"It's so vivid! I can see why some people get addicted!"

"Yes, some of my clients never want to come back to the present. They would live in the past all the time if they could. Some of them turn to unlicensed mnemologists and spend all their waking hours reliving the best parts of their lives. But let us proceed." He pushed the button again.

She was in a great amphitheater with thousands of people. The preacher on the faraway stage was stridently exhorting the congregation in English. Tall as a building, his three-dimensional image was projected above the stage. His silver hair and wise eyes looked faintly like her father's.

"The sins of the people!" he shouted.

"The sins of the people" roared the audience, Ariadne included.

"Man is born to wickedness!" he exclaimed.

"Man is born to wickedness!" they shouted.

"Man is born in shame!"

"Man is born in shame!" they echoed.

"It is bound up in his DNA as surely as I am a messenger of the Lord!"

"Messenger of the Lord!"

Ariadne's pulse was rapid, her breathing deep, and she knew without any doubt that she was hearing the Truth. Her heart was filled with love and she worshiped the preacher, who was only one step from God. The promise of salvation shot from his eyes to hers like laser beams and stirred her soul such as no one had ever done.

"And the Lord has said unto me," he continued, "that if you allow your tongue to taste alcohol, or your skin to touch V-grains, or your arms to hold another not wed to you, you shall suffer the torments of all the clones of the devil when you make that great final quantum leap from this universe!"

"From this universe!" they roared.

It was pure ecstasy.

She was back in the mnemologist's office, her heart still pounding. "I was at a sermon by the Benedictor Simon."

Stefan's eyes opened wide. "You're not a Simonist, are you?" The neo-Puritan Simonist movement had swept North America, Europe, and Asia.

"Yes, I am."

"You, a scientist?"

"That day I saw the Benedictor was the happiest day I have ever had. I had been lost in a world of mechanical laws, believing in nothing but logic and mathematics. The Benedictor made me see there was more to life than equations. It was all so clear."

"When was this?" said Giorgio.

"I remember it vividly. It was the most important day of my life: Two years ago, on August 11, 2105."

Giorgio entered the data. "Ready for another one?"

She nodded. He pushed the button.

The air was hot and humid. She was walking by a canal. People were talking in gibberish. A big black boat jetted past her. The water smelled funny. She held a green balloon in her hand. It tugged at the end of the string, trying to escape. Her other hand held one of Daddy's huge fingers. A great big dog jumped out of an alley and barked at her. She saw his enormous, terrifying teeth, drool dribbling down his jowls. She screamed and let go of the balloon. It raced upward. She cried, the loss of the balloon becoming even more horrible than the monster barking at her. Her cheeks were all wet. Daddy picked her up and held her close, patting her on the back. She licked her tears; they were salty.

Ariadne returned to the present, and discovered that tears really were rolling down her cheeks. Giorgio gave her a tissue. It took a minute to recover her composure.

"I've never experienced anything like this in my life!" she exclaimed.

"Yes you did," said Giorgio with a smile. "Once before."

She nodded, and described the scene. "It must have been Venice. I know we went there once when I was real little. My mother talked about it, but I didn't have any conscious memories of it. I must have been three or four."

"How tall were you, compared with your father?"

She visualized looking up to Daddy. "I just about came to his waist."

"How tall are you now?"

"I'm 168 centimeters."

"And how tall was your father?"

"My mother always said he was a great 184 centimeters."

Giorgio entered the data. "This will help us calculate your age more accurately."

They continued for an hour, mapping her mind. Finally, Giorgio announced, "Good! We now have enough data to home in on the memories you want. It still won't be precise, but we should be able to get your mind to within a few weeks of October 4, 2087. Now that you have been through so many memories, you should be able to control the process yourself. Just force yourself to remember that what you are seeing is a 'dream,' and this office is reality."

"When I'm under, it's hard to remember it's not real."

"Perfectly normal." He handed her a small joystick. "Push this forward to take you forward in time, and backward to reverse. The more you push the joystick, the further you will go. It will return to neutral whenever you let up the pressure, and leave you at that time for as long as you wish. If you squeeze the joystick tightly, memory-evocation stops and you return to the present. Now, the brain does not work simply or smoothly, so the memories will jump around. Ready?" She nodded and he hit the control button.

It was dark. She was in bed with her pussycat nestled against her, purring.

Ariadne pushed the joystick forward and she was at a birthday party. There were six candles on the cake.

She pushed the joystick longer and found herself in a hot, sticky place that looked like an airport. She was in front of a space shuttle. Many black people were around, doing mysterious things. Daddy had said this was Kenyatta Spaceport, in Africa.

In one arm, she clutched a pirate doll, while the other was held by Mommy. Daddy was talking in Greek. He looked very serious, an unusual expression. "And I don't want you to worry about me. We've got a good crew."

"I spoke with Costa," said Mommy. "He'll help me out with the red tape if there's any problem with your pay."

"He's a good man. Also, if you need advice, you can always trust Rafael Cuadra or Sean O'Shaughnessy."

"It's going to seem like forever."

"Remember, it's only for six months."

"Only!" said Mommy. Ariadne looked up at her face and saw tears.

"Why are you crying, Mommy?" said Ariadne.

Daddy hugged Mommy and said, "She's crying because we're going to be apart for a while. But it's just temporary. Daddy'll be back before you know it."

"That's what you always say," said Mommy bitterly. "But

it's always forever. Why can't you get a regular Earth job like a normal man?''

"You know I've got exploration in my cells. You knew that the day we married.''

"I thought marriage would cure you.''

Ariadne began to cry in sympathy. Daddy picked her up and kissed her. "Don't worry, my little pirate. Just take good care of Mommy and study your lessons. I'm going to talk to you in Italian and English when I get back, so you better be ready.''

"I will, Daddy.''

"Promise?''

"Yes, Daddy.''

"And remember the old proverb: 'Be quiet, and people will think you are a philosopher.' ''

"What's a philosopher?''

"A wise little girl.'' He smiled. "Ah, my little one, long ago Zeus gave Ariadne a crown and he set it among the stars. I'll see if I can find that crown for you, and bring it back.'' Ariadne nodded seriously.

He wrapped his wife and child in a single embrace. "Take care of each other,'' he whispered. "You're all I've got in the universe.''

A voice from the shuttle shouted, "Dr. Zepos, we're cleared for launch!''

He kissed them both again and put Ariadne down. "I've got to go now. If I miss my shuttle, I can't catch my starship, and that just wouldn't do.'' She and her mother wept again.

"I love you!'' he whispered as he turned away and climbed the steps. He stopped at the hatch and waved to them. Ariadne waved back furiously.

A black man came up to them and said something in English. Her mother translated and said, "We've got to get inside now.''

They watched from within the terminal as the shuttle taxied out like an airplane. The roar of the electrostatic engines could be heard through the terminal windows. It accelerated until its stubby wings lifted it into the air. Then it roared even louder and climbed steeply into the sky. After a few seconds, a sonic boom sounded, causing Ariadne to cry even harder.

"It's all right, Ariadne,'' said Mommy. "Daddy's all right.''

With tears in their eyes, they stared at the sky long after the shuttle had disappeared.

After a long while, Ariadne pulled the joystick back.

Daddy was showing her a model of a starship.

"This is the one I'll be taking to Beta Hydri."

"Are you going to be all alone in that big spaceship, Daddy?"

"Oh, no, sweetie. Daddy is going to have a crew of people to help him out."

"Are you going to search for pirate treasure?"

He laughed. "You'll never be satisfied till I find that treasure, will you?"

"You promised me you would find out where the pirates hid all their treasure!"

"Oh, I will, my little pirate, I will."

She squeezed the joystick tightly and returned to reality.

"That's it!" she exclaimed. "That's the question I was always asking!"

"What?" said Stefan excitedly.

"Where did the pirates hide their treasure?"

"That's *it?*"

"Yes! I remember now. Daddy used to tell me lots of stories about pirates. I was obsessed with pirates. I'd dig up beaches, always looking for treasure. Daddy must have found treasure!"

"Pirate treasure?"

"Of course not. But some kind of treasure, some mineral wealth or an Earthlike planet. Or maybe he found the ruins of an alien civilization! He found Ariadne's crown after all!"

Stefan nodded slowly and his eyes glazed over. "Treasure . . ." he whispered.

They left the mnemologist's office excitedly discussing her memories, then paused for a drink in a spherical lounge that jutted out from the side of Delphinus over a small underwater canyon, as they excitedly analyzed the possibilities. Fish swam around them unnoticed, centimeters away.

"If we could just find that treasure of your father's," said Stefan, "our careers would be assured. Not to mention our wealth."

"I don't care a leaf of kelp for the wealth or the promotions. To me, being able to see some new world before anyone else alive would be worth more than all the geodollars in the solar system!"

Stefan nodded. "But how could we locate this place? There was no indication in your father's message of where it is."

"I've been thinking about that. One of the people Daddy said we could turn to for help was a spacer, Sean O'Shaughnessy. For years, we used to get Christmas messages from him, always from some exotic place on Mars or Jupiter or whatever. He's the only spacer I ever had contact with. Maybe he can help us."

"It's worth a try. Do you know where he is now?"

"No, but the last message we got was from Aldrin City, a couple of years ago, so I could start there."

"Let's do it."

They hurried to her office. She dialed the lunar operator.

An animated cartoon of a woman appeared on the screen. "What city, please?" said the synthetic female voice in English.

"Aldrin City." The pause reminded Ariadne of the three-second time delay.

"Name?"

"Sean O'Shaughnessy." She spelled it out.

"I'm extremely sorry, but there is no one by that name in Aldrin City. Would you like me to continue the search?"

"Yes." There was a longer pause.

"I'm extremely sorry, but there is no one by that name on the moon."

"Listen, he's a spacer. How can I find him?"

"Is he with the World Space Agency or a private company?"

"Private, I think."

"In that case, I suggest that you contact the Solsys Spacers' Association in Tychoville. Shall I connect you?"

"Please do."

After a moment, a grumpy male face—a real human—stared at them and said, "SOSA Lunar Office, what do you want?"

"I'm looking for a spacer named Sean O'Shaughnessy."

The face brightened. "You looking for Sean? He's a lucky guy. I mean, having a lola like you looking for him."

Ariadne ignored the uncultured language. "You know him?"

"Sure. He and me fueled up together a few times."

"Where can I get in touch with him?"

"That's tough. He's been an isser for a few years now."

"Isser?"

"Interstellar spacer. Yeah, but he usually runs from the roids. They're not so sticky about red tape out there, bless 'em."

"The Asteroid Federation?"

"Yeah. Call the SOSA office on Ceres. They try to keep track of who's where, in case they get a call for a contract."

"Could you give me the number?"

"Dial green-blue-red and ask for SOSA Ceres."

"Thank you very much."

"You're go. And tell Sean his pal Razorback sends him an oh-two." The screen died.

She dialed the number and another cartoon woman appeared. "Interplanetary operator, what colony please?"

"SOSA Ceres."

"Are you familiar with interplanetary calling procedures?"

"Uh, no. I've never made one, unless the moon counts."

"The moon does not count. All interplanetary calls involve time delays of many minutes or hours. Ceres is currently twenty-four light-minutes away. It will take your message twenty-four minutes to get there and twenty-four for an answer to return. If we have to call other asteroids, the time delay will be even greater. Therefore, please prepare your message carefully. Ask as many questions as possible. And set your viziphone to record–answer mode."

Ariadne composed the message mentally, then said, "All right, I'm ready."

"On the word *go* you will be transmitting to SOSA Ceres. Please remember to leave your number. Three, two, one, go."

"Uh, SOSA, I'm Ariadne Zepos and I'm looking for a spacer named Sean O'Shaughnessy." She spelled it out. "I need his advice. He was a friend of my father's. Please track him down wherever he is. I'll pay for the calls. My number is yellow-green-yellow, brown-gray-purple-orange, blue-blue-white-red. Uh, that's on Earth. That's all." She hung up.

Stefan, who had watched all this in silence, said, "I wonder how much this call cost."

She hit the dollar-sign key. "Last call," said the synthetic voice, "long-distance to Asteroid Federation, 179 geodollars."

She bit her lip.

"That's all right," Stefan said importantly. "It was a business call. Charge it to your grant. I'll authorize it."

"Thank you very much," she said with relief. "Now all we can do is wait."

"I wonder," said Stefan, "how we could kill some time." He rubbed her back.

Ariadne moved away. "I wish you wouldn't do that."

He stiffened, then sighed. "Very well. Let's discuss business."

For the next several hours, they talked about the underwater excavation, future research grants, and the possibility of an interstellar expedition to locate her father's world.

*　　*　　*

Finally, the call came through. A scruffy, red-eyed face stared at them. His red hair and stubble matched his eyes, but his face was an ugly mess of black, blue, and yellow splotches. He wore a dirty Aran Islands turtleneck sweater, adding to his roguish look.

"Hello, Ariadne," he said in English. "This is Sean." His brogue, lubricated by alcohol, was so thick you could cut it. "SOSA tracked me down to this leakin' flea-suit hotel. I'm on Vesta. If I didn't have so much respect for your father, rest his soul, I'd have waited a few hours till I'd had some sleep and recovered from our little celebration and my brain was computing at 100 percent.

"But what can I do for you? If it's in my power, I'll try to do it. I'm about twenty light-minutes from you, so pack as much into your call as you can." He gave his number and signed off.

"This time-delay stuff is rapidly losing its charm!" said Ariadne with a scowl. She called the number and spoke into the viziphone. "Hello, Mr. O'Shaughnessy. This is Ariadne again. I'm sorry I disturbed your rest. This is hard to believe, but I got a call from my father. It was transmitted twenty years ago and just arrived. I'll play it for you."

She played back the recording of the interstellar call, translating the Greek.

"I think my father found some kind of interstellar treasure trove, and I want to go look for it. Is there any way you can tell where he might have been? Oh, and I spoke to a gentleman on the moon. He said I should tell you that your pal Razorback sends you oh-two. That's all." She hung up.

"Now we wait again," said Stefan.

They went out for a meal and got back just in time to catch the next message.

"This is Sean again. My, you're looking better than ever, Ariadne. You really are a Greek goddess now. I must say, that call from your father gave me a few gray hairs. It was like seeing a ghost. It was twenty years ago that I said good-bye to him when he transferred to his starship. A decenter man, I've never met.

"In answer to your question, yes, I can tell where he was when he made that call. I've put in a call to lunar farside to get the coordinates from the antenna that picked up your message. That'll tell us where in the sky the antenna was pointing. It'll give us two of the three coordinates we need to tell where he is—was.

"Then, he said you'd be getting the message in 'twenty years, five months, and three days.' That tells us he was twenty light-years, five light-months, and three light-days away, which gives us the third coordinate. I'll compute the location when I've heard back from farside.

"But I don't want you to think seriously about going out there. Mother Nature has thought up more ways to kill you than you could ever dream. Hyperspace is filled with unpredictable obstacles that get worse the farther you go. Anything that killed Alexandros and his crew would be far too tough for a young girl like you." Ariadne grimaced. "You'd need a big, well-equipped expedition to even stand a chance. And from what I hear of those taxin' 'crats on Earth''—Stefan winced—"they're not going to spend a whole lot of money for an expedition that has no guarantee of a big payoff.

"And I don't see any reason to think he found treasure out there. I'm afraid he just found a new way to die. Happens all the time in interstellar space. I'll call you back when I've got the coordinates. Well, so long for now."

There were now gleams in the eyes of both Ariadne and Stefan.

"We've done it!" said Ariadne.

"In a little while, we'll have an interstellar treasure map!" said Stefan.

In less than an hour, Sean O'Shaughnessy's scruffy face was back on Ariadne's viziphone.

"Ariadne," he said, "these were your farther's heliocentric coordinates at the time of his transmission, twenty years ago." He rattled off a string of numbers. "There's an uncertainty of about one light-day in the position, not to mention the unknown uncertainty due to the motion since then of whatever object he was exploring. I checked out these coordinates on my starship's computer and there's nothing listed. It's almost a light-year from Beta Hydri, which we know almost nothing about.

"So all we have is that he spotted something in hyperspace on his way to Beta, and stopped to investigate.

"Well, that's about all I can do for you, except to assure you that your father would never permit you to go to an unexplored world. And he'd have had my head on a platter if I'd not advised you so. If I can be of any further help, don't hesitate to call. I'll be on Vesta until I get a new contract. May the spirit of Zeus look after you. Give my best to your mother.'' The screen went blank.

"Now," said Ariadne, "where can I get a starship?"

"Let me take care of that," said Stefan.

CHAPTER 5

In pressure suits, Sean and Plum floated above their starship, still in orbit around Vesta. An insurance adjuster floated with them, examining the damage to the spacecraft. His tiny roidcycle, little more than a rocket with a saddle, was magnetically locked to the hull. Because of its low cost, the roidcycle was the standard means of personal transportation near asteroids, where feeble gravity placed few demands on the rider.

"How'd this happen?" said the adjuster, examining the massive dents all over the top of the fuselage.

"We passed through an unmapped comet remnant on our way back from 61 Cygni," said Sean.

The adjuster's skeptical frown was easily visible through his faceplate. "Mr. O'Shaughnessy, we at Mutual of Asteroids understand that you issers are an adventurous lot." He stared at the engines, which showed severe damage. "We know that you'll file a flight plan with us for a certified colony, then go off exploring some new planet. If you get a few dents and scrapes, we look the other way and pay for your repairs. But to repair this is going to cost ten, twelve thousand roidbucks. And this damage *didn't* come from a comet remnant in 61 Cygni. This looks like the marks of a hailstorm on a high-gee planet, and there's nothing like that within a thousand A.U. of 61. I'm afraid I'm going to have to disallow your claim."

Sean blushed in a manner noticeable even in the dim sunlight.

"If you'll forgive me for saying this, sir," said Plum to the adjuster, "it doesn't seem quite fair. We, after all, have been paying insurance premiums on this starship quite regularly."

"Of course," said the adjuster. "But our premiums are calculated on the statistical tables for standard flights between certified colonies with known accident rates. We make a modest profit on that basis. If we allowed every isser to get paid every time he decided to explore a dangerous planet, we'd either have to charge

37

a hell of a lot more, or go broke. You can understand that, can't you?''

"I suppose so," said Plum.

"And," said the adjuster, "your policy has a clause that specifically restricts its validity to runs between company-certified colonies, void if a false flight plan is filed.''

Sean shook his head hopelessly.

"I wish I could do more," said the adjuster. "I was an isser myself, once." He threw his hands out sympathetically. "Of course, you can always demand arbitration, but you know the arbitrator's going to have the same facts and reach the same conclusion.''

"All right," said Sean. "I know when a man's got me fair and square.''

"Sorry I can't help. Gotta move now. Got to check out a Smuggler's Policy claim. Good ions to you." He got on his roidcycle and shot off.

"There goes half our pay," said Sean.

"Ah," said Plum, "but we'll still have close to ten thousand for ourselves.''

"Don't forget the eight thousand we still owe from outfitting this expedition.''

"Eight bloody thousand? I didn't realize we had run up such a debt.''

"We'd better get this ship fixed as soon as possible and rustle up another contract.''

That evening, Stefan paid a visit to his brother-in-law, Alfred "Wolf" Wolfram, in Rome. A huge, bald man with a white scar above one eye, he had been raised in the slums of Antarctica and had worked in the nastier parts of three continents and the moon. The two had first met when Stefan was arranging an illegal diversion of lunar ballet funds to a Martian bank. They had found a common cause in the diversion of terrestrial government funds to their own, decidedly superior, uses. Eventually, Wolf married Stefan's sister, who had been attracted by his worldliness.

Wolf sat sprawled in a chair, guzzling weedbeer and smoking a kelparette. Stefan, never a beer drinker, and desiring the absence of his sister, sent her into town for more elegant stimulants. He described the recent events, speaking in English, Wolf's best language.

"If we can arrange an interstellar expedition, I can get a lot of credit out of it at the very least, and probably the minister's job.

But if, as I suspect, that Greek found the ruins of an alien civilization, there will be riches and fame beyond even your hot dreams!''

Wolf smiled a great crocodile grin. ''That would really be something, to be the first guys to find a'other civilization. Like the first guys to loot the pyramids.'' He spoke with a deep, monotone voice in the slurred mixture of Australian and American dialects characteristic of Antarctic English. ''Anything alien, mate, even a cup or a fork, would be priceless! But the jewels, gold, whatever they used, would make the biggest diamond on Earth cheap as moon dust.''

Stefan nodded enthusiastically.

Wolf had endured three years of marriage, during which his wife had almost never been simultaneously awake and silent, and he was constantly looking for excuses to travel. ''Okay,'' he said, puffing on his kelparette, ''so where do we get the starship?''

''Our best bet is to get one from your ministry. My ministry doesn't have many people with interstellar experience. And if we went through the Ministry of Science, we'd be stuck with a lot of scientists who would ask too many questions. Plus their people hate my ministry's guts. We're always battling over jurisdiction and funds. So let's arrange a joint project between your Ministry of Trade and my Ministry of Culture. It's done occasionally. We recently arranged a tour to the Alpha Centauri colony of an ensemble that specializes in twentieth-century rock music.''

Wolf grimaced. ''I *hate* classical music.''

''Out in the colonies, they appreciate anything.''

Wolf had a cushy job in the Customs Division of the Ministry of Trade, thanks to Stefan. It was a job requiring little work, and allowed much travel at taxpayer expense. Wolf was an Assistant Chief Customs Inspector, better known as a C-cop, ''a Wolf in charge of the chickens,'' as Stefan once put it.

''If we use a small interstellar freighter,'' said Wolf, ''we can pick our own crew. And one of the guys in Interstellar Freight owes me a big favor.''

''Good. Now, how small a crew can we get away with?''

''For a job like this, we'll need a' experienced isser for pilot. He'll want a copilot and a hyperspace navigator. Maybe we can find a navigator with some piloting experience, to do both. We need a' engine man. Then, there's the two of us. That'll be a good skeleton crew.'' A wail came from the children's bedroom. ''Damn—diaper time.'' He got up and left for several minutes. When he returned, Stefan said, ''We'll also need a couple of

robots. A doctrobot, in case we get injured.'' Wolf nodded.
''And I'll also want to bring a journobot along.''

''What the bloody hell for?''

''To record our great adventure. We'll get infinitely more
publicity if we've got pictures of us making our great discoveries. It will make us interstellar heroes overnight, and we can keep
the best videos secret, sell them under the table and make another
fortune.''

Wolf shrugged and lit up a fresh kelparette.

''On the way back to Earth,'' continued Stefan, ''we can store
some of our loot on an astéroid. That way we'll only turn over
part of it to the ministry, and have the rest to sell on the black
market.''

Wolf nodded. ''You always did think ahead, mate.''

''That's why we make such a good team. I'm the left brain,
you're the right.'' Stefan smiled. ''I'll arrange funds through the
Ministry of Culture. They'll pay for fuel, food, equipment, anything we need.''

''Won't your boss wonder what this money's for?''

''He's not got much up there in the old processor,'' Stefan
said, tapping his head. ''I'll tell him I'm funding a trip to Beta
Hydri, to see whether we can erect an artist's colony there, like
the one at Lalande 21185. That will explain why I'm going
along. He won't give a damn. All he cares about are old television commercials. He's an absolute fanatic when it comes to
those. Every chance he gets, he funds scholars to study them.
He's the reason why the Louvre got rid of all its paintings and
became the Louvre Museum of Ancient Commercials.'' He pursed
his lips distastefully.

''Art always bores me,'' said Wolf. ''I don't care whether it's
the 'Mona Lisa' or the 'Alka-Seltzer.' Anyway, we'll need lots
of bucks.''

''I'll divert the funds from a hundred other projects. We do it
all the time—mostly to fund studies of old commercials. I'll tell
everyone there's been a small budget cutback. That's our standard excuse.''

''What about the lola?''

''Yes, she's a problem. If Ariadne went along, decorative
though she may be, when we got back, she'd get all the publicity. 'Daughter achieves father's dream!' That's what they'd say
on the QV shows. Plus, she'd want a piece of the pie. No, I think
she's the kind who would insist on it all going into a museum.
What a waste that would be. She definitely has to stay.''

"But it sounds like she's hot to go. How you going to keep her here?"

"It shouldn't be too hard. She can't get a starship without going through channels, and with my help, that will take years."

"Suppose she decides to go to the moon or the roids, and hire herself a' independent isser?"

"Good point. She'd have to get a permit to do that. If she tries, we'll just have to make sure Customs doesn't let her through. Between the two of us, we have enough pull with friendly C-cops to ground her for life."

Wolf chuckled, a sound more nearly resembling the grunt of a Centaurian barking worm than anything human.

"Well, my fine, handsome brother-in-law," said Stefan, "it looks as if we are going to be unable to avoid becoming rich and famous. As soon as my sister gets back, we shall drink a toast to interstellar treasure!"

"Now *that's* something worth drinking to, mate!" said Wolf with a crocodile smile.

The next day, Ariadne consulted with Stefan in her office.

"I want to get a research grant as fast as possible," she said. "With this message from my father, and the coordinates from Mr. O'Shaughnessy, and your backing, it should be easy to get a grant for the first interstellar archaeological expedition!"

"Ah, my dear," said Stefan, standing tall with his hands behind his back, adopting his Noble Adviser Position Three, one of his more successful body-language forms. "I admire your enthusiasm, but the real world does not work in such simple terms. First, there is a grant proposal to be written. There are cost estimates to be made, and they will be very expensive and also difficult to compute. Accountants will have to be brought in. Personnel will have to be selected and approved. Then the forms must be submitted to the Division of Archaeology. If they approve, then the proposal goes to the Research Bureau. If they accept it, it goes to the Accounting Division, and then to the Office of Transportation and to the Operations Support Group. At each stage, someone will ask you to rewrite the proposal, and then it has to be resubmitted all the way along the line.

"Then it gets to the Office of the Deputy Minister of World Culture"—he bowed demurely—"and I give it to the minister and he says, 'Where are we going to get this two million geodollars?' or whatever it is, and I talk him into increasing next year's proposed budget. Once a year, the proposed budget for the whole ministry is sent to the Minister of World Finance, and then he says we're spending too much, cut back by a hundred mega-bucks. If we're incredibly lucky, we'll have this expedition approved in two years, and launched a year after that.''

There was fire in Ariadne's eyes. ''Three *years?* I'm not waiting three years for the greatest discovery in the history of the Earth!''

''There, there, Ariadne. It's not forever.''

''Yes it is! There must be a quicker way.''

''I'll do everything in my power to speed up the process. Just give the proposal to me and I'll personally hand-carry it to the appropriate offices.''

''I appreciate that, Stefan,'' she said softly. ''You've been a real friend through all of this.''

He held her hand in his. ''Never forget, you've always got me on your side.'' He graced her with his handsomest, noblest smile, a Number Seven.

A day later, bleary-eyed, she gave the proposal to Stefan in her office. ''I worked all day and night on this,'' she said, handing him the little white viewcrystal with her audiovisual proposal stored inside. Each atom in the crystal stored bits of data within its quantum energy-levels, giving to viewcrystals a greater infor-mation density than the human brain. Sounds, pictures, and text could be mixed at will, with the proper recorder.

''I'll take it to Rome right away,'' he said. ''I'll read it on the subexpress and make any changes I think will help.''

''I really appreciate what you're doing for me—and for the world,'' she said, taking his hand in hers.

He gave her a light kiss on the cheek, which she returned.

''With my string pulling, I may be able to cut a year off the whole process.''

''I'll be extremely indebted for anything you can do.''

He gave her his aw-shucks-'tweren't-nothing-ma'am shrug and left.

She sat down wearily in her chair, laid her arms on the desk, and rested her head on them. The silence magnified the hum from the air ducts. A janitrobot squeaked by outside, cleaning the floor.

She thought about the memories of her father she had relived in the mnemologist's office. They were more real than her twenty-year-old memories of the great man who had left her life so mysteriously and painfully, leaving her with a hurt that no amount of comfort from her mother or stepfather had ever been able to heal.

As she went over each reawakened memory, she recalled her father's advice: Three people he said could be relied on. Costa was dead. Rafael Cuadra was now her stepfather—good man, but an accountant with no pull. And Sean O'Shaughnessy— "Sean O'Shaughnessy!" she exclaimed, and dialed Vesta.

O'Shaughnessy's answer came back two hours later. "Ariadne, I think you're crazy to try to mount an expedition out there. But knowing you're the daughter of Alexandros Zepos, I know I can't talk you out of it. Maybe he'd even have wanted it that way. Maybe that's why there were enough clues in the message so you could follow him if you really wanted to.

"Well, everyone's got the right to choose his own death, so I might as well help you with yours. If you give up getting Earth to pay for your suicide trip, then get as much money together as you can and put it into an interplanetary bank account. You'll need at least ten K roidbucks, which is around a hundred K geobucks at the current exchange rate."

"A hundred thousand geodollars!" she exclaimed.

"Go up to Gagaringrad and catch a roidship to Vesta. Take the express. It costs more, but you don't want to spend a year getting here on a Hohmann transfer. And don't go orange class unless you're a masochist.

"Meet me here at the Besta Vesta Hotel in Barftown. I'll put you in touch with a good starship pilot. I'd pilot you myself, but I lack your self-destructive willpower, except when I'm in a bar. So long for now."

Ariadne stood up and began pacing the floor, making a mental list of all the people from whom she could borrow money. "A hundred thousand geodollars . . . ."

During the next two days, she borrowed all the money she could from her mother, stepfather, and friends. She went to the bank and borrowed the limit on her undersea condominium in Delphinus. She was barely able to put together fifty thousand geodollars. She put the money into a Bank of Earth account, filed papers for a leave of absence, and applied for a tourist permit to leave Earth.

She called Stefan and explained what she was doing. He tried unsuccessfully to talk her out of it.

Then he called Wolf.

Soon after, Ariadne received a call from Customs.

"I'm sorry," said the young uniformed C-man in Italian. "We're going to have to put your permit on hold for a few weeks."

"But you promised me it would be ready in a week!"

"Look, person, I don't make the rules. All I know is your application has been frozen."

"Let me speak to your supervisor!"

After a moment, an older C-man came on the screen.

"Signorina Zepos, your application has been iced, and there's nothing we can do about it."

"Can't you at least tell me why?"

"No, I'm sorry, that's confidential."

She tapped her fingers angrily on the console. "What is your name?"

"Luigi Paolini."

"And which office are you in?"

"Rome, Section Red Blue."

"Well, Signore Luigi Paolini, I just want you to know that my father's a big chip in the Ministry of Taxes," she said, exaggerating. The C-man's eyes darted guiltily around. "You've heard of Rafael Cuadra, of course."

"The name sounds familiar," said the man uncertainly.

"If you don't straighten this out right now, I'm going to ask him to do a little digging around in Section Red Blue, with particular attention to the personal tax records of Signore Luigi Paolini."

He grimaced. "Perhaps I could tell you a little."

"That's better."

"In strictest confidence, of course."

"In strictest confidence, of course."

"Well," he said, "it seems you've been dealing in the black market for antiquities."

"You're crazy! I'm a registered professional archaeologist! Just call the University of Delphinus!"

"Well," he said, "I know you haven't been convicted of anything, but the word's come down that you're under investigation. That means we can't let you go off-Earth. You might escape, or maybe you'd try to smuggle something out."

"This is ridiculous! Isn't there anything I can do?"

"Afraid not, not till the investigation is over."

"And how long will that be?"

"Who knows? These things usually drag on for months."

She slammed the off-key. "Damn!" she shouted, pounding the console with her fist.

Ariadne got up and paced the floor again. Then her face lit up and she sat down at the viziphone. She dialed her stepfather.

When his face appeared, she said, "Rafael, I have a *big* favor to ask . . ."

The next day, Ariadne and her stepfather were at Kenyatta Spaceport, weighted down with her luggage.

"Your mother will kill me," said Rafael Cuadra, "when she learns what I've done." He spoke Greek with a Spanish accent.

She ignored his remark. Her eyes darted everywhere in the spaceport. "It's so eerie, being in this place where Daddy left eons ago."

Rafael nodded silently, having long ago learned he could never compete with the memory of a dashing, star-exploring father. What could a paunchy, middle-aged tax accountant offer to compare with the famous Alexandros Zepos?

She continued, "And what makes it even weirder is that I saw this whole place just a couple of days ago in the mnemologist's office. It hasn't changed much in twenty years." She stopped, her mouth open. She dropped her luggage and ran over to a gate. Her stepfather awkwardly picked up the extra bags and followed her.

"This is where he left," she said quietly when Rafael came to her side. She stared at the Earth Spaceways shuttle on the pad. "Gate violet-blue, it was." A tear came to her eye.

She shook her head and took two of the bags back from Rafael.

They approached the Customs office. "Wait a moment," he said. They paused. "I want you to promise me again that you'll be more careful than you've ever been in your life."

She put her arms around him and hugged. "Oh, I will, I promise."

"If anything happens to you, your mother *really* never will forgive me."

"I promise that if I see anything that might seriously get me into trouble, I'll come home."

"Good. And you'll hire the best spacers you can get?"

"Of course." Another tear came to her eye. "It's strange. Now that I'm leaving you and going light-years away, Rafael, I've never felt so close to you in my life." He hugged her hard. "I know you could lose your job because of what you've done for me. I always kept Daddy's name until now. I felt it would be betraying him to change my name from Zepos to Cuadra. So now I find the only way I can follow his footsteps is to change my name to yours. Ironic, isn't it?''

"It will take them another day or two for the clerks to enter the change on all the government's computers. Until then, Ariadne Cuadra is free to go where Ariadne Zepos is forbidden.''

"If they figure out that you helped me do this, they'll fire you, if they don't throw you into jail.''

"I'll just say I didn't know anything about it.''

"And they'll wonder how I could have got the name change, the travel permit, and the new passport in a measly few hours without your help.''

"Let them wonder.''

She hugged him again. "You're wonderful, you know that, Rafael? Mother's very lucky. But you better not go into Customs with me. They might remember you.''

He nodded and helped her arrange all four pieces of luggage so she could carry them, awkwardly.

"Oh, and be sure to call Stefan and tell him what I've done. In all the rush, I didn't have a chance.'' She kissed him and said, "Tell Mother I gave her all my love. Or half of it, anyway, split between the two of you.'' He smiled.

As she struggled into the Customs area, he sadly watched her go. Her father had been his best friend. Rafael had known Ariadne since she was born, had been her stepfather since she was eight. He had wiped away her tears countless times. Now there were tears in his eyes, too.

CHAPTER 6

Sean and Plum docked their ship at Mickiewicz's Ship Repair, a station orbiting around Vesta. Ms. Mickiewicz personally inspected the starship, flying around it in her pressure suit and evapack. She whistled when she looked inside the engines.

"O'Shaughnessy," she said, "your systemdrive's got three holes in the Kawasaki, and the hyperdrive looks like it'll go critical if you breathe on it too hard."

"So give us the bad news," said Sean.

"Going to take at least twelve, maybe fourteen thousand roidbucks to fix."

"Fourteen K?" exclaimed Sean. "That's ridiculous!"

"O'Shaughnessy, the terries have raised the duties again. The cost of everything imported here from Earth went up 6 percent. That includes engine parts."

"Can't you get them on the black market?"

"These aren't tiny things you can hide in your booties. Takes big-scale smuggling to get starship engine parts out. That means big bribes, more overhead. Until we start manufacturing them here in the roids, we're going to pay through the nose cone, and the terries know it."

"There goes our profit!" said Sean.

"If it's any comfort, some guys over on Juno are tooling up an engine factory."

Plum spoke up. "We shall simply have to work harder to find a new contract."

"And to think," said Sean, "I came out here to escape Earth's damn rules and now I find they're squeezing me in the chips. This taxin' solar system is getting too small."

Ariadne disembarked from the shuttle at Gagaringrad, a colony that orbited a thousand kilometers above the Earth and served as one of the major jumping off points for the moon and other colonies. She wore a beige episuit of a conservative cut not likely to attract attention.

Two things she noticed at once on this, her first visit to a space colony: one was the phenomenal spring in her step, thanks to the half-gee gravity maintained in the outer ring of the spinning station; the other was the faint, sour smell of cabbage in the air.

She retrieved her luggage from the crowded baggage room, went through Customs, and parked the bags in three lockers. She quickly found the Interplanetary Ticket Office, where there was a bewildering number of desks, labeled in Russian and English: EARTHWAYS, INTERPLANET, TRANSWORLD SPACEWAYS, ROID RIDERS, SUNRUNNERS, PANPLANETARY, and MARS INVADERS. She went up to an idle Customs man.

"What's the meaning of all these names?"

"Just come from Earth, eh?" He spoke English with a Russian accent. "Those are all different spacelines that leave from here."

"Which one is best?"

"Depends what you want. This isn't Earth. You'll have to get used to making decisions for yourself out here. Earthways is owned by Earth government, and it goes most places, but it's overpriced and service is lousy. Others are privately owned. They have different specialties. SunRunners only goes to inner planets—you know, Venus and Mercury."

"How do I get to Vesta?"

"Ah, you want asteroid express. Roid Riders and TWS have service to most of major roids. I suggest you go to a travel agent for best deal. Here, I just happen to have card of very good agent." He pulled a business card from his pocket and handed it to her. "Tell them Gherman sent you."

The card spoke to her in its tinny synthetic voice: "Anton's Planetravel Base, where you'll find the best deals in the solar system. Just drop into our conveniently located offices in the spaceports of Aldrin City, Deimos, or Gagaringrad for the happiest trip of your life. Package tours a specialty. Geodollars, roidbucks, and all major bankcards accepted." Then a jingle started up:

> "Mars was such a dreary place,
>   Venus just a mystery,
> Then I tried old Anton's Base.
>   I made travel history.
> Anton's, Anton's, Anton's, Anton's
>   Planetary bliss-story!"

She cringed as the jingle ended. "How is it you happen to have this card?"

He shrugged. "Frankly, person, it's because I get percentage from any customers I send them."

"Where are they?"

He pointed to the exit and said, "Two blocks down that way, just under Toyota ad. One more piece advice: Don't travel orange class."

She found Anton's run-down building underneath a huge three-dimensional advertisement for two-person Toyota space shuttles.

She touched the door and it squeakily slid sideways. Inside, a short, plump woman smoking a cigar sat behind a counter, watching a soap opera.

"We can't keep meeting like this," said the sexy woman on the video.

"We have to," replied the sexy man on the video. "I love you, Carmelita." He kissed her.

Ariadne coughed noisily. The cigar lady looked up and smiled. "Welcome to Anton's." She spoke English with a Slavic accent.

"Oh, Fosdick!" said Carmelita on the video.

"Gherman sent me," said Ariadne.

"If I can't see you," said Fosdick, on the video, "I'll kill myself!"

"Good old Gherman," said the cigar lady, making a note.

"Oh no, Fosdick," said Carmelita, "I could never live if you did!"

"What can I do for you?" said the cigar lady.

"Then why won't you see me any more?" said Fosdick.

"I want to go to Vesta," said Ariadne.

"You know," said Carmelita. "It's on account of—your clone!"

"Vesta?" said the cigar lady. "Not much going on there, this time of year."

"*Him* again!" shouted Fosdick.

"I've got business there," said Ariadne.

"He's younger and handsomer than I," said Fosdick, "isn't he?"

"Okay," said the cigar lady. She tapped the travelog screen next to the counter.

"Yes," said Carmelita. "We got married yesterday!"

"We've got three good connections from here," said the cigar lady.

"*Married?*" exclaimed Fosdick. "You married my *clone?*"

"I'd like to get there as soon as possible," said Ariadne.

"I *had* to," said Carmelita.

"In that case," said the cigar lady, "you'll want the TWS Express that leaves tomorrow morning."

"*What?*" said Fosdick.

"How long does it take?" said Ariadne.

The cigar lady hit some keys.

"Yes," said Carmelita. "I'm carrying his child."

"Four days," said the cigar lady.

"No!" shouted Fosdick. "Not that!"

"That's fine," said Ariadne.

"Yes," cried Carmelita, "the doctrobot told me last week."

"The express uses one-gee acceleration," said the cigar lady.

"How do you know it isn't *my* child?" said Fosdick.

"Moves like hell," said the cigar lady, "but costs."

"Because," said Carmelita, "the doctrobot said I got pregnant the Saturday before last."

"How much is it?" said Ariadne.

"*That* Saturday?" said Fosdick. "You said you were visiting your mother!"

"What class?" said the cigar lady. "Brown class is sixty thousand geobucks."

"I lied," said Carmelita.

"Sixty thousand geodollars?" said Ariadne.

"We went on a picnic to the moon," said Carmelita.

"Private cabins," said the cigar lady, "all the luxuries."

"But you always said," said Fosdick, "the moon was *our* special place!"

"What about red class?" said Ariadne.

Fosdick pulled out a quantagun and aimed it at Carmelita.

"Thirty thousand geobucks," said the cigar lady. "Four to a cabin, no use of the brown-class lounge."

"No!" cried Carmelita.

"What about orange class?" said Ariadne hesitantly.

"Yes, you slut!" shouted Fosdick.

"Nine thousand geobucks," said the cigar lady, "including tax. But I don't recommend it."

Fosdick squeezed the trigger.

"You're frozen," said the cigar lady. "Stored with the luggage."

Carmelita fell to the floor.

"I guess," Ariadne said distastefully, "it will have to be orange class." She pulled out her interplanetary bankcard from its telcro compartment on her hip.

Fosdick dropped the gun and bent over Carmelita's body, crying. An electronic dirge rose in the background.

The next morning, Ariadne arrived back at Customs with her luggage, having spent the night in a cheap spaceport hotel.

This time, the Customs official was a woman. Ariadne stood in line behind a husband, his wife, and a seven-year-old boy.

"Why can't we go to Mars this time, Daddy?" whined the boy. "Venus is so ultra-boring!"

"Because Mommy has government business at Aphrodite," said the husband. "This way, the ministry pays for our vacation."

A janitrobot rolled by noisily, vacuuming the floor.

"I wanna go to Mars!" screamed the brat.

"Turn it off," said the wife, "or we'll send you back to Baltimore. You want to go back to the dole riots, huh?"

The Customs woman cleared the family and asked for Ariadne's papers. As she read the passport, her eyes opened wide and she pocketed the documents. "I'm afraid I'll have to ask you to come with me," she said.

"What's wrong now?" said Ariadne impatiently.

"Just come with me." She took Ariadne's arm and pulled her over into a little office. Ariadne was left in front of a chair occupied by a huge bald man in a black business suit. He had a scar above one eye and smoked a black kelparette. If Buddha had been in the Mafia, he might have looked like this.

"Hello, Ms. Zepos," the man said in English.

"I am Ms. Cuadra, if you please," she said, standing with her chin raised, putting on an air of arrogance.

"Yes, and a couple days ago you were Ariadne Zepos, daughter of the great Alexandros Zepos and resident of the city of Delphinus." He puffed on his kelparette.

She lost her arrogance and let herself slouch.

"Allow me to introduce myself. I am Alfred Wolfram, Assistant Chief Customs Inspector. Some people call me Wolf. You can call me Mr. Wolfram." With his Antarctic accent, his attempt to sound officious made his speech choppy.

"What do you want from me, Mr. Wolfram?"

He pointed at her, aiming his kelparette like a gun. "I just want you to return to Earth until our investigation of you is complete."

"What is all this nonsense about investigating me? I've never broken a law in my life! Well, hardly ever. I mean, you can't breathe without breaking some little law. But I've never stolen anything, never hurt anyone, and now I'm suddenly Public Enemy Number Brown!''

"Look, person, all we got is a' anonymous tip you were dealing in the illegal sale of antiquities. We look into it, we find you're a' archaeologist who gets all kinds antiquities all the time. Makes sense, doesn't it? In your line of work, you could clone bucks on the black market.''

"Mr. Wolfram," she said pleadingly, "I have never even thought for a moment of selling what I find in my work! These are treasures for all personkind! I'd sooner sell my body to an organfarm!''

"Okay, maybe you're truthing me, maybe not." He blew a smoke ring. "But we can't let you go joyriding around the solar system until we find out, can we?"

"But I swear I'll come back as soon as my work is finished!"

"How do I know, once you're out in the roids, beyond the reach of Earth law, you'll come back again?"

"I promise!"

"If I had a roidbuck for every promise I'd been given, I could retire to Mars."

"Look, how long is your stupid investigation going to take?"

"I don't know, maybe a month, maybe two."

"Suppose the person who gave you the anonymous tip has also planted false evidence?"

"Then you'll go to jail until we can prove you're innocent. First offense, you'd only get a year or two."

They stared at each other silently for a moment.

"Okay," said Ariadne, "I'll go back to Earth."

"That's a good lola."

She turned and opened the door.

"Where are you going?" said Wolf, rising like an asteroid of flesh.

"To catch the next shuttle back to Earth."

"Not without me."

"Oh," said Ariadne.

He took her arm, holding it with an airlock grip, towering over her, and they walked toward the Earth-shuttle area. The Wolf was arm in arm with the lamb.

"Wait," said Ariadne. "I've got to retrieve my luggage."

"Moon dust!" cursed Wolf. "Let's go get it."

They walked back to the interplanetary area and collected her four bags. Ariadne made sure he carried the biggest and bulkiest, freeing her from his magnetic grip. He held the kelparette in his teeth, smoke-signaling his annoyance.

They approached the portal to the Earth shuttle, where the janitrobot was vacuuming noisily. As she passed the robot, she bent over its microphone, pointed at Wolf, and said, "That man's face is on fire!"

Immediately, the robot stopped vacuuming and a siren sound emerged from its speaker. "Man on fire! Man on fire!" it shouted between bursts of the siren. A jet of icy foam shot from its head and splattered Wolf squarely in the face. He fell backward.

Ariadne dropped her luggage and ran as fast as possible. In the low gravity of the colony, she was able to run faster than a champion athlete on Earth. Wolf tried to rise, but slipped on the foam.

She raced around a corner and, with great strides, ran down a corridor. In the distance, she could see the Toyota ad. She ran for it, and pushed into the travel agency breathlessly.

"—not *you!*" said Fosdick on the video.

The cigar lady looked up and smiled.

"Yes, it is I," said a woman on the video who looked exactly like Carmelita.

"What can I do for you today?" said the cigar lady.

"A Customs man was trying to take me back to Earth," said Ariadne, gulping for breath.

"But I *killed* you!" said Fosdick.

"Ah, in trouble with the law?" said the cigar lady.

"No you didn't," said the Carmelita look-alike.

"Just a little," said Ariadne.

"Oh no, you aren't—" said Fosdick.

"Aren't we all?" said the cigar lady.

"Yes. I am—" said the Carmelita look-alike.

"I've *got* to get that Express!" said Ariadne.

"You're Carmelita's *clone!*" said Fosdick.

"It can be arranged," said the cigar lady.

Carmelita II pulled out a quantagun.

"Thank God!" exclaimed Ariadne.

"No, *don't!*" said Fosdick.

"It will only cost you another ten thousand geobucks," said the cigar lady.

Carmelita II shot Fosdick.

Ariadne winced and pulled out her bankcard.

Carmelita II bent over Fosdick's body.

"Spacers," said the cigar lady, "are always happy to help anyone escape Earth."

"Now," said Carmelita II, "*I* shall marry your clone!" Organ music surged up.

A few minutes later, Ariadne was sneaking into the freight entrance of a spaceliner hangar. There was a smell of grease. A tall man with a huge walrus mustache and an earring in one ear came up to her and said in English, "You Cuadra?"

"Yes."

He took her past a pile of metal crates and into a cold room. The grease smell was replaced by a faintly nauseating odor she could not recognize. "You're going to travel as freight."

"Sounds even worse than Orange Class."

He grunted. "Six of one. Either way, you get shoved into a zirco crate with your own automatic life-support system and doused with hibergas. Only difference is your crate is going to be marked *machine parts* instead of *passenger*."

"Sounds lovely."

"It's the only way to fly. You ready?"

"I guess so."

"Put this on." He handed her a plastic box the size of a shoe and helped her strap it on her left arm after rolling up her sleeve. "This'll check your pulse, respiration, whatever. It lowers your temperature too, though you don't actually freeze the way they say. If anything goes wrong, it'll inject you with whatever it thinks you need. In the event of an emergency, it'll try to wake you up."

"Try?"

"Doesn't always work. It does the best it can."

"Wonderful," she said.

He opened the lid of a metal crate, a cube about a meter on edge. He attached two cylinders and regulators inside it. "The blue one's lox for you to breathe. It also serves as refrigerant. The yellow's hibergas."

"I'm going to stay in that little thing?"

"It's either that or we can strap you to the outside of the ship. The crate's vacuum-tight. The lox has enough air to last you five days at the rate you'll be breathing."

"Suppose I wake up early?"

"Then it'll last you six, eight hours. Maybe ten, if you keep calm."

"Super."

"Get in."

She stepped into the crate and crouched down on her back in a nearly fetal position, resting her head against the cylinders. "What, no video set?"

He reached in and attached two tubes between the cylinders and the life-support control.

"How about shuffleboard?"

He pushed a key on the control and said, *"Bon voyage!"* as he unceremoniously slammed the lid down.

In the darkness, claustrophobia began to descend. The only light was from the feeble green indicators on the control box. She put her hands against the lid above her face. The metal was cold. She tried to recall the emergency procedures she had been taught in underwater training. "Stay calm," she whispered. "Don't panic. Think of something nice." She thought of a warm, sunny beach in Greece.

A tinny synthetic voice spoke from the control box: "Prepare to hibernate."

"I'm as prepared as I'll ever be," she murmured. "Hope the temperature doesn't get too cold. Hate to freeze to death after all this."

"Hibernation initiated," it said. "Sweet dreams." Some long-forgotten saintly engineer had added that little human touch to the voice synthesizer program.

A yellow indicator light lit up and a hissing sound started. A nauseous smell filled the crate. The temperature started to fall. She shivered.

"It's not enough, now the crate stinks," she whispered. "So . . . cramped in . . . can't . . . stand . . . smell . . ."

She began to hibernate. And to dream.

CHAPTER 7

Ariadne was falling in space, into a whirlpool, a cosmic Charybdis, a black hole. A huge, ugly, bald man with a long curved sword chased her, striding over space like a god. As she fell, she got colder and colder, until icicles formed in her veins. The man caught her and smiled, revealing the teeth of a vampire. He bit into her left arm, draining her frozen blood. She screamed. . .

. . . and awoke. A squat, bearded man was looking down at her as she lay in the crate.

"Where are we?" she asked in Greek.

"You speak English?" he said.

"Yes," she said weakly.

He unstrapped the life-support control from her arm. Her head felt as if it had been between the crashing boulders of Scylla, and the nauseating odor of hibergas filled her nostrils.

"Welcome to Vesta."

"Now I understand why they said not to go orange class." She held her aching head between her hands.

He helped her stand. The only reason it was possible at all in her weakened condition was the almost nonexistent gravity. She felt light as a feather, and almost was.

"Oh, I need—" she said.

"It's over there," he said, pointing to a little room marked with the symbols of a man and a woman.

She ran to it as fast as possible, bouncing off the ceiling in her haste.

After she returned, straightening her episuit, the man said, "First thing everyone needs after a few days in hibernation is a quick visit to the head."

She sat down on a crate, almost bouncing off. He gave her a tall glass of water with a straw. The liquid formed a wobbly, nearly spherical surface at the top of the glass, looking as if it would fly away at the least motion. She drained it immediately.

He refilled it and gave her a pill. "This'll help kill some of the

56

headache, but it'll take a couple of hours for the pain to go away completely. Anything stronger and you'd be unconscious.''

She swallowed it.

"Do I have to go through Customs?"

He laughed. "No Customs agents out in the roids—apart from snoops, trying to track down smugglers so they can trap them in Earth space. But they have no legal power here. No need to worry about terry 'crats out here. No C-cops, no tax men, and no Big Mother telling you what you can't do. Welcome to paradise.'' He studied her pale, unhappy face. ''Want anything to eat?''

At the thought of food, her stomach threatened to erupt like a volcano on Io. ''No,'' she murmured.

"How do you feel?"

She rested her head in her hands. She was alone, hundreds of millions of kilometers from her loved ones and friends, with a headache that throbbed and tried to split her brain into hemispheres; she was nauseated, and wanted by the police on Earth. And she had lost all her luggage.

''I feel miserable,'' she said, then realized that it was much too joyous a way to describe her condition.

After half an hour, she felt up to the journey to the Besta Vesta Hotel. Her brain was still throbbing but the nausea had receded, replaced by a growing fear that she had gotten in over her head. After getting directions, she gingerly stepped outside.

Vesta was more bizarre than she had dreamed. The videos she had seen had never given her the gut feeling of a world where you weighed as much as a grapefruit on Earth. No amount of watching could provide the stomach-churning sensation of walking like a kangaroo, jumping higher into the air than an Olympic athlete. Nor could videos prepare you for the unreal feel of mulitcolored plastic skyscrapers like houses of cards ready to blow down in the first breeze.

Thousands of people streamed by, hopping or riding the ski lift. One man flew through the air fifty meters overhead on muscle-powered wings, like Icarus. Clothing styles ranged from ultraconservative to nude, but she hardly noticed the natives' eccentricities of dress, since roiders were famous for ignoring Earth fashions.

The air smelled strangely fresh and countryish, thanks to the gardens everywhere that produced the oxygen she breathed. Flowers grew as tall as people in the low gravity, and trees towered over some of the skyscrapers. The sky was dim, thanks to the distant sun. Fresnel refractors—thin sections of sun-tracking lenses on top of the bubble dome—and reflectors outside brought more of the sunbeams into the city than nature originally provided, but it was still no brighter than an overcast day on Earth. The sun was less than half its proper size, and the sky surrounding it was black, except where sunlight glistened off refractors.

In twenty minutes, she was standing outside the Besta Vesta Hotel. One of the hotel's annunciator's vowels was defective, and it repeated "Bosta Vosta Hotol, ront by the minute or by the month" endlessly. The hotel was not one of the more memorable examples of Vestan architecture. Constructed in the Polka Dot Period, it bore large green dots on an orange field; the color combination made her stomach twinge. It stood ten stories tall and was frayed at the edges. She entered the lobby.

The first thing she noticed was the furniture: it consisted of plastic planks with footholds and seat belts. Evidently, its main function was to keep the occupant from bouncing off.

An old, bearded man was asleep on a couch, strapped in nicely. A battered janitrobot vacuumed the extremely dusty air. The young clerk was exercising in the office, bouncing off the floor and ceiling like a Ping-Pong ball.

Ariadne went up to the counter. "Hello."

The clerk stopped bouncing and hooked his legs over a bar near the ceiling. Upside down, he said, "What can I do for you, person?"

Disoriented enough by Vesta, she was taken aback further by the task of conversing with an upside-down clerk. She replied hesitantly, "I'd like to see Mr. Sean O'Shaughnessy, please."

"He's staying in room green-black-red," he said. "That's green floor. But I saw him go out a while ago."

"Do you know when he'll be back?"

"Heisenberg only knows. But if I wanted to make some easy money, I'd bet he's in the nearest bar."

A bar! Her nose wrinkled at the thought of the sinful behavior associated with bars, even on Earth. On Vesta, it was better not to think what might take place there. "Where is that?"

"It's the Loch Vesta Pub, down the street to the right, half a block."

"He often spends his time in such places?"

"They'd go broke if it wasn't for O'Shaughnessy."

Her nose wrinkled again. "Thank you very much." As she exited, the clerk began to ping-pong himself again.

She walked down the street, noting consciously for the first time the extraordinary variety of people. They were of all colors, and wore every conceivable clothing style—plus a few inconceivable ones. Some looked like escapees from jail, others like video stars. Everyone looked young, the result of the flattering effect of low gravity.

The Loch Vesta Pub was a green plastic copy of a Scottish inn, with green plastic heather on the roof. Its annunciator repeated a message in a thick Scots burr: "The Loch Vesta Pub, trrraditional Scots food and grrrog forrr the thrrrifty spacerrr wi' a wee bit o' heatherrr in his DNA." There were many cracks in the wall, some covered with green tape. It looked like patrons had exited through them. Ariadne opened the door.

Inside, there was no ceiling. The pub opened up to the air. Only around the edges was there plastic heather, giving the illusion from the outside of a complete roof. It surprised her until she realized it must never rain under the bubble.

The odor of smoke, of recreational chemicals, and of various permutations of alcohols greeted her nose rudely. Had there been a roof on the place, the smell would have been intolerable. The murmur of conversation in a variety of languages and dialects provided a soundtrack to the offensive panorama.

There was a long counter with flimsy stools, some of them occupied by seedy men and scantily clad women who looked as if their virtue was available wholesale. Behind the counter stood a large bearded man in a kilt. On the floor were a half dozen tables, several occupied by men and women in various stages of intoxication. Most of their drinks had straws, even the glasses of beer whose foam floated into the air. A robot in a kilt was cleaning one of the tables.

Additional tables and chairs jutted out horizontally from the walls, halfway up to the "roof." Beside the door was a pill-vending machine murmuring synthetically, "Hi, I'm the Happy Pharm. Would you like a pleasure pill?"

A number of the men eyed Ariadne as she stood in the door, an experience she could never get used to. In the far corner, she saw the man whose ugly face had graced her viziphone so much of late: Sean O'Shaughnessy.

She went over to him, taking careful small steps so as not to bounce too high. Sean was sitting with another man, a plump fellow who looked completely out of place in his black suit and tie. Sean himself was wearing shapeless brown slacks and his Aran Islands turtleneck sweater, now clean. He looked bigger in life than he had on the viziphone, though also more disreputable, with his stubble, red eyes, matching nose, and half-healed black-and-blue face. He was smoking a black kelparette and staring moodily into a glass filled with a green liquid that bulged upward. His companion toyed with a glass of sherry.

Her nose wrinkled distastefully, a position that threatened to become permanent on Vesta. ''Mr. O'Shaughnessy!'' she exclaimed.

He looked at her through bleary eyes and shouted, ''Ariadne! You really did do it!'' Alcohol made his brogue even thicker than usual.

''Of course, Mr. O'Shaughnessy. I always do what I make up my mind to do.''

He smiled and said, ''I haven't seen you in real time since you were, I guess, twelve years old.'' He chuckled. ''You've really improved,'' he added admiringly.

Haughtily, as if a queen were requesting permission to board a garbage scow, she said, ''Do you mind if I have a seat?''

''Oh no, have two, they're free.''

His companion rose and pulled a chair over for her and helped her strap the seat belt. ''Permit me to introduce myself,'' he said in his upper-class British accent. ''I am Pelham Chalmondeley III, copilot and partner to Mr. O'Shaughnessy, at your service.''

''I am pleased to meet you,'' said Ariadne, relieved to meet a civilized person. ''My name is Ariadne Zepos.''

''Please call me Plum,'' he said.

''You may call me Ariadne.''

Sean, oblivious to the subtleties of etiquette being enacted, said, ''Plum, Ariadne's the little girl I used to carry around the shuttlecraft when I was working for her father.''

''You must have been rather young then yourself,'' said Plum.

''Yes, I was in my late teens the last time I saw her father.'' He grew solemn. ''Poor old Alexandros. He was so good to me. I'd've done anything for that fine man.''

Ariadne, touched, said, ''I know he had the highest regard for you.''

Sean nodded. ''What kind of a filthy galaxy is it that takes a fine broth of a man like that and chugs him down and spits him out? Is this any way to run a universe, I ask you now?''

The bearded bartender in the kilt came up to the table and said, ''Och, can I get anything for the lassie?'' He spoke with a strange dialect that Ariadne could not place.

''Have you any mineral water?'' she said.

"Don't get much call for that on Vesta, lassie," he said. "But I can give you some club soda. On the roids?"

"What?"

"With ice?"

"Yes please," she said. Her stomach rumbled and she blushed. "Do you serve food here?"

"Just a few things: oatmeal, haggis, kidney pie, and tacos."

"Tacos?"

"Yes, O'Shaughnessy swore he'd never come back here unless I added something Mexican to the menu. He loves Mexican food, hates most everything else."

"I'll drink to that!" shouted Sean, and he proceeded to prove his devotion to truth by draining his glass. "MacGregor, I'll have this drink's twin brother."

"What is haggis?" said Ariadne.

The bartender recited: "It's the minced heart, lungs, and liver of a sheep, mixed with onions, oatmeal, and suet, and boiled in the stomach of the animal. Quite repulsive, actually."

Her nausea started to return. "But does it taste good?"

"Just between you and me, lassie, it makes me vomit."

"I think I'll have the oatmeal."

"You're on safe grounds there, lassie."

"And tell me something," she said.

"What?"

"Where are you from? Your accent intrigues me."

"Och, lassie, I hail from Haifa."

"Israel?" she exclaimed. "But the kilt and everything?"

"Well, you see, lassie, this place was up for sale, and I'd always wanted a bar of my own, and I'd made a few roidbucks mining, and it was cheaper to grow a beard and have a kilt made than to redecorate."

"I see."

"My name's Moshe Rabinowitz, but everyone calls me MacGregor." He shook her hand and went off to the counter.

"Mr. O'Shaughnessy," Ariadne said.

"Call me Sean."

"I want you to take me to that world my father found."

He paused briefly. "Ariadne, don't you know that you'll never come back from there?"

"I've had a lot of experience with dangerous work. In my work as a hydroarchaeologist there's been many a shipwreck that nearly claimed me for a victim."

"But what do you know about spacing? Have you ever been trapped in a vacuum with only seconds of air left?"

"I've been on the bottom of an ocean, with only seconds of air left to get to a decom chamber."

"Have you ever been on a cryoplanet," said Sean, "where it's so cold that if you stick your arm out the hatch, it will freeze like an icicle and break off if you bump it?"

Not to be outdone, Ariadne said, "Have you ever dived in an underwater volcano, with steam bubbling up centimeters from your face, ready to turn you into bouillabaisse?"

"That's different," insisted Sean. "I'll concede you probably have guts, since you're the daughter of Alexandros Zepos, but your experiences have all been on one tiny little planet. When you've spent half your life in space, then I'll talk to you about going to see your father's graveyard."

MacGregor arrived with drinks and oatmeal. He put the steaming bowl in front of Ariadne. She thanked him and said to Sean, "I'm going there with your help or without it. All I want from you is the name of a good interstellar spacer."

"Your father would never forgive me if I let his little girl go to her doom. Ariadne, I'll help you go anywhere in known space, I'll even fly you myself, but I'll not help you get to that devilish place."

"On the viziphone, you promised you'd help me find a good spacer."

Sean grumbled into his drink. "That I did, and I'm a man of my word."

"So who's the best spacer in town?"

"You're looking at him," said Sean.

"Daddy didn't tell me you were modest too."

"May I make a suggestion?" said Plum. "Since, as it happens, we are currently studying alternatives for our business plans, perhaps we might consider contracting our services to the young woman in return for a percentage of whatever we find."

"Not if it means taking her to her father's planet."

"I certainly could not consider those terms," said Ariadne. "Anything we find would be of immense historical value and would have to be reserved for museums for the benefit of all personkind."

"To hell with personkind!" shouted Sean. "What has personkind ever done for me except drive me from my beloved Ireland and into thirty-eight kinds of danger?"

"Let us be reasonable," said Plum to Ariadne. "Were we to

take you there, and were we to survive, we should deserve some reward for our efforts.''

"I'll give you all my money," said Ariadne.

"And how much, may I ask, is that?" said Plum.

"Let me see, there are almost thirty thousand geodollars left."

"Three thousand roidbucks?" said Sean. "You seriously thought you could finance an interstellar expedition for three K?"

"It was all I could get," she said defensively. "And I ran into some unexpected expenses."

"Really, miss," said Plum, "your plans are a trifle unrealistic. It would probably take at least five thousand roidbucks—approximately fifty thousand geodollars—to hire a good interstellar spacer. Then, purchasing supplies, insurance, and other necessities would run the account up quite a bit more."

"But that's all I have."

"Then you have no alternative but to accept our terms," said Plum.

"I will never permit any valuable artifacts to pass into private, greedy hands."

"Really, miss," said Plum. "Without such an arrangement, you will never get there and no one will ever see the great treasure that you seem convinced is waiting. At least our way, your museums get half the treasure. As they say on Mars, half a brain is better than none."

Her head began to throb again.

"Without us," Plum continued smoothly, "no human eyes shall ever see your father's treasure; and with us, his legacy will be found and human culture will be enriched. If a few items happen to fall into the hands of discriminating collectors who will treasure them just as much as you, where is the harm? Is that really any worse than their falling into the hands of some museum administrator who keeps them hidden in his office? Worse than allowing them to join the basement collections of the thousands of other artifacts stored by generations of scholars, never to be seen except by a handful of students and janitrobots?"

Ariadne stared at her oatmeal for a while. "I don't know what else I can do," she said. "It is agreed."

"Wait a microsec!" exclaimed Sean. "Plum, are you seriously suggesting we commit suicide for a half-share in some imaginary treasure?"

"Ah," said Plum, "but suppose it *isn't* imaginary. Think of how much it would be worth . . . And think of how often we have risked our necks for a pittance. And then, my friend, contemplate your bank account.''

Sean mulled it over moodily for a while, then slammed his fist on the table, bouncing the glasses and dish into the air. ''Agreed!''

''Excellent!'' said Plum.

''Let's drink to it!'' shouted Sean, demonstrating.

The robot in the kilt came over to their table. It carried bagpipes and began playing them at an excruciating volume.

''What's that he's playing?'' shouted Ariadne, covering her ears.

''*Hava Nagila*,'' shouted Sean.

Her head throbbed worse than ever.

After Sean and Plum had celebrated to their satisfaction, they returned to the Besta Vesta Hotel with Ariadne. Night had already fallen, a day on Vesta being only a bit over five hours long.

''I'll get a room in this imitation hotel,'' said Ariadne.

''Why don't you sleep with us?'' said Sean.

She looked at him indignantly.

''Nothing improper, I mean,'' said Sean. ''There's plenty of space on the floor, and a plastic floor on a low-gee asteroid is one of the nicest beds there is.''

''I would never consider for a moment sleeping in the same room with two strange men,'' said Ariadne primly.

''We're not that strange,'' said Sean. ''Just unusual.''

''I have my reputation to consider,'' she said.

''I've never known a woman to fail to enhance her reputation by sleeping with me,'' he said with a leer.

''Mr. O'Shaughnessy, I'll beg you to refrain from such vulgar remarks.''

''Ariadne, we're going to be spending a long time together in a tiny ship, and there are no private suites on her.''

''That's different. I'm sure we can arrange some privacy when circumstances require it. But propriety demands that we should spend the night in separate quarters when the possibility exists.''

''You realize that every roidcent you save by not paying a hotel bill is one we can spend on equipment that might save our lives.''

She nodded slowly. ''Very well. I shall sleep on the floor of your room, but only if we erect some barrier between us.''

Sean laughed and said, ''It's a deal.''

They climbed up the handholds on the outside of the hotel to the fifth floor and entered the corridor. Sean stuck his key into the keyreader and the door slid open. There in the darkness was a big man with a lightrod. He whirled and shined the lightrod in their eyes. "Don't move!" shouted the man. "I've got a gun." He shined the lightrod on his quantagun so they could see it. "Inside!" he commanded.

As the trio entered, Sean hit the lightpad and the room lights turned on. "Wolfram!" exclaimed Ariadne as she recognized the huge bald man.

Wolf blinked at the sudden light and Sean kicked himself off the wall. In the light gravity, he flew like a human cannonball.

Sean slammed Wolf's gun wrist aside with a karate chop and rammed his other fist into the man's solar plexus. The huge man toppled and his gun went flying.

Gasping for breath, Wolf snapped his knee up toward Sean's groin. Sean blocked it with his own knee and received a painful blow to the stomach. He belched pleasant alcohol vapors and grabbed the man's lapels.

Plum scooped up the quantagun and stood, arms folded, observing the scene with the air of one who has seen it all before.

Wolf slammed an uppercut into Sean's chin. Only the Irishman's grip kept him from tumbling head over heels into the ceiling.

Sean let him go and the big man jumped up at him. Dodging, Sean grabbed an anchored table with one hand and Wolf's ankle with the other and swung him slowly, like a centrifuge, accelerating. When let go, Wolf smashed into the outer wall of the building. The plastic bulged and gave way. Wolf flew through the wall out into the street.

"That was a good one," said Sean.

"About average," said Plum. "He's a rather large chap, and well versed in the art of street fighting, I'd say, but not in roidgravity."

Sean jumped through the hole in the wall and pushed off, falling gently feetfirst down the five stories, gliding to rest with his feet on the man's belly.

"Oof!" belched Wolf.

Sean flipped him over and bent his right arm into a hammerlock, sitting on him.

Plum and Ariadne climbed down the building less gracefully.

"That's the man who tried to take me back to Earth when I was in Gagaringrad."

"A cop?" said Sean.

"A Customs inspector," growled Wolf.

"A C-cop!" spat Sean. "There's nothing lower than that to a roider," he said to Ariadne, "except a lawyer or a taxer."

He retrieved the man's I.D. card. When pressed, the card lit up with a 3D picture of Wolf and said, "This is Assistant Chief Customs Inspector Alfred R. Wolfram. All citizens are required to submit to search and inspection of their bodies, luggage, freight, and any other objects of suspicion. By order of the Ministry of Trade, as authorized by the Supreme Judiciary of Planet Earth."

Sean threw it away, laughing. It sailed a hundred meters into the air. "That badge is worth its weight in moon dust out here."

"Mr. Wolfram," said Ariadne, "how did you get here so fast?"

He remained silent. "Must have caught the same ship you were on," said Sean. "But how'd he know you were coming here?"

"He saw all my papers, knew I had a ticket for this run."

"Yes, but how did he find *my* room in *my* hotel on Vesta?"

"If you'll forgive me for pointing out the obvious," said Plum, "Miss Zepos is not inconspicuous in her attractiveness. There are not as many attractive women on Vesta as the demand would warrant, nor is this a gigantic world. Thus one may surmise that it would not be difficult to follow her trail."

Sean nodded and twisted Wolf's arm. "Why did you follow her?"

"She's wanted for selling stolen antiquities on the black market."

"Now, *that's* my kind of girl!" said Sean with a smile.

"But I didn't!" exclaimed Ariadne. "Someone's trying to frame me."

"Who would want to do that?" said Sean.

"I've been trying to figure that out," she said. "There's an archaeologist who's jealous of my discoveries, and who's always trying to belittle them, but I can't believe he would stoop to such a thing."

"Who is the informer?" said Sean to Wolf persuasively.

"Anonymous," said Wolf through gritted teeth.

"That's what he told me," she said.

"Get out of here," said Sean, releasing Wolf.

The man stood up unsteadily and started to walk away. Sean booted him in the rear and he flew high in the air like a football. "And don't come near Ariadne again," shouted Sean, "because the next time, I won't be such a gentleman!"

Plum remarked, "Such a rude fellow, and on the Sabbath, too."

"Sabbath?" said Ariadne. "Is today Sunday?"

Sean glanced at his watch. "Yes, it is. We keep Universal time out here, for convenience."

"That's Greenwich time," elaborated Plum with a hint of pride.

"I must find a church," said Ariadne. "Is there a Simonist church around here?"

Both men shrugged. "You can find anything in the roids," said Sean.

A few minutes later, she walked into the little pink plastic Simonist church. A prerecorded sermon was in progress. A quantavision recording of the silver-haired Benedictor Simon, looking more than ever like her father, was addressing the half dozen churchgoers in glorious, larger-than-life 3D. His torso floated above their heads, every gesture and grimace magnified to an overwhelming intensity, while the sound thundered proportionally.

". . . to avoid eternal hell!"

"Eternal hell!" shouted the churchgoers.

"But only through the twin miracles of quantum theory and pyramidology may we understand the revealed Word of God."

"Word of God!"

Ariadne strapped herself into a pew and let the glory and ecstasy of the message of the saintly Simon roll over her.

"The deadly promise of the entropy death at the end of time is but the devil's work."

"The devil's work!"

"Verily, it will be the only reward of those who neglect the teaching of the Lord."

"The teaching of the Lord!"

"For thus it is written on the great Pyramid of Egypt, and this I have personally seen with mine own eyes and measured with mine own laser."

"Mine own laser!"

"But for the believer, has not the Prophet Heisenberg—"

"Heisenberg be praised!" shouted one man.

"—said unto us that the nature of life is uncertainty, yet we may still be confident of particular overall truths?"

"Overall truths!"

"And has not the Prophet Schrödinger—"

"Schrödinger be praised!" shouted the man again.

"—said that even as life is comprised of waves, so too must we bear with its ups and downs."

"Ups and downs!" chorused the churchgoers.

"Let us never forget that the Equation of Life has many solutions, and it is for us to choose the initial conditions for a satisfactory answer at the end of it all."

"The end of it all!"

"Verily, I say unto you, brethren and sistren, those who choose the path of truth and decency will be rewarded with quantum leaps of happiness, while those who fail to initialize their lives properly and fail to conserve their moral momentum, will quantum-tunnel through the walls of heaven and descend into the black hole of the Devil himself!"

"The Devil himself!" they shouted.

"Yet the Prophet Schrödinger—"

"Schrödinger be praised!" said the man.

"—has said that it is not possible to predict with certainty, but only to apprehend probabilities, so never should you be depressed because your actions are not immediately rewarded with happiness or success."

"Happiness or success!" muttered the group.

"It is sufficient to know that you have maximized your statistical happiness-function!"

"Happiness-function!"

"And so, my beloved fellow believers, I must leave you now once again."

"Once again!"

"I dearly hope you will find that my message has increased your probability-current to God, and that you will donate as much as you possibly can to the continuation of this teaching of the Gospel of the Lord."

"Gospel of the Lord!"

"And I pray that you will read my latest viewcrystal, available in your neighborhood food market or through the facilities of this fine church!"

"This fine church!"

"Major bankcards accepted."

"Major bankcards accepted!"

"Amen!" said the preacher.

"Amen!" shouted everyone. The floating torso of the Benedictor Simon disappeared.

Ariadne was in tears, as were several other men and women.

The donation box was handed around. Ariadne slid her bankcard into the slot and said to the box, "Ten geodollars."

After a pause, the box replied, "Bank account invalid," and spat out the card.

She stared at the rejected card in shock.

Inside Mickiewicz's orbital hangar, the great bald mass of Wolf floated underneath the starship *Shillelagh*. Because it was Sunday, the mechanics were off duty. It had been no trouble for an old lunar worker of his skills to break through the hangar's locks.

With tools from the hangar, he opened a hatch underneath the control panel of the starship. He attached a pocket terminal to one cable and entered a series of commands to the ship's computer.

Then he pulled a small metal cylinder from a thigh pocket and wired it into the hyperdrive control-line.

He pushed the ON key and smiled like a crocodile.

CHAPTER 8

"Your bankcard's invalid?" said Sean. "We needed that money for supplies!"

"I don't know what happened!" pleaded Ariadne. "I had almost thirty thousand geodollars in my account!"

"What bank is it?"

"Earthbank."

"Of course!" exclaimed Sean. "Run by the terry government. All Wolf had to do was contact them to freeze your account."

"But I had the money transferred out here!"

"To an Earthbank branch, of course."

"Naturally."

"Why in the name of the rings of Saturn didn't you transfer it to a private bank? Then the terries couldn't have frozen it."

"How was I to know they'd do this?"

Sean groaned. "What are we going to do for money now?"

"Sean," said Plum, "if I may be so bold, may I suggest that we postpone paying any debts we can, and cancel the more cosmetic repairs to the *Shillelagh*."

"I hate owing money," said Sean, "but it seems there's no alternative. Most of what we owe, we owe to the starship outfitter, Wong. I saved his life once, so he'll extend me the credit. We've got enough to pay for the repair of the engines. If we skip the other repairs, we can have enough to buy a few supplies. That's what we'll have to do."

Above Vesta, a starship freighter with Earth-government registry settled into a parking orbit. A roidtaxi rendezvoused with the starship and a huge bald man transferred to the ship.

Expedition Leader Stefan Draganescu greeted Assistant Chief Customs Inspector Wolfram. Stefan introduced him to the four-person crew: pilot, copilot–navigator, engine man, and exobiologist, the latter the only woman on the crew.

"I added her," said Stefan to Wolf as he introduced them, "in case the dangers we face include animal life."

Stefan and Wolf moved aft, into the cargo bay, away from the hearing of the others. Wolf grinned lecherously and said, "She'll also come in handy if we're away from civilization very long."

Stefan smiled and said, "That thought also crossed my mind."

"Always thinking ahead!" said Wolf with his bloodcurdling laugh.

Stefan pointed to a closet with a red cross and said, "That's where the doctrobot is stowed."

"Standard," said Wolf.

"And this is my journobot," said Stefan, pointing to a shiny red robot screwed into a shipping mount in the ceiling. Its torso was pear shaped, the size of an average man, with two twelve-jointed arms and similar legs. It had five-fingered hands and big five-toed feet that grasped handholds in the ceiling. Its head was vaguely humanoid, with large, red humanlike ears. Its two metallic eyes, on short stalks, focused on Wolf, and a green light in its chest glowed.

"How do you do, sport?" said the robot. Its rubbery lips—purely cosmetic—pretended to form sounds from the speaker within. Rubbery eyebrows added a quizzical expression for emphasis.

"I call him Homer," said Stefan. "I got him from the Ministry of Information, a very expensive model. He records 3D video as well as audio. And he has a censor program that we can use to color the stories most flatteringly. Isn't he beautiful?"

Wolf shrugged. "I still think that's a waste of space. At least we can always dump him if we need more room."

"Dump me?" squealed the robot. "Please, dear Stefan, protect me from this brute! The fate of the world's press is in your hands! And," he added shrewdly, "the fate of history's record of these events!" His Asimovian self-preservation subroutine was hard at work.

"There, there, Homer," said Stefan. "I won't let anyone hurt you. After all, you're going to make me more famous than anyone on Earth."

"Oh thank you, Stefan. You're so noble." The robot switched to his journalistic mode and his chest's green light turned yellow as he announced with a deep, resonant voice: "Dateline: Vesta. The journey had hardly begun when the expedition's journobot, Homer, named after the greatest poet in terrestrial history and the latest design from Earth's leading robot factory, was threatened with destruction by one member of the crew. Already the firm hand of a born leader could be discerned as Stefan Draganescu saved the robot from certain death, preserving the rights of the press once again.'' Then his yellow light turned back to green.

"Privacy mode," said Stefan to the robot.

"Roger, dear Stefan," said the machine in his higher-pitched conversational voice. His green light turned to red.

"Now he does not record what he hears and sees," explained Stefan. "Wolf, is Ariadne taken care of?"

"We can forget about the lola from now on."

"Excellent," said Stefan. He walked forward to the crew module and addressed the pilot: "Captain, prepare to take off for interstellar space."

CHAPTER 9

It was a week before the *Shillelagh* was ready to take off for hyperspace. Such fuel and supplies as they had been able to afford were stowed on board the battered vessel, which was still tethered inside Mickiewicz's hangar.

Sean and Plum sat belted into the pilot and copilot seats, while Ariadne sat in the removable passenger's seat behind them.

Sean turned on the voice channel of the main computer. "You okay, Snafu?" he said to the computer.

"Affirmative, Captain O'Shaughnessy," said the computer in a sexless monotone.

"Anything to report?"

"All parameters are within acceptable limits of nominal, although most of them are on the lower side of acceptability. Good enough for government work. One log anomaly to report."

"Report."

"My accelerometers measured the impact of a man-sized object a week ago Sunday, when my understanding was that the mechanics were off duty."

"Did he come inside the cabin?"

"Negative."

Sean pondered this awhile, and Plum looked worried.

Sean turned to Ariadne and said, "Do you think Wolf might try to sabotage us?"

"Oh, I am certain he would never do anything that dangerous," she replied. "After all, he is an important official of the World Government."

Sean sneered. "That's like saying he's a graduate of the Orbital Penitentiary."

Plum nodded. "I think we should assume the worst."

"Wise man," said Sean. "Let's check all the outboard hatches."

"It's not my fault!" said the computer.

The two men exited through the airlock. Ariadne followed them curiously, eager to enjoy the experience of zero gravity afforded by the hangar's orbit around Vesta. Air was present in the hangar, so they did not need pressure suits. Sean called to Mickiewicz to turn on the floodlights. The men each opened hatches and examined the wires, pipes, cables, fibers, and cryolines that lay within, while Ariadne bounced joyously from one side of the hangar to the other, like a dolphin with wings.

The starship was one of the smallest made, barely fifteen meters in length. Where most starships were designed to fly only in space, using shuttlecraft for landings on planets, the *Shillelagh* was designed to do both. Consequently, it did neither especially well; but it was adequate.

Shaped something like a flounder, its body had been designed to plough through interstellar dust when the electromagnetic deflectors were down, and to have some aerodynamic lift when flying at high speed through an atmosphere. Instead of wings, and a tail, it had electrostatic jets for atmospheric stabilization and steering.

Once it had been sleek and shiny. Now, in addition to older wounds, its top was battered, with numerous dents from the hailstorm. The front portion was occupied by the crew module and front vernier engines, the middle third by the cargo bay, and the aft by the Kawasaki, hyperdrive, and rear vernier engines.

After twenty minutes, Sean called out, "Here it is!"

Plum floated over and stared in the hatch below the main control panel. There was a small metal cylinder attached to a cable.

"Looks like it was designed to blow up when we hit the hyperspace drive," said Sean.

"My opinion exactly. The blighter wasn't satisfied with diverting us, he was willing to kill us in the bargain."

"A bomb?" said Ariadne, bouncing down to the ship and grabbing one of the cables holding it in place. "I don't believe it."

"I wish I'd killed him when I had the chance!" spat Sean. "That moon-dusty, chip-eating, son of a gynoid!" To Ariadne, he said, "Go down to the office where it's safer."

"If it's safe enough for you, it's safe enough for me," she said defiantly.

Sean muttered under his breath, an increasingly frequent occurrence now that Ariadne was around. He carefully disconnected the bomb and carried it over to a small airlock, pushed it through with waldoes and watched it drift away. When the bomb was barely visible, he grabbed a laserwelder, aimed it through a porthole, and fired.

There was a great flash that lit up the interior of the hangar.

Thanks to the vacuum of space, it was soundless, apart from some clunks reverberating as fragments hit the hangar harmlessly.

Ariadne stared out wide-eyed.

"You know," said Sean, smiling with satisfaction, "for a government-surplus computer, Snafu's not half bad." He clapped his hands and said, "Back to work!"

Plum closed up the external hatches and the trio reentered the crew module. They put on geesuits, one of which they had specially purchased from a secondhand pressure-suit store for Ariadne. The bulky suits were filled with a liquid that redistributed the pressures of high-gee acceleration. They put on close-fitting face masks that would pump air into them to keep them breathing when their lungs were too heavy to inhale. Then they plugged the suits into the seats and strapped themselves down.

"How's everything now, Snafu?" asked Sean, his voice muffled by the face mask.

"Nominal," replied the computer.

"Love to hear that word," said Sean. "Now to try out the Kawasaki," he said to Plum.

Plum pressed several keys on the yellow area of the control panel.

"Will that take us into hyperspace?" asked Ariadne.

"Praise the saints," said Sean. "A backseat pilot."

"Easy on her, Sean old boy," said Plum. "It is, after all, her first interstellar trip. Remember yours?"

Sean grumbled something under his breath.

"The Kawasaki engine," said Plum, "is used for interplanetary space, as well as for the fine-tuning of translation—movement—once one is in hyperspace. But in order to get into hyperspace, for faster-than-light movement, one needs the hyperspace drive."

Back in the twentieth century, physicists thought the universe had from four to eleven dimensions of space-time. In the next century, thousands of additional dimensions were found, and it was theorized that there is an infinite number of dimensions of space-time. Few of them are well mapped, making most of them unusable for travel.

The *Shillelagh*'s hyperspace drive translated the spacecraft along the sixty-fifth dimension, and then moved it parallel to the familiar universe—normspace—much like an ant might be lifted off a two-dimensional table and moved parallel to it through the third dimension. In this parallel translation the space-time metric shrinks along certain paths, so small hyperspace distances correspond to large normspace distances.

The ship travels in hyperspace and then translates back to normspace, but because of the different metrics, a one-kilometer movement in parallel space may correspond to a million kilometers in normspace, depending on local hyperspace curvature and the distance of the movement path from normspace.

"Why not go right into hyperspace from here?" said Ariadne.

"Because," said Plum, "the sun's gravity gradient warps space-time too much to permit the space-time resonance that allows us to shift into hyperspace. Only far from a star can we achieve the delicate conditions necessary."

"You sound like a mathematician," said Ariadne.

"As a matter of fact, that is what I read at Oxford, before going on to study hyperspace engineering."

Sean ran carefully through a long checklist, and Plum glanced at his screens, peppering his discourse with "Roger."

"I've heard that there are stars or some such obstacles in hyperspace. When my father's expedition did not return, there was speculation that they had run into one."

"Oh, I'm afraid there are, including some very strange singularities we imperfectly understand, but the ones near the routes to the nearest stars have been carefully mapped."

The first interstellar pilots used trial and error; the errors never returned. Then robot explorers went out. Thousands of robots were sacrificed to make hyperspace maps, and gradually safe paths were found to the nearby stars.

Plum called up a map on his main screen. The three-dimensional image showed a complex, color-coded spaghetti of coordinate lines. He pointed to one particularly severe convergence of spaghetti strands. "This is one known singularity near our path, which no robot—or human—has ever returned from, so we will avoid it quite carefully." He tapped the screen with his finger. "This is rather like those medieval charts that said, 'Here there be dragons.' Our dragons are mysterious objects in hyperspace that we do not understand at all, and they grow more numerous the farther one goes from the sun."

"Ah, that explains why we've never gone much beyond the twenty light-years my father went."

"Right-o. Very difficult, requiring much robot mapping. Very costly. We have enough planets within twenty light-years to keep us busy for centuries, I should guess."

"And that also explains why we've never got to the Galactic Center."

"Quite. Those mysterious signals we've been receiving from

there for the last century have caused many a spacer to dream of being the first to the Center, and not a few of them have disappeared trying, but one fears it's hopeless. After all, it is thirty thousand light-years away."

"It's all so frustrating," said Ariadne. "To know there is another civilization out in the Galactic Center, and yet to be unable to visit them or even decipher their signals. If only there were some civilization closer to Earth, one we could visit. I pray that is what my father found."

"I hope you're right."

Sean handed green pills to Ariadne and Plum, and took one himself. "Gee pills, to combat high-gee acceleration," he said.

"We're going to be accelerating at very high rates," explained Plum. "Otherwise, it would take us weeks to get far enough to initiate hyperspace translation."

"If you like," said Sean, "you can also have a sleepill so you don't have to experience it at all."

"No thanks," said Ariadne. "I had enough sleep on my trip from Earth." She shuddered.

Sean began conversing on the viziphone with Ms. Mickiewicz. "Prepare for departure," he said.

"Roger," replied Mickiewicz. "All personnel clear. Did you file your flight plan?"

"Roger, all filed."

"Crane ready."

"I copy crane ready. Tug away!"

A robot crane, magnetically attached to the *Shillelagh*, pulled the starship forward, into a giant airlock. Its great iris closed behind them.

"Inner lock closed," said Mickiewicz.

"Roger."

The outer lock irised open and air gushed out into the vacuum of space.

"Crane disconnect," said Mickiewicz. "Have a good trip, Sean."

"Thanks, Mick."

The crane let go its magnetic connection. Momentum made the starship continue to drift slowly out of the airlock.

After a couple of minutes, they were completely clear of the hangar. Sean fired the verniers and oriented the ship's engines away from the hangar and Vesta.

"Ready for Kawasaki drive, Snafu?" said Sean.

"Affirmative, Captain O'Shaughnessy," replied the computer.

"Plum?"

"We are go for Kawasaki initiation," said Plum.

"Three, two, one, initiate," said Sean, hitting the red Kawasaki key.

As a rotating spherical fuel pellet, magnetically levitated inside the Kawasaki engine, came in contact with an ion beam, the outer metatomic layers ripped off and roared aft, channeled magnetohydrodynamically.

The fuel was mined from interstellar asteroids produced by supernovas. When a supernova exploded, its planets were shattered and their matter compressed to ultradense states beyond anything made in the laboratory. Nuclei fused together to form metanuclei millions of times more massive than in ordinary atoms. As the matter flew through space, expelled by the supernova, it relaxed to form metastable superatoms—metatoms—and crystallized into metals far denser than any occurring on earth, but inherently unstable.

Such rare metatomic asteroids, captured by the gravitational field of a large planet like Jupiter, or seized on the fly during a chance passage of a free interstellar asteroid through the solar system, were the prize find of the lucky roider. They were more valuable than a moon of gold, and were the source of energy that had revolutionized solar-system travel.

Because of the instability of the metatoms, all it took was the touch of an ion to make some of them blast off into space at high speed, where a magnetic field controlled their direction. In effect, the Kawasaki drive tapped a tiny part of the energy of a supernova.

The ship began to vibrate subsonically—a silent pulsing felt in the guts—and they slowly moved away from Vesta.

"We have Vestan escape velocity," said Snafu.

"Snafu, go to one gee acceleration," ordered Sean.

"One gee acceleration," repeated Snafu. The ion current on the pellet increased and the ship began to move much more rapidly, pressing them back in their seats with the feel of Earth-normal gravity.

"After that feeble gravity on Vesta," complained Ariadne, "I feel like an elephant."

Sean consulted with Plum about their course and made some adjustments.

By now, the gee pills were having an effect; the adventurerers felt extremely relaxed and moved very slowly.

"The medicine will help you resist the abuse the high acceleration will inflict on your body," said Plum to Ariadne. "It relaxes the muscles, slows the heart, reduces tunnel vision, and does other kind things to you. The computer will increase the oxygen content of the air to keep our brains from suffering oxygen starvation. Be sure to get as comfortable in your seat as you can."

They each squirmed around in their plush gee-seats, which adjusted automatically to their contours.

"Every four hours that we're under high-gee acceleration, we'll stop the engine for a break. If you need to visit the W.C., let us know and we'll take the break early."

Sean said, "Brace yourself for some unpleasantness." Then he commanded, "Snafu, initiate high-gee acceleration program. Go to sixty gees over one hour."

"Roger," replied Snafu.

The ship vibrated more strongly and the crew members were pressed down into their seats farther and farther. One gee had been unpleasant, but this acceleration multiplied that each minute, as their weight grew truly elephantine.

Ariadne lay back miserably, feeling as if the Great Pyramid of Cheops were on her chest. Every muscle in her body was tugged down. Even with the gee pill, everything in the cabin looked like it was at the end of a tunnel. She was glad there was no mirror to see the distortions in her face, and prayed that it would not be permanently wrinkled. She discovered that there was no way to lie comfortably. The mask hurt as it dug into her face, but without its forced air, she would not be able to breathe. "How long do we have to accelerate?" she asked, each word coming with difficulty.

"Only about half a day," replied Sean.

"Half a day!" she whimpered.

"We'll take it easy on you. We'll give you a one-gee break every hour. And after the high-gee part's over, we'll relax for two days at one gee until we're safely outside the solar system. That'll be pleasant. We'll have nothing to do for two days but eat and talk, and I've loaded up our supplies with plenty of enchiladas, tacos, tamales, and burritos."

"What?" Plum said glumly. "No human food?"

"Oh," said Sean, "there's some kidney pies and other stuff unfit for consumption by anyone but an Englishman."

"Bless you," said Plum.

"Then," said Sean, "after our two-day feast, we'll decelerate, to match speed with the cosmic rest-frame. Then we'll go into hyperdrive.'' He loaded a World War I flight simulator into his computer, while Plum called up a Louis L'Amour Western in the original printed words.

Ariadne closed her eyes miserably, swearing that she would not give these brutes the pleasure of hearing her complain. She also resolved to take the sleepill at the next break.

The hours passed until glorious relief came at last. The acceleration fell to a comfortable one gee as they traveled at an appreciable fraction of the speed of light. Ariadne's body ached all over, but she gladly accepted the pain as payment for the joy of normal weight, which now felt like weightlessness.

They happily changed out of their smelly geesuits into ordinary clothing, after each had taken a shower. Sean wore his beloved turtleneck and smoked a black kelparette; Plum had an Oxford gray suit complete with regimental tie, and smoked a pipe; and Ariadne bore a form-fitting beige episuit. Her blond hair, damp from the shower, hung down to her shoulders.

Snafu spoke: ''Captain O'Shaughnessy.''

''Yes?''

''Today is the independence day of Trinidad and Tobago, and also of Malaysia.''

''Hallelujah!'' shouted Sean. ''Double rations of starshine for everyone!'' He dashed for the emergency locker.

Ariadne looked quizzically at Plum.

The Englishman sighed. ''Sean has this appalling custom of celebrating the independence day of every nation that was ever under British rule. What is today's date, Snafu?''

''August 31.''

''One loses track of time so easily in space,'' said Plum, opening his personal locker. ''Sean has programmed all the independence dates into Snafu.'' He pulled out a tiny British flag.

Sean threw Plum and Ariadne each a squeeze-bottle and raised one into the air. Ariadne read the label: ABDULLAH'S REAL IRISH WHISKEY FROM MARS. She threw it back at him.

Catching it with one hand as if it were the most valuable object in the solar system, he shouted, ''To the spirits of all freedom-lovin' souls on planets, in space, and in hyperspace!'' He squirted the precious fluid into his eager mouth.

''God save the King!'' said Plum, waving the flag and squirting the liquid into his less enthusiastic orifice.

Ariadne crossed her arms disapprovingly.

After finishing the bottle, Sean removed some food from the reconstituter and served the other two. Ariadne frowned at his whiskey breath. She picked at the Mexican and English food, unhappy with the selections, wishing for some good Greek *pastitsio*, but unwilling to complain after the ordeal she had been through. Sean broke open another bottle of Abdullah's.

They had passed the two days of one-gee acceleration by drinking, conversing, eating, playing games with the computer, listening to music, sleeping, and drinking. Then they went through a grim period of high-gee deceleration to match the cosmic rest-frame velocity.

Finally, when they were at rest with respect to the universe, Sean shut off the Kawasaki engine and addressed the computer. "Snafu, prepare for hyperdrive."

"Roger, Captain O'Shaughnessy," it replied.

While Ariadne floated happily around the cabin, the men discussed the hyperspace map on the video screen. With overlays, the spaghetti-lines tangled with numbers and mathematical symbols. It all looked like a tax-audit report after an accident in an Italian restaurant.

"We're all set, Ariadne," said Sean. "Better strap yourself in again."

"It's not going to be like that horrid high-gee run, is it?" she asked as she obeyed.

"No, this is quite different. Fun even."

"While there are some who actually enjoy hyperspace," added Plum, "there are others, myself included, who regard it as offensive."

"Offensive?" said Ariadne.

"That is the best word I can think of to hint at the strangeness of the experience," said Plum. "It offends one's senses, and is disturbing to me in a fundamental way I cannot put into words."

"Oh," said Sean, "you're just like those gravity-chauvinist terries who can't stand zero gee because they always have to know where 'up' and 'down' are."

"On the contrary, my good fellow," said Plum, "I have always rather enjoyed zero gravity, except in the beginning, before I became accustomed to it. But hyperspace is one thing I'm quite sure I shall never become accustomed to."

"Ariadne," said Sean, "you adapted to zero gee like a Centaurian tumblemouse to liquid sulfur, so it's my bet you'll not dislike hyperspace at all."

She smiled at what she sensed was the first compliment she had received from Sean since their Vestan meeting. She was surprised to realize that she even cared what he thought of her. Also, she noticed that he was beginning to look much better as the frostbite splotches faded, though she did wish he would shave his red stubble. She reminded herself that he was a crude, blasphemous, immoral brute and resolved to return to her normal businesslike attitude toward him.

For his part, Sean was pleased that she was wearing the far shaplier pressure suit after half a day of being in the bulky geesuit. He resolved, however, to turn his mind from the direction it threatened to go in, with the thought that she was a prude and a professional virgin.

Plum sat glumly glancing back and forth between the two, trying to compute the probabilities that the two would (a) become romantically involved, (b) kill each other, or (c) both.

"Snafu," said Sean, "how are the hyperdrive systems?"

"Nominal," replied the computer.

"Lovely," said Sean.

He and Plum ran through some more tests and calculations, and made some fine adjustments of the spacecraft attitude, velocity, and angular velocity with the vernier drives. To execute hyperspace translation, the ship had to be at rest with respect to both the expansion and rotation of the universe.

When he was satisfied, Sean said, "Brace yourself for hyperspace, Ariadne."

"Roger," she replied eagerly.

"Three, two, one, hyperdrive," counted Sean. He hit the barber-pole–striped key, and the powerful hypergenerator sent currents through coils embedded in the skin of the ship. As he eased the vessel's angular velocity to zero, the oscillating multipole field resonated with the metric of the sixty-fifth dimension. The stars disappeared.

Early in the twentieth century, Mach's principle had given the first clue to the peculiar phenomena that occurred when a body was not moving with respect to the universe. Mach perceived that there was a fundamental difference between a rotating and a nonrotating object: The rotating one feels a centrifugal force because it is spinning with respect to the matter of the universe. Later in the same century, the cosmic blackbody radiation left over from the Big Bang that formed the universe provided the ultimate cosmic rest frame. For the first time, it was possible to measure how fast Earth was moving against the general expansion of the universe.

In the next century, scientists performed an experiment in space, just beyond the orbit of Pluto, in which they carefully slowed a microscopic superconducting sphere until it was precisely at rest with respect to the cosmic frame, with zero spin and zero velocity. To their astonishment, the sphere disappeared. It had resonated with the structure of hyperspace and quantum-tunneled into the seventh dimension.

Years of study turned the laboratory effect into a practical means of transportation. By surrounding the vessel with an electromagnetic field of a particular spectrum and shape, one could choose the dimension into which it moved.

Each of the *Shillelagh*'s crew members felt queasiness due to tiny gradients in the changing metric. Ariadne was grateful that they remained weightless. She stared through the windows, fascinated. Outside, the familiar stars were replaced by a multicolored cobweb of crisscrossing curved lines. Sean was hunched over the videoscreen, glancing up now and then to relate what he saw out the windows to the hyperspace map. His hands flew back and forth among four joysticks that controlled their motion. With the shrunken metric of this dimension of hyperspace, gentle acceleration of the Kawasaki drive sufficed to carry them over distances corresponding to light-years of normspace.

"Each line is a hyperspace star," said Plum. "Their images are highly distorted by the irregular curvature of hyperspace."

"Are these the same stars we have in our sky?" asked Ariadne.

"Some of the lines are 'ghosts' of the gravitational fields of stars in our galaxy, extensions of their fields that happen to pass through this subspace. Much of what you see, however, are stars and topological monstrosities that exist only in *this* space. Have a look backward, Ariadne."

She rotated her seat and looked through the rear viewscreens, fed by cameras in the aft. A turbulent hurricane of red, blue, and brown streaks whirled back there.

"Those are our sun, planets, and major asteroids," said Plum, "the 'ghosts' of their gravitational and magnetic fields, whirling around millions of times faster than normal due to our motion through space-time."

She stared at the complicated, vicious dance of the "ghosts." "I can see why we don't use hyperdrive inside the solar system."

Plum smiled. "Yes, just a close perturbation from those fields would be enough to destroy us. By the bye, one of the difficulties with hyperspace is that things are not where they seem to be.''

''Why not?'' said Ariadne. ''Light travels in straight lines.''

''No, light travels curved lines—geodesics—as Einstein showed. In this highly curved space, photons of light travel as if through a swirling, heated gas, as you may have noticed above a fire on Earth. The paths are distorted by the curvature of space, and an object which seems to be on the left may actually be on the right.''

''Which must have made hyperspace even more difficult to conquer.''

''Quite right. Sean, I do believe she is a closet mathematician.''

Sean grunted, absorbed by his navigational problems.

They traveled for hours, following a complex path through the hyperspatial obstacle course. Ariadne was fascinated by the constantly changing panorama.

Finally Sean announced, ''We're all set to emerge at your father's coordinates, Ariadne.''

Her heart leapt.

Sean commanded, ''Snafu, prepare to reenter normal space.''

''Roger, Captain O'Shaughnessy,'' replied the computer.

After touching up the vernier controls, Sean hit the barber-pole key again. The hyperdrive translated them back into normal space.

''What the hell?'' exclaimed Sean. A huge white star filled their forward window—and they were rushing toward it.

''Danger course,'' Snafu said. ''I repeat, danger course.''

''I can see that, you taxin' bag o' one-bit chips!'' exclaimed Sean. He verniered the vessel to the right until it pointed perpendicular to their motion, then hit the Kawasaki hard, giving a thrust vector deflecting them toward one side of the star. The acceleration pushed them into their seats.

The star moved toward the left of the screen. Great bursts of fiery plasma flared into space all around them, the death rattle of a dying star that had once been much like the sun. Dark star spots moved across the surface as it rotated rapidly.

''Plot impact parameter!'' commanded Sean. The star image shifted instantly and a bull's-eye was superimposed, showing where the spacecraft would hit the star if it continued on its present course. The bull's-eye was near the center of the star's disk. Each second, the disk grew larger.

''It's not my fault!'' said Snafu.

''What in the name of the big blue balls of Barnard's star is it?'' said Sean.

''It is a star, Captain O'Shaughnessy,'' said the computer.

"For that I paid six K of good roidbucks?" said Sean angrily.

"There's no star near those coordinates," exclaimed Plum.

"What kind of star, Snafu?" spat Sean, hitting the Kawasaki controls harder.

"Spectral analysis indicates white dwarf," said Snafu. "Would you like to know its age?"

"I don't give one teaspoonful of moon dust how old it is!"

The star rushed toward them. Sean pushed the Kawasaki controls harder and the impact point very slowly moved toward the edge of the star. Too slowly. At this rate, they would still hit the star.

"Hell and damnation!" shouted Sean. "White dwarf! Gravity's so strong this close, we may not have enough power to get to grazing orbit before we hit! Get the geesuits!"

Plum climbed to the suit locker, fighting the acceleration of the ship. Ariadne joined him. They helped each other into their suits, popped some gee pills, then returned to their seats. Plum gave Sean a gee pill, then helped him put on his suit while the Irishman cursed and tried to control the ship with one hand.

Ariadne was frightened, more by the fear she sensed in the two men than by her own senses. Anything that would worry these men, she knew, was something worth worrying about. "Why not jump back into hyperspace?" she asked.

"Too close to the star!" muttered Plum.

"Backseat pilots!" exclaimed Sean.

When the suits were all plugged in, he accelerated to twenty gees, which proved almost intolerably painful—the gee pills had not yet begun to work. They were close enough now to the graininess of the star's hot surface, where vast cells of plasma the size of countries boiled. The cell grew larger.

"Snafu!" said Sean. "Surface gravity of the star!"

"The surface gravity," said Snafu, "is eight thousand gees, first approximation."

"Only eight thousand!" spat Sean. "Saint Anthony, get me out of this and I swear I'll go to confession next week!"

"Eight thousand gees is within normal parameters for white dwarfs," replied Snafu casually. "We are now within ten thousand kilometers of the surface of the star. Terrestrial safety regulations forbid approaching within this distance to a white dwarf. You are now in violation of Terrestrial Judiciary Interstellar Space Laws, Volume Seventeen, Section Twelve, Paragraph Three. It's not my fault!"

"You can take your space laws and shove them up your RAM!" swore Sean, sweating.

Ariadne closed her eyes, trying not to look at the growing disk of the star, but it only made her more conscious of the horrible weight of her body.

"Altitude, nine thousand kilometers," said Snafu. "You are in serious trouble with the Judiciary." The vessel shook horribly as a plasma flare struck.

The gee pill began to work. Sean increased the acceleration to sixty gees. His vision narrowed into a high-gee tunnel. The force was almost too powerful to permit him the strength to hold the controls, even with the fluidic circuits in his suit. He issued commands verbally to the computer.

"Eight thousand kilometers," said Snafu. "I wash my hands of all responsibility."

"Increase acceleration to eighty gees over ten seconds!" Sean commanded.

"I must warn you," said Snafu, "that the structural parameters of this vessel are designed for seventy gees nominal. Eighty gees will place strains beyond the limits considered acceptable, even for government work. Altitude, seven thousand kilometers."

"Do it, you dust-sucker!" spat Sean from acceleration-distorted lips.

"Don't blame me for what happens!" said Snafu.

The ship creaked as the fuselage strained under the gee forces. The vessel began to vibrate terribly. As the acceleration passed seventy gees, Ariadne blanked out. At seventy-six, Plum was out. At eighty, Sean struggled to remain conscious. The window was now one vast field of white fire, with irregular star spots darkening it here and there. Wisps of magnetized plasma from the dying star flew all around them. The ship groaned under the stress.

"One thousand kilometers," said Snafu.

Sean could see the edge of the star approaching the impact point. He shouted, "Snafu! One hundred gees, then back to eighty, over ten seconds!"

"You have been warned."

"Do it!"

Sean blanked out.

CHAPTER 10

The ship compressed under the severe acceleration and reached a hundred gees. The frame creaked, unnoticed by the unconscious crew. Seams strained at their welds. Plasma waves buffeted them like an ocean storm.

Snafu returned to eighty gees. Sean regained a foggy consciousness. He watched the edge of the star as it passed the impact point. "We've done it!" he whispered. Only the computer heard him. "Power down to one gee over ten minutes," he said weakly.

After deceleration, Plum and Ariadne revived. They found Sean had put the *Shillelagh* into orbit around the white dwarf and they were mercifully back in free-fall.

"Good God," said Plum, trying fruitlessly to rub his aching muscles through the geesuit. "How the devil did you do it?"

"Just told the white dwarf I was Irish and it turned out his grandfather's a leprechaun in County Kerry," Sean said wearily.

"I rather think you've kissed the Blarney Stone once too often," said Plum.

"That may have helped, too," Sean admitted, then gave Plum the real story as they changed into pressure suits and relaxed in the bliss of weightlessness.

"Where are we?" said Ariadne.

"I've not the slightest notion," said Sean.

Ariadne felt a chill run through her battered spine. "This must be the place my father found!"

"Absolutely not," said Sean, as if that settled the matter.

Ariadne said, "I feel like Alice in Wonderland for asking this, but if you don't know where we are, how can you be sure we're not where we're supposed to be? Perhaps this really is where my father went."

Sean shook his head, too tired to explain. Plum said, "All visible stars in the solar neighborhood have long been mapped. I can assure you that were a white dwarf anywhere near your father's coordinates, we should have known about it before we left.''

"Maybe Sean made a mistake.''

"Now, just a minute, young lady,'' Sean said indignantly.

"There, there, Sean,'' said Plum. "Even you have been known to make a mistake. I seem to remember an occasion on Ceres—''

"That was different,'' said Sean. "I didn't know she was married.'' Ariadne grimaced. "Where spacing is concerned, I am more careful than a lox handler in a hydrogen electrolyzer.''

"She's got a point, though,'' said Plum. "It is not entirely impossible that you—or even I, heaven forbid—should have made some tiny navigational error. I shall check.'' He floated over to the controls and began to play back the flight record.

"I think we have quite a lot to be thankful for,'' said Sean.

"So do I,'' said Ariadne.

"We have just survived a close encounter with a star. So let's celebrate a little.''

"How?''

"With a little bit of starshine.''

Ariadne angrily stamped her foot on the hull and floated to the other side. "We are lost light-years from home and all you can think of doing is beclouding your mind with alcohol?''

"Yes,'' said Sean.

"I don't know what my father ever saw in you!''

"Oh,'' said Plum, "I should think a bit of a drink wouldn't harm.''

"Men!'' exclaimed Ariadne.

"Women!'' exclaimed Sean, pushing off for the emergency locker.

After the two men had sipped from the squeeze-bottle of Abdullah's Whiskey, they went over the flight record step by step, while Ariadne studied the surface of the white dwarf through the viziscope, peering anxiously for any sign of an alien world or a human spacecraft.

In the middle of the record, Sean suddenly snapped his fingers. "Wait a microsec!'' he explained. "We're forgetting something. Wolf!''

"But we removed his bomb,'' said Plum. "We found no other devices anywhere.''

"No hardware,'' said Sean, "but what about software?''

"What do you mean?''

Ariadne turned away from the viziscope and said, "Of course! When he put in that bomb, he also reprogrammed your computer!''

Sean nodded angrily, Plum smiled, and Snafu said, "It's not my fault!"

"That slimy little 'crat was smarter than he looked," said Sean. "That son of a gynoid!" he shouted, growing angrier. He slammed his fist into the hull and floated backward, automatically braking himself with a hand behind his head. "The bomb was *meant* to be found!" he exclaimed, fuming. "It was a diversion!"

"It certainly was," said Plum.

"Oh," continued Sean, "he wouldn't have minded if we'd failed to find it and been blown to quarks when we entered hyperspace, but that taxin' macrocrat realized we might find his bomb. And he knew we'd be overconfident then, and not think of looking for a *software* 'bomb'!"

"It all fits quite well," said Plum.

"But why didn't your computer tell you he'd been tampered with?" said Ariadne.

"I beg your pardon, Ms. Zepos," said Snafu, "but if he tapped into my main fiber lines, I could no more tell that my software had been tampered with than you could tell if some mnemologist had inserted false memories in your brain."

"That is a disturbing thought," said Ariadne.

"Quite right, Snafu," said Plum. "The easiest way would be to alter your coordinate system so that Ariadne's father's coordinates would fall into the heart of a star."

"I told you it was not my fault," said Snafu with all the smugness his limited voice-synthesizer could muster.

"Wolf never struck me as a very well educated person," said Ariadne. "How would he have been able to do the complex reprogramming?"

"All he'd need," said Plum, "would be to buy or borrow some interstellar navigation software, and tell it to change the coordinates in Snafu's program."

"But how would he know Alexandros's coordinates?" said Sean.

"You must have told him," said Plum to Ariadne.

"Never," she said.

"My room!" spat Sean. "He was in my room! While I was in the pub, I left a viewcrystal there I use for notes. All he had to do was play it back and he'd have the coordinates!"

"Well," said Plum, "now that we have solved that mystery, we can proceed to disentangle the flight record."

"Before we do that," said Sean, "let's give this vessel a thorough search from top to bottom, inside and out."

"What for?" said Plum.

"Anything we may have overlooked. Maybe he planted *three* bombs."

"I'll go through the software and check all critical subroutines," said Plum.

"Warning!" said Snafu. "My software may not be altered except by a registered professional computer psychiatrist. World Judiciary Computer Licensing Code, Volume Twelve, Section Four, Paragraph Six."

"So report him to the nearest cop," said Sean to Snafu, smiling. To Plum he said, "I'll go outside and check everything once again."

Sean put on a pressure suit and was joined by Ariadne, who insisted on donning one as well.

"You'll be no damn good out there," said Sean.

"I don't care. I've never evaed before in space, and since this is *my* expedition, I insist on going."

"This is *our* expedition, and *I'm* the captain of this vessel, and what *I* say goes, but since you've had a little experience diving, I suppose it's all right."

"A *little* experience?" said Ariadne. She frowned but decided she had won, so she refrained from a further retort.

Sean topped off the backpack lox tanks and checked their systems out. They exited through the crew airlock.

Ariadne's eyes were agog at the alien sky. When she looked at the white dwarf, its dazzling brightness was dimmed by the suit's photochromic faceplate to a tolerable intensity. Because it was so close, it looked about the same size as the sun, even though the star was only slightly larger than Earth.

Fascinated, Ariadne started to drift away. Sean grabbed her ankle and pulled her back with annoyance.

"Your booties and gloves are telcroed, and so are patches all over the hull, so all you have to do is touch them and you'll be stuck to the ship. The backpack does have jets for maneuvering, but I don't like to waste oh-two."

"Oh-two?" said Ariadne. "Oxygen? Your friend back on the moon used that term, but it didn't make sense."

"Yes, oxygen. Spacers use *oh-two* for anything good: 'Yes,' 'You're go for launch,' 'You're welcome.' Oh-two's the most precious thing going. You can get by without food or water for a while, but not without oh-two. In fact, it's so valuable, it's sometimes used for money out in the roids.'' He proceeded to open a hatch and meticulously examine every pipe, wire, and connector.

Ariadne planted her feet on a telcro patch and looked up at the sky away from the star. The effect was overwhelming: Never before had she been in a place without a horizon to interrupt the view. Stars were everywhere. It was like stepping into the infinite. With the small ship at her feet, she felt as if she were standing on a tiny rock in the vast ocean of space, while the galaxy whirled around her, silently, infinitely slowly.

Space was darkest black everywhere except near one star, where a faint pink glow was just visible. Some of the constellations were still recognizable, yet others were disturbingly different. She wondered if her father had been here and seen the same stars and felt the same awe. As she thought of him, she remembered his last message, and his pain, and his death, and she began to cry silently.

She stood with her head in the stars forever, it seemed. Gradually, memories of her father mingled with the beauty and immensity of the cosmos, mesmerizing her. An almost religious ecstasy flowed through her body.

Finally, Sean brought her abruptly back to reality with a tap on her shoulder. Startled, she looked at him with alarm.

''All clear,'' he said. ''Let's get back on board.''

They reentered through the airlock, removed their pressure suits, and found Plum happily working away at the viewscreen, staring at long lists of program steps. Sean and Ariadne stood on opposite sides of the crew module, their feet in toeholds. They were almost head-to-head, but each was upside down to the other.

Sean removed the helmet from his pressure suit and ran his fingers through his red hair. ''We'll have to study the local star positions,'' he said. ''I'm sure we can figure out where we are. Then we can work out how to get to where we want to be.''

''You mean we are not hopelessly lost?'' said Ariadne.

''Quite right,'' said Plum.

''I'll drink to that!'' said Sean, retrieving some whiskey.

''You and that damn alcohol!'' said Ariadne.

''Having a woman on board a starship is enough to drive a man to drink,'' said Sean, proving it. ''Come to think of it, it's only the second good reason I've ever heard to have a female passenger.'' He flicked his eyebrows in a mock leer.

''O'Shaughnessy, you're hopeless!'' exclaimed Ariadne. She

decided not to argue, still filled with the afterglow of the experience of her space walk. And, she was disturbed to find, Sean was beginning to look less brutish the longer she stared at him. She frowned at the disturbing thought and focused primly on the amiable Plum.

"I'll do an interior hardware check now," said Sean, offering the bottle to Plum, who turned it down. "Then we can get ready to go back home."

"Home?" said Ariadne.

"Yes," said Sean. "We can't go on, not when we've been sabotaged twice already."

"But you've found the problems."

"I think so, but we don't know whether Wolf did any damage that we might not be able to detect until too late. We don't have a complete starship engine shop here. We can't test everything. He may have sabotaged the hyperdrive generator so it will fail when we're light-years from home. We'll just have to go back to Mickiewicz and have a thorough test made."

"After what we've been through," she said, "you're going to turn around?"

"Of course. It's the sensible thing to do."

"He's right," said Plum.

"And after we've done all those tests," said Ariadne suspiciously, "are we coming back to my father's coordinates?"

"I'm afraid not," said Sean.

"*What?*" she said, now fully returned from her space reverie.

"Look, Ariadne," said Sean, "this mission was suicidal enough when no one cared whether we got there or not. But now that someone's trying to keep us away, going on would be like trying to fly through the rings of Saturn in a luxury spaceliner, blindfolded."

"In other words," said Ariadne bitterly, "you are a coward."

Plum shook his head.

"Now, watch your tongue, young person," said Sean. "There's a hell of a difference between being sensibly cautious and being a coward."

"That's what the cowards all say," replied Ariadne.

Sean clenched his fist at her. "If you weren't a woman, I'd make your hide so black and blue, you could hang it in a museum and charge admission!"

"If you were a man, you wouldn't be running back home with your tail between your legs!"

"I swear by the Book of Kells that if you weren't the daughter of Alexandros Zepos, I'd put you over my knee and thrash the very devil out of you!''

''If you were man enough to do that, you'd be man enough to keep your word!''

''I always keep my word!''

''Hah! You promised that you'd take me to my father's place! You call this keeping your word? I'd sooner trust a goat to fly this moth-eaten toy!''

''Now, hold your thrusters,'' said Sean. ''You can insult *me*, you can even insult poor old Plum, but don't you *ever* insult the *Shillelagh!*''

''The *Shillelagh*? This thing looks like it was bought from a Turk who used it to haul garbage from Ankara to Izmir!''

Sean drew himself up to his generous height and replied with deadly seriousness, ''I'll have you know, the *Shillelagh* has saved my life more than once.''

''Then that's another good reason to curse!''

''If it weren't for this 'toy,' your atoms would right now be polluting the atmosphere of that star!'' He pointed in the direction of the white dwarf.

She stared at him silently with clenched fists, anger boiling in her eyes. After a while she said, ''And to think my father led me to believe you were a man of your word.''

He looked away guiltily.

''I can still recall his words,'' said Ariadne, ''when he said to my mother, 'If you ever need any help, you can always count on good old Sean O'Shaughnessy—' ''

He looked down at his feet.

'' '—a good friend and true,' '' she continued inventively, '' 'a man of his word, a sterling fellow, a man who would never let a woman down in her hour of need.' ''

More silence followed.

Finally Sean broke it by saying, ''Damn you, Ariadne, if it weren't for Alexandros Zepos, I swear I'd kick you out the hatch and let you orbit this star forever, but in the name of your father—and not because of any of the lies you've told today—I'm going to take you to his damn place if it kills the lot of us, as it surely will!''

Ariadne smirked. ''I had a suspicion you could be shamed into doing anything.''

Plum began a careful analysis of Snafu's guidance program while Sean angrily switched the viziscope to spectroscopic mode and began analyzing the brightest stars. He aimed the screen's camera at a random part of the sky. The stars shone in their different colors on the screen. He touched some of the brighter ones with his finger, each time hitting the spectro key. The computer sensed the star he was pointing to and replied with a spectral type. Sean scratched his red stubble.

"Tell me, Sean," said Ariadne. "Why don't you ever shave?"

"F2 IV," said Snafu.

He ran his hand over his stubble. "Oh, but I do," he said, scowling. "Whenever I return to civilization, I always try to take time for a shave and a bath. Of course, often I have to postpone it due to the press of more urgent business."

"Like getting drunk," Ariadne said scornfully.

"Of course," said Sean. He selected another star.

"M6e III," said Snafu.

"But Plum shaves on board ship. I saw him using Defoliant cream. Does it really hurt to be civilized?"

"Look, my fine young colleen, I didn't come out here to be lectured by some woman barely out of diapers who belongs in a nunnery." Ariadne crossed her arms haughtily. "When I'm on a mission, I don't believe in wasting my time with such frivolities. After all, one of the reasons I went into space was to get away from the formalities and fripperies of that mudhole called Earth."

They glared at each other for a while. He selected another star.

"B1 II," said Snafu.

Ariadne began thinking about the long and dangerous journey ahead, and made an effort to be conciliatory. "Tell me, Sean, how did you become a spacer?"

Sean chose a star and replied, "That's a long and boring story, and I'm sure you wouldn't be interested."

"O9.5 Ib," said Snafu.

"No, really, Sean, I would like to know."

"Oh, I simply always had a hankering to see the vacuumy part of the universe."

"You were born on Earth, weren't you?"

"Yes," he replied, softening, "I was born in the city of Galway, Ireland." He smiled wistfully.

"I've never been to Ireland. What's it like?"

He stared at the screen, seeing in his mind images of his youth. "Foreigners usually talk about the greenness of it all, if they get outside of Dublin. But what I remember most is the blue of Galway Bay, the boats going to and from the Aran Islands. At night, I would often lie on the beach, listening to the lapping of the waves and the deep throbbing of ships' engines as they went by, and I'd stare up at the fascinating beauty of the Milky Way. I would wonder what ships were sailing up there in the sky, and whether some of them had crews that weren't human.

"I used to play around the Spanish Arch, where the sailors from the Armada had put in after Plum's ancestors clobbered the bejesus out of them. Spaniards and Frenchmen have always been welcome in Ireland, because they were usually fighting the British. I loved the palm trees there, because they made me think of South Seas islands, and I had this urge to explore."

"Palm trees in Ireland?" said Ariadne.

"Yes." He laughed and touched another star.

"BOE IV," said Snafu.

"Nobody ever believes me, but the Gulf Stream keeps the west coast warm enough for palms to grow there. Just a handful, mind you, not a jungle." His face softened. "I had a dog there, good old Claddagh, and we'd go play with the beggarmen."

"What induced you to leave such a pretty place?"

"Ah, that's the sad part." Sean stared unseeing at the screen for a long time before continuing. "My father was a civil engineer." He spoke slowly, without his usual touch of merriment. "He worked for the World Administration Center in New York. He loved the job, because he didn't have to go to New York very often. He lived in Galway and dealt with them by viziphone and computer. Maybe if we'd moved to New York, the whole tragedy wouldn't have happened, and I might be a little 'crat myself down on that planet, heaven forbid."

"Tragedy?"

"He was assigned as chief engineer on a project called HOC—Hopwood Orbital City. Ever hear of it?"

She shook her head.

"I'm not surprised. You must have been a little girl at the time, and the Ministry of Education doesn't publicize the government's failures. HOC was to be the orbiting headquarters for the World Government. All the officials who needed or wanted quick global access would be moved from all over the world up to there, just like they do today. Only back then, just a few orbital government offices existed. The World President for Life decided that the World Police, Customs, the military, the World Revenue Service, the Ministry of Information, and many others would all be able to monitor the Earth most conveniently from there, dispatching shuttles to any trouble spots quickly. Even the president herself was going to have a suite there, though she hated space travel.

"It was a luxurious wonderland. They spared no expense. There was a zero-gee hospital for administrators and their families. Free luxury hotels were designed so Earthbound 'crats, officers, and cops could have a nice place to vacation. They built the largest low-gee swimming pool ever made.

"Things went along beautifully until a man named Bevan Milbury began to play games with the accounts. He was the chief administrator on the project. He shaved money wherever he could and diverted it into his own pockets. He altered the design of the large structural members that formed the city's backbone, so they could use less metal, kevlon, and other expensive materials. He did this by altering the plans after my father had already finalized them in the project's main computer.

"My father didn't discover this until the project was half built. He'd gone up in orbit to inspect the construction, and soon realized that something smelly was going on. He returned to New York and saw Bevan. Bevan pretended to be shocked, and said he would investigate immediately."

Ariadne, who had been listening politely, found herself growing genuinely intrigued.

"Things went on as usual for a while," continued Sean. "Every time my father inquired of Bevan, he assured him that a great, secret investigation was on the brink of uncovering the dastardly criminals. Finally, the bulk of the construction was completed and they began spinning up the city to create artificial gravity.

"My father begged Bevan to delay the spin-up, because he knew it couldn't stand the stresses. Bevan promised he would, but he didn't. By this time, much of the city was enclosed, so most of the workers no longer wore pressure suits . . . When they neared the design nominal of half a gee, the city broke open, and thousands of workers died quick, nasty deaths."

Ariadne was shocked.

"It was such a big scandal, even the Ministry of Information couldn't hide it. There was a big investigation—and who did they arrest? My father, of course. They found a couple of million geobucks in his bank account, and not one byte of the memos he'd sent on the project's dangers could be found. Bevan had carefully deleted every one of my father's critical reports and, with the aid of friends in the Ministry of Finance, had planted the money in his account.

"My father was arrested, tried, and convicted for treasonable corruption, damage to world property, and murder." He looked Ariadne straight in the eyes. "Three days after the accident, they executed him."

She looked away, unable to say a word.

"It drove my mother insane. She's still in the hospital, down in Galway. Hasn't spoken in years. Just stares at the walls. I had just started university then, in Dublin. They tried to prevent me from speaking to my father before they executed him, but I bribed my way in. He told me the truth. I tried to save him—I tried to have Bevan arrested. But he was too powerful, had too many connections. He had me arrested and held until my father was killed. Then he had me thrown out of university. I was blacklisted by the World Government, couldn't get a job.

"I met this spacer in a bar, and he needed a helper to clean and fix the robots—menial work, but it would get me off that godforsaken planet, so I hired on. I went to the moon, worked and saved enough to get a degree in astronautics from L-5 University. From there, it was one short step to becoming a roid miner, and then eventually I had enough to buy this starship. So if you make any more glowing statements about Earth and its beautiful bureaucrats, please forgive me if I fail to share your enthusiasm."

They were silent for a long while. Finally, Plum announced, "Snafu's coordinate software is now debugged, I believe. We'll have to run some self-consistency checks, but he's all yours for now."

Sean made a few more stellar spectral measurements and said, "All right, Snafu, you have a goodly number of star positions and spectral types. I want you to do a least-squares fit for our position against all catalogued stars within one hundred light-years of Earth."

"Roger, Captain O'Shaughnessy," replied the computer.

"What is he doing?" said Ariadne to Plum.

"Snafu is going to make a series of guesses as to where we are in space, and see which of them most closely resembles the sky we see out the windows. By doing this repeatedly, he'll find where we must be in order for these stars to be where we see them."

"My best fit is now ready for outputting," stated Snafu.

"How good is it?" said Sean.

"Mean deviation from input star positions is two arc seconds."

"Greatest deviation?"

"Five arc seconds."

"That's it!" said Sean "A place for every star, and every star in its place. We now know where we are."

"Where are we?" said Ariadne.

Snafu reeled off three galactic coordinates.

"Aha," said Sean. "We're about two light-years from where we wanted to be. In fact, we ought to have a nice view of that star your father was trying to get to, Beta Hydri." He did a calculation and hit the verniers, orienting the spacecraft. A bright yellow star drifted into the center of the forward screen.

"Thar she blows!" said Sean.

Ariadne stared at the insignificant yellow dot. "Can you point us to the place where he actually did go?"

"Sure thing." He did another calculation and touched the verniers a little. Beta Hydri swung off to the lower left corner of the screen. At first, nothing was visible in the center, apart from a dusting of distant background stars.

"Whatever's out there isn't visible from two light-years away," said Sean.

Ariadne stared at the screen for a long time. She began to see a red glow almost too faint to be seen against the background stars. "What's that pink color near the center?" she asked.

Sean and Plum stared at the screen more closely. "You've got the eyes of a born spacer," Sean said with new respect. "I didn't even notice it myself. That looks like hydrogen gas, perhaps excited by Beta Hydri."

"What does it mean?" she said.

"Probably nothing. Space is littered with clouds of dust and gas."

"Where do they come from?"

"Some condense from interstellar gas, aided by gravitational self-attraction. Others are thrown off by stellar winds, novas, supernova explosions. The galaxy is a dirty place, a real garbage dump, constantly throwing stuff all over, and recycling some of it as stars, planets, and Greeks. Of course, that gas could be dozens of light-years away." He turned to the screen and said, "Snafu, do a high-resolution check on the red gas in the center of the screen. Check its spectral lines. Look for absorption lines in the background stars, especially Beta Hydri."

"Roger," said Snafu.

"That's a very useful computer you have there," said Ariadne.

"Yes, considering that he's government surplus. I bought him from a used-computer dealer on Juno. He wasn't much when I got him. He'd been abused by government spacers on the lunar–roid run. They didn't give a damn about him. They were just in it for the early-retirement program. But Plum and I repaired him. We added more memory and peripherals, and wrote a whole batch of new software, until he became the fine broth of a computer he is today. Only trouble is, it would've been too expensive to change his ROM crystals, so he's chockful of bureaucratese and regulations. But if you ignore the gigo, he's all right.''

"I am ready to file my report," said Snafu.

"Shoot," said Sean.

"The absorption of the red gas is predominantly hydrogen. Would you like a quantitative breakdown?"

"No, just tell me, is the absorption present in the spectrum of Beta Hydri?"

"Affirmative."

"Interesting," said Sean. "It means that the gas is indeed somewhere between us and the star. So maybe it is connected in some way to whatever your father found."

Ariadne stared at the pink gas. "I wish my father had told us more."

"So do I," said Sean. "So do I."

CHAPTER 11

They entered hyperspace once again and made the two—light-year trip to Alexandros's coordinates. The sight that greeted them when they emerged into normal space was completely different.

The sky was black, except for a hint of pink everywhere. Most of the stars looked much the way they had near the white dwarf, but near the edge of the forward screen was a tiny red star surrounded by a pink glow.

"Snafu," said Sean, "zoom in on that bright star."

"Roger," replied the computer.

The image became larger until it filled the screen. A great, glowing, spinning disk floated in space before their eyes. Plum stared in disbelief, Sean's mouth fell open, and Ariadne gasped.

It was clearly artificial, and unlike anything they had ever seen before. Without a word, they realized they were seeing something no human had ever before witnessed and lived to talk about: the artifact of an alien civilization.

There was an impression of immense size, but its unfamiliarity gave them no scale. It was partly inclined to them and had hundreds of "grooves," making it slightly resemble the rings of Saturn, but the grooves were spaced regularly and the disk continued to the very center, with no planet visible.

The disk, though predominantly red, was a blur of many different colors that, near the center, spun so fast it was impossible to focus on. As their eyes became accustomed to it, they could glimpse features on the outer rings between the darker grooves: bumps, projections, and hollows that zipped by. But the rings revolved at different rates, a most disturbing effect to watch.

The outermost ring glowed red and revolved more than twice every minute. From ring to ring, each ring spun faster than the larger one it nested in; each was a different mix of colors, a chaotic, whirling rainbow. Toward the center, they became a complete blur.

It was dizzying, hypnotic.

The three humans stared, entranced.

Finally, Ariadne said, "What is it?"

"Never seen anything remotely like it," said Sean. "Or heard of anything."

"Nor I," said Plum.

"Snafu," said Sean, "can you strobe this viewscreen?"

"What do you mean, Captain O'Shaughnessy?"

"I'd like you to flash the screen off and on, and keeping it on for a millisecond, synchronizing with the outer ring. Freeze the screen between images."

"I was not programmed for that," replied Snafu, "but it is theoretically possible. I will have to write a new subroutine."

"Do it," said Sean.

"Done," replied Snafu after a moment.

"Run it," said Sean.

"Roger."

The image on the screen froze. At least, the outer ring did. The next ring drifted slowly, and the next ones yet faster, until another stationary one could be seen. Now it was possible to see details in the outer ring that had flashed by in a blur.

Most of the red glow of the outer ring came from what seemed to be great windows. There were bulbous structures on the ring. antennas of strange shapes, pulsating lights.

"Zoom in, Snafu," said Sean.

"Roger."

The screen slowly magnified the central portion until it became blurred from motion.

"Stop," said Sean.

It froze on a window from which red light glared. Inside, there seemed to be machinery. Something blue was moving across the window, but the image was too fuzzy to discern detail.

"It looks like someone's home," Sean said softly.

A chill ran down Ariadne's spine.

"How far away is it, Snafu?" said Sean.

"I don't know, but it's not my fault."

"Don't you have radar contact?"

"Negative."

"Does that mean it's invisible to radar?" said Ariadne.

"More likely," said Sean, "it's just so far away, we haven't had time for a reflection yet. How long have you been sending radar out, Snafu?"

"Fourteen minutes."

"Then the object must be at least seven light-minutes away," said Sean, "over a hundred million kilometers."

"But at that distance," said Ariadne, "to be visible without magnification, it would have to be as big as a planet!"

Sean looked at her with grudging respect. "Sometimes, you do seem to have something between your ears besides moon dust."

She nodded with dignity at the backhanded compliment.

"Let's see," said Sean. "We've got to know how far away it is before we can do any navigation. Snafu, what's its rotational period, for the outer ring?"

"Twenty-three seconds. Do you want more significant figures?"

"No. Use them, but just give me two sig-figs. What's its linear speed?"

"I don't know," said Snafu. "How am I supposed to tell? Nobody programmed me to compute the linear speed of an object I can't do radar off of. It's not my fault."

"Snafu," Sean said irritably, "are there any spectral lines from the outer ring? From the lights or windows?"

"Affirmative."

"Then measure the Doppler shift and do the geometry, assuming a circular ring."

"Roger." After a pause, Snafu said, "The linear velocity of the outer ring is 3,500 kilometers per second."

"Holy Heisenberg!" Sean exclaimed. "That's a percent of the speed of light! That ring's moving like a bat out of a tax auditor's office! And the inner rings are even faster! Snafu, compute its radius."

"Roger. The radius is 13,000 kilometers."

"That thing is twice the size of the Earth!" exclaimed Sean.

"Fantastic!" said Ariadne in awe.

"But no material could possibly survive such a centrifugal force," Plum objected. He twiddled his thumbs—for him, the equivalent of hysteria.

"Not unless it's in free-fall," said Sean with eyes narrowed in intense thought.

"Preposterous."

"No, wait," said Sean. "Suppose down there in the center is some incredibly strong gravitational force."

"It would have to be ridiculously massive," said Plum.

"Let's see," said Sean. "Snafu, assume the outer ring is revolving in free-fall about a point mass. How big would the mass have to be?"

"It would be 1.2 solar masses."

"More massive than the sun!" exclaimed Sean.

"You see," said Plum, "utterly absurd."

"Now, wait a microsec," said Sean. "There are two kinds of objects that could have such mass and still be small enough to be hidden in an object this size."

"Neutron stars and black holes," said Plum.

"Exactly."

"Are you seriously proposing . . ."

"Whoever built this thing was a hell of a lot smarter than us. They could have found a black hole or a neutron star and built a super-city orbiting around it."

"Preposterous. The tidal force alone would destroy it."

Ariadne interrupted, "How do we know what an advanced civilization could do? More important, how can we test Sean's theory?"

"By looking at the center," said Sean. "Snafu, zoom in on the center of the rings."

"Roger." The screen filled with the blurry image of the innermost ring. A spherical object lay in the center, like the yolk of an egg, bulging above the ring. White streaks flashed over the spherical surface, erratically, frantically, too fast for the eye to follow.

"How big is the sphere, Snafu?" said Sean.

"The radius is eleven kilometers."

"A neutron star!" said Sean.

"Incredible," said Ariadne. "I studied them in astronomy class. Dead stars, aren't they?"

"Yes," said Sean, "the remnants of supernovas."

Ariadne said, "I remember my profuter saying they're so dense, a piece the size of a grain of sand could weigh a million tons."

"Right."

"But they've never been visited by humans, have they?"

"They've never found one close enough to explore."

"Until now," said Ariadne.

"Until now," agreed Sean.

"So my father discovered the first accessible neutron star, too!"

"That's right!"

"Well," said Plum, "let's not jump to conclusions. The sphere does have the right dimension and the right mass. Also, the rings would explain why we've not detected its radio signals from Earth—energetic particles collide with them so they cannot radiate the way a proper pulsar would. But I still cannot believe that an artificial structure could withstand the stresses, that close to a neutron star. In the outer ring alone, the gravitational attraction would be about a *hundred thousand gees!*"

"Sure," said Sean, "but what difference does that make if you're in free-fall? You'd still feel zero gravity. You could build a whole ring around the star out of chewing gum!"

"That makes sense," said Ariadne.

"But the tidal force!" said Plum.

"What do you mean?" asked Ariadne.

"The fact that," said Plum, "if you're in free-fall, with your feet pointed toward the star and your head pointed away, your feet are closer to the star and hence feel a stronger force."

"Ah, like the Earth's tides," said Ariadne. On Earth, the part of the ocean nearer the moon feels a slightly stronger lunar gravity than the ocean on the other side of the planet. The moon's gravity pulls the ocean, making tides.

"Yes," said Plum. "On Earth, the force is too feeble to feel unless one is an ocean. But close to a neutron star, the force could tear one in two!"

"But in free-fall," said Ariadne, "you would not feel any gravity."

"No," said Sean, "you think that way because you've only been near the Earth's skimpy gravity, where the tidal force on you is too small to notice. But if you got close enough to a neutron star, the gravity's so enormous that even in free-fall your feet might feel a thousand gees toward the star while your head felt a thousand gees in the other direction—thanks to centrifugal force. It would tear you apart," he said, grinning with mock sadism. "Let me see, for a man two meters tall, in free-fall with the outer ring, the tidal 'gravity' he'd feel would be, let me see—how much, Snafu?"

"That's .04 gee."

"A fraction of a gee!" said Sean. "Even you'd like it, Plum!"

"But the problem gets far worse for the inner rings," said Plum. "The force goes up as the inverse-cube of the distance. At one-tenth the radius of the outer ring, the tidal force would already be a thousand times as great. You should feel forty gees! And at one-tenth *that* radius, forty *thousand* gees!"

"Perhaps," said Sean. "But these are one *hell* of a good bunch of engineers. Maybe they figured a way around it. Furthermore, this explain Ariadne's pink gas."

"How?" she asked.

"Because after a supernova explosion," said Sean, "there's a remnant of gas left over."

"But rings are gravitationally unstable," grumbled Plum.

"Only if they're not artificially stabilized. I've got a hunch whoever built this thing is way beyond Civil Engineering 101 and perfectly capable of building active stabilization into it, maybe using the neutron star's magnetic field."

"I suppose so," said Plum, keying a reading from the computer. "The magnetometer shows an extraordinary magnetic field and gradient even at this range."

"Typical for pulsars," said Sean. "They have magnetic fields around a trillion times Earth's." To Ariadne, he added, "That's how they generate their radio signals. Electrons accelerate like crazy in a field like that and radiate every kind of wave you could ask for."

"I suppose," said Plum, "one could pass electrical currents through the rings in such a way that the electromagnetic force would push the ring whichever way one wished."

"Sure. You pass a current through a segment of the ring in one direction and the magnetic force will push it away from the star. Pass it through in the other direction, and it pulls it toward it. Freshman physics."

"Yes, with a computer, a few sensors, and some rather heavy wires, I suppose one could stabilize the system in that way."

Ariadne added impatiently, "We can argue like philosophers forever and prove it's really made out of goat cheese, or we can land on it and take a look. I didn't hire you to philosophize! Let's go!"

"All right," said Sean. "But let's not forget, this thing killed some fine people who knew a thing or two about exploring unknown worlds. Let's move carefully."

"Carefully, fine," said Ariadne. "As long as we move!"

"Warning!" said Snafu. "I can find no governmental regulations covering neutron stars. Therefore it is inadvisable to approach closer."

"That's too bad, Snafu," said Sean. "If Christopher Columbus had listened to you, the only thing he would have discovered would have been the bars of Madrid. We'll just have to be pioneers."

"I wash my hands of all responsibility," said Snafu.

"You usually do," said Sean.

They continued their approach.

CHAPTER 12

Over a period of several hours, Sean piloted them on a rendez-vous course. The *Shillelagh* closed in on the alien world that now filled the windows. The tidal force could already be felt as a slight apparent weight on their bodies.

The spacecraft had begun to vibrate, so softly at first that the occupants did not notice it, but increasing as they approached the world. Finally, Sean shook his head with irritation and said, "What's that vibration?"

Plum looked around and said, "It seems to be everywhere." The entire spacecraft was humming.

"Snafu!" said Sean. "Report anomalies!"

"Practically everything's anomalous," said Snafu. "Vibration, tidal stresses, magnetic fields, electric fields, gradients. What am I supposed to do when I've never been programmed for anything like this?"

Sean snapped his fingers. "The B-field!"

Plum laughed. "Of course!"

"The B-field?" said Ariadne.

"The magnetic field," explained Plum. "We are now so close to the object that its powerful magnetic field is affecting us. And since it is nonuniform and rotates, we feel a changing field, causing the ship's magnetizable materials to vibrate."

"Warning!" said Snafu. "I can find no government regulations covering landings on objects of this type. It is suggested that landing be delayed until a committee has been authorized to investigate."

Sean and Plum chuckled. "Proceed with landing," said Sean.

"I strongly recommend aborting this mission," said Snafu.

"Recommendation noted," said Sean. "Proceed with landing."

"I refuse to accept responsibility for the consequences."

"Proceed, you chip-kissing piece of mood dust!"

"Roger, Captain O'Shaughnessy. I am passing the responsibil-

106

ity for any and all unfortunate consequences, direct and indirect, to you as captain of this vessel.''

"Responsibility accepted," growled Sean.

"Look at that!" exclaimed Ariadne, pointing. A light-pen spun around on the bulkhead near Plum's knees. They watched in amazement as the pen danced in a small circle, pressed against the surface.

"Of course," said Sean. "The magnetic field!"

"Ah, yes," said Plum. To Ariadne, he added, "We're now so close that the star's magnetic field and its gradient are strong enough to attract the DC current running in that pen. The pen moves as the star spins."

To Snafu, Sean said, "Show me a close-up of the outer ring."

"Roger," said Snafu.

The screen image zoomed in on the center of the ring. A huge window, kilometers wide, could be seen. Inside, a red glow showed what seemed to be pieces of great, softly curved machinery, moving mechanically back and forth.

"Let the strobe synch slip 1 percent."

"Roger."

The ring drifted by. Huge projections passed: cables, grills, unfathomable objects of an alien technology. A large bulge appeared, surrounded by blue lights, with a bright flashing red glow from the trailing edge.

"Hold it," said Sean. The image froze. "Zoom in to the max, focusing on the red flash."

"Roger."

The image magnified until they could see a blurred image of a great chamber, glowing a brilliant red. The edge of the chamber flashed a brighter red. "Looks like an invitation to a red-light district," said Sean.

"I suppose you're an expert on that," Ariadne said dryly.

Several blurry objects were visible, silhouetted against the light.

"Those look like interstellar spacecraft," said Sean.

"That could be where my father landed," said Ariadne.

"Plum, try viziphoning them."

Plum pushed a key and said, "CQ, this is the starship *Shillelagh* of the Asteroid Federation, calling CQ." Horrendous static burst from the speaker. Plum lowered the volume. The static roared erratically, like a massive thunderstorm. Random daggers of multicolored snow shot across the comscreen.

Plum tried several more times, with no more success, on

different frequencies. "Frightful bit of interference," he said. "I shouldn't be surprised if we'd be completely unable to receive a message even if there were one."

"Then let's go down and take a look," said Sean. "Snafu, compute a trajectory to match velocity with that chamber."

"Not only are we experiencing magnetic forces but I have no way of calculating the gravitational field of the rings themselves. I'm only programmed for simple celestial mechanics. Someone is going to be severely reprimanded!"

"Useless piece of junk," muttered Sean. "Okay, model the *Shillelagh* by a simple induced magnetic dipole, and add in the torque and force on our electric currents. Calculate the del-*mu*-dot-*B* force on it, using the observed *B*-field and its gradients, and a multipole expansion centered on the neutron star. Model the ring gravitational field by assuming azimuthal symmetry and using the relative acceleration from radar Doppler-ranging data as we approach. I'll handle higher-order corrections manually."

"Roger," said Snafu. "But I won't be responsible if we crash!"

"Prepare for landing," said Sean.

The three humans belted themselves in. Sean gripped the Kawasaki joystick. The stroboscopic viewscreen switched to normal mode, showing the outer ring rushing by like a colossal, surreal merry-go-round out of control.

"Docking mode," said Sean.

"Roger," said Snafu, putting a pulsating white dot in the center of the viewscreen to show where the *Shillelagh* was aimed. The computer added a pulsating white circle to the left, marking where the ship had to be pointed now, so it would meet its target later. Color-coded numbers indicated actual and desired velocities.

"Never matched velocities with a station at 1 percent the speed of light before," said Sean.

"I do hope you're careful," said Plum. "Even a tiny error could be rather messy at this speed."

"I'll try."

He delicately squeezed and pushed the joystick until the dot was centered inside the circle and the velocities matched. The ship moved rapidly closer and the circle-dot moved toward the glowing red chamber. Their velocity was over three thousand kilometers per second, and he began to sweat. Plum's eyes darted nervously between the main screen and the copilot's monitor; Ariadne stared wide-eyed at the onrushing world, oblivious to the danger.

The dot drifted away from the circle as accumulated errors in Snafu's mathematical models built up. Sean tweaked the joystick until it was centered again.

The chamber grew ever larger on the screen, until they could see its contents clearly. It was vast, many kilometers wide and long, but short in height. Its "ceiling" was covered with thousands of objects like spacecraft, in precisely aligned rows.

"It's a hangar!" said Sean. "I'm going to turn us upside down." He touched the altitude controls.

"How can those spaceships stick to the roof like that?" said Ariadne as the ship rolled 180 degrees. Her stomach rolled unpleasantly with it.

"Peanut butter," said Sean, eyes quickly scanning the hangar, searching for obstacles and a clear landing space.

"Centrifugal force," said Plum. "It's related to that tidal force we spoke of earlier. The outermost part of the outer ring is spinning slightly faster than orbital speed, so centrifugal force exceeds gravitational. But just slightly, just enough to give one a feeling of moderate gravity."

As they got closer, they stared at the individual spacecraft. Two of the vessels were familiar terrestrial designs, but all the others were strange, giant, squat greenish shapes unlike any ever built by humans. The huge vessels had a main fuselage shaped with a bulging forward hull that tapered to the aft, much like a whale, ending in a black tip. Each alien ship bore a pair of teardrop-shaped pods on either side. Every surface was aerodynamically smooth, as if intended for atmospheric flight, or for ultrafast flight through interstellar gas and dust.

The *Shillelagh* entered the hangar slowly and drifted toward the two human starships.

"The vibration has stopped," said Plum.

Sean nodded. "Must be shielded in here."

As they got closer, the spacecraft grew in the screen. "*Patera mou!*" exclaimed Ariadne, her heart pounding. "That's my father's spaceship!"

"Yes!" said Sean.

"The one on the left?" said Plum.

"Yes!" said Ariadne.

"Ah, yes, it's an older design," noted Plum. "But who brought the other ship?"

They were silent.

Sean landed with a heavy thump in between the two starships.

They unbelted hastily and stood up. They felt very heavy, as if the gravity was above Earth-normal.

"I feel rather odd," said Plum.

"So do I," said Sean. "Must be the tidal force."

"Yes," said Plum, lifting one foot in the air. "Our feet are heavier than our heads, and they get lighter when one raises them. Curious feeling."

"I thought you said gravity would be very small here," said Ariadne to Sean.

"Don't blame me!" said Snafu. "That was for the zero-force circle. We are many meters above it, so the gravity-gradient is much stronger."

"Zero-force circle?" said Ariadne.

"If this ring had no thickness," said Snafu, "then it would be a circle centered on the neutron star. Everywhere on that circle, gravity and centrifugal force would be exactly equal, and would cancel each other out. That's the zero-force circle."

"The farther you are below that circle," amplified Plum, "the stronger is the centrifugal force and the weaker the gravity. On the other side, the reverse is true. We're so far below it, with our feet pointing away from the star, that our feet are more strongly pulled by centrifugal force than our heads, and the whole force is much greater than the fractional gravity Snafu computed."

"But," said Snafu, "it *would* be .04 gee for a two-meter tall man at the zero-force circle as the captain originally asked."

"Quite right," said Plum.

"You see, Ms. Zepos?" said Snafu. "I was right!"

Ariadne ignored the computer and raced to the airlock.

"I was right and I deserve an apology," said Snafu, "but I know I won't get one. No one ever appreciates me," he added with a tone of martyrdom.

In her haste Ariadne stumbled awkwardly in the unfamiliar gravity. The rapid change in the gravity gradient made her slightly nauseated. She shook her head and stood up slowly.

"Hold your horses, person!" said Sean. "Put on your pressure suit! It's pure vacuum out there!"

The three suited up quickly and emerged.

They climbed down the exit ladder and stood for a while by the side of the *Shillelagh*. Ariadne stared at the old starship with the Ministry of Science emblem on the nose, a dozen meters away. Her blood was pounding as her emotions swirled: thoughts of her father, ancient civilizations, and aliens mingled kaleidoscopically.

Sean and Plum stared at the alien ships farther away and their breathing slowed to an imperceptible level. In the eerie red light of the hangar, the ships stretched as far as the eye could see. Most were identical: huge, hulking, strangely shaped vessels half a kilometer long, dwarfing the human spacecraft. They were greenish ovoids resembling dirigibles that had been squashed partway, and they had a strange black filigree at the tail where an engine should have been. Each ship looked ready to take off, as if awaiting its alien crew. The apprehensive humans half expected the aliens to appear at any moment.

After a long time, Sean turned toward Alexandros's ship and nodded with recognition. "I remember that vessel now," he said. "I was in lunar orbit getting ready for a roid freighter job, and I dropped by to say good-bye to your father. I wanted ever so much to go along. If I hadn't been on contract, I would've gone with him."

Ariadne walked over to the ship, with the two men following. She had seen many pictures of the ship, but had never gotten the feeling for its size that being next to it gave. It loomed over her, much larger than the *Shillelagh*, a purely interstellar vessel designed to hold two small planetary shuttles in its bay. She touched the metal hull, gleaming red in the hangar light, and whispered, "If only you had never left."

A ramp extended to the hangar floor from a lower hatch. They walked up it and entered the airlock.

Inside, it was dark. Sean shined his lightrod around and found some switches. The yellow emergency lights came on dimly, just enough to see by.

Sean checked the atmosphere with his suit spectrometer, and said, "Oh-two." They removed their helmets and hung them on their belts.

They walked down an empty corridor, the yellow light and human artifacts comforting after the alien hangar. The air was musty. The sounds of their footsteps echoed down the corridor hauntingly. They glanced into cabins as they passed. Tools hung from the walls; a football lay in a corner; underwear had been thrown on a bunk; a 3D picture of a woman and child hung beside a mirror.

"It's like a sunken ship," said Ariadne, shivering. "Little touches of people, but nobody there."

They passed a workshop and found a ladder extending upward.

"Top deck's the flight deck," said Sean.

They ascended past three decks, Ariadne in the lead. At the

top, Sean pointed her forward. They entered the control room. A large console spread out before them, with four empty seats. An old, faded jacket hung over one of them. Viewscreens stared blankly at them.

Ariadne sat in one of the seats. Sean and Plum sat next to her. Sean studied the control panel and pushed a key.

"Acknowledged," said the ship's computer in a monotone similar to Snafu's. Ariadne jumped.

"It still works!" said Sean. "Computer, do you have the log on-line?"

"I have the logs of the expedition leader, pilot, navigator, and chief engineer on-line."

"Give me the last entry in the expedition leader's log."

"Your voice is not in my access file. I cannot comply."

"Damn security!" said Sean. "Computer, this expedition's been dead for twenty years. Do you confirm?"

"Roger," said the machine. "Until one week ago, I had not been accessed in approximately twenty years."

"Who accessed you last week?" said Sean.

"The Deputy Minister of World Culture."

"Stefan!" exclaimed Ariadne.

"That 'crat who was with you when you called me?"

"Yes!" she said.

"Hmmm . . ." said Sean. "Things begin to take on a new smell."

"He told me it would take years to put together an expedition!"

"For you," said Sean, "it would have. But not for *him* . . ." Ariadne fumed.

"Computer," said Sean, "how did this deputy minister access you when he wasn't a member of the original crew either?"

"I calculated that the probability is nearly unity that the original crew are all dead," said the machine. "He showed me his identification and said that his was the replacement crew from Earth. I have no information to contradict his statements, so I must assume their veracity."

"Well," said Sean, "we are his backups, sent by the ministry to help him out. We were sent by the minister himself, after the deputy minister had left."

"Show me your identification, please."

Sean looked quizzically at Plum and Ariadne.

Ariadne spoke up: "I'll go get it."

Sean shot a question at her with his eyebrows, but she just disappeared down the ladder.

A couple of minutes later, she was back. She waved her Ministry of Culture Grant Identification Badge and said, "Here it is."

"Please place it on the violet key in the front of the console," said the computer.

She did so and the badge lit up and spoke synthetically, "Dr. Ariadne Alexandros Zepos, Researcher in Hydroarchaeology, University of Delphinus. Authorized by the Ministry of Culture, approved by Deputy Minister Stefan Draganescu, on grant number MWC green-blue-white, red-black-orange-orange-yellow. Expiration date, 30 June, 2108."

"Accepted," said the computer. There were smiles all around. "Please give me your names and degree of access for future reference."

The trio spoke their names and requested unrestricted access.

"Access granted," said the computer.

"Now," said Sean, "give us that last entry in the expedition leader's log."

"Roger." The forward viewscreen lit up and the face of Alexandros Zepos loomed above them. Ariadne's eyes opened wide.

"Log entry," said the face in grave, Greek-accented English, "1117 hours, 10 November, 2087. I have decided that we shall go on. The deaths of the three crew members have cast a pall on this expedition, but we all knew the risks when we started. This world is far more important than any mere unintelligent life-form we might have found had we gone on to Beta Hydri as planned. We are all in agreement that the discovery of artifacts of an intelligent alien species is the most important find in the history of the human race.

"I have instructed the pilot to set this starship on autopilot, and given the computer instructions that, should any member of the crew return, the ship must fly to the nearest colony with news of our discovery. We have agreed that, as long as at least three people survive, we shall continue to explore.

"We have outfitted ourselves with equipment and supplies sufficient to last us for a month. We will exit from this ring by means of the 'train' at the inner edge, and transfer to the next ring. We will mark our passage with black symbols. I will periodically leave viewcrystals with whatever information we have gained at that point.

"End of log entry." The screen went blank.

Sean studied Ariadne. She was bursting with excitement.

"We're going to follow in the footsteps of my father!"

Sean nodded soberly. "And let us hope we don't make the same mistakes." Ariadne calmed down noticeably. "We're not going to leave here until we've studied this log thoroughly. What we learn from their mistakes may save our skins."

"But first," said Plum. "I think it might be rather nice to pop over to the other ship for a visit."

"Oh-two," said Sean.

They entered the other ship cautiously. It had not replied to their radio signals, despite the absence of interference inside the hangar. It was even larger than Alexandros's ship, being an interstellar freighter. Inside the airlock, there were similar signs of deserted occupation: a baseball cap, a sloppily stowed pressure suit, food stains in the galley. No voices greeted them.

In the great cargo hold, there were strangely shaped pieces of alien hardware. A green lump, two meters high with pipes coming out one side, stood next to a transparent block the size of a closet, filled with blue fluids circulating through it. A plastic carton held a half kilo of tiny violet crystals, diamond-shaped, with hexagonal holes through them. Nothing was identifiable, except for a yellow vase with an intricate geometrical design on it, and even that might have served some purpose radically different from what its appearance suggested.

In the cockpit, they went through the familiar rigmarole with the computer until they had convinced it that they were working for Stefan Draganescu.

"Computer," commanded Sean. "Expedition leader's log, most recent entry."

Stefan's handsome, bearded face appeared on the screen.

"*Amesto kalo!*" spat Ariadne. Sean did not ask for a translation, but smiled.

"Twenty-eight August, 2107," said the face in elegant English with an accent that sounded vaguely Slavic. "I am going to follow the trail of Zepos. I believe that, with the knowledge he acquired, I will be able to survive the dangers ahead and bring back to Earth some of the treasures of this extraordinary place. I am going to limit my exploration to the outer ring of this world, since there are more wonders here alone than we could possible understand in a century."

"And since it's a lot less dangerous," added Sean.

"I have gone over the dangers with my crew," continued the image of Stefan, "and I am confident that they will follow my lead." He paused dramatically, raised his chin, and added theatrically, "I am determined to be the first human ever to survive this world and to bring back the news of its discovery. This is Expedition Leader Stefan Draganescu, signing off."

"And you trusted this dust licker?" said Sean to Ariadne.

"He's a very well educated man," she said defensively, "and he *is* the Deputy Minister of Culture."

"I could have told you he was as phony as a Martian pyramid if I'd had just three seconds to talk with him. I used to see this kind all the time, out in the roids. They come out there, stay in a luxury hotel, go on guided tours, then go back home and tell everyone how they lived the rugged life for two weeks out on the frontier. Terries!"

"I've been thinking," said Ariadne. "I think we've been too quick to condemn Stefan without a trial. I bet that he pulled every string he could for me and got the grant faster than he believed possible. But by then, I was gone, and using a different name. He couldn't get in touch with me. So what else could he do but come out here?"

"If you believe that," said Sean, "I've got some swamp land on Mercury to sell you. In fact, I'd bet my ship and a year's supply of Guinness that Wolf was working for him."

"Don't be absurd. Stefan would never have anything to do with a man of such monumental vulgarity."

"Hah! It explains a lot. It explains why he found you so quickly in Gagaringrad. It explains why he's been baskervilling you since the moment you left Earth, and why he sabotaged our ship."

"Nonsense," she said. "Someone has simply filed an erroneous report about me with the Customs authorities."

"Let us concentrate," Plum said diplomatically, "on deciding what we should do now."

"Let's go!" said Ariadne.

"Let's *prepare* to go," corrected Sean.

They spend the rest of the day studying the log of Alexandros Zepos.

"Log entry 1351 hours, 1 November, 2087. We have landed in what appears to be a hangar, filled with spacecraft of unfamiliar designs. We are going to explore the hangar . . .

"Log entry, 1612 hours, 1 November, 2087. We have found an airlock. It took us much experimentation to make it work. First you have to press the two blue spots in the center of the

door. They must be pressed at the same time. That makes sure
the inner door is up. Then you press the two white spots. Ignore
the dozens of colored ones. We still do not know what they do.
When you press the white ones simultaneously, the door slides
down into the floor. Then enter the chamber. Press the two white
dots on the far side, and the first door will close again. It almost
crushed one of the men the first time we tried it. If there is
a safety mechanism, it had broken down. Be sure you do not
stand over a retracted door!

"When both doors are up, the room will automatically fill with
air. When the pressure is about 1.2 atmospheres, the second door
will slide into the floor and you can enter a corridor. There is
artificial light everywhere, mostly red. We suspect therefore that
the aliens were originally from a red star. The air is breathable,
rich in oxygen, a little high in CO_2. The temperature is about
thirty degrees C, pleasantly warm. It has an unusual amount of
methane, but not dangerously so . . .

"Log entry, 1801 hours, 1 November, 2087. We have found a
map of the outer ring. It is a three-dimensional X-ray picture in
the ceiling above the corridor near the airlock, and it moves. We
do not yet understand the meaning of the moving parts, but we
have explored enough of the adjacent corridors to verify that it
really is a map of this ring. There are many strange symbols on
the map, designating particular corridors and rooms, which we
have no idea of the meaning of. We have not yet found a map of
the inner rings.

"There are signs in a written language. It is a beautiful script,
filled with curlicues, generally descending from a horizontal bar
at the top. Marie Patanjali says it reminds her of the Devanagari
script of India, which they use for Hindi and Sanskrit.

"The outer ring, where we are currently, is a strange design. It
is divided into two halves. The dividing point is evidently the
zero-gee circle where any object would be in free-fall. Outside of
the circle, the apparent gravity points outward; inside, it points
inward. The ring is divided into many floors, and each floor has
many corridors, corridors thousands of kilometers in length. We
will gradually work our way up to the zero-gee circle, then down
to the innermost floor of this ring. Then we will see if it is
possible to get to the next ring.

"This world was built by the aliens around a neutron star.
They probably started by building this outer ring, and used it as
the base of operations from which to build the inner ones. We do

not know how they solved the problem of the tidal force, which must grow horrendous on the inner rings.

"There is dust everywhere, centimeters thick, like snow. Our exobiologist, Marie Patanjali, has measured the rate of dust deposition and computed that this ring has been abandoned for eight hundred to fourteen hundred years! Yet there are recent tracks though some of the dust. Some look like they were made by machines, others by animals the size of rats or smaller. She is searching for samples.

"Marie has also found water troughs and what appear to be waste-disposal facilities. The flowing water is safe to drink, which is an exceedingly useful discovery, since it means we will not need to carry water with us. The disposal facilities are marked with blue circles on the floor, and may be used as bathrooms after some familiarization . . .

"Log entry 0906 hours, 2 November, 2087. Christopher Barkeley is dead. He was trying to disconnect a blue sphere from the floor of the first corridor. It was a small sphere, no larger than a football, and he thought it would make a good artifact to bring back. According to his companion, Vartan Kasandjian, he was trying to cut through the small copper-colored pipe on which it stood. After half an hour with a diamond ultracutter, he made a tiny pinhole. A stream of blue fluid shot out of it. It cut right through him, almost cut him in two. It must be under inconceivable pressure. He died instantly. We buried him in space, ejecting the body from the hangar. I have given orders that no alien devices are to be removed by force until we know more about them . . .

"Log entry, 1402 hours, 3 November, 2087. Vartan Kasandjian is dead. He was in a room that was filled with mechanical tracks. The room was almost dust-free and had several machines taller than a man, parts of which spun too fast for the eye to see. We could hear them spinning, like the blades they used to have on helicopters. He knew there was danger, but he was using a stroboscope to observe the operation of the machines, which seem to be connected to the air circulation and regeneration system. Suddenly, another machine entered the room. It apparently was a maintenance robot. It ran by Vartan and knocked him backward into a spinning rotor. It took him a while to die. He was too far gone for the doctrobot to save him. We buried him in space.

"We now believe that the yellow line on the floor is where the maintenance robots go. I have told everyone to avoid walking along any such lines, regardless of color. When necessary, cross over one quickly, after looking both ways carefully. These robots move quickly. There must be many other such robots following these lines. In the thousand years since abandonment, apparently some of the robots have started to break down. Their safety features may not always work. We think that is what happened to poor Vartan.

"This world must be booby-trapped with all kinds of such dangers. After all, if an alien were to land in one of our cities, he might be run over by a vehicle or trapped in a refrigerator or killed by sticking his fingers into an electric outlet. We must think of this world as one that has been unintentionally booby-trapped. And perhaps there are even intentional ones, designed to kill burglars. We just do not know enough.

"I tell the crew to think ten times before they make a move! They are shaken by the loss of Chris and Vartan. There are only five of us now, but we are still determined to learn who or what these creatures were, and what is the purpose of this place, and why they abandoned it—*if* they abandoned it . . .

"Log entry, 0907 hours, 4 November, 2087. Our exobiologist, Marie Patanjali, has found the first life-form! She had set a little trap on one of the dust-trails where tiny animal footprints could be seen. She used one of the traps we had brought with us in case we found any animals in the Beta Hydri system. It is a transparent cage with two open ends, triggered electronically.

"When she checked it this morning, there was a nasty-looking little creature inside. It is the size of a large rat, with a three-segmented body, rather like a giant ant. But it is a true animal, not an insect, with hard, dark green scales all over its body. It has sharp teeth that it flashes whenever anyone comes near the cage. One of the men called it a ratroach, and the name has stuck. Certainly, it captures the spirit of two of the more repulsive Earth creatures.

"She says that it has male sex organs different from Earthly animals, but still anatomically recognizable. She points out that this means there must be at least two sexes, and also there must be a whole ecology in the ring, animals or plants for this creature to feed on. She has now found more than a dozen other types of small animal and insect tracks.

"Log entry, 1230 hours, 4 November, 2087. Lajos Szeker, our engineer, has measured the timing of the dimming and brightening of the corridor and room lights. They are bright for about nineteen hours and dim for the same period. He thinks the aliens are from a planet where the day lasts thirty-eight hours.

"Log entry, 0315 hours, 5 November, 2087. Our exobiologist, Marie Patanjali, is extremely ill. She was bitten by that ratroach she caught. One arm is swollen and she has a terrible fever. We have returned her to the ship, and the doctrobot is monitoring her constantly. I have suspended further exploration for now. Morale is bad, and the crew is talking about giving up and going home. I have ordered the crew to carry side arms to defend against dangerous animals or machines.

"Log entry, 0812 hours, 6 November, 2087. Marie Patanjali is recovering nicely. She thinks her blood is probably just as poisonous to the alien bacteria as they are to her. Everyone's spirits have risen with her recovery. The crew is talking once more about continuing the exploration.

"Log entry, 1450 hours, 7 November, 2087. We have reached the inner edge of the outer ring, according to the map. Helene d'Albis, our geologist, was studying the moving dots on the map. Some of them move in circles, running around the ring; others go in straight lines across it, from the outer edge to the inner and back. She followed the map and located the place where one of the circumferential moving paths was. It turned out to be a huge corridor in which the floor moves in an eerie fashion.

"Helene thinks the molecules in the floor vibrate in such a way that they push you continuously in one direction. You fall down until you get used to it. It takes you at a fast pace in one direction around the ring. There is an adjacent corridor moving in the opposite direction.

"She rode the conveyor until she found a transfer point where the circular dot-paths on the map cross the straight ones. There, she found a similar conveyor going upward. You have to grab handholds and put your feet on steps. It runs rather like an old-fashioned escalator, but she says to be careful of the zero-gee point.

"She jumped on it and went to the end and back again. I had told everyone to go in pairs, and not to do anything risky without telling me, but she ignored my order. She was too curious, she said. In any event, she was not harmed and we now know how to get from here to there. We still do not know how to get to the next ring, but I am sure we will find a way when we have explored the inner edge of our ring.

"Log entry, 1722 hours, 8 November, 2087. We have been studying the innermost corridor of our ring. In the ceiling, we have found a map of the whole ring system. It is horrendously complex. There are hundreds of rings within rings.

"The map is a masterpiece of three-dimensional motional art, with magnification selectable by wall keys. In the model, each ring moves as you watch it. Marie Patanjali calls it a prayer wheel. As you go closer to the center, each ring moves faster, just as we saw during approach. There is something like a commuter vactrain system operating between the rings. The map shows the real positions of the trains as they move from one ring to another.

"You catch the train where the 'escalator' ends. Periodically, this train arrives at your ring, opens its door, closes it, then accelerates along the ring until it has built up enough speed to match the next ring, which is only a few kilometers away. Then it jumps over to that ring and climbs like an elevator to the center of the ring. There it pauses a few seconds and then it does the whole routine again to get to the next ring. It continues in this way until it has gone all the way to the innermost ring, right next to the neutron star. Then it comes back.

"Helene d'Albis and I took the train over to the next ring. We jumped off there and explored a little. The air is fine, both on the train and in the second ring. There are great fields of yellow grasslike vegetation growing throughout the parts we saw, with a massive irrigation and fertilization system.

"Since it takes the train many hours to make the round trip to the center and back, we used the conveyor system to take us a few kilometers down to the next train line, which the map showed us was due in soon on its outbound leg. We returned to the outermost ring—or 'home ring' as we call it—and took the conveyor back to the crew. They were relieved to see us again.

"It is hard to believe, but we seem to have finally mastered this world!"

CHAPTER 13

The next day, Sean and his companions examined the alien artifacts closely and studied the other logs in both ships. They learned that Stefan's copilot–navigator had been killed by laserlike energy while removing a signal plate from a corridor. That left him with his pilot, engineer, exobiologist, Wolf, the journobot and the doctrobot.

"They've got about a week's head start on us," said Sean to Ariadne and Plum. "I'm surprised they didn't just grab all the loot they could and come back. They're probably scared to move anything for fear it will blow up in their ugly faces."

"Well, *we* are ready to go now, aren't we?" said Ariadne.

Sean nodded without enthusiasm. "As soon as we load up with supplies, weapons, tools, and anything we can think of that might possibly be of help."

"For someone who talks a lot about Stefan's supposed cowardice, your words speak much louder than your actions."

"Just remember, person," Sean said sternly, "this world probably has no end of surprises. I've been on enough planets to know you can never be too smart or too cautious. I've buried more than one man who was too brave for his own good." He let the name of Alexandros Zepos go unspoken.

They unstowed the *Shillelagh*'s own doctrobot and loaded up with everything they could carry, letting the robot take the heaviest items.

In their pressure suits, laden with backpacks and frontpacks, and wearing quantaguns on their thighs, they walked toward the hangar airlock described by Alexandros. Sean led, followed by Ariadne, Plum, and the four-armed doctrobot.

"I say, old bean," said Plum. "If I never return from this jaunt, do be so kind as to drop a message to my mum and dad in Bristol, would you?"

"Of course, my friend," said Sean. "But with the three of us and the doctrobot, and with the knowledge from the logs, I think we're all going to make it back oh-two, provided we can keep this young woman from killing us.''

Ariadne sneered at his back.

At the airlock, Sean touched the two blue spots in the center of the door, then the two white ones. The door slid down into the floor with a puff of escaping gas and dust, revealing a dark chamber tall enough for even Sean to stand in without bending.

The three humans and the robot entered, while Sean said, ''Remember, don't stand over the door slot unless you want a nasty surprise.'' He touched the white spots in the second door. Immediately, the first door rose back up to the ceiling, leaving them in darkness. He switched on a lightrod and played it around the almost featureless chamber.

There was a hissing sound of gas, picked up by the exterior suit microphones. ''I sure hope these doors don't break down,'' said Sean.

''That's a lovely thought,'' said Plum, studying the red-lit interior of the chamber. ''I should hate for all of us to be entombed in this airlock forever because some little part chose this moment, after a thousand years, to fail.''

The second door slid into the floor and they stepped into the corridor, which glowed dimly with red light emanating everywhere from walls, floor, and ceiling. It was broad, nine meters wide, and it stretched endlessly in both directions. Periodically, portals opened out, presumably into rooms. The floor was covered with dust. Many boot prints and machine trails cut through it like snow tracks. Ariadne started to remove her helmet, but Sean stopped her.

''Wait until I've run an atmos check.'' He studied the suit spectrometer.

''We know the air's fine,'' said Ariadne. ''The whole crew of my father's ship breathed it.''

''We know it was fine twenty years ago,'' said Sean. ''And if your friend Stefan can be believed, it was fine last week.'' He looked up. ''Well, now we know it's fine today too.''

He unfastened his helmet and the others did likewise. The air was humid and warm, and smelled slightly foul. The dim red light made the atmosphere gloomy. They stood there as their eyes adapted, breathing the alien air and thinking private thoughts for a while.

Then Sean broke the eerie silence. ''Must be nighttime,'' he said.

Plum sneezed.

"Just think," said Ariadne, inhaling the air with gusto, "a thousand years ago alien creatures walked here, breathing this very air, thinking thoughts that would probably be incomprehensible to us."

Sean nodded slowly, feeling like an intruder in someone's home, wondering what that someone looked like.

The doctrobot stood silently, his head rotating through 360 degrees above its spherical abdomen, surveying the sights.

Ariadne looked at the ceiling. "There's the map!" she said, pointing upward.

They craned their necks and saw, spread out over the whole ceiling near the airlock, a large transparent ring floating over their heads like a crown. It contained dozens of pastel-colored circles and tubes nested within it, clearly representing floors and corridors. Two white dots pulsed at the outer edge. Sean pointed at them and said, "That must mean 'You are here.' "

Some of the circles revolved within the ring; some straight lines moved radially. Ariadne pointed at them and said, "Those must be the conveyors and escalators."

"Ariadne, take a picture of this, would you?"

She removed a cryscamera from a thigh pocket and inserted a fresh viewcrystal. She aimed it at the map and took a moving picture of it.

"Good," said Sean. "Now we've got a map to take with us."

"Most of the boot prints go to the left," said Sean.

Ariadne threw down her helmet and started to walk in that direction.

Sean picked it up and handed it back to her. She frowned and said, "It's just extra weight, and I've already got all I can carry in my pack."

"There may come a time when we are in some place where the air isn't so breathable. Their regenerator may have broken down somewhere. There could be a hole in the wall, and you could wind up breathing vacuum."

They walked on, their helmets hanging from the side of their belts, past portals that showed strange machines sitting silent, covered by dust.

They stopped at the entrance to one room from which whirring sounds came. Large black hand-drawn letters on the wall said, in English, DANGER! MOVING MACHINERY!

Sean motioned them to hug the wall while he stuck his face around the corner. Inside were great shiny red machines, with transparent pipes running in and out everywhere. The floor was almost free of dust, and a yellow stripe on it threaded between the machines.

Sean stood in the entrance and said, "This looks like the place where that man got sliced up." The others joined him, but no one stepped into the room.

They walked on until they came to an entryway bordered in green, a color made sickly by the red light. Some human had scrawled CONVEYOR in black letters on the side. Inside, they saw a shimmering green floor. "According to the map," said Sean, "this is the conveyor we want."

He touched one foot tentatively to the shimmering floor. It was swept sideways, throwing him off balance. He fell onto the ordinary corridor floor. "Damnation!" he exclaimed.

Embarrassed, he stood up and jumped with both feet onto the shimmering conveyor. He fell again, but this time landed on the conveyor. He was carried bodily along.

His companions tested the surface with their toes and jumped on. Plum promptly fell, too, but Ariadne deftly kept her balance, smiling with superiority. The doctrobot followed, having carefully observed the humans. He had no difficulty remaining standing.

"Stand sideways," said Ariadne. "It wants to spin you if you straddle it."

Sean followed her advice, albeit with much grumbling, until he was standing. Plum just remained seated, looking unhappy. "Differential motion," said Sean, struggling for dignity in words of many syllables as he observed Ariadne overtake him without apparent effort. "The inner parts move faster than the outer ones. If you straddle them, they spin you." He transferred to Ariadne's lane and found himself moving at the same speed, while Plum fell farther behind.

Plum crawled to the faster lane and busied himself by probing the surface of the conveyor, finding dignity on the floor by being studious. He removed a glove and touched the conveyor. "Feels curious," he reported. "It tickles, yet is hard to the touch. Strangely silent. Evidently it is some microscopic or submicroscopic nonlinear ultrasonic vibration, as was surmised."

They passed numerous other portals, each marked in a strange writing, until they came to a large room with a different type of conveyor moving upward. "Off!" commanded Sean, jumping with relief to the hard floor. The others followed. A black scrawl read ESCALATOR TO INNER EDGE OF OUTER PRAYER WHEEL. Underneath that was written *Helene d'Albis of Marseilles, first human here, 2087.*

"This must be the transfer point we want," said Sean.

They studied the escalator. It was a good dozen meters wide and rose from a hole in the floor, disappearing into one in the ceiling. Rods and horizontal platforms crawled up the wall, seemingly animated as they smoothly rose. The platforms, extending the width of the escalator and protruding half a meter straight out, looked too flimsy to stand on. The rods, extending the same distance as the platforms, were spaced about a meter apart, like bristles in a great brush. On closer examination, they found the escalator to be of the same shimmering green material as the conveyor, but the rods and platforms were somehow attached to the material in a way that allowed them to move upward, while the escalator material looked as if it were standing still.

"I suppose it could be a traveling wave of molecular attraction," mused Plum.

Sean stepped on the next platform to rise out of the floor and gripped one of the rods. He rapidly rose through an opening in the ceiling. The others followed suit.

They passed through several floors, each one different. One had great vats of bubbling pink liquid exuding a foul smell. The next revealed a blue robot the size of a squat locomotive with slowly spinning spiral projections on top. Dozens of metal feelers explored the floor, giving it the impression of a centipede looking for food; parallel grooves ran centimeters deep along its back, each one glowing with pulses of purple light that traveled back and forth along its length. It moved with surprising speed away from them, groaning disturbingly as they continued up.

The higher they got, the lighter they felt. As they continued on, a deep, bloodcurdling voice snarled at them in an incomprehensible language unlike any Earthly tongue. Startled, they looked around for the source but could see none.

Suddenly, their feet seemed to be pulled out from under them. Hanging on to the rods for dear life, they let their feet settle, upside down, on what had been the platform over their heads.

"Zero-gee circle!" exclaimed Sean. "Damn, I should have anticipated that."

Plum elaborated for Ariadne's benefit: "We have just passed through the point Snafu spoke of earlier, where the centrifugal and gravitational forces from the neutron star are precisely balanced for this ring. We are now within the inner half of the outer ring. Our feet now point down toward the star."

"That's what those words were!" exclaimed Ariadne. "A

recording saying, 'Fasten your seat belts,' so to speak. I wish we had recorded it. It would be a clue to understanding the language.''

At last they arrived at the end, where they jumped off into a large chamber. Ariadne spotted a message some Earthling had printed on the far wall: PRAYER-WHEEL RAILROAD, START OF THE LINE, CONNECTIONS TO LONDON, PARIS, TOKYO, CUCAMONGA.

In the ceiling was a great, three-dimensional, moving map of the whole alien world. Rings whirled within rings, dizzyingly, hundreds upon hundreds of them, like the ridges of an antique phonograph record. The outer ring revolved slowly, the next one inside a bit faster, and each smaller circle moved faster than the preceding ones until they were a blur. At the very center was a tiny, spinning sphere. Ariadne removed her little stereoscopic cryscamera and videoed the map.

The group stared at it for a long time, trying to make sense of the alien labels underlying the rings. Little blue dots traveled slowly from ring to ring. Ariadne pointed to one: "That could represent one of the trains.''

Sean nodded and timed its movement from ring to ring. "Judging by its motion, the next train is due here in about four hours. We might as well relax a bit.''

Plum sat down on the floor with relief and squirted some water into his mouth from the tube in the neck of his pressure suit.

Ariadne said, "I think I'll explore a little.''

Sean groaned and said, "If you're going to be wandering about at every opportunity, you're going to get yourself killed.''

"I'll be careful," she replied.

"If you insist on going," said Sean, "I'd better come along to keep you out of mischief.''

"Honestly," said Ariadne, "you're like Cassandra, always predicting the worst.''

"But," said Plum, "Cassandra's predictions had a habit of coming true, eh? I think I shall wait for you here." He sneezed.

"I'll mark our path," said Sean to Plum, "and if we're not back within the hour, come looking for us with gun drawn.''

Ariadne and Sean walked out of the chamber and into a corridor— the woman eagerly, the man warily.

"Quite a lot of traffic to the right," said Sean, studying the tracks in the dust. Many boot prints went to the right, only a few to the left.

"Let's follow them," said Ariadne, going to the right.

Sean marked a right-pointing arrow on the wall with a blue v-pen and initialed it *S O'S*.

Ariadne walked in the lead, quickly, staring everywhere, dashing from one side of the corridor to the other, putting her nose into each portal they passed, like a puppy sniffing out a new home.

"The light is getting brighter," noted Sean. "Must be dawn." He walked behind her, realizing he could not both keep ahead of her and proceed cautiously. His longer stride compensated for his more deliberate pace. He studied the corridor ahead as far as he could see and glanced back frequently, looking for dangers.

"They left the corridor there," said Sean, pointing up ahead, where the tracks turned into a portal. "Don't go inside until we're sure they got through it alive."

She did his bidding and her mouth dropped open. "A body," she whispered.

Sean looked inside and saw the body of a woman stretched out on the floor of a room full of small alien objects. They stared at it, neither eager to enter.

"I suppose we ought to see if we can identify her," said Ariadne reluctantly.

"Not yet," whispered Sean. "Let's see if we can tell how she died first. Maybe whatever killed her is still in there." He drew his quantagun.

There was a loud groan from the room, coming from behind a partition. Sean pulled Ariadne back from the portal and peered warily around the edge, aiming the gun toward the voice.

A male voice shouted, "Goddammit!"

Another male voice muttered something indecipherable.

"Might as well get up and have some goddamn breakfast!" said the first voice.

Ariadne peered around Sean, hugging him closely. Even through the pressure suit, Sean found her touch a most pleasant sensation.

The body on the floor stirred and yawned.

Sean and Ariadne laughed. He whispered, "She was only asleep!"

Ariadne whispered, "Why don't we go in?"

Sean said, "Let's wait a little and see what we can see."

The woman on the floor stretched, stood up, and walked behind the partition.

"I must say you are looking beautiful this morning," said one of the male voices.

"That's Stefan's voice," whispered Ariadne.

Sean nodded without surprise.

"Is anyone using the bathroom?" said the woman's voice. She spoke with a North American accent.

"Yes, Wolf is in there," said Stefan. His Romanian accent lent his speech a touch of Transylvania.

Sean looked at Ariadne and nodded a strong I-told-you-so. Ariadne looked incredulous.

"He always takes forever," said the woman's voice.

"I think we could possibly find something to do to kill that time," said Stefan.

"Get your hands off me!" said the woman. "I'm getting damn tired of reminding you that I'm engaged!"

"But your fiancé is twenty light-years away."

"Cut that out! Between you and Wolf, I swear I'm going to turn the next one who lays a hand on me into a eunuch!"

Ariadne frowned with disgust and muttered *"Mangas!"* Sean smiled the smile of the just.

"But, Millie," said Stefan, "we are stuck in this damn prison for the rest of our short lives. We might as well get the little pleasure out of it that we can."

Sean and Ariadne looked at each other quizzically.

"Oh, why did I have to come on this godforsaken expedition?" said Millie. "I should have listened to Hank! But no, I had to be the great explorer, advancing the cause of science!" There was silence.

Sean whispered to Ariadne, "Call out to him, but don't tell him I'm here." He moved back all the way into the corridor.

Ariadne stood in the portal. They continued their spat, oblivious of her. Millie was a short, rather attractive brunet in an orange jumpsuit covered with bulging pockets. Stefan was wearing a dashing silver explorer's suit with the logo of the Ministry of Culture on it.

"Hello, Stefan," Ariadne said loudly.

"What?" he exclaimed.

"We're saved!" shouted Millie.

They rushed toward the portal and were joined by a third person, an unfamiliar Asian man, who came running. "Thank god!" he shouted.

The trio stopped abruptly at a white line on the floor.

"Ariadne!" exclaimed Stefan.

"Who is she?" said Millie.

"Who cares?" said the other man. "She's human!"

Ariadne started to enter the room.

"Stop!" shouted the three simultaneously.

Ariadne froze.

"There's a barrier here," said Stefan. "Some sort of force field."

"It's one-way," said Millie. "It lets you in, but won't let you out."

A bright red robot of human manufacture joined Stefan and Millie. It put an arm around Stefan, who patted it familiarly. "Hi, sport," it said to Ariadne. "I'm Homer. I'm the journobot who's recording this expedition." Switching to his staccato journalistic mode, he said, "Hope at last! After a month of near-death from starvation and thirst—"

"It was actually a week," said Millie.

"—our daring, intrepid crew brightened like a bank of lasers at the sight of a beautiful human rescuer. Their courage and patience, and above all, the fearless, unflagging leadership of Stefan Draganescu, have been rewarded!"

"How on Earth did you get here?" said Stefan.

"I hired a ship in the Asteroid Federation," said Ariadne coolly.

"Really?" said Stefan. "How wonderful!"

"What is your name, please?" said Homer conversationally.

"Ariadne Zepos," she replied.

"Not the daughter of Alexandros Zepos?" said Homer.

"Yes."

"This is wonderful!" said the robot. In journalese, he added, "The Draganescu Expedition was saved by the beautiful daughter of the very man who had so mysteriously disappeared on the first expedition!"

"And how, may I ask," Ariadne said coldly to Stefan, "did *you* get here? I thought it was going to take years to get an expedition together."

"It would have," said Stefan smoothly, "but I used up every favor I was owed in two ministries to get a starship. Just for you. But by the time it was all arranged, you had disappeared. Your stepfather said you'd gone to Gagaringrad, but I was never able to track you down."

"The galaxy twists fates unpredictably," said Homer. "Who would have believed the lives of these diverse people would become intertwined on the distant, spinning wreckage of an abandoned, alien world?"

The hulking bald mass of Wolf Wolfram hustled into view, mouth open in astonishment.

"And what about him?" Ariadne said icily.

"Him?" said Stefan. "This chap? He's just someone who was assigned to this expedition by the Ministry of Trade."

"Alfred Wolfram is his name," said Homer. "Known to his intimates as 'Wolf,' he is the daring Assistant Chief Customs Inspector from Earth who selflessly joined the historical Draganescu Expedition to advance human knowledge at the risk of his own life, a man second in courage only to the bold Stefan Draganescu himself."

"We've met," said Ariadne sourly. Her eyes narrowed. "Did Mr. Wolfram happen to tell you how he tried to kill us?"

"Whatever are you talking about?" said Stefan.

"This man planted a bomb on our starship, and fixed the computer so we would get killed even if the starship didn't blow us up."

"That's absurd!" said Stefan.

"I never did no such thing," said Wolf.

"I was told he is a highly regarded official with an exemplary record," said Stefan.

"Fortunately," said Ariadne, trying not to look at the still-hidden Sean, "I happened to hire a pilot of exceptional skill and some intelligence, who saved our lives against great odds."

Sean smiled and leaned casually against the corridor wall, still out of sight.

"Was it that Irish ruffian?" said Stefan.

She nodded and Sean smiled again.

"To hell with all this nostalgia!" said Millie, "You've got to get us out of here!"

"What is this place, anyway?" said Ariadne.

"At first," said Stefan, "we thought it was a museum. There were all sorts of fabulous gems and *objets d'art* just lying around here." He pulled a multifaceted topazlike gem the size of a walnut from his pocket and toyed with it. "We were all entranced. We entered this room and began exploring all the other rooms. Then Wolf discovered we couldn't leave. The force field had us trapped. That was about a week ago."

"I'm surprised you haven't died of thirst," said Ariadne.

"Oh, there's plenty of water," said Stefan. "It tastes odd, but seems to be safe. The real danger was from starvation. There is some kind of alien food here. Our pilot ate some and said it was surprisingly good—just before he died."

"Oh no!" said Ariadne. "I'm so sorry."

"This accursed world has more ways to kill a human than I'd ever dreamed of, and more than our doctrobot was ever programmed to cure. We didn't touch the alien food after it killed the pilot. The irony is, it now seems this place is not only *not* a museum, it is actually a nursery.''

''Nursery?'' said Ariadne.

''Yes, or a kindergarten,'' said Stefan with some embarrassment. ''It appears it was designed to accommodate and educate the young of the species. Evidently, adults could pass through the force field, but children could not. The gems and artifacts that so attracted us are apparently nothing but toys for the young.''

Sean smiled broadly and Ariadne laughed. ''So you're trapped in a nursery!'' she said. ''How delightful!''

Irritatedly, Stefan said, ''You wouldn't think it so comical if you were in here. What you must do is find out how the alien adults were able to pass through the field. They must have had some key that allowed them through.''

''Suppose it was a voice code, some phrase that children wouldn't know?'' said Ariadne. ''Then we'd never be able to figure it out.''

''Don't say that,'' said Stefan.

''Or perhaps it simply detected the deeper sounds of an adult's voice?'' said Millie. ''Wolf, you've got the deepest voice, God knows. Try saying something real loud.''

''What you want me to say?'' he asked.

''It won't work,'' and Stefan. ''He's been speaking ever since we got trapped and it hasn't helped.''

''Well, maybe they had loud voices,'' suggested Ariadne. ''Try speaking louder.''

Wolf yelled, ''What the frigid moon dust you want me to say?''

''Try singing,'' said Ariadne.

Wolf pondered a moment, then began to sing while pressing against the force field. He sang in a voice that would have threatened to bring the aliens back to life if any were buried nearby:

''I am the very model
     of a modern stellar spacer now
  I've been to every star within
     twelve light-years of this place, I vow.

  I've stored them in my database,
     in RAM and ROM and every place.

I'm very good at finding my way
  round about in hyperspace.

I'm filled with knowledge of the creatures
  on the worlds of Sirius.
I've integrated differential 'quations
  till delirious.

In short, computers all allow,
  in RAM and ROM and every how,
I am the very model
  of a modern steller spacer now.''

"Enough!" pleaded Ariadne. It had accomplished nothing.

"I thought you didn't like classical music," said Stefan.

"We had to learn that when I was in school," replied Wolf.

"By the way," said Ariadne to the other woman, "we've not been introduced."

"Millicent Kingsley, exobiologist. Call me Millie."

"Dr. Millicent Kingsley," said Homer, "expedition exobiologist. Possessor of a bachelor's degree in biochemistry from Canaveral College in Florida and a Ph.D. in exobiology from the University of California at Pasadena, she has never been content to rest on her looks, but instead has chosen one of the most difficult and challenging of all careers, that of the student of life-forms of other worlds. Her brains match her beauty, and she is Professor of Exobiology at the University of Toronto. Winner of numerous awards and honors, she has traveled to three star systems, published extensively in the scientific literature, and is the author of the viewcrystal *Extraterrestrial Ecosystems of Earth-like Planets*. Not exactly light reading, unless you have a Ph.D. of your own. Certainly, no one can possibly doubt that this lovely woman is truly a superbly well qualified member of the extraordinary Draganescu Expedition."

"If you cut out the moon dust," said Millie, "most of that is true, except I'm only an associate professor."

"Pleased to meet a fellow scientist," said Ariadne.

Millie tilted her eyebrows quizzically.

"Hydroarchaeologist," said Ariadne. Then, to the unfamiliar man, she said, "And you, sir?"

"Takeo Miyazawa, at your service, Dr. Zepos." He was a tall, thin man with muscular arms, who spoke with a thick Japanese accent.

"Takeo Miyazawa," said Homer, "expedition engineer. A whiz at both sublight and hyperspace engines, able to dismantle and reassemble them blindfolded under high gee with one hand tied behind his back."

"Not quite," added Takeo.

"Trained at the world-famous Kawasaki factory," Homer continued obliviously, "and experienced from many interplanetary and interstellar missions, he was the perfect choice for the most critical position on the expedition, with the exception, of course, of that of the dedicated leader, Dr. Stefan Draganescu." Stefan patted Homer on the head.

Sean, convinced that nothing more could be gained by remaining hidden, stepped into the portal. The prisoners started. Homer perked up and began recording the scene, saying, "Another noble rescuer to the aid of the brave Draganescu Expedition!"

"Top o' the mornin' to you, Wolf!" said Sean. The bald man remained silent, rubbing his jaw, distaste written on his face.

"And you, Stefan," said Sean, "I recall from one of Ariadne's viziphone calls."

"How do you do?" said Stefan, his words oozing civility.

"I'm grand," said Sean with a smile, "for an Irish ruffian."

Stefan shrugged and said, "Only an expression. No offense?"

"None taken," said Sean. "It's an honor to be considered offensive by the man who tried to steal Ariadne's rightful place on this expedition, and who tried to kill us on Vesta."

Homer, sensing tension, remained silent.

"Vesta?" said Stefan. "I've never been on Vesta in my life."

"Of course not," said Sean. "You merely ordered it. Your faithful ratroach Wolf did the dirty work."

"Moon dust!" spat Wolf. "Prove it!"

"Now, see here," said Stefan, "Mr.—Mr. O'Shaughnessy, isn't it?" Sean nodded. "Evidently, someone has tried to kill you. Of that, you seem quite certain."

"Oh yes, quite certain."

"Well, a man of your, let us say, background, living as you do on the untamed frontier of civilization, has no doubt occasionally earned the ire of some undesirable miscreant who might wish to see you dead."

"That I have."

"Well, there you have it," said Stefan. "Some enemy of yours must have done the foul deed. There's no reason at all to suspect me or this fellow Wolf." He turned on his Look of Martyred Innocence, Number Two.

Ariadne began to show some doubt. "He could be right, you know," she said to Sean.

"Stefan," said Sean, "I've met some slick worders in my time, but I have to admit you're one of the best. I'm sure you can twist the facts around until you have me convinced I planted that bomb on board my ship myself. But you'll not make me believe I didn't meteor my fist into Wolf's fine, smooth skull when I found him rummaging through my room."

"Well," said Stefan, "I don't know anything about that. After all, it is the job of a Customs inspector to investigate reported cases of smuggling. And smuggling, he tells me, is what brought him to the Asteroid Federation. And you roiders are famous for your neglect of the rules of terrestrial trade—not that I hold that against you, you understand."

"And you just happened to choose as a crew member the man who ransacked my room, and just happened to stop by Vesta to pick him up?"

"Chief Wolfram came to me when he was investigating a report—no doubt malicious mischief on the part of some unknown scoundrel—that Ariadne was engaged in smuggling with you. Since I needed a man of his exceptional background, I invited him to join my expedition, after assuring him that in no way could Ariadne possibly be involved in any underhanded business. When he unexpectedly had to go to Vesta, thanks to the admittedly suspicious behavior of Ariadne, I agreed I should pick him up there on the way here."

Sean shook his head admiringly. "Seldom have I ever heard such a pile of moon dust so beautifully shoveled in front of my own ears."

"It *could* be true," said Ariadne.

"And I *could* be a leprechaun," said Sean. "And if his story is true and I'm a leprechaun, then we can all go home and sing hymns to the brotherhood of man. But since, as you can plainly see, I'm too tall by quite a measure to be a leprechaun, I'm afraid we'll have to assume that this bunch has wound up right where they belong—in a nursery-jail. I see no reason why we should trouble ourselves on their account. If they spend the rest of their lives here, it will be too good a punishment for them. I think it's time you and I said our good-byes and wished them a fond farewell." He waved and started to walk away. Ariadne hesitated.

"Wait!" said Stefan. "You can't just leave us here! We're human beings! We have the same DNA under our skin! We're your brothers! We've only got a few weeks of food left! We'll starve to death!''

Sean kept walking. Ariadne remained and called back to him, ''Sean, he's right. We can't just leave them here to die, no matter what they've done. They haven't been convicted by a court of any crime.''

Sean whirled around and said, ''Now, isn't *that* a shame! No noble Earthly judge, dedicated to the punishment of the guilty and the freeing of the innocent, has passed a sentence of death on these fine human beings! And they didn't do anything at all, but try to kill three decent people. 'Tis a shame, indeed! Is there no justice in the universe?''

Millie shouted, ''Well, *I* never had anything to do with trying to kill you!''

''Neither did I!'' said Takeo. Millie nodded strenuously.

''We've got to try to free them,'' said Ariadne. ''It's the decent thing to do. We can let the authorities on Earth decide whether they have committed a crime.''

''Well,'' said Sean, ''my belief in the abilities of the authorities on Earth to bring criminals to justice, of course, knows no bounds. In fact, I believe in them so strongly that I'm willing to trust them to rescue these people. And since I haven't the faintest idea of how to unlock their alien prison anyway, and since there has been a noticeable lack of talkative aliens to assist us, I'm afraid we shall just have to give up and wish our friends the best of luck in their new home.''

''Sean,'' said Ariadne, ''I'm not leaving here until we've done everything we can for them.''

He closed his eyes, shook his head, and sighed. ''All right, Ariadne,'' he said, walking back to her. ''I've come to know how stubborn you can be when you set your mind to it.''

He stood in front of Stefan, hands behind his back like a drill sergeant about to scold the troops, and said, ''Now, look here, Draganescu, suppose we do figure out a way to free you. What do you promise in return?''

''We'll do anything you want!'' said Stefan.

''Anything?'' said Sean. ''That's a fine word. For starters, do you agree to accompany us in our exploration, following my every command?''

''Yes, certainly,'' said Stefan.

''And you, Wolf. Do you agree to have all charges against Ariadne dropped?''

''Sure,'' he grunted.

"So, Stefan," said Sean, "you solemnly swear before all these witnesses that if we do release you from this prison, you will follow our every order, turn over all your supplies to us, and dance to whatever tune we whistle?"

"I swear!" said Stefan.

"Just a minute, Mr. O'Shaughnessy," said Millie. "Neither Takeo nor I ever had anything to do with their slimy schemes. I signed on this expedition for scientific reasons alone. I think you're probably absolutely correct about their crookedness, and I don't want to be lumped in with them."

"Damn right!" said Takeo.

"I think you're telling the truth," said Sean. "I hate to see you two mixed up with these dust-suckers. If I could free both of you and leave these gentlemen to spend the rest of their lives in this cosmic nursery, I'd gladly do it, and not ask for any thanks."

"Well, then," said Millie, "let's start thinking like aliens, and maybe we can figure a way out of this moon-dusty place!"

Everyone nodded.

"First," said Sean pointing, "pile all of your weapons in the corner there."

The prisoners removed their side arms and put them down.

"Are you sure that's all you had?" said Sean.

"Wolf has a quantarifle and another small gun back there," said Millie, pointing out of sight. Wolf grimaced.

"Would you be so kind as to retrieve them, Millie?" said Sean.

When she had piled them with the others, he said, "Now let's be aliens!"

"For a week," said Millie, "we've been trying to think like these aliens, but we have the handicap of not being able to see the outside rooms the way you can. We've replayed Homer's recordings of the adjacent corridor endlessly, looking for clues. We couldn't find anything useful, but what do you expect from a lousy journobot?"

"I bet your pardon," said Homer. "I must inform you that unless you improve your attitude, I will be forced to downgrade your historical record from 'the lovely, exemplary scientist' to 'the pseudoscientific wretch who, after joining the expedition under false pretenses, proceeded to undermine the morale of the crew, which had been so painstakingly molded by the illustrious Dr. Stefan Draganescu.' It is up to you to determine which report lives in the history crystals. I don't care."

"You can shove your database up your lying RAM!" said Millie.

"I like you, Millie," said Sean, smiling. "You're my kind of woman!"

Ariadne's eyes narrowed as they darted between Sean's face and Millie's. She could not quite put her finger on why she felt vaguely disturbed by his words.

"So this is an alien nursery," said Sean to the prisoners, "and you're young little aliens, frisky and frolicsome, who could get hurt if you were to roam around this world by yourselves. Now, Ariadne and I are adult aliens, your parents, and we've come to visit you. There's this force-field playpen to keep you inside unless you're with us. Naturally, it's smart enough to let us in and out. But how does the force field know we're adults?"

"Perhaps there are sensors in the floor, to determine your weight," said Ariadne.

"No," said Stefan. "We thought of that. Wolf tried carrying two of us through without success."

"There *must* be some way that the field knows when you're an adult," said Sean. "Maybe adults all carried identity cards, the way you do on Earth. Or maybe it had a pattern-recognition capability that was smart enough to tell an adult from a child. Do you have any idea what the aliens even looked like?"

The prisoners shook their heads. "The only art we've found has been abstract. We haven't found any pictures of them yet," said Stefan. "Apparently, they were not as artistically inclined as we."

"Or as narcissistic," Millie said pointedly.

"What about the toys?" said Ariadne. "If this is a nursery, the toys could tell us a lot about the creatures, just like in archaeological sites."

"There are many toys here," said Stefan, waving his hands widely. "All over the place." Millie went away. "And some of them are animals. But which are the aliens, if any?"

Millie returned with an armful of moving, squealing animal-like objects. She put them down. They stood up, making all kinds of animal noises. "Toy robots," she said.

All wore little metallic tunics and had rings around their necks. One, looking rather like a gorilla, grunted and muttered incomprehensible words as he crawled away on four limbs.

"He sounds like the escalator warning," said Ariadne.

Another animal, a fat snake, slithered away, squealing and uttering higher-pitched words in what sounded like the same language. A toy ratroach snarled through its pointed teeth and chased the snake. A creature rather like a two-legged cow uttered mooing sounds and spoke much like the others. A five-legged spidery yellow "octopus" crawled up Stefan's leg, rubbing against him like an affectionate cat. He pulled it off and threw it into the force field, where it bounced off, fell, and skittered away.

"Which one, if any, is a model of the intelligent species?" said Stefan.

Sean laughed. "I supposed if some alien found a collection of human toys, he might conclude that the dominant life-form on Earth was Mickey Mouse, perhaps together with another intelligent species called Donald Duck."

"Are you sure those are toys, not real animals?" said Ariadne.

"We broke one open," said Stefan.

"It was quite difficult," said Takeo. "We had to use tools from the ship. But it turned out to be purely mechanical."

They stared at the tiny robots running hither and thither. "Funny they all wear tunics," said Sean.

"It's merely a cultural sign," said Stefan. "Just as Minnie Mouse wears a skirt."

"That makes sense," said Ariadne. "Virtually all human cultures, at least, have worn some kind of clothing, even if only on their elbows. And we put clothes on toy animals to help children learn how to become adults."

"Another thing," said Sean. "The toys are all wearing necklaces." Stefan nodded. "Suppose the tunics or necklaces are only worn by adults? That would be a way for the force field to tell them from the youngsters!" The group began to study the toy robots with a new intensity.

"Ariadne," said Sean, "let's see if we can find anything like that around here."

"Good thinking," she replied.

"But let's be careful we don't get caught in their prison!"

"Just stay outside the white line," said Millie.

"We may not be able to see it in the dust," said Sean. "This is one case where we'd better not stay together, just in case the other gets caught."

"There are rooms to either side of the entrance," said Stefan, pointing. "They look as if they were for adults, presumably the teachers."

While Sean walked down the corridor to the next room, Ariadne stepped into a long chamber that was a continuation of the prison-nursery, separated by only a white line. The trapped crew watched as she studied the room with the eyes of an archaeologist, at first touching nothing. She walked slowly, mentally cataloguing details of shapes and colors.

There were waist-high, featureless rounded objects on the floor, with flat tops. She mentally labeled them *desks*. She removed her cryscamera and recorded the layout of the room.

One wall had a small greenish box projecting from it. She stood on a desk and inspected it, recording it with the camera. It had an intricate lacy pattern over a dodecahedral surface the size of her hand. She touched it, saying, "I wonder—"

Immediately, a bright violet light burst around her. Startled, she fell off the desk onto her backside.

Embarrassed, she stood up next to the desk and said, "What—" Again the violet light burst forth, but in the air above the desk.

She picked up the camera and recorded the violet light. It was a sequence of letters of the alien language, and it hung in the air like neon words in a cartoonist's balloon. There were whole paragraphs of violet alien words floating in the air, three meters wide, two meters tall, and half a meter thick.

"Beautiful!" she said. The words changed instantly.

"This is some kind of voice recognition!" she said to the crew. With each syllable, the alien words changed. Occasionally, a phrase appeared in red or yellow.

"Extraordinary!" said Homer in the distance.

"This could be the school records or lessons," said Ariadne, watching alien words flash. "A teacher might come in here and ask, 'How is little Costa doing in mathematics?' and the words would tell him."

Homer announced, "The gorgeous daughter of the famous explorer Alexandros Zepos made an incredible discovery! Hardly had she landed on the alien world when she found the records of an educational system that died before she was born."

"This is all just a theory," she said.

"In the Ministry of Information, we learn that 'One colorful guess is better than ten dull facts.' "

"That explains a lot of what I see on the news." She gazed at the changing patterns of words. "Apparently, the voice-recognizer is trying to match our words to its memories. But since we're speaking the wrong language, all it can do is produce random records. I'd give anything to know that language!"

She studied the writing some more and said, "It's boustrophedon."

"A human language?" said Homer. "Amazing! The brilliant

daughter of Alexandros Zepos deciphered the alien language with just one glance! It was the most incredible act of decipherment in the history of the human race, more phenomenal than the translation of the Rosetta Stone!''

''No, no, no!'' she said impatiently. ''That's no human language up there. But the writing is boustrophedon: 'written as the ox ploughs.' You see, it's written from left to right on one line and right to left on the next. You can tell from the way the characters are mirror images on alternate lines. Ancient Egyptian was sometimes written this way.''

''Remarkable!'' said Homer. ''The beauteous daughter of Alexandros Zepos found a connection between the aliens and the ancient Egyptians! Did these aliens build the pyramids?''

''Homer!'' scolded Ariadne. ''If you don't erase that nonsense at once, I will personally dismantle your RAM into little tiny chips!''

''Ancient Egyptian connection deleted,'' he replied quickly. ''I hope you realize that you've blown your chance to be described as *beauteous*. I don't often use that adjective.''

While Ariadne was unraveling the mysteries of the word projector, Sean found himself in a small, low-ceilinged room with nothing in it but colored dots on a part of the wall near the entrance. Struck by their resemblance to the dots in the airlock, he studied it. Each color occurred in pairs of dots. Next to each pair was a label in the alien language.

Cautiously, he stuck two fingers into the first pair. There was a hissing sound behind him. He whirled, pulling out his gun. Hanging down from the ceiling, nearly touching the floor, was a cylinder as wide as he. It was cut away, revealing neatly stacked objects on shelves. Looking up at the ceiling, he could see faint circles all over it, evidently the locations of many other cylinders. ''Closets!'' he said to himself.

He turned his attention to the objects on the shelves. *School supplies, I'd bet*, he thought. He studied them visually, hesitant to touch them. The top shelf contained white transparent hemispheres stacked upside down. Bowls?

The next bore colorful rectangular boxes the size of kelparette packs. Writing implements?

Below that, there were dozens of spheres the size of baseballs, but transparent, with wisps of color swirling inside. It was unclear why they did not roll off the shelf onto the floor. Balls?

The bottom shelf was empty except for a single rod like a conductor's baton. A magic wand?

Slowly, he reached out and grasped a sphere. It refused to move until he tugged on it, then suddenly popped free. It seemed to be held magnetically.

Up close, it showed tiny facets covering its surface completely. The wisps of colors swirled around the points where his fingers touched it. As he squeezed, the colors swirled faster and grew brighter. When he brushed it with his other hand, new swirls grew and collided with the first ones, sparkling. He played with it for a while, enjoying the sight. He named it the rainbow sphere, and put it into his backpack.

He picked up the wand, It was triangular in cross section, a dark carnelian red, with an intricate web trapped within. He ran his hands over it, tapped it, pressed the ends. Nothing happened. Then he noticed slight depressions in two faces at one end. He squeezed them with two fingers. A beam of blue light shot away. He eased his grip and examined the wall where the beam had struck. There was no mark. A pointer?

He put the wand into a thigh pocket and picked up one of the small boxes. It was colored in an intricate hexagonal rainbow pattern. He found two indentations on the bottom and pressed them, carefully aiming the other end away. A cylinder the size of a kelparette shot out and fell to the floor. He picked it up. It was covered by the same hexagonal rainbow pattern as the box and had a rectangular cross section. He sniffed it. It had a slight musty smell. He looked for finger depressions without success.

One rounded end was black, the other white. He touched the black end without reaction. He touched the white end and his fingertip turned purple. He dropped the cylinder and examined his fingertip. The part that had touched the cylinder was a bright purple. The ridges and valleys of his fingerprint were uniformly colored. Paint?

The color refused to rub off. He picked up the cylinder and rubbed the white end against the wall. At first, it turned purple wherever he touched it, but when he pressed harder, it turned indigo or blue. The harder he pressed it, the more colors he got—yellow, orange, red. The angle of tilt determined the hue and saturation. A crayon!

He wrote *Sean Seamus O'Shaughnessy* across the wall and it came out in a rainbow of colors. Fascinated, he drew a crude sketch of Ariadne, shading it as he went. It came out glistening in a multitude of colors.

Curious, he touched the black end to the wall. Where it touched his drawing, color disappeared. An eraser!

He touched it to his purple fingertip and the color vanished. He smiled and put the stylus in a pocket.

Returning to the color-dot panel, he pushed the two dots which had caused the closet to descend. It rose into the ceiling again, with a slight hiss. He touched the next two. Another cylindrical closet, next to the first, descended quickly from the ceiling. Realizing that there were dozens of closets, he just glanced in and, finding it empty, hit the dots again. It retracted into the ceiling.

He hit another pair of dots and a cylinder dropped. Three dark things jumped out and scurried around the floor, clicking and hissing. "Moon dust!" spat Sean with revulsion, pulling out his quantagun. "Ratroaches!"

He shot two dead. The other escaped down the corridor. "Ratroach alert!" he yelled after it.

He looked in the closet. There was a jagged hole near the bottom, large enough for ratroaches to enter. It smelled like a pigsty, and there were animal droppings inside. Hastily, he hit the dots and let the cylinder return to the ceiling.

He went through several more closets without excitement until one revealed a pile of copper-colored wires. He picked one up. It was a circular loop, like a large version of the necklaces worn by the toy animals. Thousands of almost microscopic beads were linked together invisibly. Sean spun it around on a finger. Could it be . . . ?

He took it back to the prison entrance. The four humans sat there gloomily. "Millie," he said, tossing it to her, "try this on for size."

She caught it and put it on over her head.

"Try touching the force field," said Sean.

She approached the white line and gingerly touched the field. Her finger went through! She jumped through the field and threw her arms around Sean, laughing. "It worked!" She danced around with him. "You're a genius!"

The trapped three approached the force field and watched the cavorting duet warily.

Ariadne and Homer joined them, attracted by the shouting. She smiled as she saw the other woman free of prison, but her expression cooled noticeably as she observed the two embracing.

"It was the necklace!" said Sean, beaming.

"It sure was!" said Millie, kissing him.

Stefan motioned inconspicuously to Homer.

Sean said, "There's a whole slew of them over in the other room."

Homer bent an ear-microphone to Stefan.

"I owe you my life!" said Millie to Sean.

Stefan put his arm around Homer and whispered.

" 'Twas my pleasure, Millie," said Sean.

Ariadne felt Millie's necklace and said, "Do you suppose all adults wore these?"

Homer walked quietly toward the weapons stacked in the corner.

"Sure," said Sean. "All kinds of information could be encoded on these little beads. Your name, where you're from, government identification number, political record, whether you owe any taxes . . . Just like home." Sean glanced at Homer, paused a second, then shouted, "Stop, you rusty chip-kissing wonder, you!"

The robot continued.

Sean pulled his quantagun and aimed it at the robot. "I mean *you*, journobot!"

Homer halted and turned.

"One step more, and it's the junk dealer for you! Now what did your boss tell you to do?"

Stefan said, "There's no need to abuse a poor, defenseless robot."

"Answer me, Homer!"

"I was just going to get two handguns for Messrs. Draganescu and Wolfram—"

"Aha!" exclaimed Sean.

"—who will be needing protection from the vicious beasts when they leave this prison. After all, their services are indispensable to this record-making expedition."

"I, for one," said Sean, "could dispense with them quite easily."

"Oh, that would never *do*," said Homer. "This is, after all, the Draganescu Expedition, destined to be famous throughout the known universe, and Dr. Draganescu is, of course, the exalted Minister of Culture!"

"*Deputy* minister," corrected Ariadne.

"And the Ministry of Culture," continued Homer, "is a branch of the Government of Earth, and who could possibly know better who is best to lead?"

"I could," Sean said dryly. "Give me that necklace." Millie

removed it and handed it to him. "Takeo, put this on and step outside."

As Takeo began to put the chain over his head, Wolf started to reach for it. Stefan held him back.

"Smart move, Stefan," said Sean, " 'cause I really would like an excuse to shoot a nice little quantum-tunnel into his gut." Wolf radiated hatred.

Takeo stepped through the force field and handed the necklace to Sean. "Thank you ever so much!" he said, shaking Sean's hand enthusiastically. "I owe you a big one!"

Sean twirled the necklace on his finger and cocked his chin at Stefan, saying, "Isn't this the prettiest sight in this world we've yet seen? A terry 'crat and his C-cop pet, locked up in a nursery. Maybe there is justice in the universe after all."

"Remember," said Stefan, "we gave you our word that if you just release us, we will do your bidding. And surely you must realize how shorthanded you are, with just a girl for your crew. Or are there more?"

Sean pointedly ignored his probing question. "Well, you've been kind enough to supply us with two additional crew members, and that should do us fine, though I do appreciate your concern for us." He smiled broadly.

"Listen, you!" said Wolf. "You'd better let us out, or I swear by the abominable snowman of Antarctica I'll kill you somehow!"

Sean laughed. "And with what do you propose to do that? Snowballs?"

"Shut up, Wolf!" muttered Stefan. He put on his Most Appealing Innocent Victim of Circumstances look and said to Sean, "Mr. O'Shaughnessy, you don't strike me as a murderer. And to leave us here when you could so easily release us would be murder, pure and simple."

Sean just smiled.

"Really," continued Stefan, "we could be of great service to you. I don't know how much more exploration you intend to do, but you know this place is one enormous booby trap. The more people you have with you, the better your chances of survival. Just look how close we came to dying."

"Now you're talking," said Sean. "It reminds me of a story I heard long ago. It seems that back in the nineteenth or twentieth century, it was the ancient custom for Arab men to walk ahead of their women. Then came some war or other, and suddenly there were land mines planted all over the place. Overnight, the custom changed, and women were ordered to walk in front of their men. You, Stefan, and you, Wolf, may now become honorary Arab women if you wish. I give you permission to enter the most dangerous-looking places ahead of the rest of us. Is that agreeable?''

"Yes," said Stefan through clenched jaws.

"How about you, Wolf?" said Sean.

"Yeah," he muttered.

"That's grand of you," said Sean, tossing Stefan the necklace.

CHAPTER 14

While the former prisoners enjoyed their freedom, running up and down the corridor and chattering among themselves, Sean and Ariadne discussed the next step.

"I'm beginning to have second thoughts about continuing," said Sean, keeping one foot on the pile of confiscated weapons and one eye on Stefan and Wolf, who conversed in low tones.

"You mean third and fourth and hundredth thoughts," said Ariadne impatiently.

A man sneezed in the distance. It was Plum, walking down the corridor toward them.

"Ariadne," said Sean, "look how close these four people came to dying. Not to mention their pilot, who did die, rest his soul. We've got enough artifacts in this one room to fill both ships. We can go home now and call it a great success."

"I'm not going home until we've gone to the center of this world like my father. What we've seen so far may be nothing compared to what lies farther in."

"Hello," said Plum. "I was beginning to get worried about you chaps. I can see I had no need. You seem to have found yourselves some companions."

Sean and Ariadne mumbled greetings and returned to their intense discussion.

"Be reasonable, Ariadne," said Sean. "We've reached the inner side of this ring, we've saved four lives, and we've got enough junk to fill ten museums."

Plum drifted away, shaking his head, and introduced himself to the members of the other crew.

"Sean, we still don't even know what these creatures looked like. We haven't the slightest idea of what happened to the aliens. We don't have any real clues to their language. There are too many tantalizing mysteries here for us to just abandon it when everything's going so well."

"It's precisely when things are going well that you should go home. As sure as Murphy is the saint of screwups, something's going to go wrong if we continue."

Homer began interviewing Plum.

Ariadne said, "Why do you always have to be such a pessimist, Sean? Everything's worked out fine so far, hasn't it?"

Faint words drifted to them from Homer: ". . . an intrepid Englishman . . ."

"I just can't understand," said Sean, "why you want to constantly take unnecessary risks."

". . . from the land of sticky wickets and stiff upper lips . . ." said Homer.

"After all," said Ariadne, "we now have four more people to make the expedition that much safer."

"Please, Ariadne, trust me when I tell you someone's going to die if we continue. Look what happened to your father's people. You wouldn't want that on your conscience, would you?"

"Sean," said Ariadne, getting angry, "you swore you'd help me explore this world, and you've done nothing but try to get out of it since Vesta. I'm not leaving here until we've followed my father's footsteps to the end! If you want to leave me alone, that's fine. I'll go on without you!"

"I'm not going to let you commit suicide," said Sean. "If you're going on, the whole damn lot of us is going, too!"

"I appreciate your enthusiastic support," she said sarcastically.

"Damn you scientists and your idle curiosity! You make the most inquisitive cat look dead. But if we're to continue, I want you to obey my instructions to the twelfth decimal point from now on."

"I shall obey them," Ariadne said haughtily, "as long as they are reasonable."

"Women!" muttered Sean, turning to the rest of the people.

"Sean," she said softly, touching his arm.

He looked back at her, scowling.

"Sean, please try to understand. It's more than just scientific curiosity. My father died here. For twenty years, I waited for him to return, long after everyone said he was dead. I have this ache in my soul that perhaps you can never understand." She squeezed his arm hard.

He thought of the last time he had seen his own father, in a jail cell awaiting execution, imprisoned but defiant. Sean's face softened. "Maybe I can understand more than you think, Ariadne."

She looked into his eyes and said, "All my life, I have felt a deep loneliness. I have felt abandoned. I have felt worthless. I have felt that somehow it was all my fault. But now the spirit of my father is everywhere around us. I have touched the jacket he wore twenty years ago. I have felt the viewcrystals he left as if it were yesterday. I can never rest until I find out how and where and why he died."

Sean clumsily touched her hair. He nodded and turned back to the others. "Tune in, everybody!" shouted Sean. "This is what we're going to do."

When they had all gathered around him, he said, "We're going to follow the trail of the Zepos expedition." With a sour glance at Ariadne, he added, "As long as it doesn't get too hazardous. I want everyone to wear one of the necklaces. It may be the only way to get through similar barriers in the future. We're going down to the train station with all the supplies you can carry. We'll leave whatever alien goodies we take from the nursery at the station and we'll catch the next train out to the second ring. Now let's move our engines!"

"But first," said Ariadne, "I must record what we have found." She took out her cryscamera.

Sean shrugged. "Everyone else, load up!"

After Ariadne had finished recording the sights and sounds of the nursery-prison, the two crews walked slowly up the corridor, laden with supplies and booty.

They waited several hours for the next train to come in. All wore side arms except Wolf and Stefan. Sean carried a quanatarifle slung over his back.

Suddenly, a recorded alien voice boomed in the chamber and a huge door slid into the floor.

"Next train to Dublin!" announced Sean. "All aboard!"

He cautiously entered the train. It was a single great room, forty meters wide and two hundred long, filled with hundreds of rows of seats with high backs. The entire room was transparent: the outer wall, floors, the front and back, even the seats.

Through the floor could be seen the next huge ring of this strange world, slowly drifting past them, some kilometers away. He stepped gingerly on it, as if afraid of breaking through thin ice and tumbling into the void.

Beyond the next ring, stars were visible, racing through the sky like a planetarium projection running through a whole day in less than a minute, except there was no moon or sun to brighten the night. The effect was dizzying and made it hard to keep one's balance; the different speeds of the stars and the other ring made the sight all the more disconcerting.

The two crews carried their equipment inside hesitantly and sat down, staring at the view hypnotically, except for Plum and Stefan, who turned green and closed their eyes.

"I think I'm going to be seasick," said Plum.

"I wonder if they allow smoking," said Sean. "I could use a kelparette."

The seats were resilient to the touch and pleasantly comfortable. Millie sat next to Sean and said, "These seats indicate the aliens were anatomically similar to us. Their legs were probably shorter, judging from the way our knees stick up. But they may have had longer torsos, because the backs are so tall."

They waited over a quarter of an hour, growing impatient. Then an alien voice boomed and the door rose shut.

The train began to move with a gentle acceleration, smoothly floating straight out toward the second ring. The wall that had replaced the door also turned transparent. In the gap between the two rings, they floated in space, stars left and right, flying between rings so gigantic their curvature was almost imperceptible. The humans felt insignificant and fragile, as though falling though space forever.

"My God!" murmured Ariadne.

"I wonder how this train works," said Sean.

"It might use the star's magnetic field," said Plum. "Give me a bit of current in this coach and the magnetic field's so strong I could accelerate it to a fare-thee-well."

"A train that runs on magnetic tracks. Like a monorail, except the track's invisible. No need for solid conductors when you've got a ginormous magnetic field to repel or attract you."

The second ring rapidly approached. It was marked by huge windows, hatches, serrated arches, and many features too exotic to comprehend. Chartreuse pulses traveled mysteriously around the rim, confined to a thin line like a racetrack.

Less than a minute after departure, the train matched speed with the second ring and landed at a rectangular hatch the size and shape of the vessel. Suddenly, the train was swallowed by the ring, the view of the outside universe replaced by the surrounding walls rushing past. A stomach-wrenching acceleration pushed them down in their seats. Then it stopped and the door-wall slid into the floor. Through the transparent floor, they could see the third ring drifting by.

"Out!" commanded Sean. "On the double! We don't know how long it lingers at local stops!"

The crews warily stepped out. They were in another chamber, similar to the room they had just left but smaller, bathed in a red light dimmed by a mold that covered the glowing walls. The floor was covered in dirt, denser than the dust of the first ring. Little pink objects grew out of the dirt like pyramidal mushrooms. Dragonflylike insects buzzed through the air. Animal tracks ran everywhere. The air was hot, thick, and humid, and smelled of dampness and decay. Something skittered away down the corridor. Within seconds of the last person's exit, the alien voice boomed, the door shut, and the train vanished. Unobserved, alien animal eyes watched the humans.

"There's something taped to the wall," said Takeo, pulling it off. "It's a viewcrystal," he said.

Ariadne saw large Greek letters, alpha and zeta, on the wall next to the tape, along with a hand-drawn arrow. "Those are my father's initials!" she exclaimed.

Takeo handed the crystal to her.

She pulled her cryscamera from her pocket; then, removing her own viewcrystal, she inserted her father's, and hit the PLAYBACK key.

The image of Alexandros Zepos stared at them through the camera's tiny screen. "I am recording this to let future explorers know my findings at this point. We have only explored this ring a little.

"From studying the map of the rings, which you should see above you, it appears that the train stops momentarily in the same way in each ring, except for the inner and outer ones.

"This ring and, apparently, all the others inward of it, are entirely on the inner part of their zero-gravity circles. Thus, you will not have to experience the disconcerting effect of turning upside down as you did in the first ring.

"We still haven't a clue as to why they built ring after ring, working their way close to the star. It hardly seems that it could have been just idle curiosity about a neutron star. We may never learn the answer if we do not go to the innermost ring.

"The ring we are in now is primarily filled with vegetation. It seems to have been a combination of a park and a farm. The crops evidently were used for food by the aliens. They've grown wild, and an ecology of animals and insects has evolved around them. I imagine these are the descendants of the pests, pets, and livestock that once shared this world with the aliens.

"Beware of the animals near the control room! One of them killed our exobiologist, Marie Patanjali." He paused with obvious pain. "There are now only four of us, plus the doctrobot. We are determined to continue on to the third ring."

"This doesn't sound like a place for us to linger," said Sean to Ariadne. "And as long as your father has already explored it, why don't we just catch the next train?"

"No!" said Millie. "This is my chance to study the local life! We could learn a lot from it, including clues to the nature of the aliens themselves."

"She's got a very good point," said Ariadne, glad to back up a fellow scientist.

"Every moment we spend here is going to expose us to greater danger," said Sean.

Homer lit up and said, " 'Far greater danger!' said the rugged space explorer, undaunted by the thought, nay, even thrilled by it."

"But I'll tell you what," said Sean. "It'll be hours before the train returns. That'll give you enough time to do a little exploration. Then we can proceed to the third ring. Oh-two?"

Millie and Ariadne nodded.

"Oh-two," said Sean. "Plum, you stay here and hold the fort. Make sure Wolf doesn't do anything nasty. Stefan will come with us. I'm happier when they're apart. We'll also take our doctrobot. Ariadne, I suppose it's too much to ask you to stay here where it's relatively safe."

"Of course it is. I wouldn't miss this for the solar system."

"Very well," he said with a sigh.

"And of course," said Homer, "I too must go, as the expedition's only representative of the fourth estate."

"If you represent the fourth estate," said Sean, "then I represent King Arthur and the Knights of the Round Table."

"Sean," said Ariadne, "he really should come. He'll provide a much better visual record than I can with my cryscamera. When we return home, it will make a wonderful documentary."

"Gutenberg would rocket out of his grave if he could see what the press has come to," said Sean. "All right, Homer, you can come."

"Bravo!" said the robot. "Well spoken! The courageous explorer, Sean O'Shaughnessy, has wisely foreseen the necessity for the people of Earth to have a top-quality journobot on this mission. Truly a leader of intelligence as well as courage, second in these qualities only to the daring Dr. Stefan—"

"Delete the moon dust!" commanded Sean. "Stefan, come here." The Romanian broke off his muted conversation with Wolf and joined Sean's group. "Now you'll have your chance to fulfill your promise to be our booby-trap detector."

Stefan cringed. "Really, Mr. O'Shaughnessy, I have absolutely no knowledge of such treks as you are embarking upon."

"Now's the perfect time to learn," said Sean.

"But," protested Stefan, "I am a simple administrator, whose exploratory experience is limited to slashing through jungles of red tape."

"Oh, that's quite all right. All you need do is put one foot in front of the other, and if anything kills you, it will come to my attention and you'll have the satisfaction of knowing you've done a fine job."

"Please, Mr. O'Shaughnessy," pleaded Stefan, "surely there must be someone here better qualified for the task."

"Undoubtedly, but you're the lucky one I've elected. I'll tell you what. If you happen to get killed, I promise to send an ecstatic note of commendation to the Minister of Culture. Who knows, you might even get a medal."

"Sean," said Ariadne, "I think perhaps you're being too harsh on him." Stefan nodded enthusiastically. "He really is, after all, an office worker, not someone used to facing danger, like you."

"Oh," said Sean, "I won't hold that against him. It takes no experience to learn how to die. This'll be good training for him, and I won't even charge him extra for it. Move to the head of the line, Stefan." Slowly, the bureaucrat obeyed.

Homer began recording Stefan's progress and announced, "Our leader, the illustrious Dr. Stefan Draganescu, courageous beyond the ability of mere mortals to comprehend, has decided to move into the most dangerous place in the group, the point position."

Sean checked his watch and turned to Plum. "If my timing of that map is right, we have more than five hours before the next train. If we're not back by then, come after us armed to your follicles. Keep an eye on Wolf. If he gives you any arguments, don't hesitate to stimulate his cooperation with your quantagun." Wolf sneered. "Now let's move!"

With Stefan in the lead, Sean came next, followed by Ariadne, Millie, the doctrobot, and Homer. "Follow Alexandros's marks," said Sean to Stefan, pointing at the arrow on the wall next to the Greek's initials. Plum, Wolf, Takeo, and the other doctrobot silently watched the group depart.

Sean glanced back at his little troop and saw Homer trailing. "Homer!" he called. "If you're going to come on this expedition, the least you can do is go up front with your beloved boss."

"But," said Homer, "the first position is the most dangerous, traditionally enjoyed by the intrepid leader, ever eager for more adventure. The rear is the safest place, which should be occupied by the most valuable equipment such as I."

"We're going to start a new tradition and let you walk up front, as well."

"But I am programmed to minimize the risk to myself. I am, after all, an exceedingly expensive robot, and government property too!"

"You'll go up front, or not come at all, you truth-cruncher!"

Homer trudged to the front of the line, saying, "The fairly good explorer O'Shaughnessy, recognizing the intelligence and wisdom of the expedition's journobot, decided to minimize the risk to the crew by moving the fearless robot to the side of the courageous Dr. Stefan Draganescu."

They followed Alexandros's arrows down a dirt-filled corridor, flying bugs and skittering things running away. After passing several portals, they stopped at one bearing a note in English: *Trail inside leads to central control. Watch out for animals and robots! AZ.*

After reading it, Ariadne noticed Sean staring at the message intensely. "Why don't we try it?" said Ariadne.

"Just a microsec!" said Sean, continuing to study the writing.

She looked at Sean's slow-moving eyes and lips. A smile grew on her face. "You're illiterate, aren't you, Sean?"

"Of course I'm not!" said Sean, his face growing as red as his hair.

"Sean O'Shaughnessy, the great explorer, is illiterate!" said Ariadne, laughing.

"Now, see here, person," said Sean angrily, "you ought to get your facts straight before you go around insulting a man. And you'd better realize I couldn't have got my degree in astronautics if I couldn't read!"

"Oh, I've got your data," said Ariadne gleefully. "I know lots of engineers at the university and most of them can only read the letters of the alphabet, and only those because they occur in equations!"

"Well, that's reading," said Sean defensively. "I can read both regular letters and Greek letters," he bragged.

"You engineer types are just like 99 percent of the human

race! You're so used to voice synthesis, and having robots read to you, that you can't even read your own language anymore. It's a wonder you can even read numbers!''

"Now that's a naked absurdity! An engineer has to know his numbers! You can't handle differential equations using that stupid color-code the civilians use!'' He unpocketed an alien stylus and wrote Schrödinger's Equation on the wall with a flourish. The symbols gleamed in a rainbow of colors. Ariadne automatically made the sign of the cross. "There!" he exclaimed. "That's writing for you!"

Ariadne took the stylus from him and wrote on the wall in English, "Who has eaten the honey? He who has a fly on his face.''

"That's a Greek saying," she said. "Read it to us."

"No problem," he said. He stared at it, tilting his head one way and another. "Your handwriting is not the easiest I've ever seen. In fact, it's almost impossible to read, but I'll do it anyway. Just to show you. Just to prove—"

"So read it!"

" 'Who,' " read Sean slowly. " 'Has.' That next word is terribly poorly written. What is it?"

"Eaten," said Ariadne with the air of a schoolmistress addressing a retarded child.

" 'The. Home. Home? Hone—honey.' "

"That's enough, Ariadne," said Millie protectively. "He's proved his point. He *can* read."

"Barely," said Ariadne.

"That still makes him more literate than most humans," said Millie.

"Very well, Sean," said Ariadne. "I'll concede you read your native language almost as well as I could read English when I was seven years old."

Sean blushed again and said, "And I'll concede that you speak Greek almost as well as I pilot through hyperspace!"

Ariadne pursed her lips in the disapproving manner of the schoolmistress and turned back to her father's writing. "This message says, 'Trail inside leads to central control. Watch out for animals and robots!' "

"I know that," said Sean.

"So shall we enter, O great scribe of the ages?" said Ariadne.

Sean immediately stepped through the portal, forgetting in his haste to let Stefan and Homer go first. The others followed.

They found themselves in a bright yellow jungle. Vegetation

grew everywhere, rising over their heads, intertwined vines so thick they could not see the roof. Violet cabbagelike flowers with waving tendrils proliferated. Something called "Vok! Vok!" repeatedly in the bushes. Flittering, long-winged blue insectoids buzzed past the humans, large as birds. The air was hot, humid, and had a sharp, unpleasant smell, like a freshly overturned compost heap. A trail could be seen through the brush.

A loud buzzing like an angry beehive erupted from the left. One of the blue insectoids was caught in the tendrils of a cabbage-flower. The crew watched with varying proportions of fascination and disgust as the flower slowly drew the struggling creature deeper.

Sean turned on his suit air conditioner and then, resisting the temptation to let Ariadne roast, did the same for her. They kept their helmets off. The others, being in ordinary plastex overgarments, just sweated.

Millie examined a blade of the shoulder-high, thin yellow leaf that grew everywhere. "Giant grass," she said happily, delighted to have a whole rich ecology to study. She examined a young shoot, barely a meter tall. "Something like timothy grass on Earth." It had tall cylindrical growths with orange spikes sticking out. She examined one of the other plants. "These vaguely resemble clover and alfalfa."

She peered at pale blue flowers the size of dinner plates that grew on vines wrapped around thick stems of grass. Their triangular petals opened up, one on top of another, in an intricate geometrical pattern. Black veins drew a complex map on each petal. "Strange, there's no stamen or pistil I can see. Never seen anything like it. I wonder how they reproduce."

She knelt in the dirt, examining the bases of the stems, and then dug down a dozen centimeters with a stylus. "There's a metal web here," she said, "below surface level. The webbed sections in the floor are where, I presume, the plants are fed hydroponically with water and nutrients. Over the centuries, decaying vegetation has fallen, animal droppings have been added, insectoids have made their contribution, until this soil has built up to the present state. In that time, insectoids could have made enormous evolutionary adaptations, and even animals could have made significant changes, even if the mutation rate is typical of earthlike planets. And here, it might be greater."

Something slithered in the undergrowth and she jumped back quickly.

"So as the machines broke down," she continued, "the environment would have changed from a controlled ecology to an uncontrolled one that would have adapted painfully to each change.''

Homer recorded Millie's lecture and then said, "The Draganescu Expedition's expert exobiologist made a lightning-fast evaluation of the nature of the steaming, deadly jungle facing the courageous explorers. 'Mutants lurk in there!' she concluded.''

Sean crouched by the jungle path. "Look at this. Looks like it was made by a robot—and recently. I guess some of the maintenance robots still work, though judging by the state of the vegetation, most of them must be worn out. The humidity, fungus, and wildlife would be a hard environment for a machine to endure for a thousand years''—Homer's head jerked around toward Sean, giving him his undivided attention—"especially after the robot-repairing robots broke down. Well, this is the only path from this entrance, so it must be the one Alexandros took. Let's give it a go.'' He motioned to Stefan and Homer. "After you, gentlemen.''

As Stefan surveyed the jungle ahead, he had the most intense expression of distaste Sean had ever seen on a human. Muttering, "Damn barbarian!'' he brushed past Sean.

Homer followed Stefan, keeping a good two meters behind. "'Plunge on!' said the invincible Dr. Draganescu, sweat streaming down his well-muscled back. 'We will make a safari trek into this jungle or die trying.' As usual, he insisted on being the first to enter the unknown. 'No mutant monsters can frighten me,' he added. His illiterate assistant O'Shaughnessy followed in the rear.''

Sean walked behind the robot, pushing branches out of the way. "Should have brought a machete,'' he said. "At least I have my roidknife,'' he said to Millie, behind him. He kept his hand on his quantagun, however.

Ariadne and the doctrobot came last.

They walked on for half an hour without incident. Stefan had kept up a constant stream of complaints as he prissily brushed away branches and insects. Homer spiced the complaints with wild speculations about the types of mutants that could be lurking, doing nothing to improve Stefan's attitude.

"—And my feet are delicate,'' said Stefan. "They're simply not used to this kind of—''

"Shut up!'' said Sean.

"You can lead me to certain death,'' said Stefan indignantly, "but you can't make me keep quiet about it!''

"Shut up!" said Sean again, pointing his gun at Stefan. "I think I heard something!"

They all stopped and listened breathlessly. There was a faint whirring sound whose direction could not be sensed. As they listened, it gradually grew louder. "Something's coming," whispered Sean.

"The mutants are coming!" said Homer.

"Shut up, Homer," whispered Sean, pointing his gun at the robot. "Everybody into the bushes!" he commanded.

Homer was the first to obey, tripping on the undergrowth. Sean holstered his handgun and unslung the quantarifle. He waited until everyone was hidden, pushing them farther in when necessary, then slipped in beside Ariadne.

By now, the noise was loud enough to make talk difficult, had anyone been so inclined. It was coming from the direction they had been heading toward.

Sean and Ariadne could barely see the trail by peering through tiny gaps in the foliage. Still, nothing was visible. A yellow, five-legged creature like a misshapen spider the size of his hand fell on Sean's shoulder. He did not notice it.

The sound grew ever louder, getting harsher until it began to pierce the eardrums. Ariadne saw the spiderlike creature, grimaced, and removed the quantagun from her holster. She hit the creature with the tip of the gun and felt a semiliquid resistance, as if hitting an octopus. It jumped off and disappeared in the brush. She shuddered.

The vegetation began to shake. A tall brown machine appeared, visible in glimpses. It had whirling blades that chopped off foliage, and spinning wheels that cleaned the ground as it slowly rolled by on invisible wheels. It was twice as tall as Sean and nearly five meters long, filthy, and covered with blades, several of them whirling, but a dozen more frozen still. They were star-shaped, thin, vicious-looking blades, each half a meter long, some broken off. They looked capable of slicing a man in two without trouble. Debris shot out of chutes on top and showered the jungle like rain. Two stubby robot heads, one at each end of the machine, screeched as they swiveled back and forth like executioners looking for work.

Sean kept his quantarifle aimed at the middle of the machine as it moved past. Ariadne felt her stomach turn as it vibrated to the tune of the mechanical monster.

Slowly, it disappeared from view. After endless minutes, its sound gradually faded, though for a long time it echoed in their minds.

"Théa mou!" Ariadne said weakly, putting an arm around Sean. He encircled her waist protectively, then helped her out of the bushes. The others joined them.

Stefan was pale. He coughed. Sean glanced at him and deduced that he had lost his breakfast in the bushes. Everyone clustered together, shaking.

"Is it okay to speak?" whispered Homer.

"Yeah," said Sean.

"Excellent!" said the robot in his usual strong voice. "The Draganescu Expedition survived its first brush with a mad killer robot! Led by the heroic Dr.—"

"Zip it up, robot!" commanded Sean. Homer became silent again. To Millie, he said, "You still want to continue?"

"Yes," she said shakily. "I would at least like to see that control room Alexandros mentioned. We might be able to tell something about the aliens from that."

"And how are you doing, Ariadne? " he said.

"I'll be all right," she said. "I want to continue also."

"And I can see," Sean said sarcastically to Stefan, "that our fearless leader wants to plunge on eagerly, too." Stefan closed his eyes and covered his face. "Oh-two!" said Sean. "Move your engines out!" Taking pity on Stefan, Sean added, "Homer, you lead this time."

"Really!" said the robot. "I must protest! Ministry of Information regulations specifically state that—"

Sean wearily aimed his quantagun at the robot again, and Homer started moving along the trail. Stefan walked so slowly that Sean pushed ahead of him, to the clear relief of the administrator. Homer began quoting Earth robot-abuse regulations at great length, dwelling on the penalties for damaging government property.

CHAPTER 15

Precisely 18 minutes and 322 regulations later, the jungle stopped abruptly at a portal tall enough to accommodate the trimmer-robot. Homer halted at the edge and turned around to face Sean. Looking beyond the Irishman to Stefan, dragging himself in the distance, the robot called out, "What now, brave leader?"

A low, swishing sound came from within. Sean looked inside and saw a machine glowing yellow. He was about to step through the portal when he noticed a white line across the floor of the entrance. He stopped and waited for the rest of the safari to catch up.

"The floor looks like it's been kept clear by machines," he said to the group. "But the white line might be another one of those force fields we've come to know and love."

"It could be working backward," said Millie, "keeping everything out except humans and robots."

"Do you have your necklace on, Stefan?" said Sean.

The administrator nodded dispiritedly, fingering the chain beneath his collar.

"Good," said Sean "because you're going to step inside and then back out again, just to make sure we're not going into another one-way trap."

Stefan shook his head violently and began walking backward. "Shoot me if you want to," he shouted, "but I'm not going in there!" His Romanian accent had thickened considerably, making him sound incongruously like Count Dracula.

Sean sighed disgustedly and stepped across the line. "See?"

"But can you come back out?" said Stefan.

Sean stepped back outside with no trouble. "No glitch," he said.

He watched a plate-sized, blue-and-white-winged insectoid fly past Stefan and into the building. "I don't think the field's even working." He took off the necklace, put it on the ground, and stepped across the white line and back again. "See, Stefan? Nothing to worry about." He removed one of his suit gloves to pick up the thin necklace and threw it back over his head, tucking it under the neck ring of his pressure suit.

He went back inside, putting his glove back on, and was followed by the other members of the crew. A pack of ratroaches skittered away into corners, accompanied by a curse and a grimace of disgust from Sean.

Massive machines stood every ten meters: great five-sided metal pyramids with their tops sliced off. Four meters high, they glowed yellow, silhouetting a network of small pipes running all over their surfaces. A loud swishing sound came from them.

"Looks like some kind of engine room," said Sean. "Or maybe generators."

Transparent oval pipes the thickness of a man's torso carried green sludge to and from the machines. "Nutrients probably," said Ariadne. "For the hydroponics."

They walked past a dozen engines. A loud shriek burst from the next room. Sean motioned everyone behind an engine.

They hugged the glowing, vibrating metal machine, while listening through its noise to the sounds from the other room. The shriek was replaced by a jackhammer pounding. Slimy many-legged insectoids crawled away from the dirt next to the machine. The sharp smell of ozone hinted at the presence of high voltage.

Sean stealthily made his way over to the entrance to the other room and cautiously peered into it. He was near one corner of a warehouse-sized room. There were robots everywhere, most of them frozen, some half-dismantled. Arms, legs, mechanisms, and shells lay randomly on the floor. Fifteen meters away, a massive, five-armed, pyramidal robot stood, a smaller, scarlet image of the yellow machines outside. Taller than Sean, with a multifaceted head on top, it faced away, three of its arms worked on the guts of a half-open robot. It was disassembling a mechanism like a power plant inside the open torso.

Sean noticed another portal a short distance from him, in the other wall by the nearest corner. Through it, he could see hundreds of glowing colored lights.

He went back to his comrades and whispered, "The next room is robot repair, and the chief mechanic is busy. I think I see the control room. I'm going to sneak into it. You all wait for me here."

"I'm coming," said Ariadne.

"It's twice as likely that two will be spotted as one," said Sean. "Remember, your father said, 'Beware of animals and robots.' "

"In that case, you stay and I'll go."

"Damn! He should have said, 'Beware of my daughter!' " He shook his head hopelessly and returned to the portal, Ariadne following closely.

Drawing his side arm, he checked that the repair-robot was still preoccupied, and ran to the control room, Ariadne at his heels.

In the room, they were hidden from the repair-robot's view. A dozen ratroaches ran away. Returning his side arm to its holster, Sean scanned the room while Ariadne darted every which way, poking her nose at everything that caught her eye. One wall was filled with the multicolored lights, each labeled in the alien language. Another was filled with vertical blue lines of differing lengths, with markings next to them. They reminded Sean of nothing so much as thermometers. There were mounds in the center resembling the chairs of the train. Ariadne recorded the scene with her cryscamera.

"Look at this," she whispered from the far side of the room, pointing to a note in her father's handwriting. Sean came over to her side. With a glance at him, she read it aloud: "Monitor-camera controls."

Next to the note were several pairs of indentations, one of them labeled ON/OFF by Alexandros. Ariadne touched that pair and the room was filled with light. She and Sean whirled around and saw the three-dimensional image of a ring floating in air, almost filling the room. It was clearly a map of the ring they were in, since tiny images of the yellow jungle could be seen almost everywhere, in transparent color. It was extraordinarily precise, with details as small as the eye could see, yet several large sections were completely without images, as if the cameras had failed.

She touched another pair of indentations and the image expanded so greatly that only part of the ring could fit into the room. Colored lines ran every which way, apparently conduits, perhaps the power and fluid circuits of the world. Some lines had rapidly moving green dots as if to show the flow of fluid or energy through them.

Ariadne found a pair of indentations that raised the image; another set rotated the ring. She rotated it until she recognized the image of the machine room they had passed through. As she magnified it, they could see small images of their friends next to the machines. With more adjustment, she imaged the very room that she and Sean were in, and they amused themselves by waving and watching the little images move in precise imitation. Sean looked around for the cameras and decided that they were too small or too well concealed to be readily visible.

"Let's take a tour," he suggested.

She rotated the image so the next room appeared. They watched the mechanic-robot conducting tests. Then they glided through the wall and into the jungle. They paused when a creature—like a cross between a giant dragonfly and a peacock—jumped into the air and flew on rainbow-colored wings into the thin vegetation near the roof. A translucent red creature with hundreds of legs grasped at the air where the creature had been, then undulated into the brush.

After a while, Sean whispered to Ariadne, "I've had my fill of jungle watching. Let's go back now."

Reluctantly, she agreed.

"Turn that thing back on the mechrobot again," he said.

They watched as the robot reinserted the mechanism he had removed. "Good," said Sean. "He's preoccupied. Let's move."

He stuck his head around the corner and verified that the robot was facing away from them as it worked on its broken brother, whose eyes stared in their direction. He gave the thumbs-up to Ariadne and ran across the gap to the engine room.

As he crossed, the robot being repaired rotated its head, following Sean, and let out a cry in the deep, alien language, a sound like a funeral march played backward at half speed. As Ariadne put one foot out, preparing to dash in Sean's direction, the mechrobot turned its multifaceted head around and made a similar bone-chilling call. With surprising speed, it rolled toward her, sliding on the floor as if on invisible wheels.

She froze halfway out the portal. Sean, witnessing the whole scene, yelled, "Run!" and drew his handgun.

Ariadne jumped back inside the control room as the large mechrobot advanced on her speedily, waving its five arms and several tools.

The mechrobot passed Sean and entered the control room. Sean fired the quantagun at its body with no effect. Ariadne ran to the rear of the room, straight through the repair-room projection that still floated in space.

The robot paused, confused by the conflicting images of the real and projected rooms. Sean shouted, "Project the control room again!'' He gave the robot a powerful side-kick, hoping to topple it over. It was like kicking a ton of lead bricks.

Ariadne ran back to the controls and rotated the image so it projected the control room, increasing the magnification until her image was life-sized. The robot's head swiveled from the image of Ariadne to the real woman and back again. Sean pulled his roidknife and jumped on its back, his feet resting on stubby protuberances near the bottom of the mechrobot. It aimed a tool at Ariadne's image. A red beam shot out, passed through the image and vaporized a hole in the wall.

Sean squeezed the knife, triggering the high-voltage supply in the handle, and pressed the blade into the robot's tool arm. It sunk slowly into the arm as the field-ion effect ripped atoms out of the robot's skin, the ceramic coating preventing short circuits between the submicroscopically parallel blades, while allowing the intense electric-field gradient to penetrate to the metal. A blue beam of neutralized ions shot out the end of the handle, which he automatically pointed away from himself.

The robot aimed its red beam at the real Ariadne. Sean sawed the knife deeper and the robot's arm went dead.

Its head spun around toward him as another arm bent backward toward Sean, a spinning blade whining. Sean shoved his knife into one of the robot's two eyes and grunted, ''Good-bye, stereo vision!'' The robot's spinning blade shot past his head, nicking the tip of his ear.

The robot flailed wildly with the blade, unable to locate the man accurately with only one eye, and Sean plunged the knife into its other eye.

Its head began spinning in circles, the knife stuck inside. Sean jumped off. ''Good-bye, Cyclops!'' he shouted with satisfaction.

The robot bumped into the wall, smashing some control lights. It backed up to the opposite side of the room—past Ariadne, who ran toward Sean—bumped into the far side of the room, and made a right-angle turn.

''The damn son-of-a-chip is computing the size of this room!'' exclaimed Sean. ''Let's get out of here before he navigates his way into us!''

Ariadne needed no urging. The two ran across the corridor and into the machine room, where the other members of the group greeted them joyfully.

''Move your engines out!'' commanded Sean, and they started running toward the entrance.

Just as Stefan, first in the retreat, reached the entrance, Sean, in the rear, felt a sharp pain in his back and fell. He cursed and looked back. There, blocking the portal to the repair shop, was a gray, hemispherical robot the size of a giant turtle. Suddenly, colored patterns flashed all over its surface in a hypnotic pattern.

Ariadne paused and looked back at him. *"Go! Go! Go!"* he shouted, and she ran for the exit. Sean stood up and a ray shot out of the robot, striking him in the belly with searing pain. He fell on the floor and rolled behind an engine.

There was a blackened spot in the pressure suit where he'd been hit, but no penetration. Most of the energy had been absorbed by the layers of insulation, and only a fraction of the heat had penetrated, but his belly ached as if scalded.

He glanced at the entrance. The other humans had escaped. Peering around the engine, he saw the hemispherical robot sliding toward him, flashing dizzying swirls of colors. He drew his quantagun and fired—with no effect.

"Damn!" he cursed and ran to the rear of the engine again.

The communicator in the neck of his suit turned on with the words of Ariadne: "Are you all right, Sean?"

He holstered his quantagun and peered around the rear of the engine. "Yeah, but the damn mechrobot must have called for his friend."

"We've stopped at the entrance portal. Millie thinks it's a vermin hunter," said Ariadne. "They probably have robots to kill ratroaches and such so they don't get in the machines. The colors could be designed to attract the vermin."

"I'd give my share of the loot to have my roidknife back!"

Sean saw the hemispherical robot at the far end of the engine. Because of the swishing noise of the engine, he could hear no sound from the robot. He jumped between the transparent pipes and hid behind the machine, peering through the pipe's green sludge.

The robot tried to follow but could not pass under the lowest pipe, so it detoured back around the engine. "Not very agile, these ratcatchers," said Sean. He climbed back through the pipes.

"Sean!" cried Ariadne's voice. "There's another one!"

"Where?"

"It just entered from the repair shop."

"Hemisphere-turtle type?"

"Yes!"

"Don't let it see you!"

He jumped through the pipes connecting the next engine,

heading in the direction of the entrance. "Only one more engine and I can join you," he said.

"The other one's coming straight back, very fast!" shouted Ariadne.

Sean ran to the first engine, and heard a hissing sound. "I think he just shot my backpack." He climbed through the pipes. "I'm at the first engine!" he shouted excitedly.

"He's coming around it!" shouted Ariadne. "He's between us and you! And the second one's on the other side of the engine!"

"Trapped!" he shouted. He glanced around and began scrambling up the huge pipes. "We'll see if the little bastards can climb!"

He reached the top pipe and balanced precariously there, four meters above the floor, the vibration of the engine threatening to dislodge him. He could just see over the flat top of the engine—which was covered with dirt and crawling with dozens of large, ugly green ratroaches. "Jesus, Mary, and all the saints!" he shouted. "I've found the mother lode of ratroaches!" Shuddering, he searched for a foothold in the engine, found some narrow ledges that looked like radiator fins, and put one foot on them and both hands on the dirty top. A stench greeted his nose and a ratroach bit his right glove, hurting almost as much as if it had pierced through to his hand. He cursed and slugged the rat-sized creature, which fell over the side, shrieking. There was a thud as it hit the floor, followed by a hiss as a robot zapped it.

"What's happening?" shouted Ariadne, but Sean was too busy to respond.

Out of the corner of his eye, he saw the robot below stop.

"Maybe they can only shoot at ground level," said Sean hopefully.

The hemisphere rotated until a dark spot was pointing at him. A beam shot out, accompanied by the hiss of vaporizing material. A glance revealed that the helmet drooping from his belt had been hit. He cursed again and scrambled up on top of the engine, slipping in the dirt. "So much for that theory."

"Millie says they'd probably be designed to shoot down vermin that are climbing around the pipes and machinery," said Ariadne.

The ratroaches shrieked and milled around excitedly, their segmented, scaly bodies vibrating with anger as they jumped on him. He struggled to shake the disgusting, poisonous creatures from his arms. One crawled up to his shoulder, flashing its sharp teeth, and tried to climb into the neck of the suit. Sean flicked it over the edge.

He pulled his gun out and shot the creatures with his right hand, while his left pounded others into oblivion. Several crawled up his legs and he grabbed them by the thorax and threw them over the side. After a minute, he was mercifully alone in the dirt and filth. "God, how I hate those creatures!" He shuddered.

"Are you all right?" pleaded Ariadne.

"Sure, couldn't be better. I've got a nice comfortable bed four meters above two killer robots. And who knows how many more are coming to join the party?"

"Is there anything we can do?" she asked.

"Not unless you have a gigawatt quantabeam on you." Remembering the quantarifle across his back, he removed it and found a black splotch in the firing mechanism where it had been hit by a robot's beam. "God damn you, Murphy!" He threw it into the dirt.

"Murphy?"

"Yes, the Irish bastard who discovered the master law of the universe: 'If anything can go wrong, it will!' "

"Oh, *that* Murphy."

"My quantarifle got zapped."

"One of the robots has stationed himself at the entrance," said Ariadne. "I guess he thinks you've got to go through it if you're going to escape."

"Wonderful, just what I need to make my day complete: a smart killer robot." He holstered his gun and stood up as far as possible, crouching to avoid hitting the ceiling. His feet vibrated with the engine as he pondered the situation. There was nothing between him and the door except the ratcatcher. The ceiling was covered with bands of wires, but they blended in too smoothly to grab. Eleven engines lay between him and the portal to the robot repair room. The tops of the machines stretched out before him, most of them crawling with ratroaches.

"What I couldn't understand," said Ariadne, "was how the civilized creatures who built this world could have produced these killer robots."

"They did, and that's all that matters."

"But then Millie said she thinks the machines *evolved.*"

"What do you mean, evolved?"

"Over the centuries, as circuits broke down and chips lost parts of their memories like old spacecraft, there would have been random changes—mutations—in their software. Some robots might have become dangerous. If that happened to the mechrobot, he might have turned all the vermin hunters into real killers. A mechanical Darwinian evolution would operate. The most vicious machines would defeat any that tried to stop them.''

Sean surveyed the scene for the umpteenth time, searching for a way out. The ceiling was a smooth pale yellow metal and offered no openings. Two more ratroaches jumped off a pipe and bit at his boots. He kicked them over the side. "Oh, moon dust!" he exclaimed.

"What's happening?" said Ariadne.

"I don't see any way out of this except possibly to go back to that repair shop."

"Why there?"

"There may be something I can use as a weapon against the ratcatchers."

"But how can you get there?"

"I'll just have to jump from one engine to another. It's only a two-meter jump," he said with false confidence.

"But it's a long fall if you miss!"

"Thanks," he said sourly, looking down the four meters to the floor. "I needed to be reminded of that."

"But the robot might shoot you in midair."

"True. I'll have to divert it." He looked around for something to throw and his eyes lit on a ratroach corpse. He picked it up with all the enthusiasm of the World President for Life removing a worm from her dinner plate.

There was enough room on the huge engine top to get a short running start. He paced out his path in the dirt, adjusting it until his last step would end with his right boot on the edge.

"Here's a gift for the ratcatcher. I hope he appreciates it." He threw the carcass to the far side of the room, where it landed with a thud. Leaning out over the side he saw the robot sitting there. It rotated as it sensed him. He pulled his head back immediately.

"I guess he's too used to the sound of ratroaches, damn his chips." Sean surveyed his domain again and spotted the broken quantarifle half-buried in the filth. He picked it up and threw it hard, after the ratroach's corpse.

Looking cautiously over the side, he saw the robot moving away.

He ran back and placed his boots into his marked footprints and began the short run to the edge. His right boot reached the edge and, as his eyes judged the gap, the thought of reconsidering flashed through his brain, but he ignored it. With his powerful right leg, he shoved off and flew through the air, landing on his left foot with three centimeters to spare. He slid in the muck and ploughed into several shrieking ratroaches. Picking himself up, he slugged a ratroach out of the way and began running again.

Sean jumped to the next machine, and the next, until he landed atop the next-to-last engine. This time, as he jumped off, his boot squashed a ratroach. Slipping, he missed the next engine, crashing against it. Frantically, he grabbed for a handhold, but his gloves slipped off the machine and he fell to the floor, cursing all the way. He landed on his feet and deliberately let his legs collapse. Rolling into a ball, he somersaulted several meters, thankful for the painful experience gained in falling on high-gee worlds.

He staggered to his feet, ran to the portal before the robots could detect him, and dashed into the repair room.

"It's leaving!" shouted Ariadne over the suit speaker. "The robot who was guarding the door is moving toward you!"

Sean skidded to a halt. He could see the big mechrobot at the end of the room, working on himself with some tool.

"So is the other one!" shouted Ariadne. "They're both coming after you!"

"The mechrobot seems to be trying to replace his eyes," said Sean. He looked around. The room was filled with broken robots of many sizes and shapes. Some were half-dismantled, others seemed complete but sat frozen.

He ran up behind the mechrobot, putting a tall, inert robot between himself and the entrance. The mechrobot seemed unaware of his presence. The robot pulled the roidknife slowly out of its eye socket with one of its working arms. It dropped it onto a workbench cluttered with other junk, including another, nearly identical, broken camera—its other eye, thought Sean. It felt around like a blind man until it found a tool, which it inserted at the edge of its eye.

Sean jumped to the bench, grabbed the roidknife and ran back behind the mechrobot. A faint hissing sound came from the entrance. "I think the ratcatchers have arrived," he whispered.

"We're coming!" said Ariadne's voice.

"No!" exclaimed Sean in as loud a whisper as he dared. "Then I'll have to rescue you as well as myself! And shut up! They might hear us!"

He spotted a large, gutted purple robot shell with an open hatch. He ran over to it, jumped inside and pulled the hatch almost shut. Something jumped on his arm. He brushed it off, cursing silently, pushed the hatch farther open and a ratroach jumped out.

He closed the hatch nearly shut again. An oily smell pervaded the shell and angular metal pieces jabbed him no matter how he adjusted his body. He watched through a crack, the roidknife firmly in hand. The mechrobot removed the silvery, broken camera from its eye and placed it on the workbench.

A ratcatcher robot glided between Sean and the mechrobot with a faint hiss. It stopped in front of the mechrobot and spoke to it in the deep flesh-crawling tone of the alien language. The mechrobot replied in the same tone and the ratcatcher continued its prowl past Sean and out of sight.

The mechrobot felt around above the bench until a cylinder filled with small metal objects popped down from the ceiling. Spare parts, thought Sean.

The robot reached up and felt around until it had grasped an object resembling the eye camera it had removed. It pushed it into its eye socket, then raised a tool and screwed the camera in.

It stopped groping like a blind man. This time it reached up confidently and removed another spare camera. It touched the wall and the cylinder retracted into the ceiling. Inserting the camera quickly, it turned around slowly and surveyed the room.

It stopped when its eyes focused on Sean's robot shell. *Damn!* he though. *It remembers the hatch was open!*

It turned back to the bench and, with two of its arms, lifted up a large gray tool of several half-meter-long cylinders surrounding a longer black rod. It looked vaguely like a space riveter, attached to the bench by a cord.

I'm not going to wait for it to zap me! Grasping the roidknife, Sean pushed the hatch open and ran over to the robot. Jumping on its back, he squeezed the knife, shoved it into the thin line where the head joined the body, and began sawing through its neck.

Its head swiveled around until it faced Sean. Then it called out in its deep voice while Sean jiggled the knife as hard as possible. He could feel it cut through—something. He hit a hydraulic line and blue liquid dribbled out. The robot touched two spots on the gray tool and a violet ray shot out, vaporizing a line in the ceiling.

Sean sawed back and forth in larger and larger arcs until the robot dropped the tool. He jumped off and grabbed the tool, disentangling the cord that attached it to the bench. The robot jerkily lurched toward him, the very picture of a mechanical Frankenstein's monster.

He heard the hiss of a ratcatcher's ray hitting his backpack. He aimed the gray tool at the mechrobot and touched the tool's two spots. The violet ray shot out and burned a hole through the robot's chest. Its forward motion stopped and it began spinning aimlessly in place.

Sean felt the red-hot sting of a thigh burn and limped over to the hulk of a long-dead robot for cover. The tool's cord stopped him short. Another hiss came as his backpack absorbed a ratcatcher ray. He pressed down on the tool's spots, shooting the ray out. Whirling around, he sliced everything in sight, including the hemispherical ratcatcher. It whistled strangely and froze. He let up the pressure on the tool and scanned around. He had sliced half a dozen broken robots in two.

A noise sounded behind him. Whirling around with the gray tool ready to fire, he spotted Ariadne with a quantagun in her hand. He jerked his hand away from the firing spots as if it were on fire and shouted, "Ariadne, you half-brained tax lawyer, I almost killed you! Why on Ceres didn't you stay where I told you?"

Millie appeared behind her.

Ariadne lowered her gun and said, "You're welcome, you air-breathing cephalopod! We came in here just to—" She yelled and fell to the floor. The other ratcatcher was behind her. It had shot her in the leg. Millie screamed and ran back into the engine room.

Sean aimed the gray tool at the hemispherical robot and squeezed the trigger spots with all his might. The violet beam shot out and bored a hole right through the robot. He wiggled the tool until he had cut the machine into a dozen pieces.

Then he held his fire, looking around for anything else that moved. Satisfied that nothing moved except Ariadne and Millie, he dropped the tool to the floor and limped over to Ariadne, jerked her to her feet, and pulled her toward the exit.

Millie was waiting just through the doorway. The trio ran through the engine room and into the jungle as fast as their wounds allowed.

They met Stefan and Homer, who huddled in the brush by the trail. "Good work, men," Sean said sarcastically.

"The rescue was a success!" exclaimed Homer. "Under the personal direction of the incredible Dr. Stefan Draganescu, the inept Irishman was rescued by the expedition's two women."

Sean was too tired and sore to retort. "Let's get back to camp and get some blister cream on our wounds," he said wearily, trudging back along the trail. The others joined him without hesitation.

After a while, Ariadne walked by Sean's side and said, "I'm sorry I panicked back there—when we came out of the control room, I mean. I guess when that mechrobot appeared, it reminded me of the time I was swimming through a recent wreck and surprised a hammerhead shark. They're really quite nasty fellows, fond of eating people. If I hadn't been able to close a hatch on him, I might have become his supper. I had nightmares about that for weeks."

"I'm kind of sorry I had to damage that mechrobot," said Sean. "Now who's going to repair those other machines when they break down? Such a waste."

"I feel like I've just been rescued by Odysseus," she said.

"Who?"

"You really are illiterate, aren't you?" He blushed. "He was the Greek hero who defeated the Cyclops by sticking something in its eye."

"Oh, I remember seeing that on video once."

"So you really are a scholar after all," she said, smiling.

"Ariadne, if I even think for a moment of giving into your idle curiosity ever again, you have my permission to slug me."

"Idle curiosity?" she said indignantly. "Mine is the professional curiosity of the trained scientist."

"Well, your professional curiosity keeps threatening to make us both professionally dead."

They continued on in silence.

CHAPTER 16

After a few minutes on the trail, Sean heard the distant roar of the robot that had almost sliced them up on the way out.

"Damn!" he cursed. "It's that moon-dusty forestrobot again. Into the bushes, everyone!"

They jumped into the jungle on either side of the trail, pushing through the brush until they were several meters back. Sean spotted something large and red moving in the underbrush behind Millie. He frowned and unholstered his quantagun.

Ariadne was on one side of him and Millie on the other. The rest were on the other side of the trail. The roar grew in its unpleasantly familiar, gut-shaking way. They peered between blue stalks like knurled bamboo.

The monstrous machine crawled past them, showering the jungle with fragments of vegetation, fewer in number now that the first pass had removed the bulk of the growth.

Suddenly, Millie cried out, loud enough to be heard above the roar of the robot. Sean spun around, aiming the gun. A huge, red creature—a python with legs—embraced Millie with dozens of orange pincer-limbs that grew along its sides like oars in a galley. Orange fluids spurted beneath its translucent skin, and hundreds of black legs dug into the dirt for leverage. The pincers moved her slowly, rhythmically toward a large, drooling red sphincter in the middle of the top of its body, opening and closing hungrily.

Sean held his fire, searching for a clear shot. There was nothing that looked like a head, or even eyes, and what *was* visible was so wrapped around Millie as to make a safe shot impossible. Ariadne aimed her gun and hesitated for the same reason. Homer recorded the scene from a safe distance, while Stefan hid behind a tree.

Sean holstered his gun and drew the roidknife. The body was over a meter thick, and at least a dozen meters long, partly coiled under Millie. Moving to within centimeters of the creature, he could see through the translucent skin at its near end a green yolk with a multitude of veins feeding it. Sean guessed it was the brain, and stabbed into it.

The knife slid in like a spike through moon dust; green blood spurted out. The creature snarled and shuddered. Millie screamed as its body convulsed. The pincer-arms on one side stopped moving, but three on the other side grabbed Sean's knife arm savagely. A tiny eye at the base of a leg seemed to be guiding its pincer.

"Damn!" spat Sean, groaning in pain as his arm was squeezed powerfully, straining the suit fabric to the limit. He weakly held on to the knife.

Ariadne stepped closer and shouted, "It probably has another brain at the other end!"

Millie screamed, her foot in the sphincter. Sharklike teeth bit at her boot.

Sean tried to grab the knife with his free hand, but a pincer-leg clamped onto the blade and pulled it away. The monster pushed him to the ground on his back and lay across his chest, almost smothering him. It stank of camphor and rotting vegetation; he could barely breathe. He punched viciously with his left fist, without effect.

"Help me!" screamed Millie. He twisted until he could see her. She gripped the base of two drooping pincer-legs, trying to arrest her descent into the sphincter, but other pincers inched her torso ever closer to the sphincter. Her leg was now swallowed up to its knee.

Sean couldn't reach his holster under the weight of the creature's body.

Reaching behind his head with his left hand, he tore open the backpack and grabbed for anything useful. He touched the baseball-sized rainbow sphere from the nursery-jail.

The sphincter opened wider to accommodate Millie's torso. Sean tossed the sphere into the sphincter opening he could barely see. Several orange tongues lapped it up eagerly and pushed it down the translucent gullet. He blessed his years of alien gravities for allowing his aim to be true.

He searched frantically for something more useful. Finding a rope, he yanked it out. He started to unravel it one-handed when the creature suddenly convulsed. It spat out Millie and she fell to the ground. Ariadne pulled her to safety.

The creature writhed and crawled partway back into the jungle. Through its translucent skin, Sean could see that the multicolored sphere in its gullet had expanded to the size of a basketball.

The monster moaned, and the ball doubled in size.

Sean painfully dragged Millie away and they watched the creature curl into a huge spiral as the ball shrank slowly back to its original size.

"I'll be damned!" exclaimed Sean.

Millie just moaned.

The ball grew large again, more rapidly this time.

"Must be something like a jack-in-the-box!" Writhing and groaning, the creature disappeared into the bush. "Activated by moisture, I bet. A toy for a swimming pool."

Millie groaned in agony.

Sean became aware of the forestrobot's noise again and looked around hurriedly, but the machine was still moving away.

Ariadne worriedly studied Millie's bloody leg. "It's cut her pretty badly," she said, "and the bone's broken. Compound fracture. At least the boot kept it from eating your foot."

Millie lay there and said weakly, "I think it broke a few of my ribs."

Sean staggered to his feet and shouted, "Doctrobot! Over here!"

The heretofore silent member of the expedition climbed through the bush on its four retractable legs and straddled Millie without touching her, its four arms poised for action. Its hemispherical head slid over its blue spherical belly, scanning with visual sensors. "Where do you hurt?" it said.

"Everywhere," said Millie through clenched teeth. "When I breathe, it's my ribs; when I don't it's my leg!"

The doctrobot tore holes in Millie's jumpsuit and placed two ultrasonic transducers gently on her abdomen. In moments, he had a holographic map of her internal bones and organs in his computer, and said, "You have three broken ribs and some internal bleeding, in addition to the leg injuries. I'm going to give you an analgesic and something to stop the bleeding." A vapor-syringe appeared in his rightmost hand and gave her two hissing injections in her abdomen and leg. Millie relaxed.

Homer and Stefan joined them. The journobot glanced at Millie and then walked cautiously over to the shuddering body of the monster three meters away and recorded it.

Stefan idly observed Millie in the arms of the doctrobot and noticed a large red marking on the spherical robot's belly. "Why does he have that mark?" he asked.

"That's the Red Crescent," replied Sean. "Like our Red Cross. We bought him from an Islamic colony on Mars."

"Tell me if you can feel this," the doctrobot said to Millie. He touched her abdomen in several places. She shook her head. "Now I'm going to tape your ribs." He wrapped her abdomen with silver rextape.

He fastened a scalpel to one of his arms and neatly sliced off the boot. He sprayed disinfectant, ultrasonically examined the bones, set and wrapped the broken one. "She needs to rest for a few days," the robot said to Sean.

Suddenly the monster crawled back out wailing and convulsing. Homer dashed back behind Sean, who had drawn his gun. The creature spat the rainbow sphere out through its sphincter and slowly crawled back into the bush, groaning. The sphere, now the size of a beach ball, bounced on the ground and stopped at a clump of grass.

"Millie can rest back at camp," said Sean. "Will it be safe to carry her there?"

"Yes, I can do it," said the doctrobot.

"Oh-two." He and Ariadne helped Millie into the two carrying arms of the doctrobot, which made its way carefully to the trail and started walking toward camp, followed by Stefan, Homer, and Ariadne.

Sean recovered the rainbow-sphere and cleaned it up. As it dried, it shrank back to its original baseball size, and he returned it to his backpack.

"When are we going to eat?" whined Stefan.

"When we get back to camp," said Sean.

Homer spoke up. "It was a close encounter with a terrifying— What do you call it?" he asked Stefan.

The administrator shrugged and Sean said, "By rights, Millie's the one who should name it."

"I don't care what you call the damn thing," she said wearily. "You name it, Sean."

"I'd call it a snakapede," he replied.

"A combination of snake and centipede?" said Homer.

"Right. A very fat, disgusting snake."

"That's terrible," said Ariadne. "It needs a Greek name, like *herpeton*—'creeping thing'—or at least Latin, such as *serpens*— 'crawling thing.' One can't simply go around breaking English words in two and sticking the pieces together at random to make a name that will be immortalized in the scientific textcrystals."

"You call it whatever you like," said Sean. "I'm calling the slimy bugger a snakapede—a good, sensible name any person can understand."

"It's easy to see you're no scientist," said Ariadne.

"It's easy to see you're no sensible person," said Sean.

"Why is it, Sean," said Ariadne, "that every time I get to the point where I could almost start liking you, you go and say something totally infuriating?"

"Well, my dear Ariadne," said Sean, "I guess you just have a remarkable talent for bringing out the best in me."

"It was a close encounter," said Homer, "with a terrifying snakapede! The vicious, two-headed, million-legged creature attacked the expedition's exobiologist, as if it sensed that here was the one person capable of understanding its evil ways. But thanks to the careful planning of the ingenious Dr. Stefan—"

"Power down, you chip-eating can of worm gears!" shouted Sean.

Stefan patted Homer affectionately on the shoulder and the safari trudged on in silence.

When they arrived just outside the entrance to the train station, Sean ordered them to halt.

"What are we waiting for?" said Stefan. "I'm hungry."

"Let's not rush inside," said Sean. "You, more than anyone else, should understand that." He smirked and Stefan looked away shamefacedly.

Sean peered cautiously into the entrance and let his eyes roam around. Equipment was sprawled on the floor in the same chaotic order as when they left, but no humans were visible. "Plum?" he called. No answer came back. "Anyone?" he called again. Nothing but the sound of flying insects returned.

"Moon dust!" he spat and wearily drew his handgun. "Stay here," he whispered to the crew. "This especially means you," he said to Ariadne. "For once, will you listen to me?" She nodded.

He stealthily slipped into the room, hugging the wall. There was still nothing obviously out of place. The footprints were human, mingled with tracks of small animals and insects, and showed no clear pattern. He did not see the eyes watching from above.

He tiptoed over to the equipment, and picked up a wisp of something draped across a backpack: an iridescent thread with a shiny, glassy core, like fiber optics, but not of a design Sean had ever seen. He flexed it; it would not break.

Pocketing it, he walked closer to the train door and bent over to look at a small object on the floor. It was Plum's pipe lighter, an old-fashioned gold-encrusted laser type used in the middle of the twenty-first century. He picked it up and flipped it thoughtfully in his hand.

He put this too in a pocket and had started to walk on, when some strands of something dropped on his head. He tried to brush them off when suddenly he was covered with them, and yellow, squirmy things landed with thuds on his shoulders and head.

"What the moon—" He tried to draw his gun but his hands were tied to his sides. He tried to run, but his ankles were tied together, and he tripped, falling on his face. His jaw wouldn't move, so he couldn't yell. He was firmly wrapped, almost in a cocoon.

Frantically he looked back and forth, but the creatures were yellow blobs, much too close to focus on. The putrid smell of the dirt mixed with a vinegary smell from the yellow blobs. His blood pounded and sweat poured from his forehead, as much from horror at the claustrophobic cocoon as from fear.

"Sean!" exclaimed Ariadne's voice from afar. "He needs help!"

Squirming, furry things burrowed under his body and lifted him off the floor. He started to move as if carried on squishy wheels.

He heard the hiss of a quantaray gun as he was carried away.

"Grab him, Homer!" shouted Ariadne, as more gun hisses sounded.

Sean felt himself lifted up by the robot. Finally, he could see what was happening: The yellow blobs were furry, octopuslike creatures with gaping mouths like heart-valves full of sharp little teeth. Their heads were twenty to thirty centimeters in diameter, with five tentacles as long as his forearm emanating from them, each bearing dozens of tiny eyes. Hundreds of them hung from the ceiling and crawled on the floor.

They had tied him with wire, knotting it with almost human dexterity. "Get the wire cutters out of the tool pack!" mumbled Sean through his gag. Homer deciphered his message and carried him to the tool pack.

Ariadne shot wildly at the yellow octopoids, screaming unintelligibly in Greek. The ones on the floor crawled away with surprising speed, while the ones in the ceiling disappeared under loose panels.

Timidly, Homer began to cut Sean free, stopping whenever an octopoid landed on him and tried to wrap wire around his limbs. Homer would merely fling the creature away with distaste and staunchly resume cutting Sean's bonds.

Sean ripped the remainder of his cocoon off and shot two retreating creatures. They curled up and lay still.

"Heisenberg damn this filthy, taxin' world!" shouted Sean, shaking.

"You're all right!" said Ariadne, hugging him. "It was awful! Those things had you all wrapped up and were taking you to only God knows where!"

He hugged her back and said, "Ariadne, I take back everything I've ever said about you. Well, nearly everything. You did an oh-two job. Now we're even."

She smiled at him. "What *are* those things?" said Ariadne.

"They resemble the octopi of Earth," said Millie weakly, "and hexapods on Ross 154 II. I suppose we should really call them pentapuses, but the general type is called octopoid, regardless of the number of limbs."

Stefan leaned against the edge of the portal, unwilling to step inside.

Millie stood up with the aid of the doctrobot and poked at the body of one of the octopoids. "Suckers allow them to hang on to the ceiling. The eyes on the tentacles give them great dexterity. They look something like cat's eyes—they're probably nocturnal.

"They've obviously evolved air-breathing ability on some planets," Millie continued. "After all, our ancestors once inhabited the sea."

"And some of us still do," added Ariadne.

"But these things weave webs like spiders," said Sean, examining the material that had bound him.

"That's evolution for you," said Millie.

"No," said Sean, "that's fiber optics." It was the same material he had picked up earlier. "That's glass or plastic inside the core, or something like it. This is artificial, I'd bet my *Shillelagh* on that."

"Maybe they use the aliens' wiring," said Ariadne. "They could pull it out and use it for their own purposes. After all, the octopus is the smartest creature in the sea, other than mammals. I've even seen them unscrew jars underwater like a child after cookies."

"In a thousand years or a million," said Millie, "they could have learned to use this artificial environment for their own needs, either by intelligence or by evolution. Every animal uses whatever is in its environment. Evidently these creatures found fiber optics in theirs. In cities, birds sometimes use wires and other artificial debris to build their nests."

"This stuff's knotted together," said Sean, squinting at his former cocoon. "They must *really* be smart."

"Incredible!" said Homer. "A herd of air-breathing octopoids attacked the expedition, capturing the illiterate Irishman in a spiderweb of alien design. Only the quick action of their daring journobot, who had been provided by the farsighted Dr. Stefan Draganescu, enabled the plucky adventurers to escape.''

Stefan smiled weakly. ''You earned that one, Homer.''

''Now we know what happened to Plum and the others,'' said Sean. ''Damn! They even disabled and carried off the other doctrobot!''

''Oh no!'' said Homer in his high-pitched conversational voice. ''I assumed that the disgusting things couldn't hurt a robot!''

''They're tough little buggers,'' said Sean.

''We've got to find them!'' said Ariadne.

''Damn right!'' said Sean. ''And fast!'' He studied the ceiling. ''Apparently, they live up there, inside the ceiling, and use the access panels to jump down on their prey. That's a lesson to us: Always keep one eye on the ceiling!''

He retraced his steps, gun in hand, to where he had found Plum's lighter and studied the tracks in the dirt, glancing at the ceiling frequently. There were smudges in the dirt leading toward a corridor exit.

He turned back to the crew. ''Millie, I want you to stay here with your doctrobot. You'll be in charge while I'm gone.'' She nodded feebly. ''Watch out for Stefan. You still have your side arm? Good. Wait just outside this room. Ariadne, you're coming with me.''

She smiled. ''You know, this is the first time you've ever invited me to do anything worthwhile.''

''Don't think I'm overestimating your wisdom,'' said Sean, lighting up a kelparette. ''It's just that you're the only one who can back me up if I get caught by those creepy critters. I'd have asked Millie to come, but she's in no shape.''

''You certainly know how to make a woman feel wanted,'' said Ariadne.

''And I too, of course, will come,'' said Homer. ''At a safe distance. The historical record must be made. Future generations demand it.''

Sean looked daggers at the robot, then smiled craftily and said, ''Of course you can come, Homer. In fact, you'll be absolutely indispensable. We need someone to go first, to attract the octopoids' attention. After all, we know they're powerful enough to disable a robot. Maybe even to dismantle it.''

''On second thought,'' said Homer, ''I have just realized that government regulations forbid me from taking such a risk with such an exceptionally valuable piece of equipment as myself. I'm sure I can trust you to tell me all about it if you get back."

"What about those future generations?" said Sean.

"What have they ever done for me?"

Sean turned back to Ariadne. "Carry these wire cutters and this lightrod," he said, attaching them to her belt. "I want you to follow ten meters behind me, with your gun in your hand. If you see anything suspicious, or hear anything, or touch anything, or even *think* anything is out of the ordinary, call out. Understand?"

She nodded. Sean picked up another pair of wire cutters and a tiny, white lightrod, slipped them onto his belt, and followed the trail into the unexplored corridor. She followed at a distance, glancing back at Stefan, who leaned against the entrance. "Poor Stefan," she murmured. "He's too delicate for fieldwork."

"Delicate?" said Sean. "He's too delicate for anything but hauling garbage to a volcanic dump on Io!"

As he walked, he felt his burn spots, wounds, and sore muscles. He was dying for rest and medication, but knew that every second delayed could be an epitaph for his friend. His eyes bounced from floor to ceiling, searching for the faintest hint of the yellow creatures. He forced himself to plant one foot after another.

He puffed on his kelparette as its mild chemicals worked their way to the pleasure center of his brain.

"A vile habit, smoking," said Ariadne.

He grunted.

"Have you ever married, Sean?" she said, changing the subject.

"No."

"Ever come close? I did once."

"No." He paused. "Well, maybe once."

"What happened?"

"She was a roidminer," said Sean, glad to occupy his mind with thoughts other than pain. "A really fine woman, I thought. I'd sworn I'd never get married as long as I was sane, but she drove me crazy. I tried to stop seeing her, but couldn't get her out of my mind. I even proposed to her! Proves I was out of my mind. Shocked the hell out of me! I never thought I'd violate my principles and get married. Fortunately, by then she'd fallen for some lousy tourist 'crat and was going back to Earth with him. 'What're you going to do on Earth, now?' I asked her. 'Mine red tape and farm concrete, and hope you don't upset some other 'crat so he has you thrown in jail or sent to Antarctica?' But she was in love, she said, and wouldn't listen to sense. Women!"

"I was in love once, but he wouldn't accept the Simonist faith."

"You and those damn Simonists!" said Sean. "Proves you wouldn't have enough sense to empty the water out of a boot if the instructions were written on the heel."

Her face flushed. "Faith has made my life meaningful. It filled the great emptiness I'd felt all my life since my father disappeared. Don't you believe in anything at all?"

"Oh, I have faith. I have faith in myself; I have faith in the equations of celestial mechanics; I have faith in the law of supply and demand; and I believe, as surely as you believe in the Benedictor Simon himself, that the bureaucrat has never been born who is better able to judge what's good for me than I am."

"That's a pretty empty religion," said Ariadne.

"I was about to say the very same thing about yours."

They trudged on silently for several minutes. Abruptly, Sean halted. "The tracks stop here," he said, looking at the ceiling. "They must have lifted them up there. Strong little beggars."

He stretched his gun-hand toward the ceiling, but could not quite touch it. "I'm going to need your help," he said.

"Of course." She walked up to him.

"I'd lift you up so you could inspect what's up there, but it would be too dangerous, so I'm going to be ungentlemanly and ask you to bend over so I can step on your most attractive engine."

She blushed and knelt down with her gloved hands in the dirt. He stepped on her and gingerly pushed at the ceiling with his gun. A panel lifted up—and something scurried away.

With a grimace, he holstered his gun and grabbed opposite edges of the opening with his hands. He pushed off Ariadne, grimacing with pain as his muscles rippled through his blistered body. He swung his feet up and caught them inside the lips of the opening, then hoisted himself up. Ariadne stood on her tiptoes and gave him a push as he climbed into the dark opening.

He grabbed his gun and peered into the gloom, lit only from the corridor below. There were wires and pipes, and bulging devices of mysterious purpose everywhere, covered with centimeters of dust. The space was less than a meter high—nowhere near tall enough to stand in. He pulled a lightrod from a thigh pocket and shined it about. The beam struck a ratroach, which screamed and ran away. There were several trails through the dust.

"Help me up!" called Ariadne.

He put the gun in his left hand and reached down with his

right. She grabbed it with both hands and he lifted her up with a grunt.

"I don't know which trail they took," whispered Sean, shining the light around. The beam hit a shiny object in the distance. "What's that?"

He crawled over to it and examined the flat object. "It's Plum's credit card. I bet he dropped it deliberately. Now we know which trail to follow." He put the card in a pocket and crawled off along the trail, shining the light ahead. Ariadne followed at a distance.

They turned a corner and clambered over some thick pipes. On the other side, Sean whispered, "Stop!" He listened for a while and heard a distant sneeze. He crawled back to the pipes and whispered to Ariadne: "That's Plum's sneeze!"

"What do we do now?" she whispered.

"I'm going to crawl as far as I can toward Plum before turning on the light. I want you to follow behind me in the dark at five to ten meters, as best you can. When I turn on the light, or if I yell, you turn yours on and shoot any beasties you see."

"Except for you, of course," she whispered back.

He oriented himself in the muffled glow of his lightrod, shut it off, and began crawling slowly forward. His left hand held the lightrod; his right, the quantagun.

The darkness was not quite complete. Red light filtered in through tiny cracks where access panels joined the ceiling, and through holes gnawed by industrious creatures.

He became conscious of faint noises, of things darting across his path in the darkness, not quite visible. A swishing sound came from a pipe nearby, and a hum from a box he crawled past. Mingled with the musty odor of the dust, a vinegar smell became evident, the smell of the octopoids. Strange shapes loomed over him, but shapes that did not move, shapes of machinery—he hoped. Sweat poured down his brow, despite the suit's air conditioner. He trembled at the remembrance of the slimy creatures' cocoon and gripped his gun harder.

To Ariadne, the experience recalled countless dives in water so dirty she could barely see her hand in front of her face; where she had to feel around in the muck for artifacts, never knowing whether she would touch a gold coin, a slimy sea worm, or a deadly scorpion fish. She bumped something that scurried away, bringing back the memory of a night dive on board a wrecked twentieth-century freighter, lying on its side, when her light failed and her partner was in a different cabin. "Up" had been impossible to tell from "down," and she had nearly panicked her way into a wet grave.

She strained for the faint sounds of Sean's movements. Plum sneezed again, much louder and closer this time.

Ahead, Sean could see bobbing things moving in the darkness toward him. The odor of stale vinegar was overwhelming. He unsheathed the roidknife and stuck it between his teeth. Clenching his jaw, he aimed the lightrod forward and switched it on.

The scene lit up like a horror ride in an amusement park: Hundreds of yellow octopoids hung from the roof above him; a huge orange octopoid the size of a desk pulsated on the floor four meters in front of him; and three men and a robot lay just to the right of it, wrapped tightly in wire cocoons.

Sean squeezed off several shots at the nearest octopoids and three fell on him with a net. He dropped his gun and sliced holes in the strands with the roidknife. Slimy tentacles wrapped around his face, blinding him, but he sliced at them with the knife and the creature fell off.

Several more octopids crawled above him. Ariadne blasted them and the corpses thudded harmlessly onto his back. He put the knife back in his mouth, too preoccupied to notice the vinegar taste of octopoid blood, and picked up the gun. Shoving the net back onto the two surviving octopoids, he shot them dead.

"Behind you!" shouted Ariadne.

Whirling around, he saw hundreds of the creatures heading toward him, some on the ceiling and others on the floor.

He squeezed off bursts into the first row, then the second, and on and on. Ariadne crawled to his side and joined the shooting. "Don't hit the cocoons on the right!" he shouted.

The huge orange octopoid squealed at a high pitch barely within human hearing. More octopoids came out of nooks and crannies.

Sean aimed his lightrod and gun at the orange beast and squeezed the trigger with all his might. It screamed a glass-shattering screech. Hundreds of yellow creatures halted, then began to retreat until they clustered all over the orange octopoid. Hundreds more formed a phalanx of troops, armed with pieces of metal for clubs and ceramic disks for shields, and began marching toward the humans. Several loners off to each side swung fiber cables like lariats at Sean and Ariadne.

A cable whipped around Ariadne. Sean blasted the creature holding it. Liquid spurted out of holes in its body and the cable relaxed. A cable whipped around his head and he blasted its owner.

Ariadne cut through the cable around her with her roidknife.

"Shoot the bastards with the lassos!" shouted Sean.

They fired at them rapidly but, like targets in a shooting gallery, each fallen creature was immediately replaced by another. Sean noticed the indicator light on his gun shift from normal green to low-charge yellow and cursed.

Suddenly, if slowly, the cluster of creatures around the super-octopoid began to move away like bearers carrying some vile orange potentate. A seething mass of octopoids crawled all over their master, protecting him and stopping the flow of blood by adhering to his wounds bodily.

The nightmarish assemblage crawled down a dark alley behind some machinery and the phalanx of troops and lasso-masters retreated with it, waving their weapons threateningly.

In a moment, the creatures were gone. Sean exhaled a sigh of relief; Ariadne was trembling and pointing her gun in the direction of the vanquished foe.

"Unzip the cocoons!" said Sean, going to the nearest one. Plum's figure was clearly visible through the mesh. Sean cut away at it with the roidknife. It hummed and its electrostatic field glowed blue as he sliced through the cables.

"Thank God!" said Plum.

Ariadne went to the second cocoon and cut it open with wire cutters. She gasped: Takeo was lying there, bleeding from large holes in his side.

Sean rushed over to him and tried to stanch the blood with his hands. Takeo looked up with glazed eyes.

"They tried to eat him," whispered Plum. "But the ones who did, got sick and died."

"We'll get you to the doctrobot," said Ariadne to Takeo, tears in her eyes. "He'll fix you up."

Takeo looked up at Sean and whispered, "I owed you a big one." He closed his eyes and grimaced. His body convulsed and then lay still.

"No!" exclaimed Ariadne. "We can get you to the doctrobot!"

Sean felt Takeo's pulse and shook his head. "It's too late for that."

Ariadne sobbed.

"Unless . . . " Sean darted over to the next cocoon, containing the other doctrobot. He cut it open, pointed at Takeo, and shouted, "Man wounded! Severe blood loss, pulse just went!"

The spherical robot crawled rapidly over to the body, retracting and pushing against any fixed object with its four legs, unable to stand in the limited space. He stuck electrodes into the man's chest and simultaneously injected the heart with stimulant. With another of his four hands, the robot pulled a respirator mask from his chest and covered Takeo's nose and mouth with it.

The last cocoon grumbled. Sean sliced it open, revealing Wolf. "Christ!" exclaimed the bald man. "I don't know what I'd've done if you hadn't come! It was hell! Worse than the South Pole at midwinter!"

"Why couldn't it have been you that they chose to munch on?" said Sean.

After several minutes, the robot shook its head. "I'm sorry. It appears that he suffered infection from the creatures' bites, and combined with the blood loss, it was just too much."

Ariadne sobbed again. Sean removed Takeo's personal effects.

"We'd better get going," Sean said. "No telling when they might come back."

"What are we going to do with . . . Takeo?" said Ariadne.

"We'll have to leave him," said Sean.

"He deserves a decent burial," she said.

"How are we going to do that, tell me?" said Sean.

"In the jungle."

Sean sighed and said, "I don't have the strength left to drag a body anywhere, and I'm sure Takeo doesn't care. I certainly wouldn't give a damn if the circumstances were reversed."

"The doctrobot can carry him," said Ariadne.

"All right, so be it," said Sean, too weary for further argument. "Let's just get out of here." He started to crawl back the way he had entered.

"Sean," said Plum, "there's an access panel right here. I saw them come and go through it."

They lifted up the panel. The red-lit corridor below was like paradise to their eyes.

They lowered the body and climbed down. Sean headed in the direction he believed was home, and said, "I hope I haven't got too turned around, and there isn't some maze awaiting us on the way."

They marched off down the corridor, warily studying the ceiling as they went, until they came to a jungle portal. They stopped and Ariadne ordered the doctrobot to dig a hole in the dirt, into which they laid the body.

"Who wants to say the service?" said Ariadne.

"You might as well," said Sean. "You're the religious . . . person here."

"Very well, although I don't know the proper procedure. But he does deserve a Simonist funeral."

"We don't even know he was a Simonist," said Sean, turning to Wolf. "Was he?"

Wolf shrugged.

"God will understand," she said. "Let us all bow our heads."

The three men, the woman, and the robot all lowered their heads.

"Please, O Savior," she intoned, "in the name of the Benedictor Simon, the prophets Heisenberg and Schrödinger, and the Great Pyramid, please take the soul of our dear colleague, Takeo— What was his last name?"

Wolf shrugged. The doctrobot spoke up: "Miyazawa."

"Please take the soul of Takeo Miyazawa," she resumed, "and tunnel it to heaven across whatever potential-barriers may exist. Let him fly there through the endless dimensions of hyperspace and make that great forbidden transition to paradise, for he died in the search for knowledge, and what better way could he have served Thee! I h-bar, d psi by d t, equals capital-H psi," she said, quoting the Schrödinger Equation. "Amen."

Men and robot echoed, "Amen." The robot covered up the body and the group returned to the corridor to begin the trek back to camp.

After a false start, Sean's group found their way back to what was left of the crew. As the doctrobots tended their wounds, Sean explained what had happened. He finished by saying, "Let's get back to our ships and out of this hell-singularity."

Everyone but Ariadne muttered agreement. She said, "We didn't come this far just to go back! What's the matter with you? There's a world out there for us to explore!"

Sean was about to explode, but Stefan stepped in and said in his more oily diplomatic style, "Ariadne dear, please reconsider." He adopted Pious Martyrdom Position Three. "Think of Takeo's life, now lost due to the totally unpredictable dangers of this world. Think of Millie, who is gravely ill and in need of rest. Think of the rest of us, who need the amenities of a good spaceship to recover from our extreme weariness. And think of Sean, who, with all his faults—minor ones, I hasten to add"—he nodded deferentially to Sean—"is an experienced explorer whose cautions must be respected as the words of a man who knows that which he speaks about."

"For once," said Sean, "Stefan is making sense, bless his little bureaucratic soul."

"All right," Ariadne said angrily. "The rest of you can turn around and go home. I know that's all any of you wanted anyway: to rob this world of its treasures and reward your greedy little hearts. I don't care. *I* am continuing!"

"By all the gods of the silicon chip," said Sean, "I swear I don't know whatever possessed me to take this woman with the short-circuited brain to this god-ionized world! If you weren't the daughter of Alexandros Zepos, I'd kick your engine so hard it would knock you into hyperspace! But since you *are* his daughter, I know as surely as Newton knew falling apples that you're going to continue unless I tie you up and ship you home. And since I've always been of the belief that the greatest of all human rights is the right to make an ass of yourself, I can't very well force you to go back if you don't want to. And since the memory of Alexandros Zepos would haunt me if I let you go to your doom alone, I'm coming with you, though I'm sure I'll live to curse this moment—though not for very long."

Ariadne cooled down visibly.

Stefan said, "But there's no need to condemn the rest of us to a probable death. Why don't we go back to the ship and wait for you there?"

"Oh-two," said Sean, "provided Plum goes with you, to see you get up to no mischief."

"I am not going back," Plum said softly.

"Ah, Plum," said Sean. "You've been through enough. You very nearly became dessert for some five-legged octopuses. You've earned some rest, and you can look after our chums."

"Sean," said Plum, "I don't have to remind you of the times you've saved my life, not the least of which was scant minutes ago."

"You've returned the favor more than once," said Sean.

"If you're going on, then so am I."

Sean sighed. "So be it. Millie has to go back to the ship in any case, but one of the doctrobots can take her. And I'll be damned if I'm going to trust Stefan or Wolf back there, so you two fine gentlemen have just volunteered to accompany the expedition."

"But, Mr. O'Shaughnessy," said Stefan, turning his oiliness quotient up to its maximum, "I give you my word that we'll wait for you as long as it takes."

"My dear Stefan," said Sean, "the Lord knows I would trust you with my life—if I valued it as little as a spoonful of moon dust—but I'm afraid we desperately need your great experience as a mountaineer of paperwork, just as we need the scintillating intellect of your colleague, Wolf. So it grieves me terribly to report that your company will be required.''

Wolf stepped toward Sean and growled, ''You clone of a lunar joyboy!''

Sean raised his fists eagerly and Stefan stepped in between the two.

''I appreciate your reasoning,'' said Stefan, ''and I can see there's no way to change your mind.'' He pulled Wolf away. ''Very well, we will accompany you further on this expedition.''

''A wise decision,'' said Sean.

Homer piped up: ''The dynamic Dr. Draganescu, undeterred by the tragedy that has stalked the expedition like a lion hunting for mice, decided to forge onward. 'No mere encounter with death could ever stop me,' he said to his admiring crew.'' Stefan embraced the robot.

Plum spoke up: ''Why don't we all sit down and have a good, restorative meal? I'm famished.''

''I'd just as soon get out of here as quickly as possible,'' said Stefan.

''He's right,'' said Sean. ''Every moment we wait here increases the chances of becoming someone *else*'s meal.''

''Well, I've been doing some calculating,'' said Plum, ''and it seems it's over two hours before the next train arrives.''

''Well,'' said Sean, ''in that case, we might as well dine.'' He broke open the food and handed it around. ''I'll stand guard,'' said Sean, picking up a foodbar. ''Sure wish this were a taco.'' He moved a few meters away from the group and called out, ''Homer, you might as well keep your eyes out, unless you want to share our rations.''

''Why, thank you for the kind thought,'' said the robot, ''but I have no need for human nourishment. I do think I'll follow your suggestion to watch for nasties, though.'' His head began to oscillate back and forth, 320 degrees in each direction, and up and down, like a clown mimicking a lighthouse.

Stefan walked over and sat next to the robot, putting one hand on a leg of the robot while the other fed himself a foodbar.

Homer said, ''The incredible expedition of the tireless Dr. Stefan Draganescu counted on the eagle eyes of their exquisitely designed journobot to detect the innumerable hideous monsters that constantly threatened to tear their bodies into bloody, bite-sized pieces. Would they become fast food for some loathsome creature of an alien jungle? Only time would tell.''

CHAPTER 17

When the train arrived on its outbound leg, they put Millie and her doctrobot aboard and said good-bye, with instructions to take off for Earth if the rest of the crew had not returned in a month. She was told how to activate the sophisticated autopilot on Stefan's ship, which was programmed to jump to the nearest colonized star, where a human pilot could be called by emergency radio.

A few minutes after her departure, the train returned on its inbound leg. The remainder of the crew jumped on board with their gear: Sean, Ariadne, Plum, Wolf, Stefan, Homer, and the other doctrobot. Each crew member carried a month's supply of food in a backpack, an easy task since the water, carbon, and nitrogen had been extracted by the manufacturer. Every day, they would load a day's food supply into the backpack processor, which over a period of hours extracted the carbon, nitrogen, and water from the air, and reconstituted the food.

The train left the second ring and headed toward the third. They sat mesmerized in the transparent vehicle as the universe flashed by to the left and right. The third ring approached rapidly with few windows visible, but there were more mysterious bumps and spikes projecting from it than had been the case with the second ring. It had a character of its own.

They flew over a great, red-glowing, ellipsoidal bulge in the third ring. Larger than the great vehicle they were in, its transparency revealed a nearly featureless bowl inside—mirroring the bulge—of no obvious purpose.

Before they knew it, they had mated with the third ring and descended to the next station. The door slid down into the floor, revealing a red-lit room similar to the last, but much cleaner.

Ariadne jumped out, followed at a more cautious pace by the others. "There!" she said, pointing to a circle on the wall. "Another message from my father!"

The train door rose and locked, leaving them irretrievably

stuck on the third ring for hours. Sean felt trapped. He walked over to the exit, gun in hand, scanning the roof and floor as he went. Ariadne anxiously retrieved the viewcrystal from the wall.

"Very clean," reported Sean, holstering his gun as he rejoined the group. "No signs of animal life. Looks almost sterile."

Ariadne fitted the viewcrystal into her palm-sized viewer.

"After the last ring," said Plum, "I could grow quite fond of sterility."

Ariadne pushed the PLAYBACK key and her father's lined, wise face appeared on the little screen. Her face softened in adoration and she held the precious memento of her father gently, as if she were holding him in her arms.

"This is the summary of two months of study in the third ring," said Alexandros's voice. "We have remained here that long because of the importance of this ring. It turns out to be a combination of library and museum, a fantastic discovery. We now know what the aliens looked like, what their history was, and how to speak their language to some degree.

"A dictionary of the spoken and written alien words that we have managed to decipher will be found following my message. Be aware that it is incomplete and probably, in some cases, inaccurate.

"We have learned some astonishing facts about their civilization, but this knowledge was purchased at a terrible price. We have lost two more men. Lajos Szeker, our engineer, and Jomo arap Moi, our pilot, were killed in accidents, although *killed* is, as you will see, not the proper word for what happened to Jomo.

"Jomo was the first. When we lost him, we debated whether to return. We had survived a week here. Jomo had been exploring the museum. Once we understood what had happened, we knew how to avoid that particular trap, and thought we were safe. We had found so many incredible wonders that we decided to stay on.

"Then, two weeks later, Lajos was killed by what we think was a maintenance robot whose programming had developed a defect. We disabled the robot afterward, so it does not present a hazard now.

"That left only Helene d'Albis and myself. Neither of us could tear ourselves away from this forest of knowledge. I understood better than ever before how Adam was drawn to the forbidden fruit.

"Now I must warn you about the museum, and how it caught Jomo, because if any intelligent being ever comes here again, his life may depend on knowing about the bizarre traps with which the museum is filled.

"It seems that the museum animals are kept frozen in a perpetual stasis field. There were once force-field shields surrounding each stasis field, to keep the visitor from touching the stasis field. Unfortunately, many of the shields in the museum have failed, apparently the result of a breakdown in the energy-line that feeds them. The stasis fields are now exposed. Jomo, not knowing this, climbed into the exhibit, to look closer at one of the animals. Unknowingly, he entered the stasis field.

"The field slows down time inside it, in much the way Einstein showed that a gravitational field slows down time for anything near it. Apparently, the aliens had learned much more about the relationship between gravity and space-time than we have. They had to learn this in order to cancel out the tidal force, which would have made it impossible to get close to the neutron star. In learning this, they discovered how to create local distortions in space-time without the enormous masses that Einsteinian physics would require.

"Where Einstein showed that the bigger the mass, the slower time passes for an object near it, these creatures found some way of creating the same effect through, I suppose, a pseudogravitational field. Time could be arbitrarily slowed down within it, creating a stasis field. Thus these creatures could put animals into exhibits in which time, for them, was slowed down to an infinitesimal pace.

"Of course, photons of light from within the field would be slowed down too—reddened—but they had a way of blue-shifting and amplifying the photons, so they could look into the exhibit and see the animal in normal color, just as if it were alive— because, of course, it *was* alive."

Alexandros shook his head sadly. "We did not know this when poor Jomo explored the exhibits. Apparently, the stasis field engulfs you, much like a bubble, as soon as you touch it. Otherwise, he would have felt like he was walking through a brick wall as the molecules in his hand slowed down and the blood piled up on the way from his heart.

"Jomo had no way of knowing what was happening. He moved close to an animal and was immediately caught by the stasis field. Time slowed down for him so completely that we almost couldn't measure it.

"But we can still see Jomo, frozen in time as he makes his way toward the animal in the exhibit. We thought he was not moving until we discovered that he is blinking. With great difficulty, we measured the rate of his blinking eyelids. You see, he was—and is—still alive. But we found that it will take him about two million years to complete his first blink!

"We have learned that the aliens were very respectful of animal life, like Buddhists and Hindus. They hated to kill, and so developed the stasis field for their museum. Even vermin were normally stunned when possible, back when the robots were working properly. They were then placed in stasis. All the animals in the museum are alive, but billions of years will pass before they have lived another hour! This galaxy will die long before their next meal is due.

"We have tried to find how to turn off the field that trapped Jomo, but our knowledge of their language and technology is completely inadequate to translate the instructions for the museum controls. There is a control room in the museum, but we tried every combination of controls we could think of without freeing Jomo. One day, I pray, humans will understand these mysteries, and Jomo may yet walk out of here long after I am dead.

"In effect, he walked into the most fiendish booby trap this world has yet presented us. *Beware of this museum!* Never step over the white lines encircling the exhibits. Those mark where the force-field shields should be.

"The nearest entrance to the museum is eighty meters to the right of the nearest exit from the train station, on the right side of the corridor as you walk toward it.

"Helene and I are all that are left. We should return home, but we are driven by the mysteries of this place: Why did they abandon it? Where did they go? What is at the final ring? That's what comes of being scientists. Curiosity may kill us like the cat in the English proverb. If one of us had just been a thickheaded pilot, we might have been able to resist the temptation."

Sean winced and Ariadne smirked.

"We have agreed that we shall continue to explore as long as at least one of us survives. If one of us dies, the other must return to Earth with the knowledge we have acquired.

"We have now decided to go straight to the end of the train line, if possible. We are just going to get onto the train and hope that we can survive whatever is at the last stop. What we have learned here indicates that the secret of what happened to the aliens lies in the innermost ring of this strange world, next to the neutron star.

"Now you are ready to experience for yourself the tantalizing world of the third ring. We have placed instructions in English at those controls we have deciphered. And we have prepared a sampling of the highlights of the alien culture in a special exhibit.

"Nothing I could possibly say could demonstrate what has happened as well as actually seeing the aliens' own images. And what I could tell you about them would be unbelievable without the actual images in front of your eyes, produced by the aliens themselves.

"I want you to follow my instructions carefully. Go to the nearest exit and turn right. Walk 230 meters down the corridor, well past the entrance to the museum. There will be a portal on your left. Enter it. You will find yourself inside a large amphitheater. Next to the entrance, there is a set of controls. Push the following pairs of indentations in the precise order I show here." His face was replaced by a series of beautiful, cursive alien words.

His face and voice returned. "If you make a mistake, press the white pair and start again. We have stored a sample of the alien recordings there, along with some of our translations and thoughts. You will learn more in a few minutes by watching that recording than I could tell you in a year. Prepare yourself for sights and sounds the likes of which have never before been seen by human beings."

The image on the screen blinked off, then on again. "The following is a dictionary of the alien words and symbols that we think we understand. First, the alphabet—"

Ariadne stopped the viewer. "Let's go!" she said eagerly.

"No," said Sean. "We need to rest."

"That's all right," said Ariadne, walking toward the exit. "You rest and I'll go to the amphitheater."

Sean strode over to her and grabbed her arm. "When are you going to learn, Ariadne?"

"My father said it was safe."

"Your father said this ring killed two good men, and in the twenty years since he died, Heisenberg only knows what else could have happened."

"I'll be careful."

Sean squeezed her arm painfully hard and growled, "It's time you learned who's in charge of this expedition, and it's not some little colleen from Earth on her first outing to another world. You'll stay here while the rest of us get some well-earned sleep if I have to tie you up like an octopoid! Understand?"

Anger flared in her face for a moment and then she relaxed and nodded. "Very well," she said. "I'll wait until we've all had some sleep."

"You give me your word? In the name of your father?"

"Yes."

He released her triumphantly and went back to the others. "Make yourselves as comfortable as you can. After we've had a nice pleasant sleep and a hearty breakfast, we'll follow Alexandros's instructions and see what we can see. We'll do two-hour watches. I'll take the first watch, followed by Plum and then Ariadne. Wolf and Stefan, you're exempt, you lucky devils." Sean pulled off his backpack and sat down against a wall, facing Wolf, Stefan, and Homer, who had all lain down on the floor.

"As long as we're relaxing," said Ariadne, "we ought to program one of the robots with my father's dictionary."

"Good idea," said Sean. "Why don't you input that viewcrystal to the doctrobot?"

Homer, whose lap now cushioned Stefan's head, spoke up. "Why not me?"

"Because I don't trust a robot programmed by the Ministry of Information and personalized by our distinguished deputy minister."

"But I'm programmed to manipulate words and ideas," said Homer.

"Of that," said Sean, "you've given us plenty of evidence."

"A doctrobot has a much more limited capability," said Homer.

"He is right," said the doctrobot. "My programming is highly specialized."

"In that case," said Sean tiredly, "why don't the both of you robots absorb whatever you can from the viewcrystal?"

Ariadne gave the viewcrystal to Homer, who put it in a slot and digested the information in a few seconds.

The doctrobot then did the same.

Homer looked up at the ceiling, where the usual ring map floated. "Amazing!" he said. "I can read most of the symbols now!" In his reportorial voice, he continued: "The expedition's journobot was given the task of becoming the chief linguist. In a trice, he had learned the alien language fluently and become at once the most valuable member of the expedition, with the exception, of course, of the handsome Dr. Stefan Draganescu." Homer patted Stefan's head. The latter smiled and closed his eyes.

Sean broke out some whiskey from his backpack. Ariadne frowned but remained silent.

Sean took a swig and passed it to Plum, who drank some with a grimace and returned it.

Soon, everyone except Sean was asleep. He put the whiskey away reluctantly, to make sure he did not join the rest.

He whiled away the next two hours by smoking kelparettes and cataloguing his cuts, burns, bruises, sore muscles, and endless miscellaneous aches and pains, and by watching the snoring bodies of the other humans. His eyes lingered more often on Ariadne's sleeping form than on her companions. He marveled that one so heavenly while sleeping could be so thoroughly diabolical while awake.

After two hours, his suit-clock said synthetically, "Time to change watches."

He shook Plum awake. Ignoring the Englishman's grumbles, Sean stretched out and fell asleep almost immediately.

Sean was awakened with a start by a booming alien voice. He went for his gun before he realized that it was just the alien train's automatic announcement of its return on the outbound journey.

He smiled, relaxed, and closed his eyes again. Then Ariadne's voice cried, "What are you doing? Get back here this instant!"

He opened his eyes again and saw her running to the train with her gun drawn. Adrenaline pumping, he jumped to his feet and drew his own gun.

Ariadne was standing at the train, pointing her gun at Wolf, who was on board the train. "Out, quickly!" she shouted.

With hatred engraved on his face, Wolf emerged and walked up to Ariadne. The door slid up into the ceiling, cutting him off from the train. He cursed and grabbed her gun hand. She screamed and Sean aimed his own gun, two-handed, at Wolf, but the bald man skillfully maneuvered Ariadne so Sean could not get a clear shot. Plum rose to his knees with gun poised, but he too could not shoot without endangering Ariadne.

Wolf pulled the gun from her hand almost casually and held it to her head, holding her wrist painfully with his other hand. "Down with your guns, you sons of chips!" he spat.

Sean and Plum glanced at each other. "Don't!" said Sean in a low voice. "Just watch out for Stefan!"

Plum turned around, and saw that Stefan was sitting down next to Homer, looking with complete astonishment at the scene.

"Down-throw your guns, you roidscum!" shouted Wolf. "Or you want me to scramble this pretty lola's brains for you?"

"You try that," Sean said in his deadliest voice, aiming his gun toward Wolf, "and I will personally teach you just how many painful ways there are to die in space."

"Drop them or I shoot!" Wolf shouted.

"You don't dare shoot," said Sean. "You may be a C-cop, but you're not *perfectly* stupid. She's the only thing keeping you alive. She's your oh-two, and if you kill her, you're going to wish you had died breathing vacuum."

"Wolf!" shouted Stefan, standing up. "Please reconsider. There's no need for this messy confrontation."

"Shut up, you wimpocrat!" said Wolf. "If it hadn't been for you, mate, you and your chip-brained schemes, I wouldn't be in this mess. I'd be sleeping in a nice warm bed with a nice warm lola on a nice warm planet. Because of you, I'm whirling around on this insane interstellar merry-go-round twenty light-years from home, and I wouldn't give you even money on my ever getting back. So don't tell *me* what to do!"

"Drop the gun and let her go," said Sean, "and we'll forget this little diversion ever happened. You have the word of a spacer."

Wolf laughed nastily. "The word of a spacer? When I was growing up in the worst Anty slum, I learned quick there were only two words to trust. One was *money* and the other was *power*, and right now, I've got the power."

"You can't hold her forever," said Sean. "One of us is going to get you when you fall asleep. And you're not going to like what we do to you then, really you're not. And that's one more word you can trust."

Wolf edged over to the exit, picking up a backpack of food as he went. "You'll have to catch me first. There's thousands of kloms of halls on this world, and you can't cover them all. Just don't try to follow me, or I'll damage the little lola." He backed out into the corridor with Ariadne shielding him.

Sean impotently watched him leave.

"All we have to do is go back to the ships," whispered Plum, with the logic of a mathematician. "He has to come there sooner or later."

"And what's he going to do to Ariadne in the meantime?"

Plum remained silent.

"But you're right," said Sean. "You do that. Go to the ships. Take Homer and his pal with you. Just leave the doctrobot here, in case he hurts her. I'm not giving up that easily."

Plum nodded, knowing further argument was futile. "As soon

as the train comes back on the next outbound leg, we'll catch it. But that will be hours from now."

Sean ran over to the exit, saying, "So your job is to keep your eye on Stefan and Homer and keep them out of mischief. I'll just see what I can do out there." He pointed to the corridor and stuck his head around the exit.

"They went to the right. I can see them running away," said Sean. After a few moments, he said, "They disappeared to the right. Wasn't that the museum?"

"Yes," said Plum.

"Good God!" said Sean. "Maybe he *is* stupider than I thought." He ran out into the corridor.

Plum went over to the exit and watched his friend run quietly in the same direction. It reminded him of the times he had seen Sean stalk dangerous animals on dangerous worlds. But never had he stalked an animal as dangerous as Wolf.

Sean halted at the museum entrance and listened carefully, straining his ears to their limit. Strange, distant sounds came from the museum, like roars of wild beasts.

He dropped to the floor, gun in hand, and peered around the edge. Nothing moved. A musty smell greeted his nose, emanating from the floor. It mingled with faint, spicy odors that reminded him of the smells of a dozen alien planets. The floor felt warm. He glanced down and observed an intricate interleaved pattern of fine lines. *Not so much dust here*, he noted. *Janitrobots must be working. Hard to follow a trail.*

He focused on the exhibits. An animal the size of a grizzly bear reared into the air a few meters away, frozen in a perpetual snarl. Its face was blue and fishlike, with rows of daggerlike teeth, resembling the killfish of Epsilon Eridani. Its green body seemed to be covered with feathers, and a dozen clawed arms sprouted from its sides. Decidedly unfriendly-looking.

As far as Sean could see, spread out endlessly, were other animals—large and small, flying and crawling, swimming and slithering—hundreds of them, all frozen as if in ice. Some exhibits contained one animal; others, many. Some were familiar, from planets Sean had been to; a few were even from Earth. A humble terrestrial milk cow on a pedestal looked out of place amid the bizarre creatures of countless alien worlds. Each exhibit was encircled by a white line, which he paid very close attention to.

He got to his feet and cautiously stepped into the museum.

Another animal roar sounded in the distance. Puzzled, he walked in the direction of the sound, avoiding the white lines with exquisite care.

He walked past the fishlike monster. A horrible animal bellow sounded beside him. He whirled, aiming his gun at the sound. It was the fish monster, unmoving, with the sound seeming to come from its frozen mouth.

Damn! Must be a recording triggered when you get near the beast. Have to stay farther away.

He stealthily made his way through the museum, weaving between exhibits, keeping equidistant from them whenever possible.

After he had gotten a hundred meters without triggering any more sounds, his confidence grew and he began to run at half speed, sure that he would catch up to a man slowed down by a reluctant hostage.

He had almost run past an exhibit of two large animals, when he did a double take and stumbled in shock, nearly falling into the field of another exhibit.

One of the two animals was a human in a green pressure suit similar to Sean's own, but old-fashioned, and without a helmet. Sean stared at the man. His face was familiar. He was a tough-looking black man with a sprinkling of gray in his curly hair: Jomo arap Moi, of Kenya, Earth. Alexandros had introduced Sean to him at the start of his last voyage. Sean remembered the awe he had felt at meeting the first interstellar pilot he had ever known.

The spacer's hands were stretched out in front of him, toward a three-eyed creature that resembled a large barrel of rippling, violet flesh. Three great mouths gaped open, one under each eye. Hundreds of snakelike tentacles, lined with sawtooth barbs, radiated from the hideous beast, each with a tiny eye on its end.

Sean moved closer to Jomo. Suddenly a hideous, bone-chilling shriek arose from the creature. Sean jumped back and the shriek stopped. *Damn sound effects!*

Sean looked into the pilot's eyes. They were glassy pools of darkness, staring perpetually at the monster. Even at a distance, each eyelash stood out as clear as life; the very pores of his face were distinctly visible. He looked as if, in a moment, he would open his mouth and greet Sean.

Knowing that Jomo was, in some sense, still alive, making a blink that would take millions of years to complete, made the sight unnerving. By the time Jomo inhaled his next breath, Sean and everyone he knew, and their descendants for generations to come, would be dead, and human civilization would be unrecognizably changed.

He shook his head and slowly walked away, glancing back once in disbelief.

Sean resumed his cautious run through the booby-trapped obstacle course of the museum, pausing occasionally to listen to animal sounds triggered by Wolf and his hostage. Once, he heard Ariadne's voice shout, *"Xekoumbisou, ap' etho!"* It did not sound encouraging.

Finally, he spotted Ariadne thirty meters away, standing behind an exhibit near the wall, her back to him. Her hands were taped behind her. She looked pitifully helpless. Wolf was nowhere to be seen. Sean stopped, sensing an ambush. He scanned through 360 degrees, but could see nothing but more exhibits. Several of them held animals or vegetation large enough to hide Wolf's great bulk.

Her pressure suit reminded him of the communicator. He turned it on and whispered into the neck microphone, "Ariadne."

Her head jerked up and she turned around, searching. She spotted him and began shaking her head wildly. Her mouth was taped, and only muffled noises came over the communicator. She hopped a little toward him, and it became clear that her feet were also bound.

"Stay where you are," whispered Sean. "Just answer with nods." She nodded. "Is Wolf trying to ambush me?" She nodded vigorously. "He must have heard those damn sound effects." She nodded. "Where is he?" She pointed with her head to the right. Sean strained to see, but could spot nothing but some exhibits too small to hide Wolf.

He moved cautiously in that direction, examining the exhibits with care. They were large snakapedes similar to the one that had almost eaten Millie. He stopped ten meters in front of them and studied the wall behind the exhibits. There was a small control panel with the familiar pairs of keys. Black words were scrawled next to them, in Alexandros's style, but too small to read at this distance.

Centimeter by centimeter, he approached the panel. The first phrase he could make out was CONTROL ROOM. He scrutinized the wall for signs of a door, but found none.

A grunt emerged from his communicator and he spun around, gun at the ready. Ariadne, a dozen meters away, had tripped and fallen on the floor, dangerously close to a stasis field. He fought the impulse to go to her, steeling himself to her plight, knowing she was the bait.

He looked behind the nearby exhibits, but they were as bare from the rear as they had looked from the front. Where the hell was Wolf?

He stepped closer to the control board to read the other labels. Muffled sounds came from his communicator. He glanced at Ariadne. She was still on the floor, frantically shaking her head.

There was a faint hissing sound behind him. He wheeled and raised his gun. A large cylinder descended from the ceiling just behind him, like the closets in the nursery-jail, but this was the size of an elevator. Wolf was inside it—and pointing his quantagun at Sean.

Sean dived for an exhibit next to the elevator.

Wolf squeezed the trigger.

The beam grazed Sean's gun arm, burning a hole through the pressure suit and flesh. He cursed, hit the floor, rolled over, and fired a wild shot at Wolf. It hit an exhibit, without effect. Searing pain shot through Sean's arm and his gun flew away. He stumbled behind the elevator. The gun hit the stasis field of an exhibit. The field hummed, flared green, and the gun stopped, frozen in midair.

Sean leaned against the back of the elevator, holding his burned arm, gritting his teeth to keep from crying out his agony. There was a smell of burnt plastex and skin.

Ariadne shook her head violently and tried to get to her feet, her eyes crying out in terror.

Wolf squinted cautiously around the edge of the elevator and spotted the gun floating in the stasis field. He smiled and stepped out boldly, his gun pointing directly at Sean.

The bald man chuckled his deep, skin-crawling laugh. "You roiders all think you're goddamn brainers, don't you? You think us terries are just squishies crawlin' around down in the gravity well, nix? Maybe it's true for your average terry, but I'm Antarctic, and they don't build squishies down there. They only build real men. And I've got info for you, ratbag. There's more real brains in a' ice-cuber like me than in any ten roiders."

Sean rose to his feet with difficulty and spat between clenched teeth, "Then how come, terry, you weren't able to vaporize a simple interstellar vessel crewed by two mere roiders and a terry girl?"

Wolf's expression soured momentarily. "Luck, that's the parameter. You just maxxed your luck, that's all. But now your luck's at min." He walked up to Sean and aimed the gun at the middle of his forehead. The Irishman tensed all of his muscles and braced himself against the elevator.

Ariadne uttered a muffled scream through her gag. Wolf glanced over at her. Sean let fly the most powerful kick of his life and hit Wolf squarely in the groin.

The blow struck body underarmor. Even so, the shock was enough to send a wave of pain through the bald man's frame. The impact knocked him backward, quantagun clenched with one hand, groin with the other.

Sean moved in and struck a throat-blow with the cutting edge of his right hand, but the seared muscle hurt him more than it did Wolf. He struck a kidney blow with his left fist, but it bounced off underarmor.

Wolf shook his head sluggishly and raised the weapon. Sean cursed, ran to the other side of the elevator, and jumped in. There were only two indentations on the control panel inside. He struck them with his left-hand fingers and the elevator rose rapidly into the ceiling. A black line crawled along the bottom of the elevator as Wolf's gun-beam seared the floor. Sean crowded against the wall, praying the metal wouldn't give under the beam.

The elevator popped into the next floor and he stumbled out, wincing with pain from his injuries. He found himself inside a control room similar to the one for the second ring. *Got to jam the elevator!* he thought. He grabbed the first movable object he found, Wolf's heavy food-supply pack, and shoved it halfway into the elevator. *Hope the safety still works!*

As the elevator started to descend, he pushed the pack halfway inside. The elevator stopped, sensing an obstacle. *Hooray, something works right for a change!*

Wolf's curse sounded from below, carried up through the elevator's opening. "O'Shaughnessy, you roid-eater, you can't stay there forever!"

"I've no intention of doing so," Sean muttered to himself as he looked around the room. An image of the museum floated in the air near the ceiling. A large elevated screen, like a transparent table, gave a video image of the museum below. Surrounded by fierce animal exhibits, Wolf was in his element. He looked up toward Sean, shaking his gun. Ariadne tried to crawl away.

So this is how you watched me, you little terry dust bag.

"I'm going to get that Greek girlperson and start dismantling her slowly,'' announced Wolf. Ariadne squirmed and inchwormed away faster. "But first I'm going to have a little rec with her.''

"Hell, damnation, and taxes!" shouted Sean. He scanned the complex control board furiously. There were hundreds of indentation pairs and a few scrawled notes in Alexandros's writing: VIDEO MAGNIFICATION, MAP ORIENT, and several other useless labels. *If he couldn't figure out the controls in two months, what can I do in two minutes?*

He looked at the ceiling and recognized access panels like those he had crawled through in the second ring. He climbed up on the window-table, grimacing with the pain in his arm, and pushed open the ceiling panel.

Some ratroaches screamed and ran away. There was a maze of cables of various thicknesses and colors. He glanced at the image beneath his feet and saw Wolf reach Ariadne.

Sean remembered his father's once saying, "When everything looks completely hopeless, do *something*. *Anything's* always better than *nothing!*''

He felt in his pockets and found the wire cutters. Awkwardly, with his left hand he reached in with the wirecutters and squeezed. The first cable was too thick. The second was too tough. The third sliced through after a struggle.

He looked down at the scene below. Wolf had lifted Ariadne up by the hair.

Sean cut a second cable. It sparked at the break and some of the red lights in the museum died. Wolf cut Ariadne's bindings with a knife.

Sean cut a third cable. Wolf began to rip Ariadne's pressure suit off her.

Sean cut a fourth. Wolf threw away Ariadne's suit. She stood in her thin undersuit, quivering.

Sean found a flat cable and cut into its edge. It arced with an intense blue-white light. He took one end and touched it to a cut cable. There was a flash! Half a meter of cable vaporized. His glove was scorched and his hand felt like one great blister, but he was lucky to still have a hand at all.

He glanced down. Wolf tore away at her undersuit, then stopped. He looked around wildly.

Sean paused. One of the animals in the stasis field moved! A snakapede was crawling out of its exhibit case! A chorus of strange growls, squeaks, roars, and buzzes emerged from below, as if all the exhibits' sound effects had been turned on at once.

Dozens of animals were loose! Some flew through the air.

Some writhed on the floor. Others crawled. The majority were still frozen. *Must have cut one of the stasis control lines!*

Wolf aimed his gun at a three-legged creature the size of an ostrich, with three arms under its three eyes, lumbering toward him with a bizarre gait: front leg down, rear legs swiveling forward in the air; then the front leg slipped through the two and repeated the cycle.

Ariadne screamed. Wolf fired. The creature screamed and jumped at him. He fired again. It hit him, knocking him down. Ariadne began to run. The creature went into convulsions. Wolf stood up and began running after the woman.

"Need a weapon!" muttered Sean. He recalled his gun, frozen in the stasis field and smiled. "Please let it be in one of the dead fields!" He looked down, but could not tell which exhibit it had been in. He jumped into the elevator, cringing with pain as he hit his arm, and pulled the foodpack in with him. The elevator promptly descended.

A snarling snakapede greeted him when he reached the floor. He kicked one of its heads and it crawled away. He went to the exhibit only to find his gun still there, floating in the air. "Damn!" he cursed. "Murphy strikes again!"

Something flew overhead. On the floor, a brown creature like a giant crab with acne lay writhing, dying in what was clearly a hostile atmosphere for him.

A blue, many-legged creature the size of a horse came slowly toward him. It sniffed the air with several hollow tentacles and snorted at him, coming closer. Sean backed away. Glancing back, he was horrified to discover he had touched the white line encircling a still-working stasis field.

He jumped sideways and the blue creature advanced some more. It opened a huge mouth that spanned the entire width of its body. Rows of sharklike teeth grinned at him. The tentacles waved, inviting him within.

Backing up, he frantically searched his suit for a weapon. He threw the wire cutters down its throat. It swallowed them without ill effect.

He pulled something long out of a thigh pocket. It was the puzzling triangular red "wand" he had found in the nursery-jail. He aimed it painfully at the creature with his right hand and pressed the two indentations on the end with his left. The blue beam shot out and hit the creature's gullet. It roared, closed its mouth, and paused, startled. He shot the beam into an eye. The creature roared again and backed away.

After several more doses, the creature decided it was needed elsewhere and slowly lumbered away. Sean sighed in relief. "Maybe they punished bad students with it," he muttered, staring at the wand.

An animal roar drew his attention ahead. In the distance, he could see Wolf dragging Ariadne with one hand, shooting with the other. Sean ran after them, his wounded arm screaming pain at each step.

He paused several times to shoot threatening animals with the wand's beam. In each case, the animals protested with snarls and roars and backed away, but none was seriously injured.

He weaved between still-frozen exhibits, trying to keep them between himself and Wolf as much as possible. After several minutes, he was a mere five meters behind them. He stopped and aimed the wand at Wolf.

Sean was breathing hard by now and the wand bounced up and down while he waited for a clear shot as Wolf dragged Ariadne along. He shouted, "Hit the dirt!"

Ariadne looked around with surprise, then fell to the ground. Wolf held onto her hand and dragged her half a meter. Sean aimed carefully and squeezed the trigger indentations.

The blue beam shot out and struck Wolf squarely in the back. He yelped and released the woman.

Wolf whirled around as Sean fired a second beam. The bald man screamed again but kept his gun gripped in his right hand. He aimed it at Sean.

Sean held the triggers down and sliced the beam across Wolf's arm. Wolf screamed and dropped the gun, holding his arm, though no damage was visible.

Ariadne reached for the gun. Wolf kicked her in the face, sending her sprawling backward. He reached down with remarkable speed and swept up the gun with his left hand.

Sean shot a beam into his bulky abdomen. Wolf cursed, his body jerked, and he stepped backward, but he held on to the gun. Ariadne lay stunned on the floor.

Wolf pointed the gun toward Sean, who fired a beam straight into the bald man's forehead. "Moon dust!" spat Wolf, stepping back and raising both arms to protect his face; but he still gripped the quantagun.

Wolf protected his face with one arm while he fired at Sean with the other. The shot went wild and Sean beamed another ray into Wolf's head. Wolf stepped backward again.

Damn! thought Sean. *Mexican standoff! Time to change tactics.*

He looked around and spotted a still-operational stasis field several meters behind Wolf. A red flying creature hovered frozen in air like a huge buzzsaw blade with five eyes on top.

Sean held the beam on Wolf's face. Wolf kept both arms across his face, stepping backward haltingly and uttering a continuous stream of curses in the gutter languages of Antarctica and the moon.

Sean nudged Wolf with the beam, using it like a cattle prod, from his head to his side and back again. Wolf got off several shots, but the Irishman jumped back and forth. Wolf could not uncover his face long enough to get a good shot in.

Finally, Wolf stepped on the white circle of the stasis field, raising the quantagun toward Sean. The roider gave him another blast with the blue beam. Wolf made one more small step backward.

The stasis field hummed, flared, and encompassed Wolf in a green glow. He froze, left hand over his face, right hand with the gun aimed at Sean.

Instinctively, Sean jumped to one side and then stared at the man. Behind his raised arms, the big man's hate-filled eyes could still be seen. The process had happened so fast that no trace of surprise could be detected. His gun stuck out without the slightest tremor, like a manikin in a wax museum.

Sean turned away and went to Ariadne. She was struggling to her feet, facing Sean and Wolf. One side of her face was covered with an ugly bruise, and she wore only the flimsy, torn undersuit. He helped her rise.

Ariadne collapsed into his arms and began to cry. Sean comforted her awkwardly, stopping now and then to shoot a discouraging beam when some animal threatened them. The warmth of her body and the smell of her hair did disturbing things to him.

After a while, her sobs stopped and she said in her thickest accent, "Oh, Sean, I don't know how to thank you." She stood on her tiptoes and kissed him.

Her lips were warm and sweaty, but they tasted sweeter than a Centaurian daiquiri. They stood kissing until an animal roar interrupted their reverie. A hairy, legless creature the size of a bear undulated toward them, displaying a mouthful of drooling spikes in its gaping jaws. Its black body was covered with blinking, pink, phosphorescent lights. Sean fired a shot down its throat. It squealed and undulated away with surprising speed.

Sean patted her head and said, "We'd better rescue your pressure suit. It cost us enough."

She nodded and they unfolded their arms from about each other. She walked unsteadily over to the stasis field and stared at Wolf. The huge buzz-sawlike beast hovered over his shoulder, hundreds of sharp claws around its rim, a gaping mouth in the center filled with needlelike teeth. "That flying monster," she said, "will haunt him forever, like the Erinyes of the ancients, the winged Furies who sought vengeance among the living and the dead. He's somewhere between the two, and I pray he will always remain there."

"I'm sorry he didn't know what was happening to him in time to appreciate it."

She turned to look at Sean, who was studying her with more than avuncular interest. She noticed for the first time the revealing tears in her garment and blushed. Covering herself with one arm, she took Sean's good arm in the other. They limped back toward the control room.

After she had donned her pressure suit, they walked slowly through the museum, nervously avoiding the stasis fields and crawling animals. The animals had thinned out, Sean deduced, from eating each other and from blundering into stasis fields. He fired the wand occasionally to discourage hungry and curious survivors.

As they neared the entrance, a large, three-eyed barrel of rippling, violent flesh charged out from behind an exhibit. Great mouths gaped open under each eye, uttering hideous, bone-chilling shrieks. Hundreds of snakelike tentacles, lined with sawtooth barbs, swirled around the obscene beast, each ending in a tiny eye.

Ariadne screamed in horror. Sean gave it a continuous burst of the blue beam. The creature hissed and its tentacles swirled madly. It slowed a little but continued to advance.

"Doesn't seem to have a central brain," said Sean, backing up with Ariadne.

"Pain must be too localized to stop it!" said Ariadne.

"This just is not my day!" said Sean. "I'll keep it occupied Run like hell!"

"I'm not leaving you," she said defiantly.

"Moon dust!" After a moment, he added, "Then keep an eye behind us."

She guided him away from stasis fields. As the creature advanced on them, Sean said, "Where's the nearest working stasis field?"

"Behind you, to your left, two meters."

He glanced backward and said, "Let's run behind it!"

They ran behind a white circle containing a bulky seven-footed humpbacked creature beneath a flying creature with double-decker wings and large pincers.

The monster approached closer and stretched out its tentacles toward the humans. One tentacle touched the stasis field. The exhibit hummed, flared, and a green glow enveloped the monster. It froze.

"Thank God!" said Ariadne, embracing Sean again.

"This place really grows on you," said Sean sourly. "Just when you think you've had all the fun you can possibly stand, they serve you another treat."

"Come on, complainer," she said warmly, tugging him toward the exit.

He stared at the monster as they passed it. "That's the one that got Jomo!" he exclaimed, pulling her back.

"What?"

"Yes! That's the one that trapped your father's pilot!"

"The black man! Yes! We passed that horrible scene shortly after we entered the museum. Wolf thought it was funny!"

"Well, now at least he knows just how funny it was. But you see what this means? Jomo's alive! His stasis field was one of those I killed!"

"He can tell us all about my father!" she exclaimed.

"Yes. Let's look for him." They walked over to where the pilot had been frozen.

The pilot's old-fashioned green pressure suit lay stretched out in front of the exhibit, a gun in his hand. Where his head should have been was a bloody mess.

"*Théa mou!*" exclaimed Ariadne. She turned away and vomited.

Sean looked away. "Twenty years the man waited for freedom. Twenty years! He must have had it for all of ten seconds. He was staring right at the monster when the field went off. He would have seen the creature coming for him. He saw it move. Must have scared the moon dust out of him. He drew his gun, probably fired several times, but the creature hardly noticed. Jomo didn't have his helmet on. His head was the only exposed part of him. The monster tasted him. Probably spat him out. Twenty years for this!"

Ariadne embraced Sean and put her head on his shoulder. "You were right. My father was right. We never should have come here."

They walked out into the corridor in silence.

CHAPTER 18

Sean and Ariadne limped toward the train station, arm in arm, each lost in thought. Sean paused occasionally to beam his wand at animals that had escaped into the corridor.

They reached the station and found the rest of the party still there. Plum's face opened into a broad, cherubic smile. "By Jove, you did it!" he shouted and slapped his friend on the back.

Sean winced and Plum noticed his arm wound. Instantly solicitous, Plum clucked, saying, "Bit of a quantagun bite there, eh?"

Sean nodded and sat down. Plum called the doctrobot over.

"Where's Wolf?" said Stefan.

"Oh, he's waiting for us in the museum," said Sean with a weak smile. The robot cut away the pressure-suit arm around the wound.

"Damn it, robot," said Sean, "this suit cost me an arm and a leg, and now you want the other arm."

"Wolf's just waiting there?" said Stefan.

"Yes," said Sean. "He has all the time in the world."

"May I go see him?"

"Certainly. Take your time. A million years if you want—he'll still be there."

Ariadne explained what had happened, while the doctrobot medicated the wound.

"My God," said Stefan. "How will I tell my sister?"

"Your sister?" said Sean. "What has she got to do with this?"

"She's Wolf's wife," Stefan said softly.

"Wolf's wife?" spat Sean. "You're his brother-in-law? That C-cop you never met in your life till he began investigating Ariadne? I always knew you two were snakes of a feather!"

Ariadne, shocked, said, "Stefan, you lied to us!"

"It wasn't really a lie," said Stefan, slipping into his bureaucratic mode. "It was an expedient exaggeration, necessitated by the need of a lawful agent of the Ministry of Trade to undertake an investigation of alleged criminality while maintaining requisite confidentiality.''

"Yes," said Sean, "that's what it was—a lie."

"Perhaps," Ariadne said hesitantly, "he really was just obeying lawful instructions."

"Yes," said Sean, "and I could be the father of ten thousand Epsilon Eridanian sea behemoths and a robot. Ariadne, aren't you ever going to wake up and see that a Ph.D. and the ability to read and write and lie prettily in twelve languages doesn't make a man a paragon of virtue?"

"My poor sister," said Stefan, trying to divert the conversation.

"Just tell her," said Sean, "that her husband is a Popsicle in an alien museum, a unique exhibit that is an honor to his memory. In fact, very likely it's the only honorable thing he ever did in his life. And he isn't even dead, he's just a trifle sluggish. If it's any consolation, tell her he won't be able to cheat on her for a few million years. If some joygirl winks at him, it'll take him that long to wink back." He winced as the doctrobot taped his arm.

"We knew something had gone wrong," said Plum, "when strange beasts began cavorting in the corridor. Had to negate the more bothersome ones." He pointed to some carcasses.

The doctrobot shot Sean with a painkiller.

"*Ohhh,*" said Ariadne, bending over the body of a large blue-green furry creature, something like an ocelot with wings. "Did you *have* to kill it?"

"Afraid so, my dear," said Plum. "It was either that or become its next *hors d'oeuvre.*"

"I wish she'd show half as much concern about *me,*" said Sean, touching his bandage gingerly.

"Oh, Sean," she said softly, rushing to his side. "I have been *so* selfish, failing to think about the abuse you have suffered." She stroked his forehead.

"Abuse," said Sean, relaxing. "There's the word, good and proper. Someone's abused the hell out of me, and every cubic centimeter of my body is screaming like it's just been battered about on a curragh in a hurricane."

"Well, now that you're here," said Plum, "we can all take the next train back to the ship and home."

"Negative," said Sean, yawning. "I'm not leaving this Einstein-forsaken world until I've seen that recording Alexandros advertised."

Plum sighed. "That means I'll stay here too, which means we all do."

Sean's eyes closed and he fell asleep.

A few hours and one meal later, the group entered the amphitheater described by Alexandros. It was a vast, ellipsoidal room stretching several hundred meters in its longest dimension. The ceiling was the tallest they had yet seen, fully eighty meters over their heads, so high it seemed almost to merge with space. It was transparent and looked out onto the second ring, which slowly moved past, creating a disturbing feeling of being on a merry-go-round. There were no seats, just a dark red concave floor.

They sat down while Ariadne studied the control panel. She replayed the viewcrystal instructions and touched the pairs of indentations in the prescribed order. The room went dark and she heard a gasp. She whirled around. There, floating in the air above them, as large as the Sphinx, was the three-dimensional, silver-haired head of her father. It was like the head of God.

"Welcome to Hecatomb," the voice boomed. "That is what I have named this world, for reasons that will be clear later.

"I am Alexandros Zepos of Greece, Earth, and together with Helene d'Albis of France, Earth, I have prepared this recording to present the highlights of what we have discovered in our studies of the third ring of Hecatomb.

"To try to comprehend an intelligence so different from our own, in the space of a mere two months, is an idea bordering on arrogance. It has been possible to translate only portions of their language. You may be absolutely certain that we have made errors, but you will see for yourself that some of their pictures speak more eloquently than any human words.

"We have but sampled a tiny portion of the records of a civilization that was more than a billion years old when it died. They were reading and writing when man was but a tiny shrewlike creature crawling through the forest, striving not to be stepped upon by dinosaurs.

"It is difficult for us humans, with only a few thousand years of written history, to grasp the amount of art, history, and culture that these creatures amassed in their time." Strange, disconcerting music began to play, gliding up and down scales without stopping at distinct notes, and changing abruptly in unexpected ways. "This music you are hearing was composed almost two hundred and fifty million years ago, when the highest form of life on earth was the cockroach.

"Now, we will show you their home." A nondescript red star floated in the center of the amphitheater, speckled with dark star spots. "This is their home star."

A yellow planet appeared, half-covered by clouds and criss-crossed by lakes, rivers, and oceans. "This was their home world.

"And these were the creatures who built Hecatomb." A stout, muscular brown creature floated in the air, vaguely humanoid, with two short, massive legs and two short, thick arms, wearing a metallic tunic that covered it from shoulders to knees. The arms ended in two long, flexible fingers, joined directly to the arms without true hands. The face slightly resembled a human's, with the same number of eyes and ears, and with the nose and mouth in the usual places, but it differed in disturbing ways. It had huge, sad, circular green eyes that seemed portals to infinite wisdom. A massive white snout protruded from the center of the face, with large, flared nostrils. A short horn stuck out from either side of the head, just above large, leaflike ears.

The creature opened its mouth and a deep, resonant voice filled the amphitheater with alien words that sent shivers down Ariadne's spine.

Alexandros's voice replaced the alien's, while the creature's mouth continued to move. "These beings were descended from creatures similar to our cattle. For this reason, we have named them the bovoids. They were plant eaters with a reverence for all animal life. Their histories say that since they first evolved intelligence, their home star has revolved around the center of the galaxy almost five times—that's more than a billion Earth-years."

The air above the arena was filled with images of a bovoid city. It was strangely flat, consisting of one-story buildings spread over hectares of land, with grassy pastures in between. Along tree-lined conveyor-roads, thousands of bovoids sped on their way.

"The bovoids were intelligent, but it was a different type of intelligence from ours, much slower and more resistant to change, and they lived in a culture in which the herd instinct was over-whelming. Social change was very slow."

An image of a crude airplane flew in the air. It had swept-back, birdlike wings and two pusher-propellers. The image dis-solved into one of a stubby rocket with curved delta wings. It took off horizontally and rose slowly into the sky. "From the invention of the airplane to the launch of their first spacecraft, thirty thousand years elapsed.

"Still, because of their infinite patience and a billion years in which to develop, they eventually traveled through interstellar space, at first in spaceships that took centuries to get from star to star." A huge interstellar rocket appeared, flying away from the yellow planet. It had seven separate parallel fuselages, like bullets in a revolver, each with its own engines, all interconnected in a spiderweb of metal.

"Long before they discovered the principles of faster-than-light travel, they had explored many of the livable planets in the outer realms of the galaxy. They met other civilizations. One of those attacked them, and they discovered *war*. It sickened them. Never had they experienced the killing of an intelligent species by its own members, with the exception of mental defectives.

"They never became warriors, but instead learned ways of rapid retreat and defensive shields. They were almost wiped out before they perfected the shields and built artificial worlds similar to Hecatomb.

"In the course of exploring the galaxy, they found many planets with pre-intelligent life, and they experimented with evolution. On one world, they found intelligent squidlike beings living in the sea, and they made suits for them so they could explore the land and discover fire and metalworking. On another, they bred dumb dinosauroid creatures for intelligence for thousands of years until they had brains large enough for thought. In each case, once the ability to think and manipulate tools was reached, they ceased interfering in order to let the civilization develop uniquely.

"Then, half a billion years ago, the bovoids discovered our Earth. At that time, life on our planet consisted mostly of primitive creatures such as trilobites that lived in the sea. But they realized its potential to evolve intelligence, so they introduced carefully engineered mutations designed to accelerate that development. Even they could not predict the exact consequences for all species of an evolution that darted from one species to another as random mutations and environmental fluctuations occurred, but they hoped to help evolve creatures as intelligent as they.

"They began by stimulating the evolution of mammals, which did not exist when they arrived. Every million years or so, they visited our planet and nudged evolution a little closer to their plan. Now you will see pictures from their extensive library of images from Earth, starting with images made several hundred million years ago."

A crablike creature crawled through murky water, raising a trail of sediment.

Something like an octopus with a dunce cap swam by.

A strange fish with a crude tail and a huge, semicircular head undulated through the amphitheater.

Primitive ferns grew by the side of a beach. There was a sound of waves lapping. The humid salt air of an ocean shore filled the room.

Another beach showed a slimy fish with handlike fins crawling out of the ocean and laying eggs in black sand.

The air grew more humid and smelled of dirt and decay. A huge reptile lumbered out of the water and roared. It had the body of a crocodile and a long, birdlike mouth filled with teeth.

A flying reptile with an elongated head soared overhead, crying plaintively. Its great, mottled claw-wings stretched from one end of the amphitheater to the other.

A tiny shrewlike creature darted through a bush and climbed up a tree, squeaking. The air filled with the smell of a greenhouse. "Take a good look at this," boomed Alexandros's voice, "for this is one of our ancestors." The creature squeaked.

A dinosaur stomped by, its voice rumbling so low and loud that it shook the amphitheater. It was an allosaurus, its huge, drooling head glistening, the claws of its two tiny hands flexing hungrily. Its massive tail dredged a trail through the dirt. The air stank like a zoo.

A proliferation of color spread out before them; flowers sprouted everywhere; insects buzzed and perfumes wafted through the amphitheater.

"The bovoids gradually evolved the bovine species—the cows, oxen, buffaloes, and such. A million or so years ago, they were shocked to realize that an animal they considered a mere colorful zoo attraction had discovered fire and invented language."

The air filled with a group of dirty, hairy, naked, scarred cave people with apelike faces, huddled around a camp fire, chanting a monotonous song. "These were the first human beings." The smell of smoke, grease, and waste filled the air.

"It became obvious that these creatures would dominate the Earth before the bovines ever could. Being extremely ethical creatures, the bovoids stopped interfering, even after primitive humans acquired a taste for beef. It disturbed them profoundly to observe bovines being slaughtered and eaten, but their respect for intelligence transcended their distaste.

"They observed us as we built villages, invented the wheel,

and spread all over the globe. They were watching when we invented war. They were horrified, but their ethics forbade them from intervening directly. Humanity was so violent and irrational that, after thousands of years, they decided to accelerate the progress of our civilization by bringing writing and other knowledge to Earth. They visited the most advanced civilization of that time—advanced in terms of ethics, not technology—ancient India.

"They continued monitoring Earth until their disappearance about a thousand years ago. Here are a few samples from their massive archives of the modern history of Earth."

A half-built Egyptian pyramid stood on the sand. Hundreds of men pulled ropes, tugging a massive stone on round logs up a dirt ramp while others poured oil on the rollers.

An exquisitely beautiful, multicolored city stood by the side of a river, surrounded by terraces laden with trees, shrubs, and flowers, on which fountains sprayed, and through which marble staircases rose. "The hanging gardens of the lost city of Babylon," said Alexandros.

A man in an ancient Greek tunic sketched a right triangle in the sand and drew squares on each side . . . Vikings with horned helmets raided a village . . . A tiger tore out the throat of a man in the Roman Colosseum . . . Three wooden crosses stood on a hill, each with a man nailed to it.

Alexandros's face returned. "Of late, we have concentrated on the great mystery of this world: where did the bovoids go, and why?

"From the records, we have learned this much: In their hundreds of millions of years of space travel, they often tried to penetrate to the inner regions of the galaxy. Like us, they discovered indecipherable signals coming from the Glacatic Center. But every attempt they made to go there failed. Some spacecraft returned after experiencing inexplicable diversions. Other spacecraft never came back at all. They were not able to get within three thousand light-years of the Center. It was as though a barrier were preventing them.

"They became convinced that there was a tremendously advanced civilization on the other side of the galactic barrier, and they were determined to meet it. So they began a research program that took millions of years. They decided that the only way to get through the barrier would be to quantum-tunnel through it in hyperspace. But the only source of energy powerful enough would be a supernova explosion. Worse, they had to engineer the explosion in such a way that it would create a space-time singularity passing through the Galactic Center.

"So they sent out expeditions around the galaxy until they found two giant stars on the verge of going supernova—on opposite sides of the galaxy."

Alexandros disappeared and the Milky Way galaxy appeared, floating above them like a flying saucer. Billions of stars swirled slowly like a vast, glowing beehive in the center, thinning out to a disk at the edge. Each tiny dot was colored: red, blue, yellow, all the colors of the rainbow. Black lanes of dust cut through the disk; strange, nearly straight wisps of glowing matter arced through the center.

The scene zoomed in simultaneously on two stars on opposite sides of the Center. Two hot, red stars floated at either end of the amphitheather, surrounded by shells of gas, embedded in which were dead planets.

"For centuries, they brought in matter from circumstellar rings and planets, adding it in just the right amounts to accelerate the supernova instability."

Endless series of spacecraft like wagon trains scooped up refined asteroids, accelerated toward the stars, and shot their payloads in. Empty spacecraft returned to repeat the cycle.

"When the day came, they stood back many light-years for safety. Robots shot the last of the triggering matter into the stars. They exploded *simultaneously!*" The amphitheater filled with blindingly white light. "Each star exploded with the energy of all the stars in the galaxy *put together!*

"For weeks, the two stars exploded, lighting up the entire galaxy, though it will take fifty thousand years for that light to finish crossing the Milky Way.

"As they hoped, the two exploding stars had created singularities in hyperspace that attracted each other gravitationally and linked up, passing through the Galactic Center." A mathematical model appeared in the air, connecting the two stars with a hyperspace tunnel—a wormhole.

"But this was only half the battle. Next, they had to harness the hyperspace path they had created. Centuries later—the bovoids were *patient*—when it was relatively quiet, they returned to the places where the stars had been. In place of each star, a pulsar remained, a young, rapidly spinning neutron star. These served as the anchors for the ends of the hyperspace connection."

An artificial ring appeared around one of the pulsars—a ring just like the first one they had encountered in this world.

"The bovoids built a large ring around one of the pulsars, to serve as a base of operations for their work. They built it at a great distance from the neutron star, to protect them from both the terrible tidal gravitational force and the intense radiation of the pulsar, generated by the rapidly spinning magnetic field and the plasma trapped in it.

"With huge electrical conductors, they captured some of the magnetic energy, transforming it into electricity just like a dynamo. With that energy, they began to be able to control the gravitational field near the ring, reducing the local space-time curvature and diminishing the tidal force; they magnetically deflected the energetic particles. Then they built a second ring, closer to the neutron star, where the magnetic field was stronger, and harnessed yet more energy. Then another ring, even closer." Ring after ring appeared inside the first.

"In this way, over thousands of years, they were able to build rings closer and closer to the neutron star, using its own energy to overcome the terrible hazards that threatened them. Thus was born Hecatomb.

"At last, about a thousand years ago, they built a ring orbiting at incredible speed next to the neutron star, almost touching it. That is where the record ends.

"Something they found there made them leave, or possibly it killed them. We have no idea what happened then. This is why I call this world Hecatomb, after the ancient Greek sacrifice of a hundred oxen.

"Helene and I have decided that the only way to solve the mystery is to go to the center of Hecatomb. We will stay on board the train until the end. I wanted her to return to Earth, but she said I would have to shoot her before she would give up this chance to be the first human to reach the innermost ring. We have agreed that, as long as we both live, we will continue. If one of us dies, the other must return.

"We are leaving this record here in case we do not survive." The image faded out and the amphitheater lit up.

The humans sat in silence for minutes, their minds reeling with the images they had seen. Homer started to speak, but Sean gave him the cut-throat sign and he stopped.

Finally, Ariadne spoke. "You realize this means we must go to the innermost ring too."

Sean nodded and said, "Not even I can resist that temptation. But someone will have to go back to the ship, in case we don't make it." Stefan lit up. "No, not you, Stefan. I meant someone I can trust. That leaves only Plum."

"Good God, man," said the Englishman. "You don't think for a moment I'd give up the chance to see what's there? After all we've been through on this bloody Hecatomb?"

Sean shook his head resignedly. "That means we all go."

"Look on the bright side, my Celtic friend," said Plum. "Alexandros had but one person with him, and he almost survived. His interstellar viziphone message proves that. With four humans and two robots, our chances are multiplied."

"If you say so," Sean said without conviction. "But this world must have a few surprises left, and they may be numerous enough to take care of four humans and two robots."

"Perhaps I would be more useful guarding the ship," said Homer.

"No," said Sean, "we may need you as translator. Also, you'll make a recording of our findings. Oh-two, let's go."

They walked slowly out of the amphitheater, each mind replaying the sights it had seen, the sounds it had heard, and the smells.

Ariadne thought of her father's godlike invocation of alien mysteries.

Plum was obsessed with the image of his shrewlike ancestor, dodging dinosaurs.

Stefan uneasily contemplated the men on the crosses.

The doctrobot thought of the possible hazards of the trip, and inventoried its medical supplies.

Homer silently composed a description of the alien images, filled with wild speculation and lurid adjectives.

Sean brooded over what had killed Alexandros and his companion. Whatever it was was powerful enough to have caused the disappearance of millions of extremely intelligent creatures, whose knowledge of the forces of the neutron star was far beyond any human's. The thought did not fill him with optimism.

CHAPTER 19

When the train arrived on its next inbound journey, the explorers were ready. Three of the humans and the two robots jumped on board quickly with their equipment. Stefan hesitated, but was assisted by a push from Sean.

The door slid up and the train took off. They crossed the gap to the fourth ring, still awed by the sights through the transparent vehicle.

The door opened and the alien recording made its eerie announcement. They glimpsed a station very much like the one they had left, clean and empty. A moment later the door shut.

"Must sense when there's anyone near the threshold," said Sean. Plum nodded.

They traveled uneventfully to the fifth ring. The passengers sat back and started to relax. The door slid open and the vehicle filled with loud, erratically changing sounds and blinding colors, drowning out the automatic announcement. Iridescent cusps of light danced among a kaleidoscope of radiant bubbles. Sean drew his gun and the door slammed shut before anyone else could do more than open his mouth.

"Homer," said Sean as they traveled to the next ring, "you recorded the map of the rings, didn't you?"

"Yes," Homer said, taking his arm from around the trembling Stefan.

"Then tell us what that was."

Homer replayed the ring-map directory in his mind. " 'Ring of Celebration' is what it says, according to Alexandros's glossary—whatever that means. Incidentally, that's also what the voice announced."

The vehicle stopped at the sixth ring. Everyone stared with anticipation as the door slid down and the announcement boomed. The station was as bare as any they had seen. The door slid up and they relaxed.

"What's this ring?" said Sean.

"Untranslatable," said Homer, holding Stefan's hand.

"What's the *next* ring?"

"Warehouse."

Sean shrugged.

When the door slid open at the seventh ring, a huge, red robot almost like a locomotive stood staring at them. It was eight meters long and three wide, nearly reached the ceiling, and had dozens of arms of different shapes and sizes jutting out from its sides. A glowing window in the front showed fluid pumping through pipes inside. A large, spherical head on a long, unreeling, articulated tube jutted into the vehicle and traveled from one end of the car to the other, surveying the contents like a pest inspector.

Two powerful metal arms telescoped out of the front of the great robot suddenly, wrapped around Homer, and picked him up.

"Help!" shouted the journobot.

"Oh no!" shouted Stefan. "Anything but him!"

"Must be robot inspection time," said Plum.

Sean drew his gun. The big robot carried Homer, moving as if on invisible wheels, to a conveyor.

Homer screamed, "Rape!"

Sean ran after them, shouting, "Someone stand over the door! Don't let it leave without me!"

The huge robot wrapped Homer in metal bands and placed him on the conveyor while the journobot shouted protests and cited government regulations. Homer moved on the belt toward a black opening in the wall, bouncing violently with his struggles but unable to free himself.

Sean ran over to him and jumped up onto the conveyor.

"Thank God!" shouted Homer. "Journalism is saved!"

The alien robot paused and stuck its head over to the pair.

Sean knelt down next to Homer. The two continued moving toward the black opening, from which grinding and sizzling noises emanated. Sean stuck his quantagun in between Homer and the bonds. The huge robot's head moved closer, inspecting the action.

Sean squeezed the trigger and the wire vaporized.

"Magnificent!" exclaimed Homer. They unwound the wires and jumped off the conveyor just ahead of the blackness.

The alien robot rolled in front of the pair, stuck its head down at Sean and telescoped out four arms, two toward Homer and two toward the Irishman.

Sean aimed his quantagun point-blank at its head and fired.

The head sizzled and jerked out of the way. An alarm arose from the robot and it rolled away with startling speed.

"Superb marksmanship!" shouted Homer.

They ran for the train and jumped in. Plum and Ariadne grabbed them and pulled them farther inside, hugging them and slapping them on the back.

The door closed, Homer hugged Stefan, and the train took off again.

"Dr. Draganescu's daring journobot," said Homer, "was taken by a monstrous super-robot. He was saved from a fate worse than death by his finely programmed instincts, in a daring dash for freedom. He received some assistance from Sean O'Shaughnessy, in the Irishman's first noteworthy act of usefulness."

"Let's all move away from the door," suggested Sean. The others obeyed without hesitation and stood against the far wall.

They entered the eighth ring. Sean said, "Homer, what is this ring?"

"Untranslatable," he replied.

"Wonderful," said Sean, drawing his gun.

The door opened, the announcement boomed, and the four humans held their breath. Nothing was there but a bare room. The door slid closed again.

For the next few dozen rings, there were no major surprises until they found themselves in a roomful of singing rainbow crystals at the eleventh ring: a factory. A great pile of the musical crystals sparkled in the station.

Stefan and Ariadne could not resist the temptation and jumped out while Sean and Plum reluctantly blocked the doors to keep the train from departing. The latter scanned the station, weapons in hand, searching for danger.

The jewellike crystals changed color rhythmically, each with a different beat, while humming in tones that varied with the colors. Stefan and Ariadne scooped up handfuls.

A tall, funnel-shaped machine suddenly entered and approached the humming pile.

"Into the train!" commanded Sean.

Ariadne and Stefan dashed inside.

The funnel was suspended from the ceiling as if on invisible overhead tracks, and it stopped at the edge of the pile.

As the train door closed, rainbow crystals poured forth from the funnel and added to the pile.

The train took off.

"Must be a freight train running through here, too," mused Plum. "One hopes we do not crash into it."

Ariadne held a jewel the size of a walnut in her palm, trying to fathom its use. She watched it change colors hypnotically, while it hummed up and down in pitch. She squeezed it and it brightened, the hum increasing in volume and pitch until it sounded almost like a kitten mewing.

The next few stations passed uneventfully and everyone began to relax.

Then, at the seventy-first ring, labeled *Dormitory*, the door slid open and a red, twelve-legged monster the size of an elephant greeted them. It had one massive head supported by three necks that sprouted from a huge doughnut-shaped body. A stench of decay emanated from it.

It entered the train and the door slid shut.

The crew ran to the far end of the train. The creature stared at the humans and opened its huge jaws, revealing dozens of rows of wicked-looking incisors. It uttered a deep roar, waved twelve claws that sprouted from its doughnut-torso at the end of long tentacles, and ran to the *opposite* end of the train.

It sat there trembling until the next stop, when it ran out as fast as its twelve legs would take it. It was greeted by three little doughnut-shaped monsters, miniatures of the big one. They squealed.

The door slid shut and the humans collapsed onto seats in disbelief.

"How in space would a creature like that get into a dormitory?" said Stefan.

"Probably traveled the same way we did," said Plum. "By train."

"Maybe it was in a stasis field that failed," said Sean. "Could have been an exhibit for the amusement of the guests."

"How would such a creature evolve?" said Stefan. "A doughnut-shaped body?"

"Probably it is aquatic, or at least amphibious," said Ariadne. "Such a shape would give it bistable equilibria. Like some aquatic birds, the bulky body would effortlessly keep its head out of water, to search for enemies, and still it could flip upside down to hunt easily for fish. It might have evolved from something like the Portuguese man-of-war—a colony of cells which form a circular bladder, from which descend long filaments."

"Walking doughnut terrified by fearless explorers," mused Homer.

More rings went by. At each ring, they experienced wrenching deceleration and changing tidal forces, then paused for a few seconds while the door opened. Sean and Plum kept their guns ready to shoot any hostile life-forms.

When they uneventfully passed the hundredth ring, Sean celebrated by refueling himself with a little whiskey, and Plum lit his pipe.

At ring 137, Homer announced, "Swimming River." A green, centimeters-deep lake of smelly, oily fluid sloshed in. They climbed onto the seats until it drained out at the next stop.

At 174, the Music Ring, their ears were assaulted by deep, pounding rhythms and grunts like a humpback whale with a megaphone.

Hours passed. Hundreds more rings came and went. The alien words of the automatic announcements, translated when possible by Homer, engraved a rudimentary vocabulary into the minds of the explorers. Vistas of strange sounds, bizarre smells, and improbable sights flew by until their minds were whirling with an overdose of the alien. The sky, visible between rings, whirled faster and faster, like a merry-go-round out of control.

At 218, the Gravity Modulator Ring, the increasingly powerful, stomach-churning tidal effects stopped.

"This must be where they turned on their space-time curvature-smoothing devices," said Plum.

"It's about time," said Stefan miserably.

At 249, the Ring of Material Processing, a huge, brown, pitted rock almost as big as the car sat near the entrance. An alien recording boomed.

"Asteroid," translated Homer. "Used as raw material for the rings."

The next ring, Inside Our Body, was covered with soft, dripping green objects like hives. Red stalactites hung from the ceiling. A pulsating, wet carpet began at the door, disappearing into a black tunnel. Fluids flowed through tubes inside its translucent surface.

"Our tongue," translated Homer. "Follow the gullet for a tour of the stomach. Turn left for the brain."

Ring 331—untranslatable—was black except for violet ribbons flying through the air like phosphorescent bats.

At 442, another untranslatable ring, they were shocked when the train stopped and they saw *themselves* staring back. Their alter egos floated in air, but each was younger: Ariadne was a little girl in a party toga, laughing. Sean was in his twenties, in rough spacer's clothes, drunk, singing, "Kiss me again, Mollie!" Plum was thinner and wore a suit and tie, saying, "I could not *possibly* agree to such a plan." Stefan was clean-shaven, wore pajamas, and was amorously kissing someone invisible.

As they watched, they got younger, their bodies shrinking continuously, limbs flailing, clothes flashing stroboscopically. Ariadne became an infant and disappeared. The men became little boys.

The door closed and they took off.

"What the hell was that?" said Sean.

"Our world-lines, one suspects," said Plum.

"Of course!" exclaimed Sean.

"As in relativity?" said Ariadne.

"Yes, quite," said Plum. "Each of us is a strand in many dimensions. In particular, we each have the three familiar dimensions plus time. Einstein, as usual, understood this first. He realized that any object has a length in the fourth dimension given by its life span, a length measured by multiplying its duration by the fundamental velocity of the universe—the speed of light. An atom that formed a billion years ago from an electron and a proton might live another billion years before being torn into its original components, so it would be a strand two billion light-years in length, along the fourth dimension."

"But the atom is made up of the electron and proton. Don't they have strands, too?"

"You are quite right. The atom's strand is itself made of other strands. The individual electron and proton might have started at the beginning of time and run until its end, but the atom as a whole exists only as a twisted strand of the pair for two billion years, so we say the atom has a world-line two billion light-years long. If I may be so bold, how old are you, my dear?"

"Twenty-six."

"Then, your strand—the fourth dimension of your world-line—extends back in space-time for twenty-six light-years."

"I think I see."

"How far forward your personal strand extends, no one of course knows. It depends upon your life span. One sincerely hopes yours is lengthy."

"I doubt it very much," said Sean dryly.

"Evidently," said Plum, "the bovoids somehow found a way to view one's past world-line as we use a mirror. Frightfully clever."

Ariadne smiled. "I have this vision of herds of bovoids coming to that ring just to look fondly at their past. We should call it the Ring of Nostalgia."

Finally, just before ring 512, Homer announced, "Terminal Ring next."

"That has an ominous sound," said Plum.

In silence they watched the last ring approach. By now, they were orbiting so fast around the neutron star that the sky was nothing but circular streaks. They were near the speed of light. The space between the last two rings glowed blue as if some kind of energy filled it.

The ring spun by rapidly until they matched velocities. It had a different character from any of the others. Giant pipes wound around the outside of the ring, conduits two hundred meters in diameter.

Their vehicle mated with the ring and promptly stopped. The alien recording boomed its announcement as the door slid into the floor. Earsplitting neutron-star thunder reverberated through the hall and the very floor and walls shook in time with it.

"We must be walking on the damn neutron star," said Stefan, trembling.

"We're orbiting just above it," said Sean, none too confidently, as the floor vibrated along with another burst of thunder.

"But what could possibly cause thunder?" said Ariadne, stepping tentatively out of the car. "Surely it is not rain."

"Pulsars occasionally have neutron-star-quakes we can detect from Earth," said Sean. "They cause glitches in their radio signals. It wouldn't surprise me if they have more frequent microquakes, disturbing their fantastic magnetic fields."

"Which would generate intense electric fields," elaborated Plum, "which could cause electrical discharges in the plasma near the star. In a word, lightning."

"And when they hit the ring," said Sean, "thunder." As if to confirm his point, a boom sounded and the floor danced a millimeter.

They gingerly set foot into the station. This room was different from the other stations. A broad conveyor-tunnel started at the train door and disappeared in the red glow of the lightning.

Ariadne jumped onto the conveyor and it gently carried her into the tunnel. She maintained her balance with some difficulty, despite the occasional shaking. The erratic bursts of thunder echoed down the tunnel, which brightened in time with the noise.

Sean held his gun before him and stepped cautiously onto the conveyor. He kept his balance awkwardly. "Follow us at ten-meter intervals," he called back. "Stefan next!"

Plum gently assisted the reluctant Stefan onto the conveyor and then followed ten meters behind. Stefan fell down and Plum simply sat down and let it carry him along. Then the doctrobot and Homer joined the rest.

With difficulty, Sean advanced to Ariadne's side. "I wish we knew where this is taking us."

"We'll find out soon enough." Ariadne's eyes were alight with excitement.

As they traveled, the thunder grew painfully louder, accompanied by brighter flashes of light. Before long, they entered an enormous room filled with massive machinery, gloomy in the red light. Incredible noise roared through the cavernous hall and the floor shuddered. Massive conduits crisscrossed over their heads like highways in the sky. Sean glanced at the floor and exclaimed, "Look down there!"

The floor was transparent. The naked surface of the neutron star stared at them two meters below, visible in its nightmarishly rapid motion by the stroboscopic action of the window that was the floor.

The surface of the star looked metallic, silvery, with jagged cracks everywhere, illuminated by the neon-sign glow of the plasma that filled the gap between the ring and the star, through which immense currents flowed, generated by the spinning magnetic field. Quakes too small to see flicked that magnetic field—a billionfold stronger than Earth's—and sparked bursts of lightning that might have vaporized a city. Inconceivably hot magnetized plasma splattered against the ring beneath their feet. Even through protective insulation, the floor shook and the room was filled with searing light and horrendous thunder. The neutron star, unbelievably dense, a mere twenty-two kilometers in diameter, spun below, unleashing terrifying electromagnetic and gravitational forces demanding a vastly superhuman science to protect them from annihilation.

So overwhelmed were they by the sights and sounds that they almost drifted past a large sign in English: STOP! DANGER! GO NO FARTHER!

Sean tugged Ariadne to the side and they jumped off. While he made sure the rest of the party disembarked, she looked around, walking on the transparent floor gingerly, as if she expected to fall onto the star at each step.

She yelled. Sean left Stefan to gather the others and ran with his gun behind the large machine from which her voice had come. He stopped when he saw her standing unharmed in front of an assortment of small pieces of equipment, next to a transparent wall showing the stars in the sky whirling by. As he looked at the area, recognition dawned. "This is where your father broadcast from!" he whispered.

"Yes," she said, trembling. "This is where he died, or somewhere nearby. His . . . body . . . must be here. Somewhere. If it hasn't been carried off by robots."

Or vermin, thought Sean, but he held his tongue.

He studied the machines further, looking for signs of Alexandros's last moments, and found a viewcrystal taped inside a black circle.

Ariadne loaded the crystal with quaking fingers and hit the PLAYBACK key. Alexandros's pale, haunting face stared out from the device. Blood covered one shoulder, but below that was off-screen.

The others crowded around Ariadne, to hear Alexandros say gravely, strain audible in every syllable, "Helene and I were attacked by thousands of large insectoid creatures with vicious claws, on the two hundredth and twelfth ring." Tinny recorded thunder counterpointed eerily the real-time thunder. "We killed many of them, but not before they had killed Helene and torn my arm off.

"I buried her in the next ring, and sent a message over the alien communication system ordering an antivermin robot squad to clean up the ring that killed her, for the benefit of future travelers.

"This ring is the entrance to a giant portal of a type I have never seen elsewhere in Hecatomb. I found instructions telling the passengers on the conveyor to stay on it until they enter this portal, but it is not clear what its purpose was.

"I have studied all the information I could find here, mostly technical viewmanuals like those in a laboratory on Earth. Their science is much too advanced for me to understand, but it seems that this whole ring was built as a way to use the energy and the distortions of space-time of the neutron star to somehow connect with the tunnel in space-time from this pulsar to the Galactic Center. But there are many things I do not understand.

"Apparently, the bovoids traveled into the portal, but where they went is unclear. It seems suicidal, but they apparently thought they could enter the hyperspace tunnel here.

"I am dying. The bites from the insectoids have infected me

with alien bacteria. Before they die from eating my blood cells, I will surely be dead myself. Our doctrobot disintegrated in a room of energy beams many rings ago."

Alexandros's image coughed harshly several times, then resumed speaking. "I am certain I would lose consciousness before I could get back to our ship. I have sent a message to Earth; now there is obviously only one thing left for me to do: I must follow the footsteps of the bovoids through this portal.

"In all likelihood, I will die there. But at least I will die seeing whatever it was they saw in their last moments. That knowledge is worth the price.

"Strangely, I do not regret coming here. The curiosity that has always driven me has made me grateful for this chance to see what no other man has ever seen. That is all I ever wanted from life. I have no regrets, but for the separation from my wife and daughter."

Tears came to Ariadne's eyes.

"So now I will take the conveyor through the portal. If it is possible, I will return immediately, and leave a message on this viewcrystal with my findings. If there is no such message following this one, then do not ever follow me."

The message ended. They waited several minutes for a second message. There was none.

At last, Ariadne broke the silence. "Through the portal is where I must go."

Sean angrily grabbed her arm. "Are you even more insane than I thought? Your father himself died there. Can't those warped hemispheres of yours understand? If he'd survived, there would've been a message. There wasn't. Therefore it is *not survivable*. Q.E.D."

Ariadne looked determinedly into his eyes. "My curiosity is no less than his. Perhaps he survived, but was unable to return. No one guaranteed me a round-trip ticket. Besides, you have all the artifacts you could hope for. Just take them back and you're a rich man. What do you care what happens to me?"

"I don't know why, but I care, damn it! It's stupid, I know, but I hate to see a young, semi-intelligent person throw away her life on a whim."

"A *whim?*"

"Yes, a whim. And I feel some responsibility for you, because your father was one of the finest men I've ever known."

"That's all?"

"Damn it, woman, perhaps if I were to scrape the bottom of

my brainpan, I might find a microgram of irrational affection for you there, though I'd have to wallow through a hell of a lot of irritation, anger, and bitter memories. You're not totally unattractive, and more important, you've got a spirit I respect, though I wish to Schrödinger it was coupled with some common sense.''

"You certainly know how to flatter a woman."

Sean took her other arm and looked down into her eyes. "Ariadne, you are possibly the most . . . *interesting* woman I've ever known. I've even thought that it might be possible sometime to . . . for us to become friends.''

"I consider you to be a friend," she said stiffly, "even if I have occasionally had doubts. I had hoped you would grant me the same favor."

"Oh, I do. But I hoped we might become . . . more than just friends.''

"Drinking companions?" she said with distaste.

"That too."

She held him closer and looked into his eyes. "I must confess that I have occasionally found myself drawn to this vulgar Irishman against my will. Had things turned out differently, I might have dared hope we could be more than just friends, too." She stood on her toes and kissed him somberly on the lips, and he returned the favor, at first hesitantly, then with increasing enthusiasm.

Stefan observed the scene with resentment, Plum with amusement, and Homer with the detachment of a journalist calculating the lurid possibilities.

After a prolonged period, during which Ariadne and Sean communicated solely through body language, she broke off her kiss and said with a flushed face, "Sean, I truly wish it were otherwise, but—can't you see?—I must go through the portal."

He held her possessively and said, "No, I damn well cannot see why you have to throw away your life, and I'm not going to let you. You're not going there even if I have to break both your legs and tie you up in a bundle to prevent it!"

"I thought you said you believed in the right of everyone to do whatever stupid things they chose, even suicide. Or was that a lot of moon dust?''

He glared at her for a while, battling with conflicting principles, then angrily said, "Very well, if that's what you choose, so be it! But I'm coming along, so help me, Einstein!"

"Don't be foolish! What purpose would you serve by endangering your life, too?"

"If there is anything on the other side, I might be able to save your neck."

"I don't want you coming with me," she said. "You're right. It probably is suicide. I don't want your death on my conscience."

"I was just thinking about something," said Sean, an unfamiliar hollow tone in his voice. "If it hadn't been for a microscopic twist of fate, I would have been one of your father's crew members. I would have died here twenty years ago. I gained twenty years of life by that. If the universe was kind enough to give me twenty extra years of life, maybe I can do something in return. I just can't let Alexandros's daughter go in there alone."

"You mean you can't bear the thought that you'd be known throughout the planets as the spacer who let a girl go where he was afraid to."

He blushed. "Perhaps, Ariadne, there is a bit of that in my head, too. Maybe you are a pure Greek goddess and your mind is untrammeled by the devious currents that flow through the brains of us wretched mortals. But maybe—just *maybe*, mind you—you too have your sly little reasons for doing this. We have a saying in Ireland: 'If the best man's faults were written on his forehead, he'd have to pull his hat down over his eyes.' Maybe, deep inside that thick skull of yours, you're nothing but a little girl running to Daddy to kiss away all her tears and make everything well.

"Or maybe you're searching for God—not the plastic god of that con-person, the great Benedictor Simon, but the real McCoy. In fact, I'm beginning to think your daddy's the real god you worship, even if you've deceived yourself into thinking Simon's a useful imitation of the real thing. Have you noticed how, ever since we arrived on this godforsaken world, you've hardly mentioned Simon and his fanciful teachings?"

It was her turn to blush. "I am quite sure you are a great judge of character. You have told me that so often I cannot possibly doubt it. But we have a saying in Greece: ' "I am a great judge of salad," said the man as he ate the hemlock.' "

"I'm afraid it's the woman who's eating the hemlock today!" She glared at him.

"Well, by God or by Heisenberg," said Sean, squeezing her arms until they hurt, "I'm going into that goddamn portal if you are! But it's not too late to change your mind."

She tore away from his embrace and shouted, "I'm going in, and I don't give one speck of moon dust whether you come with me or not!"

Plum came over and stood between the two of them. "Lady

and gentleman," he said, "if you will forgive a person for interfering where he's not been invited, I say I think your proposal is exceptionally foolhardy."

"I have no argument with you, Plum," said Sean.

"Really," continued the Englishman, "I think we should all sit down to a good, hearty meal and then sleep on it. A decision as momentous as this should not be made hastily."

"He's right, you know," said Sean.

Ariadne shook her head and said, "Plum, you're a dear man, and I appreciate your concern, but I'm going through that portal whether it is today or next year, so it might as well be now."

"So be it," Sean said unhappily.

Plum shook his head with resignation and looked at his friend. "Would you like me to come, too?"

"Einstein forbid!" said Sean. "Just because two of us are bullheaded mules doesn't mean you're obliged to be just as stupid. Someone has to stay here and nursemaid the great deputy minister back to Earth and see that our debts get paid off. Under no circumstances would I permit you to join us on our merry little jaunt."

"I honestly can't say I was looking forward to it," said Plum. "I think the two of you are pigheaded and harebrained, and if I could shoot some sense into you with my quantagun, I'd do it."

Sean patted his friend on the back. "I'm sure you would." Turning to Stefan, he said jocularly, "How about you? Want to join the picnic?"

Stefan shook his head rapidly and backed up.

Sean, Plum, and Ariadne checked their pressure suits and equipment, and repaired the damaged parts as best they could.

They walked to the conveyor with all the enthusiasm of the condemned marching to Death Row.

At the edge of the conveyor, they said their good-byes. Homer, arm in arm with Stefan, observed, "The two intrepid explorers prepared to embark on a mission of certain death. Dr. Stefan Draganescu, his heart aching to go with them but burdened with the responsibilities of command, watched them go with profound sadness. The expedition's crack reporter, the journobot called Homer, regretted too that government regulations forbade his joining the two explorers on their suicide mission."

Plum and Sean shook hands. Sean said, "May Heisenberg send the devil to the wrong planet when he comes looking for you."

"You're the best friend I ever had," said Plum, his voice

trembling, "and if I could stop you by cutting off an arm or two of mine, I should do it without hesitation. But I know it would be of no use, so I shall just wish you the best of luck and hope we meet again somewhere in space-time."

Sean and Ariadne stepped onto the conveyor.

The star beneath their feet flashed and roared.

CHAPTER 20

The conveyor carried Ariadne and Sean toward a great violet arch at the end of the hall. Nothing but blackness was visible through the arch, and the conveyor seemed to end there.

The vast chamber lit up with lightning flashes and booming neutron-star thunder resounded, making the tiny humans feel even more insignificant.

As they approached the arch, an alien recording boomed down at them. "Damn," said Sean, "I wish Homer were here."

"I thought you hated him."

"I do, although he does grow on you—like athlete's foot. But he could have translated for us just now."

"They were probably saying, 'Secure you seat harness.' "

"Or maybe, 'No oxygen beyond this point.' In fact, we'd better helmet up, just in case."

They detached the helmets from their belts and put them on. Sean checked Ariadne's seal, then she examined the repair in his suit's arm where the doctrobot had tended him. He cursed the pains in his cut, burnt, and bruised body.

"Sean," she said tenderly over the radio, "despite what you may think, I really do appreciate what you are doing." She touched his gloved hand with hers.

"What about Stefan? I thought that dust-sucker was more your type."

The room flared and reverberated to a crash of thunder.

"That *mangas?* I must admit I was attracted to him for a while, just as I regarded you as a brute barely out of the caves. But seeing the two of you beyond the protective embrace of civilization has quite changed my attitudes. I would rather leave him to the affections of his robot."

"It's just my luck to learn I'm appreciated by a beautiful woman just as I'm about to get myself vaporized."

"Beautiful?" Ariadne said softly. "I thought I was only 'interesting' and 'not totally unattractive.' "

"It varies from moment to moment. Right now, you look positively angelic behind that faceplate."

She smiled and put her hand around his waist.

"O'Shaughnessy," he muttered to himself, shaking his head wearily, "I always told you women would be the death of you."

The conveyor stopped at the foot of the great arch of braided violet cables, wound together in a bundle two meters thick and reaching thirty meters overhead, framing a massive black slab upon which were inscribed incomprehensible alien words.

Slowly, the black slab slid into the floor, revealing a vehicle with hundreds of rows of seats, much like those in the train, but so much larger that they had the feeling of being in an amphitheater.

They timidly walked down an aisle. Sean held a gun in his right hand and Ariadne's hand in his left.

The alien voice boomed again and the door slid back up.

The room seemed to tilt and a queasiness struck them. They threw themselves into the nearest seats, trembling arms about one another. The room and seats turned completely transparent. The neutron star was visible below them, crackling and bursting with electromagnetic storms, but strangely elongated, as if viewed through a distorting lens. Even the sounds were subtly different. Bursts of thunder came more slowly and at a lower frequency, and the flashes became redder and redder, until they all disappeared as the star stretched endlessly into space.

"We're in some kind of spacecraft," said Sean. "It feels like we just entered hyperspace—next to a neutron star! It's suicide!"

As they watched the star through the transparent floor, the vessel seemed to glide along its surface, which became a huge cylinder with helical grooves in it, twisting ahead to infinity.

Sean recognized the pattern. "The helix—that's the lightning on the spinning star."

Ariadne raised her eyes and gasped. They were surrounded by hundreds of helical springs, weirdly elongated versions of the rings of Hecatomb, each stretching to infinity, intertwined in an impossibly complex pattern.

At breathtaking speed, they raced along the pulsar helix, moving faster yet feeling no acceleration, threading an intricate path through the forest of ring-helices.

The encircling helices diminished in number until finally they left the last one and continued to accelerate. The stars were rainbow-colored cobwebs in the sky, the world-line of each sun drawing a thread through space. The cobwebs gradually stretched and changed hues. One part of the web, directly ahead, was much brighter and thicker than the rest, and it slowly grew larger as they traveled the pulsar helix.

"Great God in heaven," said Sean. "It looks like we're heading for the Galactic Center."

"I thought that was impossible."

"For humans, yes."

He checked his suit spectrometer, found the air breathable, and removed his helmet. She did likewise and they sat there, his stubble pressed against her silky cheek, holding each other tightly as the surreal cosmos flowed all around them.

The center of the web grew ever closer until it filled the sky in front, erupting into a blaze of millions of lines of different colors and thicknesses, each one from a different star.

A red line approached and whizzed by, giving them the momentary glimpse of a red giant's space-time image in the unknown dimensions they were flying through.

More and more of the lines flew by until they were immersed in the intensely glowing web. They sped along the pulsar helix, through the cosmic threads, shooting inexorably to the very center of the web.

The rainbow-cobweb sky grew thicker and thicker, and became almost blindingly bright. They soared between star-threads so rapidly that collision seemed impossible to avoid.

Ariadne gripped Sean's hand with both of hers.

A dark line appeared forward, outlined against the glowing web. It rapidly grew larger until they could see that it too glowed, but faintly. They were headed straight into it.

The dark, radiant line grew into a broad cylinder and still they moved on a collision course.

The queasy feeling returned and the cylinder collapsed into a dark ellipsoid; the dazzling star-spiderweb became billions of tiny dots in the sky, like a Milky Way brightened a thousandfold and spread across the entire sky. The pulsar helix had disappeared.

"We're back in normal space," whispered Sean. *"Inside the Galactic Center!"*

As they got closer, the vessel deviated from a radial course, though still moving toward the ellipsoid. Features appeared on the ellipsoid's surface—a crazy quilt of irregularly shaped sections, each in a different color, like a map of another civilization. Some of the colors pulsed, others changed slowly as they watched; some glowed steadily. The spacecraft headed toward a black triangular patch, the only colorless area visible.

The patch grew until it filled the forward half of the sky,

blotting out everything else. Blue lights appeared, scattered over the darkness in clusters and lines.

As their eyes adjusted to the dimmer light, the black became dark gray.

A triangle of blue lights, with a fourth in the center, appeared directly ahead and grew swiftly larger. They headed toward the central light until a gentle bump told them they had landed.

Their vessel lay flat on the ground. Through the transparent floor of the spacecraft they could see a dark gray mat that seemed to spread everywhere, featureless but for crisscrossing metallic fibers throughout.

The rear end of the spacecraft opened up and air hissed in. Sean and Ariadne rose and turned around. Sean grabbed his helmet but found the air breathable. It smelled of clover. He reattached the helmet to his waist.

A blue light glowed in the distance. Nothing else was visible except for billions of stars in the brilliant, crowded sky, and the endless gray metallic desert.

Cautiously, they walked down the aisle to the exit. The gravity was less than it had been on Hecatomb.

They stepped out onto a springy surface, a mat that depressed slightly under their boots. They stared at the sky and saw more stars in one glance than any human astronomer had ever seen with his naked eyes in his entire life: the stars of the Galactic Center.

Stars of every color covered the sky; there were rivers of stars in the sky, and lakes, and oceans. There were clusters too, some arrayed as regularly as petals on a snowflake.

Ariadne whispered, "I have never in my life seen such beauty!"

Sean was speechless.

"If I die now," whispered Ariadne, "my life will have been worthwhile." She looked shyly up at him. "I am so happy I can share this moment with you, Sean."

He looked down at her, smiled softly, and kissed her.

After a while, they walked toward the blue light.

A figure was silhouetted against it, walking slowly toward them. Its costume glowed, changing color as it walked, from red to yellow to green to violet and back again. As they approached, it looked increasingly humanoid.

Ariadne screamed, "*Patera mou!*" and ran toward it.

It was Alexandros Zepos.

CHAPTER 21

When he heard his daughter's words, Alexandros too broke into a run.

They embraced. He lifted his daughter into the air and swung her around. They laughed and cried with joy, and kissed each other tenderly.

Sean watched the two chatter in Greek, tears streaming down their faces, bathed in the light of a billion stars.

Alexandros's hair was as silvery as it had been twenty years before, but he looked younger, and there were no signs of injuries. He had both of his arms—and he used them to lift Ariadne as if she were a child. His garment, a tunic that covered him from his neck to his feet, changed colors in complex patterns. When he turned to face Sean, his eyes radiated profound wisdom.

Alexandros stretched out his hands and said in English, "Welcome, Sean." They shook hands solemnly and stared at each other in silence. Ariadne clung to her father blissfully.

Eventually, Sean spoke. "Alexandros, how is it that you're the first person we meet? You knew we were coming?"

"I was informed as soon as the portal was entered—the pulsar portal. It is automatically monitored, and we have faster-than-light signals."

"*We?*"

"My civilized friends."

"Where are we?"

"This is the center of the galaxy," said Alexandros, waving at the sky, "where true civilization exists."

Sean nodded. "What kind of place is this?"

"This is what you would call the capital of the galaxy, to the extent that such a terrestrial concept has meaning. It is an artificial world, built from an old star, on a scale you could scarcely grasp; this one world is large enough to encompass the entire solar system."

Sean's eyes opened wide. Ariadne just blissfully hugged her father, eyes closed.

Alexandros said, "When I first arrived, I could not believe the size and complexity of this civilization. I will never forget the first time I visited one of their museums. It had two hundred planets in it. Not models—real planets."

"Why haven't they visited us? Why haven't they helped us?"

"That is difficult to answer. No human language even has the words to discuss many of the concepts of their principal language. Even after studying it for twenty years, I can only understand the most rudimentary ideas.

"You see, these creatures are as far beyond us as we are beyond the ants. They live on the billions of worlds of the Galactic Center, and their idea of a pleasant journey is a visit to another galaxy. Outside the Center lies wilderness, which they let lie in its natural state. Humanity is the victim of what I call the galactic conservation program. The aliens regard the outskirts of the galaxy, such as where humans live, as a place either to avoid or to picnic in, nothing more. And they would no more invite humans to the Galactic Center than we would invite ants to a picnic."

"Ants?" said Sean. "I'm a hell of a way beyond an ant!"

Alexandros smiled. "That is what I thought when I arrived. I could not have been further from the truth."

"Then why do they let an ant like you live here?"

Alexandros's smile broadened. "Because, you see, I am one of the exhibits in their zoo."

"No!" exclaimed Ariadne.

"I am sorry, my little pirate," said Alexandros, "but that is the only condition under which I am permitted to live here."

Sean touched his gun and looked around suspiciously.

Alexandros shook his head and said, "You need not worry about their capturing you, as long as you are with me. I am your. . . guide. You will not be held against your wishes."

"But you're allowed to walk free?" said Sean.

"In a manner of speaking, yes. This garment is actually a sort of leash. It identifies me to truly intelligent beings as a tame animal from the zoo. If I were to try to hurt someone, or to damage anything, it would freeze me until a zookeeper could pick me up."

"That's disgusting!" said Sean. "That's slavery! No man should have to put up with such a thing!"

"No, Sean," said Alexandros. "Do not judge them too quickly.

I am here voluntarily. I could return to Earth anytime I wanted. I am held here by nothing but my curiosity, and by my hope that I can learn something of value to the human race. I am studying them even as they study me.''

For the first time, an emotion other than bliss crossed Ariadne's face. ''You mean you could have gone home?'' she said disbelievingly.

He nodded.

''For twenty years?'' said Sean. ''For twenty years, you've let them hold you here without returning to your daughter, your *wife?*''

Sadness crossed Alexandros's face. ''It has been difficult. Twenty years ago, I had to choose between my family and this place. As a husband, I had been a failure.''

''Never!'' protested Ariadne.

''Yes, a failure. My marriage was coming apart because of my wanderlust. I only saw you, sweet Ariadne, when I was between expeditions. Your mother swore she would divorce me if I went away once more.''

''She never told me.''

He nodded. ''I had made a mess of my life on Earth. I knew you would both be better off without me—Ariadne shook her head vigorously—''and I felt if I could just learn a little here, I might be able to accelerate humanity's progress away from the barbarous, evil state we are in, and toward civilization. That would benefit you and your mother more than anything else I could ever do.''

''How?'' said Sean. ''What good is it if you can't communicate with us?''

''Oh, but I would have come home eventually. In fact, I did try to go back once, after my first year here.''

''So they didn't let you go after all,'' said Sean suspiciously.

''Quite the contrary. But you see, I had already begun to have my mind rebuilt.''

''*Rebuilt?*'' said Sean with distaste. Ariadne looked at her father's hand with growing fear.

''Yes—at *my* request. I had found that my mind was too slow, and my memory too imperfect, and my grasp of their concepts painfully inadequate. But their understanding of the minds of animals is as profound as your understanding of computers. I had them go through my brain—rewire it, if you will.''

There was a hint of distaste on Ariadne's face, too.

Alexandros smiled. ''I know it sounds terrible, but it was

wonderful. They fixed synapses that had once contacted each other but which age had disconnected. They repaired mistakes of nature, the bad interconnections between the different parts of the brain. I never had much of an ear for music. They fixed some bad connections in my mind and now I have perfect pitch, and more important, I can *enjoy* music deeply, which I never could before.

''They improved the connections to the memory which cause most people to forget almost everything they experience. Now I can remember every fact I was ever exposed to and relive any moment of my life, whenever I choose.

''They speeded up my responses and removed the constant *noise* of irrelevant thoughts that goes on inside us, but which we are rarely conscious of. My brain became *clear!* It was as if a fog were lifting from within my head. For the first time in my life—for the first time in *any* human's life—I began to truly *think*.

''And they added some *new* sections, areas which the human mind has not yet had time to evolve.'' He touched his head softly, while continuing to embrace Ariadne with the other arm.

''They gave me senses that you don't even have *words* for. The ability to 'see' mathematical relationships the way you see patterns of flower petals. The ability to *enjoy* a whole personality as if it were a concert.'' He looked down at Ariadne's face lovingly.

''And many other senses. The ability to *see* beyond the conventional three dimensions to which the human mind is confined.''

''You can see *hyperspace?*'' said Sean.

''Yes, partly. I can only see into a few dimensions just yet.''

''Including *time?*''

''Yes, but only backward. I cannot see the future—yet. That is a more difficult skill. *They* can, though, at least to some degree.''

''I don't believe you,'' said Sean.

Alexandros smiled and looked at him, or more accurately, *through* him. ''I see you embraced Ariadne in a *very* friendly fashion just before you passed through the portal.''

Sean's mouth dropped open and his face reddened. Ariadne blushed. ''Anyone could have guessed that,'' he snapped.

''You left two men and a robot there. A plump man and one with a beard.''

He continued to look through Sean. His eyes darted around as if watching a video. ''It still bothers me a little,'' he muttered, ''following a creature's world-line this way, watching everything happen like a video run backward.'' He nodded several times, muttering ''good,'' and winced occasionally. Once he smiled and said, ''I see you met the doughnut creature.''

Moments later, tears came to his eyes. *''Jomo!''* he exclaimed. ''He was such a good man. I always hoped one day to return and release him from the stasis field and invite him to join me.'' He shook his head sadly.

''I believe you now,'' said Sean softly.

Alexandros's eyes returned to the real world and looked at Sean. Gravely, he wiped the tears with a corner of his tunic, and said, ''I thank you for saving my daughter from that vile man in the museum.''

They stood in silence awhile. Then Sean said, ''So why didn't you go home after that first year?''

Alexandros smiled and said, ''The zoo has strict rules about interfering with the wildlife of the galaxy. They sometimes heal injured animals and return them, but they do not permit artificially *improved* animals to return, if it might drastically upset the natural order of things.''

''So you're in a prison after all,'' said Sean, scowling.

''Not at all. I simply had to have the added sections of my mind removed.''

Sean grimaced and Ariadne looked at her father quizzically.

''I told them to do it. It's quite painless. They operate through hyperspace, no surgery. They just reach in through another dimension and pluck out their microscopic devices. At least, there was no *physical* pain.'' His eyes became distant as he reminisced.

''I don't know if I can describe what it was like in any way that you could understand. To have my new senses removed, one by one . . . to watch the universe diminish, step by step.

''Try to imagine what it would be like, to have your intelligence turned down like the volume of a video. You descend, from the level of a man to that of a chimpanzee, to a dog. You can remember being able to think, you see things you know you once understood. You look at a book and know you once could read those markings but now they are gibberish.

''And imagine that, at the same time, your hearing is shut off. Then your sense of touch. Then, smell. Taste. Color vision. Then your ability to see moving objects. Then your last bit of vision.'' He shuddered.

''It was inexpressibly horrible. And when it was done, I asked myself, what could I do now? If I returned to Earth, I would still be the person who made life so miserable for my wife, who was going to divorce me anyway. I would be no better a father for little Ariadne than a billion other men whom your mother could find easily."

"No!" she protested.

"All I wanted to do was to go there briefly and return to the Galactic Center as soon as possible. I would just cause Ariadne and Katerina new pain."

"You could have brought us with you!" said Ariadne.

"Your mother would never have come. She refused even to go to the moon. And what kind of a place is this for a girl, with no other human companionship than your parents? Raised in a zoo?"

"Anything would have been better than being without you!"

"But the government might have prevented me from coming back, so they could extract all of my knowledge. And finally I realized I could do far more for Earth right here, by learning as much as possible about this civilization, so that one day I might somehow send some of that knowledge back home."

Alexandros sighed. "No, in the end, I could not go back. Perhaps it was really cowardice. I don't know. But I stayed here and had them reassemble my mind. And ever since then, I have lived blissfully, acquiring knowledge beyond the most extravagant dreams of humanity, like a miser hoarding gold." He smiled dreamily. "It has been a scholar's heaven."

"But living in a zoo!" said Sean.

"It is a nice zoo," Alexandros said with a smile. "In fact, it was a veterinarian who healed my wounds when I arrived. They take good care of us. I may live thousands of years—it gives you a different perspective on time. We animals *love* this zoo."

"It must be horribly humiliating!" said Sean.

"Humbling, not humiliating," said Alexandros. "It is not so different from the promises of heaven in Earth's religions: A vastly superior being watches over you constantly. Billions of people have always found that concept attractive." Sean glanced at Ariadne, who blushed.

"Every facet of this place," said Alexandros, "is endlessly intriguing, enigmatic, fascinating. Each bit of information I learn is a tiny piece in the vast puzzle of this culture. But sometimes I feel like an ant crawling across a page of Hamlet, unable to comprehend the ink I walk on."

"What about us?" said Sean. "Are they really going to allow us to go back?"

"Certainly," said Alexandros. "These are civilized creatures."

"But suppose we told everybody about this place? A hell of a lot of them would want to come here, zoo or no zoo."

"That would be forbidden," Alexandros said gravely. "An ant or two in a jar is one thing. Millions would be bothersome. They would close the portal."

"We could make another one!"

"Could you? The Galactic Center is surrounded by a screen to keep wild animals and vermin out. The Tu-kii-vno who built the portal were clever. Slow to learn, but clever enough to devise a way through the screen after working on it for millions of years. The screen serves another purpose, you see. Not only does it keep out the undesirables, it keeps out the stupid. Only creatures intelligent enough to invent a way through the screen are considered for admission to galactic civilization."

"The portal is an IQ test?" said Ariadne.

"Yes," said Alexandros, "but one that tests the IQ of civilizations, not individuals."

"The bovoids passed the test," said Sean.

"They passed the *first* part of the test," said Alexandros. "But that is the *easy* part. The hard part is to show that your culture is mature, that it has left the infantile behavior of primitives behind. The Tu-kii-vno did not war on each other and they respected other peaceful, intelligent species, no matter how repulsive their appearance. Humans, I fear, are millions of years from this stage, unless we can speed up the process with what I have learned."

"What would have happened if they'd failed the test?" said Sean.

"They would have been sent back and their portal made inoperable."

"But suppose they built another?"

"Their ejection would have simply been repeated as often as necessary, until their culture had become sufficiently civilized, or until they made such a nuisance of themselves as to require that their entire civilization be frozen in stasis forever. That has been done to other cultures, and it may yet be done to ours."

"What did they do with the bovoids?" said Ariadne.

"They are now happily grazing in the shine of a billion stars, only a few hundred light-years from here. Would you like to meet them? There is a herd of them here visiting the zoo."

"Oh, yes!" exclaimed Ariadne gleefully.

"What are they going to do to us?" said Sean.

"You are invited to join the zoo, if you wish," said Alexandros. "Otherwise, you will have to return."

"I'm not going to live in any zoo, alien or otherwise!" said Sean, looking at Ariadne.

"I am staying," she said to her father. "I just want to live with you. I don't care where it is. Now that I've found you, I'm never going to leave."

Alexandros shook his head slowly. "No, my little Ariadne, much as I would dearly love your company, a zoo is no place for a young woman to live."

"I'm not going! I have as much right to live here as you!"

"Come back in ten years," said Alexandros. "After you have lived more of life. Then, perhaps, you may have the wisdom to decide whether you wish to stay here. I will still be here."

"No! In ten years, I could be dead! I might not be able to get a starship to come here! I'm not leaving you!"

Alexandros sighed. "Please, Ariadne, listen to me carefully. This is not the place for you—yet. It would be unhealthy for your mind. You are not ready. I am not even certain that *I* am ready, even after twenty years. Can't you see what it would be like? Imagine that you were living in Einstein's ant farm. You could not even speak his language, though he might be smart enough to understand some of your feeble attempts to imitate his sounds. Imagine asking him what he writes on pieces of paper, what does $E = mc^2$ mean, what is the meaning of life? Being brilliant, he could translate some of these concepts into faint echoes of the truth in tiny ant-thoughts. But the strain of living in a culture so alien that the ants seem human by comparison just cannot be imagined."

"Then surely I can stay for just a while."

"Only for a day. An Earth day. This place is seductive. If you were to stay here much longer, you would ask a thousand questions immediately, and each of those would suggest a thousand more. Days would turn into years. I know. It happened to me."

"But you need human companionship!"

"Don't you think I crave the company of human beings?" said Alexandros. "My principal friends now are other animals in the zoo. My best friend is a lizard who consistently beats me at chess. Now, as good a friend as he is—and I have never met a nicer lizard"—he smiled—"it still has been twenty years since I spoke with someone who knew what a rose was, or who had ever played football, or who knew what it was like to swim on a warm day in the Aegean Sea. Until today."

"I can't leave you, *Patera*. I love you too much."

"The father you loved died twenty years ago. Today, I am more alien than human. My left arm was eaten off by the insectoids that killed Helene. The veterinarian replaced it with an artificial copy, much better and stronger than the old one." He looked at his left hand as if it were a stranger.

"Even my heart is not human. The one I was born with was breaking down, but it was replaced with a smaller, better one that will last thousands of years. But the real reason I am not fully human now is my mind. I have been living, breathing, thinking alien thoughts for twenty years. I do not even think in Greek very often anymore. This morning, when I awoke, my first thought was whether I could *zfirnb* a little today. That is a concept which I could not even explain to you in less than a month!"

"I don't care what you've learned here, you're still my father! Your love hasn't changed, has it? Has it?"

Alexandros smiled sadly and shook his head. "No, Ariadne, it has not changed at all, not my love for you, nor my love for your your mother. But that is why you must believe me when I say that this zoo is not for you, not at the present time of your life. You must go home."

Tears returned to her eyes and she squeezed him in her arms with all her strength.

"Let me show you my world," he said to her. "You will see I am far better off than ever could be the case on Earth." To Sean, he added, "Would you like to join us?"

"Only if I'm a visitor, not an exhibit."

Alexandros laughed. "Agreed." He touched a spot on his tunic and the gray ground beneath his feet turned into a crimson disk a meter and a half in diameter.

"Step into the circle," he said. Sean joined the two of them and held Ariadne's shoulders. The vista shimmered slightly in a subtly disturbing way beyond the circle, and even the grass nearby had a metallic sheen.

Alexandros touched the tunic again and the crimson circle began to move swiftly, carrying them with it though their feet seemed to touch the ground.

"First," he said, "I want you to meet some friends of mine."

The crimson circle crossed the edge of the gray plain and entered an endless, red, grassy landscape with occasional yellow trees. They flew straight through a tree. Sean jerked Ariadne to one side.

Alexandros laughed. "No need to worry. The beings handle

space-time as easily as we do bricks. What we are standing on is a machine a few molecules thick, creating a more or less cylindrical field running from the bottom of the disk up a couple of meters. Everything inside is then slightly displaced in space-time, an angstrom or so. We cannot collide with anything.''

''But how can we still see?'' said Sean.

''Every atom extends at least a little into other dimensions, and what we see now is their higher-dimensional images, closely resembling their familiar forms.''

They approached a herd of cattle and stopped. The crimson disk disappeared.

''And where did your circle come from?'' said Sean. ''It appeared as if by magic, and now it's gone the same way.''

''I store it in hyperspace, an angstrom away from our universe. It senses me and follows me around like a dog, parallel to this universe. It is a fairly intelligent machine.''

The cattle wore metallic tunics and belts, and munched on the grass, which smelled like clover. Calves frolicked on the periphery of the herd. Several adults stood on their hind legs and stared at the newcomers. They were stout, muscular brown creatures, slightly humanoid. The arms ended in two long, flexible fingers; their faces held huge, sad, circular green eyes, and short horns protruded from some of their heads, just above large, leaflike ears.

''The bovoids!'' exclaimed Ariadne.

''Holy cow!'' exclaimed Sean.

''Well put,'' said Alexandros.

One of the standing creatures opened its mouth and began to speak with the familiar deep, slow, resonant voice they had heard so often on Hecatomb. Alexandros replied in the same language, though his voice lacked the depth and resonance of the creatures; then he translated: ''He says hello, and asks who you are.''

Alexandros replied, and the Tu-kii-vno came over and shook the hands of Ariadne and Sean. ''I told him of our hand-shaking custom,'' said Alexandros. ''He says that, as representative of the herd, he communicates that they are pleased to share pasture with you.''

''So they're animals in the zoo just like you,'' said Sean.

''Oh, no. They *passed* their test. They are *civilized*. They can go anywhere they want to in the universe. These folks are here on a family picnic at the zoo. This area is kept as a memorial park for them, since it is near where they first entered galactic civilization.''

Three calves came over and nuzzled the humans. Ariadne got down on her knees and fondled them playfully.

One of the calves spoke in a high-pitched voice.

Alexandros laughed. "She wants to know if she can feed the monkeys." He reached into his tunic and brought forth some warm *pastitsio*, which he gave to the calf.

The little bovoid stood clumsily on its rear legs and took the Greek pasta in his two fingers, placing it awkwardly in Ariadne's mouth. Sean scowled at her.

Ariadne smiled, wiped the excess off, and ate it.

"Thank you," she said to the calf. Alexandros translated.

"Would you like some, Sean?" he said.

"No thanks," he said with dignity, though his stomach had started to growl.

"It's vegetarian. Knowing we would come here, I thought it would be rather rude to use beef—even if it is synthetic."

Alexandros and the adult Tu-kii-vno conversed for several minutes. "Galactic gossip, you know," explained the Greek.

"Did *all* of the bovoids come here?" said Ariadne.

"Yes, eventually," said Alexandros.

Sean scowled. "Wasn't there even *one* bullheaded sonovabitch who refused to go?"

Alexandros translated the question into more diplomatic Tu-kii-vno language.

"You have to realize that these creatures possess a herd mentality far beyond anything we could ever understand."

"Or want to," said Sean.

"He says that, millions of years ago, there were occasional mutants and psychopaths who deviated from the herd's will, but as they became more civilized, they learned to weed out defective genes and to educate all young Tu-kii-vno into proper behavior."

"In other words, they were all brainwashed."

"Perhaps—by our standards. But by their standards, we are a vicious race of psychopathic animals who prey on each other."

The calves ran off, chasing toy octopoids.

"Are all galactics like that? Isn't there any individualism left in 'civilization'?"

"Oh, no, these are just one type of citizen. There are other species dedicated to individualism far more than we. They simply learned to curb their violent behavior. And they learned to respect the rights of others to do as they wish, another thing we too are woefully deficient in."

"Amen," said Sean.

"Indeed, the Galactic Center only accepts those species which can tolerate others having different beliefs. But perhaps we should move on. I have another friend I would like very much for you to meet."

They waved to the Tu-kii-vno, who mimicked their movements. One of them slowly waved a bracelet at them and circled them, aiming it toward them.

"I think we're in someone's home video," said Sean. "They'll probably call it *Picnic at the Zoo with the Monkeys*."

"Thank them for building Hecatomb," said Ariadne.

Her father translated and they boarded the crimson disk again.

They sailed over the plain and into a city. Its buildings were strange tall structures with concave roofs that came to points at the edges, like soap bubbles suspended from pillars. They were colored in pastel shades that slowly and continuously changed. The trio traveled speedily through broad avenues, curving here and there to avoid buildings but passing through pedestrians and other obstacles, protected by their hyperspatial displacement.

"Why don't we just go straight through the buildings?" said Sean.

"That would be impolite, violating people's privacy. How would *you* like it if traffic passed through your living room?"

"You've got a point there."

On the other side of town, they stopped at a building as tall as a football stadium, the size of a small town. Its walls changed subtly among various shades of pink. They walked toward the nearest wall.

"This is where my best friend lives," said Alexandros.

"The lizard?" said Ariadne.

He nodded with a smile.

A creature came through a triangular hole in the wall and approached them. It was five meters long and rolled on eight black wheels. It had black and red stripes across its heavily ridged, armored back running to its two long, scaly tails. A large, single eye stood upright on its wide, stubby, flat head. Its mouth hung open, showing rows of hollow, tubular teeth.

As it came closer, it became clear that its wheels were organic and grew like limbs out of its lower torso. They resembled disks of soft black rubber, and the joints were like the rotating tail-linkage of the terrestrial flagella microbe. The creature waved a tentacle at Alexandros and rolled past them. He waved back and continued toward the building.

"Was that your friend?" said Sean, eyeing the creature suspiciously.

"No, although he is a friendly chap whom I have taught to play a rather good game of poker. He's one of the zoologists. He evolved on a very volcanic planet where lava beds often formed lengthy smooth lanes resembling highways hundreds of kilometers long." He touched his tunic and a triangular section of the wall in front of them disappeared, revealing a lush botanical garden of blue ferns and giant flowers. A blast of warm, moist, fragrant air greeted them. Nibbling on the blue vegetation, there stood an enormous dinosaur.

Alexandros boldly walked toward the creature. Ariadne and Sean followed hesitantly.

Something like a brontosaur, it was sixty meters long, with a mottled blue-and-yellow skin. Its six elephantine legs were three meters across. Its huge belly was so far off the ground Sean could have walked under it without bumping his head. The neck was oddly thin and flat, ribbonlike, and so flexible that when the creature pulled its tiny head back, it folded like an accordion. At the base of its neck, like a tiny napkin, was a colorful cloth similar to Alexandros's tunic. On the other end, a stubby tail stuck out like a duck's.

Alexandros called out, "Nnnuuubuuut!"

The creature's head swung down toward them while the body remained broadside. "Aaaal-eeeex-aaaaan-droooos," boomed the creature. *"Tiiiii-kaaaa-niiiiis?"*

"*Kala, kala!*" replied Alexandros.

"He speaks *Greek?*" said Ariadne.

"I had to teach *someone,*" said her father, "so I could relax in my native tongue occasionally."

"I'll be a son of a lawyer!" exclaimed Sean.

"And he taught me dinosauroid," said Alexandros. "Meet my best friend, Nnnuuubuuut."

Ariadne delightedly chattered away at the dinosaur in rapid-fire Greek, interrupted occasionally by lengthy, slow, booming dinosauroid-accented replies in the same language.

Sean stood silently in wonder, shaking his head now and then, and studied the creature's head. The size of a hippopotamus skull, it only seemed small against the huge body. Its two eyes were *underneath* the jaws, on little wrinkled turrents that swiveled independently. The lower jaw was rigid while the upper one moved like a crocodile's mouth, displaying hundreds of huge molars spread in a mosaic on the floor and roof of the jaws. Bits of blue vegetation stuck between some of them, and his garlicky, moist breath induced Sean to back up several meters. There were dozens of tongues lapping at the teeth, and these seemed to be modulating the sounds that ushered up from the gullet, forming them into approximations of Greek syllables. Out of the neck, just below the eyes, sprouted two surprisingly delicate arms terminating in seven fingerlike digits.

"He seems to be very happy here," said Ariadne. "His planet was becoming cold and his species had just invented fire. He hates cold very much and loves the environment they have created for him here. Someday, he will return to his world to find a mate and raise a brood of wise little dinosaurs."

She chatted some more until her father interrupted, saying, "Our zookeeper is here now," Sean scowled. "Our teacher, if you prefer. You really must meet him."

Sean looked around. "Where is he?"

"You cannot see him yet with your limited senses. He is displaced into another dimension. I'll invite him in." He stared into space above the two humans, his lips moving silently.

Three walnut-sized, moist, pink objects appeared in the air over their heads and grew rapidly, changing shape and texture and color until they each resembled wrinkled, football-sized aqua pincushions. They hovered together for a moment, then flew down to the humans. Two of them flew around Ariadne while the other orbited Sean's head. He ducked as if it were a hornet.

"Relax," said Alexandros. "This is my teacher."

"Which one?" said Ariadne.

"All of them. They are extensions of one creature who lives in several dimensions you cannot perceive. They are all connected, but their body is not visible in our space. Each part is something like one of our brain hemispheres, except he has three of them."

"He is male?"

"No, they have sexes only in adolescence. These are an adult. I merely call him 'he' for convenience."

The three objects changed places, two inspecting Sean and the third going to Ariadne. Whenever they moved, they changed shape and texture slightly, simultaneously, as if they were invisibly linked. Each had a dark blue, glistening, triangular depression that stared at the humans like eyes. A row of red beads encircled each object like pearls on tiny stalks, forming an eyebrow. On top, an orange depression pulsed slowly.

Alexandros pointed at the one by Ariadne and said, "That one,

I call Patéras.'' Then, pointing at the two hovering in front of Sean's grimacing face, ''Those are Yiós and 'Ayió Pnéuma.''

''The Father, the Son, and the Holy Ghost,'' translated Ariadne.

''It is easier than trying to pronounce the being's real name, and each of his brains has a different personality.''

Alexandros looked at 'Ayió Pnéuma as if listening to a private communication, and nodded. ''He asks if he may visit your minds for a while.''

Ariadne smiled and Sean frowned. ''Not while I'm inside it,'' said the latter.

''I'm sure that it would be all right if Father thinks so.''

''It is quite harmless,'' said Alexandros, ''though you may find it disconcerting. It involves an exchange of mental images. You will see something of his mind just as he does of yours.''

''No, sir,'' said Sean firmly. ''Thank you for the honor, but I'm afraid I must decline. I just can't ask you in today.'' He tapped his skull, smiling. ''It's such a mess, and the maid hasn't been in there for days.''

''Very well,'' said Alexandros. He looked at 'Ayió Pnéuma and it moved toward Ariadne. Apprehensively, she watched it approach. It reached her face, then merged smoothly with her head until it was completely inside. Sean's eyes bugged out. He ran over to her and held her hands.

''Have no fear,'' said Alexandros, as much to Sean as to Ariadne. '' 'Ayió Pnéuma is completely in another dimension now, looking down into her mind much as you might look down into the bodies of the inhabitants of a two-dimensional world without harming them.''

A dazzling array of lights sparkled inside Ariadne's mind. Then, in rapid succession, there was a series of disconnected sensations, some hers and others completely alien: a tingling in her elbow; a repulsive, unfamiliar smell; the taste of spicy wine; a glimpse of a striped fish; a vision of red rain; a voice intoning *''This, too, shall pass''*; the Parthenon; a city of white turrets among which flew aqua-colored, toadstool-shaped creatures with three triangular eyes.

The kaleidoscope of sensations continued awhile, mirrored in the quickly changing expressions on her face that baffled Sean. Then 'Ayió Pnéuma emerged from Ariadne's head and was immediately replaced by Yiós.

Rapid-fire emotions flooded through her: excitement, as she wrestled with a moray eel at the end of her spear gun under the Ionian sea and—on an unfamiliar world—as she chased a rippling fuchsia creature the size of a fox through a forest of cinnamon stalagmites; anger, as she fought with Wolf and as she floated in a cloud of acidic fumes, suspended upside down from an ovoid vehicle; love, as she felt her father's arms around her when she was an infant, and when tentacles caressed her crinkled trunk; lust, when she eyed the lanky boy with the embryonic mustache across the classroom aisle, feeling her face flush warmly, and when the aqua toadstool-creature displayed her red photoreceptor beads at him lasciviously. Fear, happiness, greed, hunger, hatred came and went, half human and half alien.

Then, Yiós left and Patéras took its place. This time the sensations were muted and instead, concepts, relationships, complex images flooded her mind, as if she were outside her head, looking through a window into it. At first, they were all human: She saw regions of her mind where lived abstract models of herself, her father, her mother, and her stepfather, like intricate geometric shapes, interconnected in many ways. She saw her love for her father and her feelings of abandonment transform into resentment toward her stepfather and subtle hostility toward her mother. For the first time, she understood how harsh she had been toward her mother and stepfather, and how understanding and loving they had been.

There was a great, jagged gap left by her father twenty years ago, partly filled by the Benedictor Simon and his religion, and she realized that Simon was her substitute for the father who had disappeared.

A spiderweb of emotions tied together dark regions of anger and hatred, and bright ones of lust and love and forgiveness. Lines from these regions converged on Stefan and Sean. Thick barriers surrounded the bright regions, and only the tiniest threads of the spiderweb penetrated them, most of these to Sean. She focused on the barriers and saw that they were like mazes, with ways through them, paths she had never taken, but which she now knew were there, waiting to be used.

And then her head filled with a warm glow. A multitude of alien emotions swept over her, some of them recognizable, many of them ones for which she had no name. Some were intellectual concepts so sublimely integrated with the alien's mind that they had become instincts: senses of fairness and justice, compulsions for honesty and ethical behavior. There was a cosmic morality transcending the petty obsessions of humanity, embracing dizzyingly diverse societies—one had seven sexes; another, none. And embedded in it all was a love of logic and a passion for reason, an endless search for the meaning of existence.

Her mind was a spiderweb of concepts and emotions with a handful of central concentrations; his was a vast tapestry connecting countless concepts to one another.

She settled on one bright nexus. Planets flew into her mind, worlds of every color and size, populated by creatures ranging from intelligent fungi to islands of mind-colonies floating in an ammonia atmosphere. These were the worlds of the Galactic Center, connected by thought and culture, by travel and commerce, by reason and decency. These were the places where one day humanity might join the others, if it could just attain sufficient wisdom.

Finally, Patéras withdrew and Ariadne was alone again in her mind. It raced giddily with strange ideas and new perceptions, as if she had just returned home like the Prodigal Son, and was seeing it with new eyes.

Sean squeezed her hand anxiously. "Are you all right, Ariadne?"

She nodded, looking at him as if she had never seen him before, a faint smile on her face. "I am better now than I have ever been before."

"Well, Einstein damn it!" said Sean, whirling to face the three parts of the alien now hovering above Alexandros. "Tell your friend I'm not going to let it be said that Sean Seamus O'Shaughnessy wouldn't go where a woman has trod. Come on in, Patéras and your kin! Visit a strong Irish mind and feast your eyes on all the wonderful sights!"

Alexandros smiled, nodded, and looked at 'Ayió Pnéuma. It flew into Sean's face and his world became one of brilliant lights. He felt the valves of his heart beating rapidly, sloshing blood filled with tiny corpuscles that jostled against the pulsating muscle; he tasted delicious, hot grains of some unknown substance with his *foot;* he slugged a man in a bar and felt the satisfying but painful impact of fist against jaw; he jumped into a seething volcano and swam in refreshing, red lava . . .

'Ayio Pnéuma left and Yiós took its place. He felt the poignancy of an indigo spiral-creature, falling to its traditional doom on the ammonia glacier, after mating on a high-gravity world; the exhilaration of bounding like a kangaroo across Mare Orientale on the moon, the distant rim mountaintops glistening in sunlight, leaping high with nothing between him and the vacuum except an ultrathin pressure-suit; the desire that overwhelmed him when he kissed the willing waitress at the Triple Zero Exchange on Deimos, with the vast face of Mars in the sky outside the dome; the exquisite taste of the throbbing thorax of the toadstool-being he loved . . .

And finally, through Patéras, Sean saw the spiderweb of his own mind: the part of his brain that was his father, living on inside the son after death; his mother, source of nurturing and love in boyhood, driven insane by her husband's execution, unable to comprehend why Sean chose to leave Earth. Jagged scars crisscrossed back and forth between the two. From his strangely detached viewpoint, he saw how to block off the painful areas and how to keep the healthy ones connected. And, between some parts of his mind, he saw paths he had never used.

Little blobs—the other women in his life—floated here and there, connected by threads with the centers of love and lust, anger and jealousy. One, larger than the rest, was filled with images of Ariadne, a few from when she was a girl and many from the last weeks. Patterns emerged, and he began to understand her loves and hurts, her attraction and repulsion toward him, and the forces that drove them to this place at the center of the galaxy.

A warm glow came over him and he swam through a stream of alien emotions, recognizing some, bewildered by others. He felt the being's longing for rationality and an intense curiosity about everything in the universe. In one vast area of the creature's mind, he dimly recognized concepts of mathematics and physics far beyond those of the human race, so interwoven into the mind's fabric that he did not need computers to solve problems. He *absorbed* data and *saw* solutions instinctively, in a way that only the greatest human minds began to approach.

Sean's own curiosity made him plunge deeper into this part of the mind, seeking answers to the structure of the universe yet unknown to humans. He found he could see into thousands of dimensions beyond the four in which humans lived. He could see backward and forward in time. When he looked at Ariadne through the being's mind, he saw an endless strand as if she were stretched out forever, passing through the hyperspace barrier toward Hecatomb, entwined with another strand he recognized was his own world-line. Looking forward, he could see only a short distance ahead in time, where his world-line and Ariadne's curved back toward Hecatomb, but quickly blurred.

He understood that this creature lived simultaneously in the past, present, and future, though it could only see a short distance ahead in time, due to a kind of Heisenbergian uncertainty.

Then, Patéras withdrew. Sean suddenly felt deafened and blinded, imprisoned in three dimensions, with but a feeble ability to see the past and none for the future. But at least Ariadne was there, holding his hands, peering into his eyes.

Sean squeezed her hands, then looked beyond her at Alexandros and nodded. "I understand for the first time how you must have felt when you attempted to return to Earth."

"Yes," said Alexandros. "Being a superman is addictive. And you have felt only a small part of what *I* have . . . Incidentally, you now can read and speak the Tu-kii-vno language."

Sean and Ariadne looked at Alexandros. "How could that possibly be?" said Sean. Startled, he realized he had just said it in the bovoid language.

Alexandros replied in English, "I asked the zookeeper to add it to your language centers when he was sharing minds with you. It will help you get safely through Hecatomb."

"I pray to Darwin I can still speak English!" said Sean, relieved to find he had spoken in his native tongue.

Ariadne walked over to her father, pulling Sean until she touched each of their hands. "Father," she said, "why don't the three of us stay here together. We could be so happy!"

"No, my love," he said. "This is no place for a young woman who has seen so little of human life yet."

She looked at him with large, pleading eyes.

Alexandros shook his head. "There is another reason why you must return. I will give you something to take back with you." He touched the sleeve of his garment and a viewcrystal fell into his hand. "This contains the most important knowledge of this civilization that I can pass on to you." He handed it to his daughter gravely. "I did bring you treasure after all."

She cupped it in her hands like a jewel, tears welling up in her eyes.

"Aren't they going to be annoyed," said Sean, "if they find out you've smuggled the state secrets out?"

"This has the zookeeper's approval," said Alexandros. "When we received word of the Hecatomb ship's departure, he examined my mind to see whether I had included any censorable concepts on this crystal. He knew I had been keeping a record for just such an event as your visit. There are only a few concepts that minds as primitive as ours can grasp that are too dangerous for us, or that would make it too easy for us to wipe out our competitors in the wilds of the galaxy.

"There is an eternal conflict among civilized beings, between the desire to conserve the natural environment, and the wish to see primitives become civilized. This crystal represents a compromise between those two goals.

"They do not mind if certain knowledge is transferred which *accelerates* the intellectual evolution of a species, as long as it does not interfere too much with the growth of other beings. There *are* dangerous things in this crystal, but nothing so dangerous that it matters to them if the wild animals of Earth know of these." He clasped Ariadne's hand around the crystal and said, "Now it is time for you to go home."

"No!" exclaimed Ariadne. "Let us stay a few more days."

"The longer you stay, the harder it will be for you to return. And Earth desperately needs this knowledge. Each day here might mean a year of human progress postponed. I am ashamed that I lacked the courage to bring it back myself."

She embraced him and sobbed on his chest. He put his arms around her and tears came to his eyes, too. "I won't go!" she cried. "Send Sean back with it."

"Alone?" said the Irishman, hurt.

"I'll join you later," said Ariadne, mollifying him.

"Hecatomb is too dangerous," said Alexandros, "although I will advise you on ways to minimize the hazards. You are safer together." He held on to her while she pleaded more.

Finally, he softened. "I fear that twenty years of alien knowledge is no match for six years of fatherhood. Very well. You can stay one week, but only if you promise to leave then."

She brightened immediately with the joy of a little girl and said, "I promise."

"I suppose," said Sean, "a week in paradise wouldn't hurt me either."

And so they spent the next week exploring the Galactic Center, meeting other inhabitants of the zoo, having their bodies repaired by the veterinarian, conversing with visitors from a dozen civilized worlds, and learning as much as they could absorb of true Civilization. And catching up on twenty years of life.

Then, finally, Alexandros dragged the reluctant pair back to the Hecatomb ship.

"Can't we just stay another week?" Ariadne pleaded, her arm around her father.

"One week only, we agreed," said Alexandros, walking to the ship.

"I can't say that I would object to another week here," said Sean. "Earth's beginning to look less and less like home and more and more like a jungle village without indoor plumbing."

"I warned you," said Alexandros. "But now you have work to do." They stepped onto the ship's ramp.

Sean gently pulled Ariadne away from her father.

"Sean," said Alexandros, "I know I can trust you to take good care of my daughter."

"That you can," he said, and shook Alexandros's hand.

Ariadne and Alexandros hugged each other for dear life. Tears fell from both faces.

"Take good care of this knowledge," said her father. "It could advance our civilization greatly if used wisely. Do not allow it to fall into unscrupulous hands, because it could hurt as much as it could help."

Sean stepped into the spacecraft.

Alexandros paused and breathed deeply. "And there is one other thing. The zookeeper and I have been debating whether we should tell you. We finally decided it is best that you know, though it may give Earth an even greater inferiority complex than it will have when you tell them about this civilization."

"Yes?" said Ariadne.

"If ever you think of me with shame for living as an exhibit in a zoo, just remember this: This civilization travels as easily between galaxies as we do between stars. Yet there is a cluster of galaxies they have never visited."

"Why?" said Sean.

"They cannot. There is an artificial barrier around it through which they cannot pass. Do you understand?"

Sean's eyes opened wide. "There's another civilization there . . ." he whispered.

"Yes," said Alexandros, nodding serenely. "And this civilization in which I live is not yet wise enough to enter."

Sean nodded dumbly.

Ariadne lingered, kissing her father. Sean pulled her gently aboard. The door slid shut, and they stared through its transparency as the vessel lifted off.

CHAPTER 22

As the ship rose, Alexandros rapidly diminished and merged into the blue signal light. Ariadne stared tearfully back at the blue light until it too was lost in the distance.

Sean touched her hand. It opened and he picked up the viewcrystal delicately.

She continued to stare into space with unseeing eyes.

He held the crystal delicately and contemplated it. "For the first time since my father died," he said, "I have something to live for."

The trip back reversed the headlong dash through hyperspace they had entered by. Ariadne did not notice the universe racing around her.

When the spacecraft set them gently down back in Hecatomb, they emerged reluctantly. Neutron-star thunder boomed all around.

Sean found an unmoving path alongside the conveyor that had brought them to the spacecraft. "I guess the bovoids didn't plan on anyone returning," he said.

The black slab rose, admitting them into Hecatomb.

As they walked back, Sean was delighted to effortlessly read the alien signs: VESSEL CAPACITY 32,768 ADULTS; FIELD WARPER ACCESS HATCH; and a scrawled message, VUNITNIV LOVES NOKUVLA.

"I can read bovoid even better than English!" he exclaimed happily.

Ariadne paid no attention.

He looked back as the black slab closed down and read on it: ENTRY TO CIVILIZATION.

They returned to the place where they had left their companions. To their surprise, Plum and Stefan were still there, asleep, wearing earplugs to keep the pulsar thunder to a minimum.

Homer spotted them and exclaimed, "Blessed be the name of Asimov! Our intrepid adventurers came back from the hellhole of

Hecatomb!'' He removed the earplugs from the sleeping men, rousing them.

Stefan sat openmouthed on the floor. Plum rushed to Sean's side and slapped him on the back. "Never thought I'd see you again, old chum!" he said with emotion.

"Neither did I, you can count on that!" said Sean. "But why haven't you gone back yet?"

Plum shook Ariadne's limp hand and said, "I refused to return until we'd used up all our supplies. Just in case, you know."

Homer stuck his face into the group. "In the name of the press, what happened?"

Sean smiled. "Have we got a story for you!" Not even you will be able to sensationalize it any more than the truth already is."

Ariadne just sat down and stared unseeing at the neutron star underneath her feet.

After Sean had related the story, he was barraged by questions while Ariadne moodily sat, her arms wrapped around her knees.

"Let's see the sensational Alexandros viewcrystal," said Homer, to a chorus of enthusiastic yeas from Stefan and Plum.

Sean shook his head. "Not until Ariadne and I have screened it carefully first. There's stuff in there you primitives aren't ready for yet." His eyes twinkled at the word *primitives*.

They argued, but he would not change his mind. At last he said, "Let's get away from this noisy ring. Ariadne and I need to go someplace calm, where we can think. I'd like to visit the Ring of Celebration for a while."

"Wouldn't that be dangerous?" said Stefan.

"Alexandros said it's safe, if we stick to the areas he visited."

"I think we should get back to Earth with our treasures as fast as possible."

"So Homer can make you a fearless interstellar hero, the idol of every man and, especially, every woman."

"I'm not ready for Earth yet," said Ariadne quietly.

Sean put his arm around her solicitously.

"I need time," said Ariadne, "to rest and study the viewcrystal. It's a terrible responsibility. I want time to think before I'm surrounded by journalists and crazies anxious to talk to Our Lady of the Galaxy, as Homer calls me."

"Then it's settled," said Sean. He snapped his fingers, getting Homer's attention. He pointed at the camp.

"Yes, sir!" said Homer. The robot began scooping up equipment and packing it.

At the Ring of Celebration, they emerged from the train amid loud, deep, alien music and glaring, colorful flashes. Mesmerized by the light, Sean, Ariadne, and Plum did not notice Stefan and Homer sneaking back aboard before the doors closed.

The train departed. It was several seconds before Sean realized what had happened. He raged, shouting, "That dust-suckin', mother-crunchin' son of a Sirian glowskunk and his chip-lickin' cyberidiot!"

Plum shrugged and Ariadne smiled, putting her arm around Sean, saying, "I am glad to be rid of them. As long as we have the viewcrystal—and each other—that is all that matters."

Sean scowled. "At least I put a couple of surprises on board his ship when we visited it."

"Nothing dangerous?" said Ariadne with a trace of concern.

"No," said Sean. "I must confess I was tempted—just a bit—to do to his navigational program what Wolf did to ours, but I knew you'd disapprove."

"I would have."

"I'm glad now I didn't, because Millie will be aboard, too. However, I made some log entries revealing what I know of his crooked schemes, and tucked away a program in the ship's computer that will transmit some embarrassing information to the Ministry of Justice when he gets back. They may not care much about justice there, but I'm sure they'll be interested in the list of artifacts he took on board, which is bound to be longer than the list he reports to the government."

"How do you know he is going to cheat them?"

"Because I'd do the same if the situation were reversed."

She swatted him lightly.

"But," he continued, "just as long as we're safe, and we have your father's viewcrystal, I really don't mind if he gets back oh-two."

Ariadne patted the thigh pocket where she kept the crystal, then yelled, "It's missing!"

"What?" said Sean.

She tore open the pocket and ran through all her other ones. "The viewcrystal!" she cried. "That dust-sucker stole Daddy's viewcrystal! We've got to stop him!"

Sean smiled. "No problem," he said as he pulled a crystal out of his own thigh pocket and handed it to her.

She cupped it in her gloved hands. "How . . . ?"

Sean laughed. "I had a hunch he'd pull something like that, so I switched an old viewcrystal for yours, back when we were returning to Hecatomb. Wouldn't you love to see him when he discovers that instead of the secrets of the universe, he's got a viewcrystal on pressure-suit maintenance?"

She began to laugh harder than Sean had ever seen, holding on to him for support. She laughed on and on, joined by Sean and Plum. It was the first good, healthy laugh he had seen from her since the journey's start. Finally, she subsided and said weakly, "Why didn't you tell me?"

"Well, at the time, you were incapable of hearing anything I might've said. And later, I thought you might not be able to keep a secret from him, so I protected you from yourself by shutting my mouth. Your father would have approved."

She hugged him. "So do I."

"Say, Ariadne," said Sean with a twinkle in his eyes, "your father told me there's a huge room where you float in zero gee and all around you, you see and hear and smell and feel the best sights the bovoids ever found in their millions of years of exploring the universe—all the most beautiful planets and stars and civilizations they've ever visited. It's like being there, floating in air. I wonder if you'd like to visit it before we go home? We could send Plum off to the library to amuse himself. Would you like to tour the universe with me? Just the two of us. Just for a few hours."

She pondered his words. Lacing her fingers in his, she replied with an angelic smile and a devilish gleam, "Maybe for a few weeks?"

AFTERWORD

The reader may be curious about the reality ratio of this book: the ratio of real science to speculation. How much of it is already nonfiction? You might be surprised.

Take the cryogenic world at the start of the story. Although most scientists would say that life could not exist at the temperature of liquid oxygen, there is remarkable research recently hinting otherwise.

Normally, chemical reactions slow down as the temperature gets lower, because heat is nothing but molecules bouncing around. When they cool, the bouncing slows down and they bump into each other less often, so reactions slow down. Until recently, it was assumed that the colder you got, the slower they'd be, until everything would come to a halt at the coldest possible temperature, absolute zero (minus 460 degrees Fahrenheit or minus 273 degrees centigrade)—the ultimate freeze-frame on nature's videocassette.

However, measurements near absolute zero show this doesn't happen. Instead, the weird phenomena of quantum physics take over. The quantum theory—the modern theory of the atom and all its particles—says that particles can *tunnel* through barriers that would be impossible to penetrate according to old, prequantum physics. Tunneling means that, if you lean against a locked door long enough, you will fall *through* the door. You may have to wait billions of years, so you'd better be very patient, but it will happen. Thus, atoms can overcome barriers once thought to be impassible. Chemical reactions at ultralow temperatures work! That's not theory—that's experimental fact.

Soviet chemical physicist Vitalii Goldanskii has theorized that the chemicals of life itself might have started in the depths of space at temperatures near absolute zero. My speculation is that life got started on the cryogenic world during warmer days, and, as its star cooled off and the planet got colder, life adapted. Creatures evolved to live with ever colder temperatures, and quantum processes became increasingly important. (Strictly speaking, quantum physics already runs life on planet Earth. Quantum theory explains the molecules out of which we are made. We are quantum machines!)

If the cryogenic world is at least conceivable, how plausible is Hecatomb? For decades, the neutron star was just the daydream of theoretical physicists who said that, if a star exploded in a supernova, what would be left over could be an incredibly dense object unlike anything ever seen in the laboratory: all of the mass of our sun could be compressed down to something the size of a city. It would be like a giant atomic nucleus, consisting mainly of zillions of neutrons. They called these beasts neutron stars.

Then, in 1967, an object in the sky was found emitting radio signals like the ticking of a clock. These "pulsars" were first nicknamed Little Green Men because they sounded so artificial, but now we know they are neutron stars. Hundreds have been found.

Pulsars are bizarre objects so dense that they strain the very laws of physics as we know them. Matter there has a density of a thousand *tons* per cubic centimeter, and the force of gravity at the surface is a hundred billion gees!

Getting close to a neutron star will be very difficult. In practice, a pulsar radiates huge amounts of energy that will cook you long before you encounter more subtle dangers. However, if you could shield yourself (perhaps with magnetic fields), you could get close enough to encounter the next problem: tides.

We think of tides as something to do with oceans, but in fact, ocean tides are just a side effect of gravity. As Sir Isaac Newton discovered, the gravitational force of a body gets weaker the farther you go from it. Thus, if you're standing when the moon is overhead, your head—being slightly closer to the moon than your feet—is attracted a tiny bit more toward it than are your feet. You are light-headed. This is the tidal force—the force due to the *difference* in gravity between two places.

If you got very close to a neutron star, the tidal force would pull your head off, so the Hecatomb engineers built the first ring far enough away that the tidal force was moderate. The ring also has the virtue that it absorbs the high-energy electrons and protons from the neutron star, making it safe to approach.

The design of the first ring resembles Larry Niven's classic novel, *Ringworld*, which was built around an ordinary star like the sun. Ringworld, in turn, was a section of a Dyson Sphere—a structure that physicist Freeman Dyson imagines an advanced civilization might build entirely enclosing its star.

Having built one ring, the bovoids could build another inside the first. Being closer to the neutron star it would revolve faster. In this way, ring by ring, they could live and experiment closer and closer to the star during the millions of years it took to figure out how to control gravity and survive the trip into the Galactic Center.

One of the nice things about a neutron star is that it has an enormous magnetic field, about a trillion times Earth's. This field could be used by engineers to generate vast amounts of electrical power. Spacecraft could be built with their own magnetic fields to repel and attract the pulsar field, allowing shuttlecraft like the "trains" to move around.

Eventually the bovoids figured out some method—unknown to us—of canceling out the tidal force on the smaller rings, perhaps through some form of antigravity powered by the neutron star. Certainly, a lab orbiting a neutron star would be one of the best places in the universe to learn more about gravity. Near such a star, space itself is highly distorted and is on the brink of breaking down completely. If the star were a little more massive, space would break down altogether and you would get a black hole—a place where gravity is so strong that not even light itself is fast enough to escape.

And what about hyperspace travel, an old standby of science fiction? Throughout the twentieth century, physicists have been adding dimensions to our universe in their theories. Einstein really started this game, although mathematicians before him had speculated that there could be more than the familiar three dimensions of height, depth, and width.

Imagine for a moment that you are a flatworm who has lived all his life on a tabletop. We'll make you a perfectly two-dimensional flatworm—your eyes see only along the surface; you can't raise your head at all. You live on bread crumbs that magically appear in your world like meteorites. You don't know they've fallen from a *third* dimension. All your life, you think you live in a two-dimensional universe. You cannot even imagine there's an "up" or a "down."

Perhaps we are just like that flatworm. There could be a *fourth* dimension that we can't intuitively understand because we've spent all our lives experiencing a measly three dimensions.

Mathematicians have wild imaginations, often undisturbed by reality. They invented the geometry of N dimensions, a way to describe with equations the lines, curves, cubes, spheres, and other objects in four, five, six, or N dimensions—hyperspace, where N can be any whole number.

Einstein toyed with the laws of electromagnetism and discovered that the equations of electricity and magnetism look much *simpler* in four dimensions. The equations were far more "elegant," as physicists describe a particularly nifty theory. But to make the equations look elegant, the fourth dimension had to be *time* (actually, he used time multiplied by the speed of light, to give it the unit of a distance, and this choice simplified the equations even more). This four-dimensional universe is often called space-time. Time seems to be just another dimension, although it's one we can't travel in as easily as the others.

Currently, physicists are increasingly hopeful about being able to explain all the laws of physics with ten dimensions: the familiar three plus time, together with six more spatial dimensions. Throughout the twentieth century, physics has increasingly resembled science fiction.

The barrier surrounding the Galactic Center could theoretically be made by distorting space. The supercivilization could build a spherical barrier around itself by warping space. (Technically, this would be a hypersphere, since it extends into higher dimensions.) A severe distortion in space causes tremendous gravitational and tidal forces similar to those in a black hole, and would be very difficult to penetrate.

We currently know that the center of our Milky Way galaxy is one of the weirdest places yet discovered in our universe. Radio signals from it penetrate the gas and dust that keep us from seeing it by light, showing huge arcs and almost-straight lines light-years in length. The first time I saw radio images of these structures, I gasped, because they looked like interstellar traffic lanes of a supercivilization. We don't really understand what they are, but they seem to be natural, produced by magnetic fields acting on plasmas of electrons and protons. In addition, there is much evidence that there is a giant black hole at the center of our galaxy, a place where matter millions of times the mass of the sun has disappeared from our universe. Vast amounts of matter are still falling into it, creating powerful radio, X ray, and infrared signals we pick up at Earth, thirty thousand light-years from the Center.

Building a shield around the Center would no doubt take a lot of energy. But Soviet astronomer Nikolai Kardashev has proposed that civilizations may evolve through three stages: Type I, consuming energy comparable to 20th century humanity; Type II, using the energy of a star, as in Dyson's Sphere (around a hundred trillion times a Type II), and Type III, controlling the energy of a galaxy (about a hundred billion times that of a Type II). If that seems a little hard to believe, just compare the amount of energy available to a caveman (in muscle power or camp fire) with that which we have so conveniently packaged in a hydrogen bomb.

Penetrating the hypersphere barrier would be difficult, and might well require the energy available in a supernova. In theory, you too can build your own supernova. Simply find a massive star of the type that eventually will become a supernova. Then add matter to it (*lots* of matter), and that will compress the star and increase its internal heat, cooking the gases inside faster, until the point is reached at which it burns out. Then it starts to collapse, but the collapse itself heats up matter and you have an explosion on your hands. It can have the energy of a hundred billion stars for a few days. WARNING: *Do not sit too close to your supernova. It is hazardous to your health.*

The universe we already know is strange and mysterious, filled with unexplained phenomena. It's a big place—plenty of room for the bovoids and their friends. Let us never forget the words of British scientist J.B.S. Haldane, who said, "I have no doubt that in reality the future will be vastly more surprising than anything I can imagine. Now my own suspicion is that the universe is not only queerer than we suppose, but queerer than we can suppose."

I'm sure he was right.

—TMcD
Pasadena, California
March 9, 1987

BIO OF A SPACE TYRANT
Piers Anthony

"Brilliant...a thoroughly original thinker and storyteller with a unique ability to posit really *alien* alien life, humanize it, and make it come out alive on the page." *The Los Angeles Times*

A COLOSSAL NEW FIVE VOLUME SPACE THRILLER—
BIO OF A SPACE TYRANT
The Epic Adventures and Galactic Conquests of Hope Hubris

VOLUME I: REFUGEE   84194-0/$3.50 US/$4.50 Can
Hubris and his family embark upon an ill-fated voyage through space, searching for sanctuary, after pirates blast them from their home on Callisto.

VOLUME II: MERCENARY   87221-8/$3.50 US/$4.50 Can
Hubris joins the Navy of Jupiter and commands a squadron loyal to the death and sworn to war against the pirate warlords of the Jupiter Ecliptic.

VOLUME III: POLITICIAN   89685-0/$3.50 US/$4.50 Can
Fueled by his own fury, Hubris rose to triumph obliterating his enemies and blazing a path of glory across the face of Jupiter. Military legend...people's champion...promising political candidate...he now awoke to find himself the prisoner of a nightmare that knew no past.

THE BEST-SELLING EPIC CONTINUES—
VOLUME IV: EXECUTIVE
89834-9/$3.50 US/$4.50 Can
Destined to become the most hated and feared man of an era, Hope would assume an alternate identify to fulfill his dreams ...and plunge headlong into madness.

VOLUME V: STATESMAN
89835-7/$3.50 US/$4.95 Can
the climactic conclusion of Hubris' epic adventures:

AVON Paperbacks

JODI
THOMAS

78844 RANSOM CANYON   ___ $7.99 U.S.   ___$8.99 CAN.

(limited quantities available)

TOTAL AMOUNT $ _____
POSTAGE & HANDLING $ _____
($1.00 FOR 1 BOOK, 50¢ for each additional)
APPLICABLE TAXES* $ _____
TOTAL PAYABLE $ _____
(check or money order—please do not send cash)

To order, complete this form and send it, along with a check or money order for the total above, payable to HQN Books, to: **In the U.S.:** 3010 Walden Avenue, P.O. Box 9077, Buffalo, NY 14269-9077; **In Canada:** P.O. Box 636, Fort Erie, Ontario, L2A 5X3.

Name: _____
Address: _____ City: _____
State/Prov.: _____ Zip/Postal Code: _____
Account Number (if applicable): _____

075 CSAS

*New York residents remit applicable sales taxes.
*Canadian residents remit applicable GST and provincial taxes.

HQN™
www.HQNBooks.com

PHJT0216BL